THE CHRISTMAS WEDDING

THE CHRISTMAS WEDDING

Essex 1867. The first flakes of snow are falling when Daisy Marshall finds herself jilted at the altar. After losing her job as governess to the Carrington family, she is forced to leave London and everything she knows. Heartbroken, Daisy finds herself in the small coastal village of Little Creek in Essex. There she is warmly welcomed — but the village is poverty-stricken and hit by a cholera outbreak.

Determined to help, Daisy makes new friends with earnest doctor Nicholas and dashing smuggler Jay — but also dangerous new enemies, who threaten to destroy everything she's built. Can Daisy save the village and find happiness in time for Christmas?

THE CHRISTMAS WEDDING

by

DILLY COURT

Magna Large Print Books

Anstey,
Leicestershire

British Libarary Cataloguing in Publication Data.

A catalogue record of this book is
available from the British Library

ISBN   978-0-7505-4790-1

First published in Great Britain by HarperCollins*Publishers* in
2019

Published in Large Print 2019 by arrangement with
HarperCollins*Publishers* Ltd.

Library Magna Books Ltd.

Printed and bound in Great Britain by
T. J. (International) Ltd., Padstow, Cornwall, PL28 8RW

For Daisy Richards

1

The Carrington House, Queen Square, London, December 1867

Daisy Marshall put aside the garment she had been mending for Master Timothy.

'What is it, Franklin?' she asked, gazing warily at the butler, who had entered the morning parlour without bothering to knock. Such small infringements of etiquette from the upper servants were not unusual, and obviously designed to put her in her place.

'For you, miss.' With disapproval written all over his face, Franklin proffered a silver salver on which lay a sealed envelope.

Daisy's breath caught in her throat as she recognised the writing, and she snatched it up, hoping that Franklin was not familiar with the bold cursive script belonging to Julian Carrington, the elder son and heir to the family fortune.

'Thank you, Franklin.' She made an effort to sound casual and unconcerned, but Franklin had a way of reducing her to the lowly status of a scullery maid.

He looked down his long nose. 'Mrs Carrington wishes to see you in the drawing room, miss.'

'I'll be there directly.' Daisy waited until he had left the room. The Carringtons' butler had

1

never approved of her — he had made that plain from the outset — and neither had Mrs Thompson, the housekeeper. The lot of a governess was not a happy one, as Daisy had discovered to her cost. She had found herself occupying a nebulous position where she belonged neither upstairs nor below stairs, but all that would change very soon. Daisy raised her hand to touch the gold ring set with a sparkling diamond that Julian had placed on her finger, although it now hung round her neck on a silk ribbon, hidden from view. The Carringtons' money had come originally from coal mining in Yorkshire, and it was no secret that they hoped their son would marry into the landed gentry, but Julian would be twenty-one on Christmas Eve, and he planned to announce their betrothal at his birthday party.

Daisy opened the envelope carefully, not wanting to tear the expensive hand-made writing paper, and she inhaled the scent of Julian's favourite cologne. It was almost as if he were sitting beside her, and she closed her eyes, revelling in the exotic blend of aromatic essences and spice. She sighed happily: in two days' time it would be official. When he returned home Julian would place the ring on her finger in front of his whole family. Daisy Marshall from Whitechapel, the orphaned daughter of a leather merchant, would be raised from her humble status of governess to that of fiancée to the elder son of a well-to-do family. Quite how it had happened was still something of a surprise. The dashing twenty-year-old Oxford undergraduate, who had hopes of a career in the diplomatic service, was much in demand during the London season. Daisy was well aware that his domineering mother and ambitious father had their sights set on someone from a good family for their future daughter-in-law, but Julian had other ideas. He had convinced Daisy that for him it was love at first sight, and she had been similarly smitten. Now all that remained was to break the news of their engagement to the family.

Daisy broke the seal and opened the letter carefully, a smile curving her lips, but as she read the contents her hands began to tremble and the words blurred, running together until they made no sense.

Oxford
December 1867

My darling Daisy,
You can't imagine how difficult it is for me to find the words that will inevitably break your heart, as it is breaking mine when I put pen to paper. The truth is that I cannot marry you. There, I've said it and it cannot be undone. I still love you dearly, but I realise that for us to wed would be a dreadful mistake. My parents will never accept you as one of the family and I will be cut off without a penny. I cannot hope to earn enough to make a proper home for you and any children we might have, and to marry you under such circumstances would be irresponsible, if not downright cruel. I

love you too much to see you brought down by poverty and disgrace, therefore I am breaking our engagement, even though it has remained a secret and was never an official obligation on my part.

I will return home for my birthday party, but afterwards I will be leaving for Paris, where I have been fortunate enough to obtain a very junior position in the British Embassy.

Please keep the ring as a token of my undying affection and esteem, and I pray that you will find someone more worthy of you than myself.

Your loving friend,
Julian Carrington

Daisy crumpled the letter in her hands and clasped them to her bosom. She was trembling from head to foot with shock, but tears would not come. Pain, sadness, despair and finally anger flooded her with emotion, but still she was dry-eyed. *Jilted* — the word would be engraved on her heart for ever.

A timid knock on the door preceded the appearance of a housemaid. 'I'm sorry to interrupt, miss, but the master is getting impatient. He sent me to fetch you.'

Daisy tucked the crumpled sheet of paper into the pocket of her plain grey woollen dress and she rose to her feet. 'I'm coming.' Even to her own ears her voice sounded strained and edgy, but she had her feelings under control. Whatever it was that the master had to say could not be as earth-shattering as the contents of Julian's letter.

The drawing room on the first floor was furnished in the height of fashion with heavy mahogany furniture upholstered in crimson velvet, matching velvet curtains and a carpet with such thick pile it felt like walking on a croquet lawn. The former Adam-style mantel had been ripped out on Mrs Carrington's instructions and replaced by a huge, black marble fireplace that dominated the whole room, and a fire blazed up the chimney. An enormous Christmas tree took up one corner of the room, and was lavishly decorated with tinsel and glass baubles imported from Germany at enormous expense. At any other time Daisy would have been delighted, if only for Master Timothy's sake. He was what her aunt Eleanora would have called 'an afterthought', being eleven years younger than Julian, and his parents were invariably too busy to spend much time with him. It was Daisy who read him a story each evening when he was tucked up in bed, and Daisy who took him for outings to the park or the Zoological Gardens.

'I sent for you ten minutes ago. What kept you?' Albert Carrington stood with his back to the fire, glaring at Daisy through the thick lenses of his gold-rimmed spectacles. 'Well, what have you to say for yourself?'

Daisy had never felt comfortable in Mr Carrington's company. He was said to have trebled the family fortune by investing heavily in the stock market, and it was rumoured below stairs that the master would receive a knighthood for his services to industry and his generous gifts to charity. Even so, his manner was cold and calculating, and all the servants were in awe of him.

'I'm sorry, sir. I was mending a garment for Master Timothy.'

'That's no excuse.'

Mrs Carrington held up her hand. 'Let me handle this, Albert.' She fixed Daisy with a hard stare. 'I won't beat about the bush, Miss Marshall. As you know, Master Timothy will be starting school in January, and therefore we will no longer be in need of your services.'

'Yes, that's right,' Albert said, frowning. 'This is the end of the quarter and you will receive your wages from Mrs Thompson, together with a character, which should assure you of a position elsewhere.'

'I'm to lose my job?' Daisy looked from one to the other. 'But who will look after Master Timothy during the school holidays?'

'That is not your problem,' Mrs Carrington said icily. She rose majestically from the sofa and ushered Daisy from the room. She lowered her voice. 'Don't imagine that we haven't noticed what's been going on between you and our elder son. I've seen the way you flirt with him, and it is just as well your time with us had ended naturally, otherwise I'm afraid I would have had to terminate your employment.'

Daisy stared at the floor, unable to meet her employer's angry gaze. 'I'm sorry. It wasn't intentional.'

'It never is.' Agnes Carrington lowered her voice. 'When you find another position, keep yourself to yourself. Nothing but ill can come of any relationship you enter into with members of the household. And beware of male servants, too. That's the best advice that I can give you. Now pack your bags and leave. Don't upset Master Timothy by saying goodbye. I'll tell him you wish him well at school.' She whisked back into the drawing room and closed the door in Daisy's face.

★   ★   ★

The hansom cab trundled through the city streets, weaving its way through the carts, carriages and brewers' drays. Snow was falling steadily from a leaden sky and it was bitterly cold. Workers hurried homeward, mufflers flying out behind them and their hats pulled down over their brows so that the only parts of their faces visible were the reddened tips of their noses. Less hurried were those out shopping for last-minute presents. The pavements were crowded with men and women laden with packages wrapped in brown paper, or baskets overflowing with festive food. Costermongers' barrows illuminated by naphtha flares offered a tempting selection of oranges, lemons, rosy-cheeked apples and mountains of walnuts, together with bunches of red-berried holly and waxy white and green mistletoe. It was almost Christmas, a time for rejoicing, but all the way home Daisy could think of nothing other than

7

the letter that Julian had written, ending their brief relationship. The rumbling of the cab's wheels and the drumming of the horse's hoofs sounded to her ears like a repetition of his name, over and over again, until she could think of nothing else. The ache in her heart intensified with every turn of the wheels and the further they drove from Queen Square, the deeper her despair. The last time she had seen Julian they had been deeply in love and filled with excitement for the future, but now he had severed the delicate thread that had bound them. She had left the house with a shadow over her name, and she had not even been allowed to say goodbye to Master Timothy, who would imagine that she had deserted him. He was too little to be sent away from home, too sensitive a child to face the rigours of public school life, and it was almost Christmas. She had planned to fill his stocking with oranges, nuts and small toys she had purchased from the bazaar in Soho Square. She had left the packages in the nursery, but she doubted if he would receive any of them; Mrs Carrington would make sure that nothing was left to remind her younger son of the governess who had loved him like a mother.

Daisy stared blindly at the crowded pavements, seeing nothing but a blur of shapes and colours, misted by the thickly falling snow. It had promised to be the best Christmas she had ever had, and now it was going to be the worst. She had told her aunt about her romance with Julian, and now she would have to face the consequences. Questions would be asked to which

Daisy had no answer. Aunt Eleanora had drummed the importance of a good marriage into Daisy from an early age. Now she had to face her aunt's disappointment as well as her own heartbreak.

The cab drew to a halt outside the leather merchant's premises on Whitechapel Road. Situated within earshot of the Bell Foundry, with the Earl of Effingham pub conveniently close by, and the New Royal Pavilion Theatre just across the street, it was a thriving commercial area. Sidney Marshall was a successful leather merchant, having inherited an already thriving business on the death of his elder brother, Daisy's father, in the cholera epidemic of 1849. Shortly afterwards Daisy's mother had died in childbirth, leaving two-year-old Tobias and the infant Daisy to the care of her brother- and sister-in-law.

Daisy and Tobias had been brought up above the shop and had wanted for nothing as children. Toby had attended a good school and had gone on to study medicine at the London Hospital. Daisy herself had also benefited from a good education at Miss Lonsdale's Academy for Young Ladies, but having left school with a prize in just about every subject Daisy had found herself with little purpose in life other than to sit at home and wait for a suitable husband to appear. That was what her aunt expected, but not what Daisy wanted, and, after a battle with both guardians, she had applied for the position of governess in the Carrington household. Now she was returning home, broken-hearted and struggling to believe that Julian could have treated her in such a way.

Daisy alighted from the hansom cab and hefted the valise containing all her worldly possessions to the pavement. It was now snowing so heavily that she did not see the man who was walking with his head bent against the storm, and he sidestepped in order to avoid tripping over her case, almost knocking her off her feet.

'I'm so sorry.' The stranger steadied her with both hands. 'Are you all right?'

Daisy nodded. 'It wasn't your fault. I had to put my case down in order to pay the cabby.'

'No harm done, but the pavements are very slippery.' He picked up the valise. 'Have you far to go?'

'No, this is home.' Daisy pointed to the name above the premises. 'I live above the shop.'

'Marshall's, a well-known name in this area. So you must be Miss Marshall? Are you Toby's sister, by any chance?'

His smile was irresistible and she noticed that his hazel eyes were fringed with impossibly long lashes. Aunt Eleanora would have said it was unfair for a man to have such an asset. Daisy dragged herself back to the present and managed a smile.

'Yes, I'm Daisy. How do you know Toby?'

'I'm Nicholas Neville, but my friends call me Nick. Toby and I studied at the London.' He proffered his arm. 'Allow me, Miss Marshall. We don't want any accidents.'

She would normally have rejected such an offer, but there was something about Nicholas

10

Neville that made it impossible for her to refuse, and she leaned on his arm. He picked up her valise and they made it to the shop door.

'Thank you,' Daisy said breathlessly.

'I shan't be seeing Toby for a while because I'm going home for Christmas, but I hope we meet again, Miss Marshall.' Nick placed her valise on the floor.

'I'm sure we will. Anyway, thank you for your help.' Daisy turned her head at the sound of footsteps on the bare boards and her heart sank when she saw her uncle's clerk scurrying towards them with his peculiar crab-like gait.

'Miss Daisy, what are you doing here?' Jonah Sawkins cast a hostile glance at Nick.

Daisy had disliked Sawkins from the moment they first met, but her generous uncle had rescued Jonah from the workhouse and trained him to be his clerk. Sidney Marshall believed that there was good in everyone, and he would not have a word said against Jonah. Daisy knew her uncle's clerk to be sly and devious, and she was tempted to snub him now, but Jonah Sawkins had a way of getting his own back for any slight, real or imagined, and she held her tongue.

'Would you be kind enough to take my valise upstairs, Jonah?' Daisy turned to Nick. 'Thank you once again for your help. I hope I didn't delay you, too much?'

'Not at all. I've just come off duty at the hospital, so no harm done. Anyway, it was a pleasure to meet you, Miss Marshall.' Nick gave Sawkins a sympathetic smile. 'The bag is rather heavy. Perhaps you'd rather I took it upstairs?'

Daisy held her breath. She knew that Sawkins was sensitive about the abnormal curvature of his upper spine and his legs bowed by rickets in childhood. His deformity and his early years spent in the workhouse seemed to have twisted his personality, but although he had had a poor start in life Daisy had realised some time ago that Sawkins was ambitious, and she suspected that he could be ruthless if challenged.

He hefted the valise onto his bent shoulders, shooting a malicious glance at Nick. 'I can manage on me own, ta very much.' He hobbled behind the counter and opened a door leading to a flight of stairs. The red Turkey carpet glowed like a hot coal in the dim light, and Sawkins negotiated the stairs with surprising speed.

'He's been here for years,' Daisy said by way of an excuse for his rudeness.

'Yes, I believe Toby has mentioned him in the past. Anyway, I must be going.'

Nick let himself out into the street and Daisy raised her hand in farewell, but he had already disappeared into the swirling snow. She closed the door and was enveloped by the all-too-familiar smell of leather and dubbin, which she only noticed when she had been absent for a while. She was about to go upstairs when Sawkins appeared behind the counter, glaring at her beneath his shaggy eyebrows.

'I told the mistress you was here,' he said with a sly grin. 'She weren't expecting you. Got the sack, did you?'

'It's none of your business, Jonah.' Daisy had

not meant to snap at him but her nerves were frayed, and she was afraid that she might break down and cry if her aunt questioned her too deeply. She slipped past him and made her way upstairs where she was greeted by Hattie, the Marshalls' cook-housekeeper, who had been with them for ever. Daisy could not remember a time when Hattie had not been there to tell her wonderful stories about mermaids and unicorns, or to bandage a cut knee.

'Welcome home, Miss Daisy,' Hattie said, wrapping her in a comforting hug. 'We wasn't expecting you, so this is a real treat.'

Daisy returned the embrace. 'It's good to be home.'

'I'll go and put the kettle on.' Hattie gave her a peck on the cheek. 'Your aunt is in the parlour. She'll be so pleased to see you, my duck.' She waddled off along the landing, leaving Daisy to make her way to the parlour.

Eleanora Marshall was standing by the fire. In early middle-age she was a fine-looking woman with a good figure, glossy brown hair and an air of authority. She turned with a start at the sound of the door opening. 'Daisy, my darling. Sawkins told me you were here. What a lovely surprise.'

'I know you weren't expecting me, Aunt.'

'Why are you here? I thought you would be spending Christmas with your fiancé and his family.'

Daisy clenched her gloved hands in an attempt to stem the tears that suddenly threatened to overcome her. 'Julian doesn't want to marry me,' she said softly.

13

'You mean he's jilted you?'

'He's been offered a position in the French Embassy. It was too good to turn down, and our engagement was never official.'

'I don't see what that has got to do with anything,' Eleanora paced the floor, her high-heeled boots tip-tapping on the polished boards. 'There's more in this than meets the eye. Has his mother interfered? Has he met someone with more money and better connections?'

'I don't know, Aunt. He wrote a letter — '

'You mean that the coward didn't even have the decency to tell you face to face that he's reneged on his promise?'

'He was in Oxford when he sent the letter, and I've lost my job because Master Timothy is being sent to boarding school in the New Year.'

'A likely story. I think that woman has got wind of the romance and it's her way of putting a stop to it. I know what it's like, Daisy. I saw the way your parents suffered at the hands of your mother's family, and they wanted nothing to do with you or your brother. We'd better not mention this to your uncle,' Eleanora concluded. 'He wouldn't take kindly to someone toying with your affections.'

'You haven't told him of my engagement?'

'No, my dear, I wanted to be certain before I gave him the news. I know how delicate these matters can be.'

'Julian might change his mind,' Daisy said hopefully. 'I'm sure his mother knew something, and maybe she persuaded him that he was making a mistake.'

'To be swayed so easily is not a good sign. He sounds like a weakling. You'd be better off with a decent local man than a milksop who's afraid to stand up to his mother.'

Daisy gazed at the daguerreotype on the mantelshelf portraying her parents on their wedding day, which was the image that she had clung to during her childhood. She could see how pretty and appealing dark-haired, dark-eyed Marguerite must have been to young James Marshall, and Aunt Eleanora swore that Daisy was the image of her late mother. Daisy never quite believed her aunt, but she loved to hear the story of how her parents had met. In fact she had heard it so many times that she could recite it word for word. It was a true romance of a young woman whose family considered themselves to be upper middle class and a man whose family were in trade. James had come to their house in Finsbury Square to deliver a new saddle, and it had been pure chance that had led him to the front door instead of the tradesmen's entrance at exactly the moment when Marguerite Gifford had just returned from a shopping expedition. It was, as Eleanora was fond of telling her niece, love at first sight. After that the young couple had met secretly, and in the face of much opposition from both families they had eloped to Gretna Green. Daisy studied the smiling faces of her parents in their bridal finery. Perhaps she would never know the love and happiness they had shared, albeit so briefly, but she owed it to their memory to stand firm. She would not waste her tears on someone who was too weak to fight for the woman he loved.

'You're right, Aunt. But now I must look for another position. At least Mrs Carrington was fair enough to give me a good reference.'

'A sap to her conscience,' Eleanora said with a wry smile.

'And I'm fortunate to have you and Uncle Sidney and a nice home,' Daisy added hastily. 'You've always been good to me, Aunt. Both Toby and I know how lucky we've been.'

Eleanora sank down on the nearest chair. 'I have something to tell you, Daisy. Take a seat, please. Looking up at you is making my neck ache.'

'What is it? You seem upset.' Daisy perched on the edge of a chair. Surely there could be nothing worse than the news she had received earlier that day?

'Your uncle has sold the business and we intend to retire and move to the country. There, I've said it. Don't look at me like that, Daisy. We were going to break it more gently, but you've forestalled us by leaving the Carringtons.'

'It wasn't my choice, Aunt.' Daisy hesitated for a moment as a confused jumble of emotions threatened to overcome her. The apartment above the shop had been her home ever since she could remember; she knew all the shopkeepers in the vicinity, and the names of all the residents of Meggs' Almshouses, who benefited from Aunt Eleanora's generosity at Christmas and Easter. She had enjoyed theatrical presentations at the New Royal

Pavilion Theatre, including pantomimes, and she had taken omnibus rides to the West End, where exciting department stores were being opened. Daisy's lips trembled — it was all too much to bear, and it was Christmas.

'I know you're upset, Daisy, and this doesn't help, but I had to be honest with you.'

Daisy took a deep breath. She must not cry like a baby, even though her heart was breaking. 'Where are you going to live?'

'An elderly aunt has died and left me her cottage in Essex. It's where I grew up and it has enough land to enable us to keep a pig and some chickens, and grow our own vegetables. The country air will be good for your uncle, and I don't want him to work himself into an early grave.'

Daisy stared at her in astonishment. 'But I thought you were happy here. Uncle Sidney isn't an old man.'

'He's been in this business since he was a boy, and we've saved enough to keep us quite comfortably. The dirt and smoke in the city isn't good for his health, nor mine, come to that. We'll have a better life in the country.'

'But what do I do if I can't find another position?'

'We'll be here for another week or two, Daisy. I'm sure you'll find something, or you can come and live in the country with us. It's not a huge cottage, but there is room enough for you, should you decide to accompany us.'

'But what about Toby? I know he lives in at the hospital but he's about to qualify. Where will he go then?'

Eleanora smiled. 'You can ask him yourself. He's just walked into the room.'

Daisy jumped to her feet, turning to face her brother. 'Did you know of this, Toby?'

'That's a nice welcome. I haven't seen you for weeks. Is that all you can say?' Toby crossed the floor in long strides and enveloped her in a brotherly hug.

'Did you know that Uncle Sidney is retiring to the country?' Daisy demanded as he released her and went to kiss his aunt on the forehead.

Toby straightened up, facing her with a sympathetic smile. 'Yes, I did, but why are you here? I thought you were spending Christmas with the Carringtons.'

Daisy sent a warning look in her aunt's direction. Now was not the time to tell Toby about Julian. Her brother was fiercely protective and she knew he would be furious. She would tell him later, when she was feeling less fragile. 'I'm no longer needed there,' she said calmly. 'Master Timothy is being sent to boarding school, but Mrs Carrington has given me a good reference.'

'I'm sorry, Daisy. I know you liked the little fellow.' Toby's concerned expression gave way to a wide grin. 'But I've got news that will cheer you up.'

'You've passed your exams?'

'Yes, I'm a qualified doctor.'

Daisy reached up to brush his cheek with a kiss. 'Well done. I knew you could do it.'

'Yes, well done indeed,' Eleanora added, smiling. 'Your uncle will be so proud.'

Toby slipped his arm around Daisy's shoulders. 'There's something else, too.'

'What is it?' Daisy asked anxiously. 'I don't think I can take another shock. What are you trying to tell us, Toby?'

2

Toby looked from one to the other, obviously savouring the moment. Daisy could see that he was enjoying himself, but her nerves were on edge, and she was not in a mood to cope with another piece of earth-shattering news.

'All right. Don't look daggers at me, Daisy.' Toby paused for effect, but a stern glance from his aunt made him continue hastily. 'I've always wanted to specialise in surgery, and I've been offered a position as a junior houseman at the London.'

Daisy flung her arms around his neck. 'Congratulations, Toby. That's wonderful.'

'But what will you do now, Daisy?' Toby's smile faded. 'Have you applied for another position?'

'I've told Daisy about our move,' Eleanora said firmly. 'I hope she'll decide to come with us.'

'That sounds eminently sensible.' Toby took Daisy by the hand, giving it an encouraging squeeze. 'The change of air would do you good, and who knows? You might get swept off your feet by a handsome landowner.'

Daisy snatched her hand free. 'Why does everyone assume that marriage is the answer to everything? I want to prove that I'm worth something in my own right, if only to myself.'

'Good heavens, Daisy! You're not turning into

one of those bluestocking women, are you?'

'No, of course not, Toby. I just want to do something worthwhile.'

'You're upset, dear,' Eleanora said softly. 'Think it over, but you really don't have much alternative now that you're not living in Queen Square. We wouldn't think of leaving you on your own in the city, and you have no income to support yourself.'

'I spent years at Miss Lonsdale's Academy learning Latin and Greek and solving complicated mathematical problems. Are you saying that it's all been a waste of time?'

'Calm down,' Toby said, chuckling. 'I don't know why you're getting yourself in such a stew. You were only a governess, after all.'

Daisy knew that Toby had not spoken out of spite, but his words seemed to echo Mrs Carrington's opinion of the girl her son had wanted to wed, and she felt a shiver run down her spine.

'You're right,' she said slowly. 'I was just a governess, but I'll prove one day that I can do more than that. In the meantime,' she added, turning to her aunt and forcing a smile, 'I will come with you, of course, and I'll find out if living in the country suits me.'

★ ★ ★

Despite the fact that Toby was at home for Christmas it was going to be a subdued celebration. Eleanora's mind was obviously on the forthcoming move to the country, and she

21

spent most of her time sorting through her clothes or packing up small objects that had some sentimental value. Sidney disappeared to the pub at the first opportunity on Christmas Day and Toby went with him, leaving Daisy to wonder how things had come to this. Christmas was supposed to be a joyous occasion, but she had been jilted by the man she loved and had lost her job. It was not so much the money, it was the fact that she had grown fond of young Timothy, and he returned the affection. She had looked forward to being part of the Carrington family — now that was never going to happen. She was emotionally bruised, and although she tried to be positive, she could not summon up any enthusiasm for life in the wilds of Essex.

But it was Christmas Day, and Uncle Sidney and Toby were in a merry mood when they returned from the Earl of Effingham, having imbibed rather too much rum punch. Aunt Eleanora was not amused, but the table was set and, as was their custom, Hattie and Jonah sat down with them to enjoy the roast turkey with all the trimmings. Uncle Sidney did his best to be jolly, but Daisy was very conscious of the underlying current of anxiety felt by all at the move. Jonah was sullen and silent throughout the meal, and Daisy could feel his eyes upon her although he turned away hastily when she glanced at him. Toby was in fine fettle and did his best to raise their spirits, but it was a relief when the last of the Christmas pudding and brandy butter was eaten. Toby left, having a prior engagement to meet up with friends, while

Eleanora and Sidney retired to the parlour, no doubt to snooze by the fire. Hattie went to the kitchen to begin the washing-up, and Daisy was clearing the table when Jonah closed the dining-room door.

'What are you doing?' she demanded. 'I have to take these dishes to the kitchen.'

Jonah sidled up to her, grinning stupidly. 'It's a pity we got no mistletoe. I'd have an excuse to kiss you, miss.'

'You're drunk.' Daisy stepped aside. 'You'd best get on with whatever you're supposed to be doing, Jonah.'

'I've got money saved and Mr Marshall has persuaded the new owner to take me on. In less than a year I reckon I'll be managing the business, and we could live here above the shop. I'd make you a good husband, Daisy.' He moved closer and attempted to put his arm around her but she pushed him away.

'It's the wine talking, Jonah. I'll excuse you because it's Christmas, but you're forgetting yourself.'

His smiled faded and his lips twisted into a grimace. 'Not good enough for you, am I? What happened to the toff who was supposed to marry you?'

'You've been listening at keyholes,' Daisy said angrily. 'It's none of your business. I'm sorry if it hurts your feelings, but I don't want to marry you and never will.' She dodged round the table and opened the door. 'Come one step closer and I'll scream. My uncle wouldn't take kindly to this sort of behaviour.'

'You'll be sorry. One day you'll regret turning me down, Miss Marshall. I might have a twisted body, but I'm nobody's fool. You'll seek me out one day, begging for my help and see what you get then.' He brushed past her and limped off, cursing beneath his breath.

Daisy sat down at the table and reached for her wine glass. It was still half full and she downed it in one gulp. At least Jonah had helped her to decide what course she would take. The wilds of Essex seemed much more attractive now.

⋆ ⋆ ⋆

Jonah did not bother her again, although she was very conscious of his presence every time she went through the shop, but she did her best to ignore him. The next two weeks were spent sorting out what they would take to the new house, filling even more packing cases and trunks. Each day Daisy hoped she might get word from Julian, and every time she heard a male voice in the shop below, she strained her ears, willing it to be the man who had professed to love her. But Julian Carrington had not had the decency to write and apologise for her sudden dismissal, or even to enquire if she had found another position. For all he knew she might be selling bootlaces on street corners or working in the nearby blacking factory. Daisy had to face the fact that he had gone to Paris to take up his new position, leaving her to break her heart and suffer the humiliation of being jilted.

On a bitterly cold day in the middle of January, Daisy and her uncle and aunt left their home in Whitechapel. Toby had not officially started his new position at the hospital, and as he had time on his hands he had decided to accompany them. Daisy suspected that his decision was motivated more by curiosity than anything else, but Toby had said vaguely that he had a friend who lived somewhere in that part of Essex and he might pay him a visit. Her gregarious brother seemed to have friends everywhere and Daisy had not questioned him further. It was good to have the family together again, no matter what the reason.

It was snowing again, but Jonah insisted on seeing them off. 'You'll return soon enough,' he whispered as Daisy edged past him. 'And I'll be waiting.'

She did not look back as Toby handed her into the waiting hackney carriage, but even as they drove off she was aware that Jonah Sawkins was standing in the shop doorway, watching until they were out of sight.

'Cheer up, Daisy,' Toby said, grinning. 'You might even enjoy living in Little Creek. Let's hope it isn't as dull as it sounds.'

★   ★   ★

As the train pulled out of Bishopsgate Station, Daisy's last hope of seeing Julian evaporated like the great puffs of smoke and steam belching from the massive engine. Although she knew it was unlikely, she had thought he might have

25

written to her. She had been tempted to return the ring, but she would not give him the satisfaction of acknowledging his cowardly behaviour. It was tucked away in her jewellery box, along with a few cheap trinkets and the rope of pearls that her mother had worn on her wedding day. Daisy sighed and settled down to gaze out of the window.

The train trundled through rural Essex, stopping at every station to disgorge people and livestock onto the platforms, and to pick up more passengers. Daisy stared out of the window at the countryside as it flashed past, but all that registered were the stark bare branches of the trees, stretching towards the grey sky like dead men's fingers. Ploughed fields lay dormant, imprisoned by neatly trimmed hedgerows, and muddy rivers slithered like snakes, heading for the sea.

Daisy had seen little of Toby during the journey as he had joined a group of young men in another compartment and she could hear their raucous laughter above the clickety-clack of iron wheels as they crossed the points, and her uncle's stertorous snores. Aunt Eleanora was supposed to be reading a novel, but she too kept nodding off, leaving Daisy alone with her thoughts.

When they arrived at Little Creek Station Daisy stepped out onto the platform, taking deep breaths of the ice-cold air, sharpened by the briny tang of the sea and the smell of brackish mud from the saltings.

'Godforsaken place,' Toby said as he hefted a

couple of carpet bags onto the platform. 'Are you sure you're doing the right thing, Uncle?'

'Take deep breaths, boy.' Sidney inhaled deeply and exhaled with a satisfied smile. 'That is fresh air. We're going to enjoy a long and healthy retirement in the country. You ought to join us, Toby. Set up a practice in the village and live a long life.'

'And die of boredom,' Toby said, laughing. 'No, thank you, Uncle.'

'Find a cab to take us to the cottage, Sidney.' Eleanora glanced up at the sky where clouds were forming rapidly, threatening even more snow.

Daisy looked round, liking what she saw, but feeling slightly nervous. Had she made the right choice? There was no way of telling. She followed her uncle as he strode along the platform to speak to the stationmaster.

'Ho, there, my man. Where will we find a conveyance to take us to Creek Cottage?'

The stationmaster smiled wearily. 'Begging your pardon, sir, but this ain't a big city. We don't have the luxury of hansom cabs and such like.'

'But there must be someone who can transport us to our destination.'

'It's barely a mile to Creek Cottage.' The stationmaster stared pointedly at the pile of luggage. 'I dare say I can find someone to deliver your cases to you later this afternoon.'

'Are you saying we'll have to walk to the cottage?' Daisy cast an anxious glance at her aunt, who was dressed for the city in her best gown and high-heeled boots, totally unsuitable for traipsing along country lanes.

'Yes, miss. Unless you want to wait around on the off chance of someone turning up with a farm cart.'

Sidney turned to Daisy with a worried frown. 'You'd better warn your aunt. I told her to dress suitably, but you know how she is.'

Daisy knew only too well. It was hard to imagine fashionable Eleanora Marshall rolling up her sleeves and tending to livestock, or baking bread, although that would not be necessary now, for Hattie had decided to join them in their move to the country, and she had gone on ahead to make the cottage ready.

'I'm afraid there is no transport,' Daisy said breathlessly as she hurried back to where her aunt was waiting with Toby. 'We'll have to walk to the cottage.'

'Out of the question.' Eleanora folded her arms across her bosom. 'Last time we were here my cousin's solicitor met us and transported us to our destination.'

Daisy and Toby exchanged wary glances. 'I'm afraid that's not going to happen today, Aunt,' Daisy said gently. 'You could always sit in the waiting room and hope that someone comes along with a farm cart, although it might be filled with straw and animal droppings.'

Eleanora tossed her head. 'Out of the question. I'll walk, but if it rains I'll be very angry. Thank goodness I sent Hattie on ahead. I told her to light fires in all the rooms, so at least the house will be warm.' She marched off to join her husband and the stationmaster.

'This should be fun, Daisy,' Toby said, chuckling. 'I can see that life in the country will suit Aunt Eleanora down to the ground.'

'I'm glad you find it amusing.' Daisy suppressed a giggle with difficulty. She doubted whether her aunt and uncle would see the funny side to their predicament, and she did not want to make matters worse when they were obviously in a state of distress. She hurried over to them. 'Perhaps if Toby and I were to walk to the village we might find someone to help.'

'Yes, yes, whatever you wish,' Sidney said irritably. 'For heaven's sake go and sit in the waiting room, Eleanora. I'll stay with you while the youngsters look for a suitable conveyance.'

The stationmaster was about to walk away when he paused, cocking his head on one side. 'Someone is coming, so you might be in luck, ladies and gentlemen.' He hurried off in the direction of the ticket office.

'I can hear the rumble of carriage wheels,' Daisy said eagerly. 'Toby and I will go and see what we can do.' She followed the stationmaster with Toby striding along at her side.

'I'm glad I came, if only for the show.' Toby was first through the gate, but he came to a sudden halt. 'Well, I'll be blowed, look who it is.' He rushed over to the man who leaped off the box, handing the reins to the messenger boy who had been loitering by the ticket office.

'It's you,' Daisy said dazedly. 'What a strange coincidence.'

Toby released his friend, turning to Daisy with

raised eyebrows. 'Do you two know each other?'

Nick Neville smiled and bowed. 'Miss Marshall, delighted to meet you again, although I'm astonished to find you and Toby here in Little Creek.'

'We bumped into each other outside Uncle's shop when I arrived home before Christmas,' Daisy said by way of explanation. 'I meant to tell you, Toby, but with the move and everything I forgot to mention it.'

'Instantly forgettable, that's me,' Nick said, chuckling.

'But what are you doing here, old boy?' Toby demanded, grinning. 'I thought you said you were going home to sort out some family matters.'

'And that's what I'm doing. My father died a couple of months ago, leaving Creek Hall to me. I've been down here since before Christmas, trying to get things straight, but it's an uphill task.'

'I knew your pa was a doctor in rural Essex, but I thought it was Colchester or thereabouts.' Toby gazed at his friend in amazement.

'I used to tell people it was Colchester because no one had ever heard of Little Creek, and it saved a lot of explaining. I'm not ashamed of my roots; I suppose it was just laziness.' Nick smiled ruefully. 'Anyway, I might set up a practice in Little Creek. The people in the village seem to rely on an ageing midwife, or else they have to travel the eleven miles to Maldon.'

'But you'd hardly scrape a living, old boy.'

Daisy nudged her brother in the ribs. 'It's

none of your business, Toby.'

'But it is, Daisy. There's no money working in an out-of-the-way place like this, and Nick was the top student in our year.'

'Even more reason to devote myself to those who most need my services.'

'You could have had the job they've offered me, Nick. I only scraped through by the skin of my teeth.'

'You'll work your way up to Harley Street, if I know anything about you, Toby old chap. Anyway, where are you going? Maybe I can give you a lift.'

'Do you know Creek Cottage?' Daisy eyed him hopefully. 'My aunt and uncle would really appreciate a ride in your chaise. Toby and I can walk.'

'As it happens I do know the place, and it's not far from Creek Hall. In fact I believe at one time it belonged to the estate. Anyway, I'll just check if the parcel I was expecting has arrived and then I'm at your disposal.' With a cheery smile Nick strode into the ticket office, leaving Daisy and Toby to explain his presence to their uncle and aunt, who had also heard the approaching vehicle and had come to find out if they were in luck.

Toby had just finished telling them about Nick when he reappeared carrying a small package, which he deposited beneath the seat, and after introductions and explanations, Eleanora and Sidney clambered into the chaise and Nick drove off, promising to return and meet Daisy and Toby on the road. He drove off just as it started to snow and Eleanora's black umbrella disappeared into the distance, bobbing up and down like a dancing mushroom.

'Give me the city any day,' Toby said grimly. 'You can hop on a bus or hail a cab, or find a nice coffee shop and wait until the rain passes.'

'Stop grumbling.' Daisy took his arm. 'I've just had a thought, Toby. I don't know the way to Creek Cottage, and neither do you.'

He shrugged. 'Someone will know. We'll enquire when we get to the village.'

★ ★ ★

They walked on despite the fact that it was snowing, although it stopped eventually and a pale wintry sun emerged from behind the clouds. The village of Little Creek was spread over half a mile or so. The sound of hammering emanated from a smithy at the edge of the village, and they came to a school, where ragged children were racing about the yard, splashing in icy puddles, chasing each other and screaming with laughter. A Saxon church was surrounded by a graveyard, which was overlooked by the vicarage, and the village inn was conveniently near, as if to entice the worshippers to stop for a glass of ale before returning home to the terraces of thatched cottages on either side of the main street. Toby was about to enter the inn and ask for directions when Nick returned with the chaise and reined in beside them.

'It's not far,' he said cheerfully, 'but you both look a bit bedraggled and you might as well finish the journey in comfort.'

Daisy allowed Toby to help her into the vehicle and she sat beside Nick, who waited until Toby had leaped on board before flicking the reins and urging his horse to walk on.

'You've seen the cottage,' Daisy said shyly. 'What is it like?'

Nick turned to her with a wry smile. 'Put it this way, I would gladly swap cold, draughty Creek Hall for Creek Cottage any day. Your aunt and uncle's house might not be large, and I only saw the front parlour, but it's warm and cosy. I really envy you.'

'You don't mean that, Nick.' Toby clutched the side of the chaise as it lurched forward, the horse seeming to sense that it was going home. 'Is your home as grand as it sounds?'

'It's seen better days.' Nick flicked the whip above the horse's ears, urging it to a steady trot. 'Anyway, I have to go to Maldon tomorrow to see my late father's solicitor. Whether I stay or not depends on the terms of the will. If there's no money for the upkeep of the house and grounds I might be forced to sell and move back to London.'

Daisy shot him a curious glance. 'Has Creek Hall been in your family for a long time?'

'Almost two hundred years. An ancestor of mine built it, having sold his interest in a shipbuilding business, and moved south with the idea, I think, of becoming a country squire.'

'What made you choose medicine as a career?' Daisy studied his profile and decided she liked what she saw. A high forehead, a straight nose and a firm chin, all of which, as Aunt Eleanora would have said, added up to a man of character.

'You don't ask that sort of question, Daisy,' Toby said impatiently. 'It's a calling. Nick and I decided to serve mankind.'

It was Daisy's turn to chuckle. 'You went to medical school because you didn't want to take over the business from Uncle Sidney. Be honest, Toby.'

He grinned. 'Yes, that too.'

Daisy turned to Nick. 'Are you as cynical as my brother?'

'Toby likes to make out that he doesn't care, but I've seen him at work and I can promise you that it isn't so.'

Daisy smiled and squeezed her brother's arm. 'I'm very glad to hear it, but what about you, Nick?'

'It seemed natural to follow in my father's footsteps. He served the people of Little Creek and the surrounding area for the best part of thirty years, hence the dilapidated state of the family home. A country physician barely makes a living.'

'Join me in Harley Street when I get there,' Toby said airily. 'We'll have the best practice in London.'

Daisy shook her head. 'Dream away, brother. You know that Uncle Sidney hasn't enough money to set you up in a venture of that sort.'

'I'll think of something.' Toby sat back against the padded squabs and they lapsed into silence.

Daisy's curiosity was aroused by the brief glimpse into Nick Neville's life, but she refrained from asking questions, sensing that he was a private person, disinclined to talk about himself, and she concentrated on the scenery. The lane skirted the edge of a wood and followed the course of the creek to a bend in the watercourse where the land opened out to reveal a smallholding.

'That's your new home,' Nick said cheerfully. 'That is Creek Cottage.'

Her first impression was favourable and the setting would have made an artist reach for his brushes. Trees and bushes grew down to the water's edge on the far side, and in the distance, through a gap in the foliage, Daisy could see what appeared to be a very grand house.

'Is that Creek Hall?' she asked eagerly.

Nick threw back his head and laughed. 'No, indeed. My home is much nearer. That is Creek Manor, the residence of Squire Tattersall.' Nick's smiled faded. 'He owns most of the land round here.'

'Well, our place looks pleasant enough.' Toby slipped his arm round Daisy's shoulders. 'What do you think?'

Daisy nodded. 'It looks cosy.' Her first thought was of the doll's house that her uncle had made for her one Christmas when she was eight or nine. The door in the centre of the building was shielded from the weather by a tiled porch, which she imagined would be smothered in roses in the summer. There was a window either side of the porch and three more nestling beneath the eaves like sleepy half-open eyes, smiling down at the newcomers. The whitewashed walls had a look of solidity and permanence that Daisy found very appealing.

'That's your new home.' Nick glanced at Daisy with a questioning look.

'It seems very well kept and welcoming,' Daisy said slowly. 'You said that Creek Hall isn't far from here . . . ?'

'About a mile. You must come to dinner one evening. I can guarantee a good meal because Cook opted to stay, even though I can't afford to pay her until I start up in practice.'

'Please don't go to any trouble on our account,' Daisy said hastily. 'But I would love to see your home.'

'I wouldn't mind a decent meal before I return to London. Our cook could do with a few lessons on the subject, if you ask me.' Toby patted his belly and grinned. 'Hattie will probably leave anyway. She's a Londoner through and through, as am I, and I can't imagine you living here for long, Daisy. You'll be back in London before the month is up.'

Daisy shook her head. 'I'm prepared to try, if only for our aunt and uncle's sake. They've done a lot for us, Toby.'

'I know, but we're grown up now.' Toby gazed at the cottage, frowning. 'What on earth will you find to occupy your days as a country doctor, Nick?'

'I have more than enough to keep me busy.' Nick brought the horse to a halt and leaped to the ground. He held his hand out to Daisy. 'I'm sure there is much you could do for the village, if you put your mind to it.'

Daisy accepted his help to alight. 'We'll see. At least I'm willing to accept change and take it as a challenge. My dear brother is a stick in the mud.'

Toby sprang from the chaise, landing in a puddle left by melting snow, which made Daisy laugh.

'There,' he said crossly. 'I told you the country is no place for a gentleman, let alone a qualified doctor. My boots are wet and the polish is ruined. Who's going to clean them?'

'You are.' Daisy knocked on the door. 'Don't you dare ask Hattie or she really will give in her notice.'

'Maybe we can get a girl to come in from the village to do the housework.' Toby grabbed Nick's hand and shook it. 'Thanks for the ride, old chap. I'll certainly be a guest at your table whenever you say, but make it soon because I doubt if I can stand being here for more than a day or two.'

Nick smiled and nodded. 'Always grumbling, Toby. Maybe one day you'll look on the bright side of life instead of seeing problems, real or imagined.'

'I'm a realist and you're a dreamer.' Toby glanced over his shoulder at the sound of the door opening.

'Toby, dear,' Eleanora said urgently. 'Your uncle needs a hand to move a trunk that was left in the entrance hall.'

'Maybe I'll come to the Hall with you, old chap.' Toby sighed. 'I can see I'm going to be worked off my feet if I stay here.'

'Don't you dare run off and leave me.' Daisy

grabbed his arm. 'I hope you're joking.'

Aunt Eleanora chose to ignore his remark. 'The furniture will arrive later, but the carrier has left our trunks in the most awkward place and you know how your uncle suffers from his back.'

'Come on, Toby. The two of us will make light work of it.' Nick looped the reins over the horse's head and handed them to Daisy. 'Would you mind holding on to Hero? He's old and docile, so he won't give you any trouble. I'll be as quick as I can.'

Daisy took the reins, eyeing the animal warily. 'Are you sure he won't make a sudden bolt for home? I'm not used to horses.'

'Have you ever ridden one?'

'No. I was brought up in Whitechapel. There are plenty of cabs and omnibuses to take you wherever you wish to go.'

'You'll find it very different here,' Nick said, chuckling.

'Please hurry,' Eleanora called over her shoulder as she retreated into the house. 'Sidney is stuck halfway up the stairs and Hattie is struggling with the kitchen range. I think there might be a bird's nest in the chimney.'

'I think I might get the train back to London,' Toby said grimly. 'Life in the countryside is far too hectic for my taste. Give me peasoupers and smoky taverns any day of the week.'

Nick shooed him over the threshold. 'Stop grumbling and do something useful.' He glanced over his shoulder, giving Daisy an apologetic smile. 'I won't be long.'

'Don't worry about me.' She stroked the horse's velvety muzzle. 'I'm new at this, Hero,' she said softly. 'Please be a good creature and don't bolt or do anything silly.'

Hero rolled his eyes and nodded, as if complying with her request. She sighed with relief. Perhaps she could get used to being this close to such a large creature, although she hoped that Nick would return quickly. She cocked her head on one side, listening to the rushing sound of the water and the cawing of crows. The countryside seemed almost too quiet after the constant din of traffic and the babble of voices in the city. Here there was nothing but the gentle whispering of the wind in the trees and the sounds of nature . . .

The idyll was shattered by the sound of her aunt's voice raised to a shriek and a loud thud emanating from the cottage. Forgetting her charge, Daisy dropped the reins and ran towards the house.

3

'Are you all right, Aunt Eleanora?' As she reached the doorway Daisy saw Nick and Toby lifting Uncle Sidney from beneath the wood-bound leather travelling trunk. 'Oh, my goodness, is he hurt?'

Aunt Eleanora clutched her hands to her bosom. 'Is anything broken? Are you all right, Sidney, my love?'

Sidney struggled to his feet, aided by Toby and Nick. 'Stop fussing, woman. Of course I'm all right. I'm not a fragile flower.' He stomped off. 'I'll be in the parlour. Tell Hattie to bring me a glass of brandy — for medicinal purposes, of course.'

Eleanora turned on Toby. 'You're a doctor. Go and look after your uncle.'

'He's fine, Aunt. What do you want us to do with this?' He poked the trunk with the toe of his boot.

'Leave it there. The removal men should be here soon. They're trained to heft boxes and heavy objects. I can't be doing with any more falls. I'm going to the kitchen to see how Hattie is getting on with the range or we won't have anything to eat today.'

Daisy glanced anxiously out of the door, but Hero had his head down and was munching the grass. 'I'm sorry, Nick,' she said hastily. 'I should have stayed with the animal.'

'Don't worry, he's not coming to any harm.' Nick turned to Toby. 'I'll go now and leave you to settle in.'

Toby leaned over to brush his aunt's flushed cheek with a kiss. 'I'll get out of your way, dear aunt. I'm not much use when it comes to unpacking and that sort of thing.' He turned to Nick. 'How about I come with you now?'

'That's fine with me, if your aunt and uncle don't need you?'

'No, take him away,' Eleanora said crossly. 'Toby might be a good doctor, but he's useless around the house.'

'Will you be all right, Daisy?' Toby asked anxiously. 'I mean, I could stay, but . . . '

Torn between annoyance and amusement, Daisy gave him a gentle shove towards the door. 'Go, for heaven's sake. We'll do better without you.'

'I'll bring him back after supper, but perhaps you would like to come to the Hall some time, Daisy.' Nick hesitated, frowning. 'Not tomorrow, of course, because I won't be there, but maybe the day after?'

Daisy smiled and nodded. 'Thank you. That would be lovely.'

'Come on, Nick,' Toby hurried outside, glancing up at the lowering clouds. 'I think it's going to snow again. Let's get going. I'll see you later, Daisy.'

'Yes,' she said as she watched them climb into the trap. 'You'll come home when all the work is done. Nothing changes.'

'Daisy, will you go and help Hattie in the

kitchen?' Eleanora said anxiously. 'If there's a nest in the chimney there might be a trapped bird and they make me nervous. I'll go and make sure your uncle is all right.' She bustled into the parlour without waiting for an answer.

Daisy sighed and shook her head as she made her way to the kitchen where she could hear Hattie shouting and crashing about. A gust of smoke enveloped her as she opened the door.

'I'll never get used to this brute,' Hattie said, flicking a cleaning cloth at the stove. 'Maybe there's a nest on top of the chimney pot. Whatever it is, I can't get the fire to draw properly.' She wiped her face with the back of her hand, leaving a streak of soot on her cheek.

Daisy looked round the large kitchen and spotted a besom propped up against the back door. 'Maybe I can clear the blockage,' she said hopefully.

'You're never going to push that broom up the chimney, are you?' Hattie demanded anxiously. 'You'll bring a fall of soot.'

She spoke too late. Daisy had snatched up the besom and was poking it up the chimney. A shower of soot, dried leaves and bits of twig covered everything, including Daisy. She stood for a moment, coughing and gasping for air.

'I told you so.' Hattie threw up her hands. 'Look at the mess you've made. Well, I ain't cleaning it up. I warned you, but would you listen? No, you would not, and everything is covered in soot. I'm going to tell the mistress.' She stomped out of the room.

Left to clean up, Daisy stared down at her

once clean travelling gown, which was now ruined. Soot was still settling on every surface and she could only be thankful for the fact that most of their china, pots and pans had yet to be unpacked. She was wondering what to do when someone knocked on the back door.

'Come in.'

The door opened and a pale-faced young woman stepped inside. She was muffled against the cold and her fair hair hung limply from beneath her bonnet. 'You've had a bit of a mishap, miss,' she said calmly.

'The chimney was blocked.' Daisy eyed her curiously. 'Can I help you?'

'It looks like I can help you.' The stranger took off her bonnet and shawl and hung them on a row of pegs. 'I was on my way home when the young doctor stopped to enquire about my mum — she's been took sick these last few days. I told him that she was getting better, thanks to the medicine he gave her.'

'That must have been Dr Neville, but why have you come here?'

'You're Miss Marshall, aren't you?'

Daisy gazed down at her sooty clothes and smiled ruefully. 'Yes, although I doubt if my friends would recognise me now.'

'I'm Linnet Fox, from the village. Dr Neville knew I was looking for work because I'd been to Creek Hall to enquire, but he said you might need some help, miss.'

'I don't know how much my uncle would pay, Linnet, but we do need someone.'

Linnet rolled up her sleeves. 'Let's clean the

range first then, miss. We'll get the fire going and then we can heat up some water and sort out the rest.'

The door burst open before Daisy had a chance to reply and her aunt came to a sudden halt, with Hattie peering over her shoulder. 'Good heavens! I've never seen anything like it.' She glared at Linnet. 'Who is this?'

'Dr Neville sent her, Aunt Eleanora,' Daisy said hastily. 'He thought we might need some assistance in getting things straight.'

'Who is she and how do we know she's trustworthy?'

Linnet bobbed a curtsey. 'I'm Linnet Fox, ma'am. My pa was gamekeeper at Creek Hall when the old doctor was alive, but he's too poorly to work now, and my mum is sick with lung fever. I'm a hard worker and honest.'

'I've got to have someone, ma'am,' Hattie added, peering over Eleanora's shoulder. 'I can't be expected to cope on me own.'

Eleanora glanced round the room. 'You may have a trial period, at the usual rate, whatever that might be. My husband will sort that out, but consider yourself hired, and please get this disaster sorted out as quickly as possible. We've been travelling for hours and we need a hot meal.'

'Don't worry, Aunt,' Daisy said firmly. 'I'll help Linnet. We'll get the kitchen cleaned up in no time.'

Eleanora nodded and turned on her heel, bumping into Hattie, who was still grumbling. 'I told her not to poke the broom up the chimney, ma'am. I told her not to do it, but she done it all the same.'

'Yes, thank you, Hattie. I think I get the gist. You can unpack my things upstairs while they get to work, and let's hope that Pickford's manage to get our furniture here before dark, otherwise we'll be sleeping on the floor.' She shooed Hattie away and closed the door behind her.

'You might like to wash your face and hands first, miss,' Linnet suggested tactfully. 'Soot burns something chronic if it gets in your eyes. I'll make a start sweeping up.'

It took almost an hour to get the kitchen clean, and Linnet had proved herself invaluable as she set about the work methodically, managing to get the fire going so that it blazed up the chimney. She showed Daisy where the pump was situated in the back yard, and the privy, which was in a small wooden hut that had been built to straddle a narrow stream.

'Does the night soil collector get this far out?' Daisy asked.

Linnet's laughter echoed off the outbuildings. 'Lord, no, miss. Lean closer and you'll hear the brook racing down to the creek. You sit on the seat and let nature do the rest. No need to dig latrines or such.'

Daisy felt a blush rise to her cheek. As a person raised in the city she knew she had a lot to learn. 'Thank you, Linnet. An excellent idea, I'm sure.'

'And don't worry about the pump water,' Linnet said, smiling. 'You're luckier than most of

45

the people in the village: this one taps into a spring deep down. The water is crystal clear and safe to drink.' She lifted the pump handle and began to work it vigorously. 'But this will be my job. You're a young lady and you don't need to know this.'

'I'll have to find something to do with my time.' Daisy watched closely. 'I never gave a thought to how hard servants have to work, but I'm beginning to appreciate it now.' She went indoors, leaving Linnet to her labours. It was little wonder that the servants at the Carringtons' establishment had treated her with scorn. They must have considered her to be ungrateful and idle, while they had to slave from dawn until well after dark in order to please their employers. Daisy felt a twinge of sympathy for them as she looked down at her reddened hands. She held the door open for Linnet as she staggered past her, hefting two wooden pails filled with water.

'Thank you, Linnet,' she said earnestly. 'I don't know how I would have managed if you hadn't come knocking on the door.'

'Thank the young doctor, miss. He's so good and kind — I just hope he decides to stay in Little Creek, but I'm afraid he'll go away and leave us without a physician again.'

'Was it so very bad before he came to live here?'

'I doubt if you could imagine it, miss. I mean it's obvious you're used to better things. You're a lady for a start and you've got hands that have never known hard work, but for us in the village it's a matter of life and death to have a doctor nearby. My cousin died in childbirth, and the babe soon after. If Dr Neville had been at Creek Hall I dare say they'd both be alive now.'

'I'm so sorry,' Daisy said gently. 'How sad.'

'Life is hard, miss.' Linnet filled two large pans with water and placed them on the hob. 'We can finish up when the water is warm enough. Then your cook can make a start on supper and I'll head off home. Mum will be wondering where I've got to.'

'But you will come tomorrow?' Daisy asked anxiously.

'Yes, of course, miss. I'll be here early, so no need to worry.' She cocked her head on one side. 'That sounds like your furniture has arrived. I can finish up here if you want to go and help the old lady.'

Daisy smothered a giggle. 'My aunt is Mrs Marshall and she wouldn't thank you for calling her old. I will go and help, and I just want you to know I'm very grateful to you, Linnet. You've worked so hard.'

'That's what I'm here for, miss.' Linnet wiped her hands on her apron.

Daisy left the kitchen and went to help her aunt, who was firing instructions at the delivery men like an army sergeant.

'Perhaps they'd like some refreshment, Aunt,' Daisy said softly. 'There'll soon be enough hot water to make a pot of tea and they've had a long journey from London.'

'Let them do their job first. Time for tea when they're finished. You can help by unpacking the linen. It's in that wicker hamper.'

'It looks as if they're unloading the beds first. I'll make them up, if you wish.'

'That's a job for Hattie or the girl.'

'I need to be usefully employed, Aunt. I can't spend my days idling.'

'You've been brought up to be a young lady, Daisy. I owed it to your parents to see that you have the best chance in life. It's just a pity you allowed Julian Carrington to get away. Rich husbands don't grow on trees, my girl. I'm afraid you've lost your chance now, and that nice Dr Neville isn't likely to stay for long. No doubt he'll go where he can earn a decent living. I'm afraid you'll be on the shelf if you don't do something about it, and you know how hard life is for women without means, as well as the disgrace of being an old maid.'

'I'll find something to do with my life, Aunt. I don't intend to be a burden on you for much longer. I just need to work out what is best for me, and then nothing will stop me. I promise you that.'

4

Eleanora and Sidney had retired soon after supper, and Hattie had gone to her room on the dot of ten, leaving Daisy to wait up for Toby. She spent the time unpacking boxes of linen, but she was tired, and when he had not returned by midnight she decided to go to bed, leaving the key under a flowerpot outside the front door. Despite the lateness of the hour she was not worried — she imagined him and Nick playing cards after a good dinner, or sitting by the fire chatting about their student days. Toby, she knew, kept London hours and she suspected that Nick was glad to have his company. It must be lonely living in a large house without the comfort of a family to fill the rooms with laughter. Although, thinking back, there had not been much jollity in the Carrington household, and Master Timothy had often come crying to Daisy when his father had punished him severely for some minor misdeed. Julian had been the only member of the household who had had a kind word and a smile for Daisy, and now she was away from Queen Square she realised how easy it must have been for him to charm her into believing his promises of undying love and devotion.

All these thoughts passed through Daisy's mind as she lay in her bed with the covers pulled up to her chin and prepared for sleep. It came eventually, and she awakened to the sound of the wind rattling the branches of a tree close to her window, and the scrape of thorns on the windowpanes as the stems of a climbing rose brushed against the glass. It took a moment or two for her to work out why she was sleeping in a strange room, and then the memories of the previous day came flooding back. She sat up and yawned, but the chill in the room was even greater than that of her small bedchamber in Queen Square. Mrs Carrington had not allowed the governess to have the benefit of a fire, no matter how cold it was, and Daisy had often had to break the ice in the pitcher before she could pour the water into the washbasin. She reached for her wrap and was about to get up when someone tapped gently on the door.

'Come in.'

The door opened and Linnet entered carrying a jug of steaming water in one hand and a cup of tea in the other. 'I took the liberty of bringing this up to you. The mistress was asking why you wasn't at breakfast.'

'That's very thoughtful of you, Linnet. Thank you.' Daisy took the cup and saucer from her and sipped the tea. 'It's so cold. Is it snowing again?'

Linnet placed the jug on the oak washstand. 'The east wind got up in the night. It blows in off the sea — straight from Russia, so my pa says. If it goes round to the north, there'll be more snow.'

'It feels much colder here than it does in London, but I dare say I'll get used to it. Would you be kind enough to tell my aunt that I'll be down soon?'

'Yes, miss.' Linnet bobbed a curtsey. 'I could light the fire for you, if you so wish.'

'Maybe this evening. We don't want to waste coal.'

'There are plenty of logs in the shed. I lit the fires downstairs and helped Hattie to get the range going. She's still grumbling about it, but I dare say she'll get used to it, given time.'

Daisy sipped her tea, which was still quite hot and more than welcome. 'I'm afraid she might leave and return to London. It's very different here in the heart of the countryside.'

'There's plenty who would be more than willing to take her place, miss.' Linnet backed towards the doorway. 'There's not many jobs to be had in Little Creek and times are hard. We just hope that the doctor will stay, but people are saying he'll go back to London.'

'I think that's up to Dr Neville.' Daisy placed the cup and saucer on a small table near the window. 'I must get dressed and I mustn't keep you from your work, but it's good to have you here, Linnet. We need someone young and capable like you.'

Linnet's plain face flushed scarlet. 'Ta, miss.' She hurried from the room and her booted feet clattered on the bare boards as she hurried downstairs.

Eleanora was about to rise from the table when Daisy walked into the small dining room. 'Your uncle has been up for hours,' she said, sighing. 'I hope he isn't going continue like this or I'll never get any peace.'

51

Daisy suppressed a smile. 'Where is he now, Aunt?'

'Goodness knows. He put on his hat and coat and went out muttering something about fishing, although he's never shown any interest in such a thing before.'

Daisy took a seat at the table and helped herself to porridge, adding a generous amount of sugar and cream. 'It would be good for him to have something to occupy his time. A man who's worked all his life might find it hard to do nothing.'

'I suppose so, and we could eat the fish he caught. At least it gets him out from under my feet and I have such a lot to do.'

'I can help you.'

'Thank you, dear, but I need to do things my way, and I'll get the village girl to help. She has to learn our ways.'

'You mean Linnet. She has a name, Aunt.'

'I don't want to be too familiar. Servants get above themselves in such a situation.'

'You call Hattie by her Christian name.'

'Hattie has been with me for twenty years or more, and I don't want to lose her. Anyway, I know how to handle my servants, thank you, Daisy. Why don't you wrap up and go for a walk? Get to know the area, and if you see your uncle tell him to keep away from the river-bank. He can't swim.' Eleanora left the room and Daisy was able to finish her breakfast in peace.

She was about to clear the table when Linnet appeared, carrying a tray. 'I'll do that, miss. Your aunt sent me.'

Daisy knew better than to argue. 'Thank you.' She hesitated in the doorway. 'I seem to have nothing to do so I thought I'd walk to Creek Hall and fetch my brother. Which way is it?'

'Creek Hall is on the edge of the wood overlooking the saltings. Just follow the creek.'

'The saltings?'

'It's a salt marsh that's covered by the sea at high tide. It's not the place to go walking unless you know the area well.'

'Don't worry, I'm not that adventurous, but I will take a stroll.'

Having left Linnet to do her work Daisy retrieved her bonnet and cape from the row of pegs in the entrance hall before setting off. The sun was shining and the threat of more snow seemed to have passed, but the bitter east wind made her eyes water. The ground was uneven and she had to take care not to trip over the ridges created by wagon wheels or to step into the ruts filled with snow melt. Despite the chill, the air was bracing and the sun's rays reflected in the water, trapping the pale blue of the winter sky in the ripples, although as she approached the woods the shadows grew longer and the water lost its sparkle, appearing muddy and menacing. Daisy walked on, wrapping her woollen cape tightly around her. She quickened her pace and it was a relief to come out into the open where the saltings stretched out in front of her in a mass of vegetation growing haphazardly like a jigsaw puzzle tossed into the brackish water.

To her left she spotted Creek Hall, standing on its own at the edge of the wood with an uninterrupted view of the salt marsh. Sea birds circled overhead, mewing and crying like lost souls, while others waded in the shallow water, probing the mud with their long beaks in the search for food.

As she drew nearer she could see that the carriage sweep was losing the battle with couch grass and weeds, and some of the windowpanes in the upper floor were missing, but there was something about the warm red bricks of the Tudor house that spoke of permanence and solidity — two factors that appealed strongly to Daisy. She trod the gravel path, avoiding the patches of fast-melting snow, and went to knock on the door. After a while it was opened by a young woman who bore a striking resemblance to Linnet.

'Good morning,' Daisy said, smiling. 'I came to see if my brother, Dr Marshall, is still here.'

'You'd best come in then.' The girl, who was probably a year or two older than Linnet, stood aside, staring curiously at Daisy as she crossed the threshold.

Daisy returned the stare. 'Are you related to Linnet Fox, by any chance?'

A slow smile curved the girl's generous lips. 'I'm her sister, Dove.'

'Dove?'

'Yes, miss. Our mum loves birds. We all had such names.'

'Dove, who is it?' Nick's voice rang out from somewhere at the far end of the entrance hall.

'It's Miss Marshall, Doctor. She's come for her brother.'

Dressed for riding, Nick came to greet her. 'Miss Marshall, this is an unexpected pleasure. I hope you weren't worried when Toby failed to return home last night.'

Daisy smiled. 'Not at all. I'm afraid it was blatant nosiness that brought me this way. I was eager to see Creek Hall.'

'And here you are. I'd be delighted to show you round, although you might be disappointed.'

Daisy eyed his riding boots and topcoat. 'But you're going to Maldon to see your solicitor. You mustn't let me hold you up.'

'Another ten minutes or so won't make any difference, but first you must have some refreshment. It's bitterly cold and you've obviously walked here.' He turned to Dove. 'We'll have coffee in the dining room.'

'Yes, Doctor.' Dove hurried off.

'Toby is just finishing his breakfast and there's a fire in the dining room. I only use a couple of the downstairs rooms — the others are under covers all winter, although I'm afraid that does encourage damp.' Nick eyed her, frowning. 'Would you like to take off your cape, or would you prefer to keep it on?'

'I'll keep it on for the time being, if you don't mind.'

'Not at all. I'm wearing several layers myself. Come this way.' Nick led her across the wainscoted hall, through a door at the far end and down a long corridor to the dining room, where Toby was seated at the table. He pushed his plate away and jumped to his feet.

'Good Lord, Daisy. Are you checking up on

me? I thought Aunt Eleanora was bad enough, but this takes the biscuit.'

'Don't be so touchy, Toby. I've already admitted that I was curious to see Creek Hall, and I'm not disappointed.'

'You aren't?' Nick said. 'It's not exactly a grand house.'

'It feels homely, unlike the Carringtons' mansion in Queen Square. It was grand and expensively furnished but it wasn't a home.'

'If you equate homely with shabby, then you'll love Creek Hall. I'll show you round,' Nick said cheerfully. 'Although I'm afraid the rest of the house is even colder than it is in here.' He turned to Toby, who was munching a slice of toast and marmalade. 'Are you coming with us?'

Toby shook his head. 'No, thank you. I'm not nosy like my sister. I'll sit here and finish my breakfast in peace.'

Daisy chose to ignore her brother's teasing and she followed Nick from the room. The floorboards creaked as they negotiated the narrow passageways, and there were patches where the plaster had crumbled away from the walls, leaving the laths exposed. But if there were whispers from the past in the old house, the memories were happy ones.

'I'll introduce you to my housekeeper, Mrs Boynton, or Mrs Bee as I call her,' Nick said over his shoulder as they approached the kitchen at the back of the house. 'Mrs Bee has been with the family ever since I can remember, and she's a wonderful cook. I don't know why she stays on but she looked after my father in his last days

56

— she was devoted to him.'

Daisy gathered from his tone that Mrs Bee's opinion mattered, and as they entered the kitchen she braced herself for the inevitable interrogation. But it was the size of the kitchen and the height of the beamed ceiling that took her by surprise. At the far end of the room there was a huge open fireplace as well as an ancient range. The heat from a blazing log fire contrasted sharply with the chill rising from the flagstone floor.

A thin elderly woman, dressed in black from head to foot apart from a spotless white apron, rose from a chair at the table where she had been writing something in a ledger. 'Good morning, Master Nick.'

'I've brought Miss Marshall to meet you, Mrs Bee. She's Toby's sister.'

Mrs Bee looked Daisy up and down and a slow smile softened the harsh lines on her face. 'You'll be the young lady who's just moved into Creek Cottage.'

'I'm staying with my aunt and uncle, although I might return to London. I haven't quite decided.'

'We need new blood in the village. I hope you'll make your home in Little Creek, Miss Marshall.'

'If anyone can persuade her I'm sure you can, Mrs Bee.' Nick leaned over to brush the housekeeper's thin cheek with a kiss. 'I don't know what I'd do without you.'

'You're just like your late father: he could charm the birds from the trees if he so chose.'

'He loved Creek Hall and so do I, but everything depends upon my visit to the solicitor today.'

'It will be all right. There's nobody going to take Creek Hall away from you. It's been in the family for over two hundred years. You tell him that, Master Nick.'

'I will, and if all else fails I'll take you with me next time, Mrs Bee. We'll leave you in peace, but I had to show Miss Marshall the beating heart of Creek Hall.'

'Get away with you.' Mrs Bee shook her head, but she was smiling as she sat down and picked up her pen. 'Good day to you, Miss Marshall. I hope we'll see more of you at Creek Hall.'

'It was nice meeting you, Mrs Bee,' Daisy said over her shoulder as she hurried after Nick, quickening her pace in an attempt to keep up with his long strides. 'Do you really think you might lose Creek Hall?'

'My father left considerable debts. He was a good doctor but a poor businessman, and he rarely charged any of his poorer patients. Unless I can find a way to pay all or even some of the money back to the creditors, it looks as though I'll have to sell Creek Hall.'

'That's terrible. I can see how much it means to you.'

He came to a halt as they reached the entrance hall. 'You don't think I'm being overly sentimental?'

'Heavens, no! Why would I think that? If I owned a property that had been in my family for so many years I'd do anything to hold on to it.'

A smile lit Nick's hazel eyes. 'I believe you would.' He glanced at the grandfather clock as it chimed the hour. 'I didn't realise it was so late. I'm sorry but we'll have to finish the tour another day. I have to leave for Maldon right away.'

'I understand. Of course you must go, so don't worry about me. I'll go home with Toby.'

'Explain to him for me, please.'

'I will.' She stood aside as he made a grab for his hat and riding crop. 'Good luck.'

He smiled. 'Thanks. I'll need it. Tell Toby I'll call round this evening and let him know how I got on.'

Daisy nodded but he was already out of the door and she found herself alone in the hallway surrounded by echoes of the past. She could imagine the Neville ancestors pleading softly for someone to save their old home. If this house belonged to her family she would fight to the last to keep it.

'The coffee is getting cold,' Toby said crossly when she returned to the dining room. 'What kept you so long?'

'I met the redoubtable Mrs Bee.' Daisy picked up the coffee pot and filled a cup, adding a dash of cream. She sat down beside her brother. 'Nick had to leave, but he said he'd call round this evening and let you know how his meeting with the solicitor went. I do feel sorry for him.'

Toby shrugged and took another bite of toast. 'He could sell this old pile of bricks and move on. That's what I'd do if I were in his position.'

'But this is the family home, Toby. One of

Nick's ancestors built it.'

'It's old and it's crumbling. Besides which, who in their right mind would want to live in the wilds of Essex? It would be impossible to make a decent living round here.'

'But the people need a doctor. Doesn't that mean anything to you?'

'Then they should move to the nearest town. I intend to do my stint at the London, and then I'm heading for Harley Street where I can make a fortune and retire early so that I can enjoy the fruits of my labours.'

She shook her head. 'You have no soul, Toby Marshall.'

'And you are all heart, Daisy.' He leaned over to kiss her on the forehead. 'Have you fallen in love with the house or with my friend Nick?'

She chuckled but, even so, she felt the blood rush to her cheeks. 'The house, of course. I'm done with romance. It leads to heartbreak.'

He squeezed her fingers. 'Only if you fall for the wrong man, little sister. If I ever meet that cad Julian Carrington I'll give him what for.'

'He's not worth it, Toby. Forget about Julian — I have.' Daisy drank the lukewarm coffee in two gulps and replaced the cup on its saucer. 'We'd better go home.'

'It's not my home, Daisy. I'm going back to London tomorrow.'

'So soon?'

'There's no point staying any longer. I have to find lodgings near the hospital and I take up my position on Monday.'

'I'll miss you.'

Toby eyed her speculatively. 'Come with me, then. I'm sure we can find somewhere suitable for the two of us. You can keep house for me.'

The thought of being her brother's house-keeper made her laugh. 'I can't imagine how that would work out, Toby. We'd argue all the time, and anyway, I want to do something for myself.'

'Do you want to find another position like the last one?'

She shook her head. 'No, never. I wasn't cut out to be a governess, but there must be something I can do. There simply must.'

★　★　★

Toby caught the train to London next morning, once again offering to share his accommodation with Daisy should she change her mind. She was tempted, but she knew that if she were to leave now it would upset her aunt and uncle, and she put a brave face on it, waving goodbye to her brother as the train puffed out of the station. She set off to walk back to the cottage at a brisk pace and was approaching the village when she saw a group of small boys clustered around one of their friends, who was lying prostrate on the ground.

'What happened?' Daisy asked anxiously.

'He were climbing the tree, miss. The branch broke and he fell.' The boldest of the group wiped his runny nose on his sleeve. 'Is he dead?'

Daisy went down on her knees beside the child. 'What's his name?'

'Jack Fox, miss.'

61

'Fox? Is he related to Linnet and Dove?'

The boy nodded. 'He's their brother.'

'He's killed hisself,' cried a smaller boy. 'Run and get help, Danny.'

Daisy laid her hand on Jack's chest and she could feel his heart beating rhythmically. 'He's not dead.' She could see that one arm was twisted beneath him and she lifted him gently, straightening the injured limb. 'I think he's broken his arm. We need to get him to the doctor.'

'It's too far to carry him,' Danny said, sniffing.

Daisy glanced round in desperation. 'Don't just stand there, boys. Find me some straight sticks. I'll make a splint for his arm while he's unconscious and then we'll see about moving him.' She sat back while the boys scurried off to find the wood. 'Jack, can you hear me?' She brushed his dark hair back from his forehead to reveal a large egg-shaped bump that was rapidly turning blue. A head injury could be serious, but there was nothing she could do about that; the main thing was to get the boy home and send for the doctor. Daisy looked up as Danny returned carrying a bundle of twigs, some bigger and thicker than others.

'How far is it to Jack's home?'

'About half a mile, miss.'

'Is there anyone big and strong who could carry him? Or is there someone close by who owns a pony and trap?'

'The vicar has one, miss,' the smallest of the boys piped up eagerly. 'I can run fast. Shall I go and fetch him?'

Danny grabbed him by the arm. 'Don't be stupid, Alfie. We're supposed to be in school.'

'I wouldn't worry about that at the moment.' Daisy took off her cape and laid it over Jack's inert body. 'The important thing is to get help. Run along, Alfie. See how quickly you can get to the vicarage.'

Alfie puffed out his chest. 'I'm a fast runner.' He pushed past the silent boys, and sped off.

'Don't look, boys,' Daisy said firmly. 'I'm going to tear a strip off my petticoat so that I can use it as a bandage. We'll make Jack as comfortable as possible until help arrives.' She lifted her skirt and ripped a long strip from the hem of her undergarment. She could see the boys peeping through their fingers, but this was not the time for modesty and the sight of a shapely ankle was not going to do them any harm.

'He's groaning, miss,' Danny said importantly. 'He's coming round.'

Daisy worked quickly. She had read about the treatment of fractures in one of Toby's medical books, although she had never imagined that one day such knowledge might come in useful. She immobilised the arm by making a splint from three of the stronger pieces of wood bound with the material from her petticoat. Jack was moaning and his eyes fluttered and opened. He attempted to sit up, but Daisy restrained him gently.

'You're all right, Jack,' she said softly. 'You've had a fall, but you're all right now.'

He stared at her blankly. 'Who are you?'

63

'I'm Daisy Marshall. Your sister Linnet works for my aunt and uncle at Creek Cottage.'

'I got to go to school.' He attempted to rise once again, but Daisy shook her head.

'We need to get you home, and you have to see the doctor. I think your arm is broken, so please don't try to move.'

He pulled a face. 'I'll be for it when I get home.'

'So will I,' Danny added grimly. 'I'll get a beating from my dad and from Mr Massey.' His remark was accompanied by a groan of assent from the rest of the boys.

'Mr Massey?' Daisy shot him a questioning look.

'The schoolmaster. We don't like him.'

Daisy tried to think of something appropriate, but she could remember teachers at the academy for young ladies whom she had hated with a passion. Some of them seemed to have taken pleasure in tormenting the pupils under their care, and she sympathised silently with the boys. She looked up at the sound of hoof beats and the rumble of wheels.

Danny leaped to his feet. 'It's the doctor, and Alfie's sitting beside him in the trap. You'll be all right now, Jack.'

5

'You've done well, Daisy.' Nick lifted Jack gently and placed him on the seat. 'You'd best sit beside him,' he added in a low voice. 'We don't want him to fall off and suffer even more damage.'

Daisy nodded and climbed up to sit beside Jack, who was very pale and obviously in pain. 'It's all right, Jack, you'll be home soon and Dr Neville will look after you.' She glanced down at Danny and Alfie, who were watching intently. 'I think you'd best go to school and tell your teacher there's been an accident, but Jack is in good hands now.'

Nick eyed them sternly. 'Do as Miss Marshall says, and think twice next time you decide to wag school. Jack was fortunate — he only broke an arm — it could have been his neck.' He leaped onto the seat and picked up the reins. 'Walk on.'

Jack was trembling, either from shock or the pain or both, and Daisy placed her arm round his shoulders, holding him close. 'It was fortunate that Alfie met you on his way to the vicarage, Doctor.'

Nick urged the horse to a trot. 'I was called to tend to a difficult birth. The locals have been used to sending for my father and they seem to assume that I'll be taking his place.'

'Will you?' Daisy eyed him curiously.

'I don't know whether it's possible, although

'I'd like to carry on my father's work.'

'We didn't see you last evening. How did you get on at the solicitor's office?'

'I'm sorry, I intended to come and see you and Toby, but it was very late by the time I reached home.'

'What did the solicitor say?'

'He showed me my father's will and statements from his bank. Unfortunately my worst fears were confirmed. Father had tried to get a mortgage on the house, but the bank refused and probably as a last resort he borrowed money from the squire, who now owns at least half the properties in the village.'

'Is that a bad thing?'

'You wouldn't have to ask had you ever met Esmond Tattersall. Unfortunately my father was so desperate that he agreed to pay an exorbitant rate of interest on the loan.'

'Did he keep up the repayments?'

Nick shook his head. 'Apparently not. I always knew that Pa had a soft heart, and it seems I was right — he rarely took money from his poorer patients. According to Mrs Bee they paid him with produce from their gardens, a chicken or some eggs, but hardly ever with actual cash.'

'What will you do now?'

'I'm afraid I'll have to sell Creek Hall in order to pay off Tattersall, and I'll move to a more lucrative practice elsewhere.'

Jack's eyes flew open. 'Don't go, Doctor. My sister needs the job at the hall.'

'Not a word of this to anyone, young Fox,' Nick said firmly. 'It won't be for a while, and who knows? Maybe a miracle will happen and I'll be able to take up where my father left off.'

'There's our cottage.' Jack pointed with his good hand. 'Don't tell me mum that I was wagging, sir. She ain't well and neither is me dad.'

Nick drew his horse to a halt outside the house. 'I'll be tactful, but only if you promise to attend school regularly, when your arm is healed. A bright boy like you could go far, providing he's had a good education.'

'I promise, sir.'

Daisy climbed down and stood aside while Nick lifted Jack gently in his arms.

'Would you be kind enough to bring my medical bag, Daisy?'

'Yes, of course.' Daisy reached into the foot well and picked up the bag, which looked as though it must have belonged to Nick's father, judging by the well-worn leather. She followed them into the cottage, and she had to wait for a moment or two for her eyes to adjust to the darkness indoors. The rancid smell of tallow mingled with the pervading odour of damp, and a desultory fire burned in the small black-leaded range. As her eyes grew accustomed to the dim light Daisy could see that the coal scuttle was filled with pine cones and furze, and the temperature indoors was barely higher than that outside. She had always been aware that people lived in poverty, but this was the first time she had seen it first hand, and it came as something of a shock.

The sound of coughing from upstairs echoed

round the small room and a man, whom Daisy assumed must be Jack's father, rose from a chair by the range. He was tall and gaunt with several days' growth of beard masking his features.

'What's happened?' he demanded hoarsely.

'Jack had an accident, Lemuel. I need to take a look at his arm and make sure he has no other injuries.'

'I fell out of a tree, Dad,' Jack said warily. 'The branch broke.'

A bout of coughing prevented Lemuel from replying, but he pointed to a truckle bed placed beneath the stairs, and Nick laid Jack gently on the straw-filled palliasse.

'I'm just going to take a look, Jack. I'll be as careful as I can.' Nick kneeled down on the flagstone floor. 'I need some light, Lemuel.'

Daisy looked round for a lamp or some candles, but there were only a couple of rush lights, which would account for the smell of burning animal fat. She could see that Lemuel Fox was embarrassed by the doctor's request, and she felt a rush of pity for the man who was reduced to living in such straitened circumstances. It was easy to see why his daughters needed to work for low pay in order to provide even the basics to keep the family alive.

'Would you open the door wider, please, Daisy?' Nick said urgently. 'I need more light.'

Daisy held the door and winter sun shone palely into the room. Nick worked quickly, soothing Jack with a few words as he dealt with the fracture. He set the bone with a deft movement and Jack cried out, but was silent while his arm was bandaged.

Nick rose to his feet. 'I don't suppose there's much point in telling you to rest, Jack, but take things easy — no tree climbing for the foreseeable future.'

'Yes, Doctor.' Jack turned his head away, but not before Daisy had seen tears running down his cheeks. He was a little older than Timothy Carrington, who always tried hard to be a brave little soldier, and her heart went out to the boy. She put her hand in her skirt pocket and took out a poke of peppermint humbugs, a treat she had been saving for Hattie, who had a passion for the sweets. But Jack's need was the greater and Daisy pressed the paper package into his good hand.

'I'm sure the doctor would prescribe these to be taken freely, Jack. I believe they are very good for sore limbs.'

Jack's eyes lit up and he crammed a sweet into his mouth. 'Ta, miss. Ta, ever so.'

'Don't speak with your mouth full, boy,' Lemuel said crossly. 'You shouldn't spoil him, miss. Jack wouldn't have injured himself if he'd been in school. It's God's way of punishing him.'

Nick hesitated as he was about to close his medical bag. 'It was an accident, Lemuel. I think Jack has learned his lesson, and he won't be doing much climbing for a while.' He gave Lemuel a searching look. 'How long have you had that cough?'

'It's nothing, Doctor. Just the usual winter ailment, same as the missis upstairs, only she's took to her bed.'

Nick took a small brown bottle from his bag and laid it on the kitchen table. 'You might find this helps. The instructions for taking it are on the label.'

'I don't want it, Doctor. I can't pay.'

'It's a commercial traveller's sample; it cost me nothing, so it's just taking up space in my bag.' Nick snapped the locks together and made for the doorway. 'I'll call again tomorrow. Make sure you behave yourself, young Fox.' He placed his hat on his head as he stepped outside into the cold, clear morning air.

Daisy followed him to the cart. 'That wasn't a free sample, was it?'

'It will give Lemuel and his wife a little ease from the chest complaint.'

'Consumption?'

'That would be the worst diagnosis, but it could be simply inflammation of the lungs caused by the damp conditions and poor food. It's what happens to people who live in poverty, and I've seen it all too often at the London.'

'Is there nothing you can do for them?'

Nick handed her onto the driver's seat and climbed up to sit next to her. 'I wish there were, but all I can do is to hand out laudanum and advice as to their diet, which I know they cannot follow on such a limited income.'

'You've employed Dove and you sent Linnet to us,' Daisy said gently. 'At least the girls are looked after, but what will happen to Jack?'

'The boy will have to leave school and look for work. He has an elder brother, but Jay fell foul of the law and came to no good, according to Mrs

Bee, who loves to fill me in with all the village gossip.' Nick flicked the reins. 'Walk on.'

Relieved to get away from the depressing subject of illness, Daisy was intrigued by the Fox family. 'The girls have birds' names, but Jack is presumably short for James or John.'

Nick laughed and encouraged the horse to trot. 'I believe he was christened Jackdaw, but understandably prefers the shortened version.'

'And the other son?'

'Jay is the black sheep of the family. We used to play together as boys, but then I went to boarding school and university and we went our separate ways.'

'Perhaps someone ought to inform Jay that his parents are ill?'

'You're right, of course, although I wouldn't know how to contact him. I've been away from the village for a very long time.'

'But Mrs Bee might be able to help. You said that she knows everyone.'

'Again, you're quite right. I've learned how to diagnose and deal with disease, but it seems I still have much to learn about dealing with patients' problems. Maybe I'm more suited to working at a big hospital or in Harley Street. Perhaps Toby has the right idea.'

'My brother isn't like you, Nick. I think you would make a very good country doctor, and I suspect that the people in places like Little Creek are in desperate need of your services. London is full of hospitals and doctors' practices, but you said yourself that the villagers have had no one to look after them since your father passed away.'

'That is true but my position is untenable. If I can't make the repayments to the squire I'll have to sell the property.' He concentrated on the road ahead. 'Anyway, that's my problem. Will you stay in Little Creek? You didn't seem too keen on the idea yesterday.'

'It's different for me,' Daisy said, sighing. 'I really don't want to go back to being a governess, but I'm not qualified to do anything else.'

'Then we're both at a crossroads, and neither of us knows which way to go.'

He drove on in silence until they reached Creek Cottage, where he reined in and drew the horse to a halt. 'Come to dinner this evening, Daisy. I'll show you the rest of Creek Hall and you'll see the extent of my problem. Nothing has been done to preserve the old house for many a year despite my father's attempts to renovate the building. I'm afraid it might be too late to save it now.'

'That's not the most exciting invitation I've ever had,' Daisy said, laughing. 'But I would like to see more of the house. It just needs some loving care to bring it back to life.'

Nick leaped to the ground and helped her to alight from the chaise. 'I'll call for you at six, if that's convenient.'

'Thank you. I'll look forward to it.'

⋆　⋆　⋆

Dove served their meal in the dining room. Candlelight reflected off the old oak panelling, adding to the feeling of warmth and comfort, and the steak and kidney pie was excellent, but Daisy's thoughts were with the Fox family, living in squalid conditions less than a mile away.

'You aren't eating, Daisy,' Nick said gently. 'Isn't the food to your liking?'

She looked up with a start. 'No, I mean yes. The pie is delicious. I was thinking of Jack and his family.' She hesitated, at a sudden loss for words.

Nick sat back in his chair, eyeing her thoughtfully. 'Their situation really bothers you, doesn't it?'

'Yes, but I hope I didn't show it in front of Jack's father. I should imagine he's a very proud man.'

'You were very quiet. It's more what you haven't said than anything else.'

'Is their home part of your estate?'

'It was once, but my father sold the properties in the hope that the new landlord would make the necessary improvements. Sadly this doesn't seem to have happened.'

'Did you say that the squire owns them now?'

'Yes, I did. The wretched fellow lives in the manor house on the other side of the river, and I should think he owns half the county. He's also the local Justice of the Peace.'

'Perhaps someone ought to tell him that his tenants are living in slum conditions.'

'He's not the sort of man who would take kindly to criticism, even if well meant.'

'I don't like the sound of Squire Tattersall. Thank goodness my aunt owns Creek Cottage.'

'She might own the building, but I dare say the squire retained the leasehold. I believe he is an astute businessman, whatever people say about him.'

'I'll have to ask Aunt Eleanora, although she might not be aware of such a thing. The cottage was left to her by a relative.'

'Then I suggest she takes advice from a solicitor. Tattersall is not the sort of man to be sentimental when it comes to money.'

'Maybe if he saw how the condition of the cottages affects the health and wellbeing of his tenants he might do something about it.'

Nick smiled and shook his head. 'You have more faith in mankind than I have, Daisy. Let's enjoy our meal and then I'll show you the rest of the house. It looks slightly less shabby by lamplight.'

Dove brought the dessert, and after a generous helping of jam roly-poly smothered in creamy custard, Daisy was ready for the promised tour of the house. But Mrs Bee hurried into the morning parlour with the news that it was snowing again, and the road might soon become impassable.

'You'd better take the young lady home, Doctor,' Mrs Bee said in a tone that did not invite discussion.

'You're right, of course.' Nick rose from the table. 'I'll fetch the trap and bring it round to the front door. You will see the rest of the house one day, Daisy. I promise.'

Mrs Bee followed him from the room, returning moments later with an umbrella and a travelling rug, which she handed to Daisy. 'You'll need these, miss.'

'Thank you, Mrs Bee. And thank you for a wonderful meal.'

'You're welcome, miss. It's good to see the doctor so cheerful. I've known him since he was a little boy and he took his pa's death very much to heart.'

'You'll miss him if he decides to go away again.'

'If that happens it will be the end of Creek Hall. He'd almost certainly have to sell it and who knows what would happen then? I wouldn't want it to get into the hands of Squire Tattersall.'

'You're the second person who's led me to think that the squire isn't a good man.'

'I can only repeat what I've heard, but apparently he's ruthless in business and shows no mercy as a magistrate. His poor wife died young, and they say that he drove her to an early death, but I wouldn't know about that. All I do know is that he's a bad landlord and his tenants live in fear of him.'

'Well, I don't think I want to meet the squire. I'll take care to avoid him.'

'Very wise, miss.' Mrs Bee walked over to the window and peered out into the darkness. 'I thought I heard the rumble of wheels. The doctor is waiting for you. Best hurry, miss. The snow seems to be falling faster.'

Nick was waiting to help her on to the driver's seat and he wrapped the rug round her knees. 'I'm sorry we've had to cut the evening short, but we'll do this again when the weather improves.'

Daisy unfurled the umbrella and held it over him while he climbed up to sit beside her. 'I look forward to it. I think I'm falling under Creek Hall's spell even now.'

'Walk on.' He tapped the horse gently with the tip of the whip. 'The old house does that to people. I can remember visitors coming when I was a child, and some of them stayed on for days, if not weeks. There were people around all the time and the place was alive. Now it feels as though it's sleeping, but I don't want it to slip away from me.'

'You talk about the hall as if it were a living entity.'

'Do I? I didn't realise I was so fanciful. I suppose everyone feels like that about their childhood home, especially when it was a happy one. What about you, Daisy? What made you leave London and come to live in the wilds of Essex?'

'A broken engagement.' She had not meant to tell anyone outside the family, but Nick was different and he invited confidences.

'I'm sorry. Do you want to talk about it?'

'Not really. Julian is the elder son of the Carrington family and I was employed as governess to his younger brother. I don't know how it happened, but Julian and I fell in love. He asked me to marry him, but he wanted to keep our engagement a secret until his twenty-first birthday.'

'His parents might have objected?'

'Yes, they would, although it didn't come to that. Julian wrote to me from Oxford, telling me that he'd been offered a job in the diplomatic service in Paris, and was leaving immediately.'

'I don't see why that would matter. In fact, it would seem ideal for a young married couple to set up home far away from the disapproving family.'

'Perhaps, but Julian obviously didn't see it like that. Maybe he had second thoughts. I don't know.'

'I'm sorry. I didn't mean to upset you, Daisy.'

'I'm all right.' Daisy shot him a sideways glance and smiled. 'In fact, I'd forgotten about Julian for a while. I've had more important things to think about.'

'Meaning the Fox family?'

'I really would like to do something for them, Nick. But I wouldn't know where to start.'

'You are helping by giving Linnet a job, and you could call on Jack each day to see how he's getting on. His mother and father are obviously too sick to look after him properly.'

Daisy stared ahead into the swirling snow. 'I wonder if they would allow me to take him to Creek Cottage. He's not ill, he just needs someone to make sure he gets proper food and rest until his arm heals. I could help him with his lessons, if the schoolmaster would allow such a thing.'

'I think that's an excellent idea. You'd have Linnet to help you, and I could put a word in with Lemuel, if you wish. Again, I've known him since I was a boy, and he trusts me.'

'I'll have to ask my aunt and uncle, but I'm sure they'd agree. There's plenty of room in the cottage, and it would give me something to do. I'm not the sort of person who enjoys being idle.' Daisy huddled beneath the travelling rug, holding the umbrella so that it shielded Nick as well as herself from the driving snow. They lapsed into silence as the horse plodded along the now familiar road with the wood on one side and the creek on the other. The water gleamed silkily in the cold light reflected off the snow, and the trees in the wood stood out dark and mysterious against a silvery background. The cold was intense and soon Daisy had lost all the feeling in her toes and fingertips.

It was a relief when the lights from Creek Cottage beamed at them like a welcoming smile. Nick climbed down to help her to the ground and they stood for a moment, so close that she could feel the warmth of his breath on her cheek.

'Thank you for supper and for bringing me home.' Daisy moved away as the front door opened and they were caught in a beam of light from the lantern Eleanora held in her hand.

'Is that you, Daisy? I was beginning to worry.'

'I brought her home safe, Mrs Marshall,' Nick said cheerfully. 'You must excuse me if I don't linger, but I want to get back before the snow gets any deeper.'

'I wish we'd never come to this godforsaken place.' Eleanora reached out to grab Daisy by the hand. 'Good night, Doctor.'

'It isn't always like this, Mrs Marshall.' Nick tipped his hat, sending a shower of soft snow into the air. 'Spring can't be far off and it's really beautiful here in the summer.'

'I doubt if we'll be here much longer if this dreadful snow persists.' Eleanora dragged Daisy into the cottage and slammed the door. 'I didn't mean to be rude, but it's too cold to stand there and discuss the weather.'

'I still have his umbrella.' Daisy opened the door in time to see the chaise disappearing into the darkness.

'It will probably be pelting with rain tomorrow,' Eleanora said grimly. 'Give it back to him when the weather improves. Anyway, your uncle has gone to bed and I'm about to follow him. I was just waiting up for you, Daisy.'

'But it can't be much later than nine o'clock, Aunt.'

'It feels much later.' She put the lantern on the hall table and lit a candle. She headed for the stairs, holding the chamber candlestick in one hand and clutching the banister rail with the other. 'Good night, Daisy.'

'Good night, Aunt.' Daisy watched her aunt as she marched up the stairs, accompanied by the shadow cast by her candle. She had made her feelings about living in the country quite clear, and Daisy decided that this was not the right time to ask if Jack could stay with them while his broken bone mended.

She shivered and flexed her fingers, which were tingling painfully. A cup of hot cocoa would be just the thing to settle her for the night and she made her way to the kitchen, but as she entered the room she was aware of soft, even breathing. She held the lantern higher and she could just make out Linnet's sleeping form, curled up like a kitten in front of the range.

'Linnet, are you all right?'

Linnet stretched and opened her eyes. She scrambled to her feet. 'I'm sorry, miss. I didn't know you wanted anything.'

'I didn't mean to disturb you,' Daisy said hastily, 'but you shouldn't sleep on the floor. You'll be stiff and aching in the morning.'

'It won't be the first time, miss. At home I used to sleep on a mattress top to toe with my sister, with Jack snoring away in the truckle bed.'

'I thought you went home every night.'

'The missis said I could stay because of the snow.'

'Then at least she should have made sure you had a proper bed to sleep on.'

Linnet scrambled to her feet. 'No, miss. Please, it's all right. I don't want to make a fuss or I'll lose my job.'

Daisy placed the lantern on the table. 'I understand, but we can't have you lying on the floor like an animal. I'll fetch some bedding and I think we both could do with a cup of cocoa. Do you know how to make it?'

'It's our Christmas morning treat, miss. I made it this year, so I know what to do.'

'Lots of sugar,' Daisy said, smiling. 'You do that and I'll see what I can find to make you more comfortable.' She hesitated in the doorway. 'You heard about Jack's injury, I suppose?'.

'Hattie told me, miss. She said that you and the doctor had looked after him. He's a young

80

limb if ever there was one, always in trouble, but he's a good boy at heart.'

'I believe that, Linnet. He was very brave when Dr Neville set his arm.'

Daisy left Linnet to make the cocoa while she went upstairs to take the coverlet and a pillow from Toby's room. It was unlikely that he would come to stay in the foreseeable future, but she did not want to offend her aunt by allowing a servant to sleep in his bed. There were a couple of small attic rooms beneath the eaves on the top floor. Hattie had one and with a little effort the second could be made habitable for Linnet. It would be up for discussion tomorrow, when, she hoped, Aunt Eleanora would be in a happier mood, and Daisy would bring up the subject of taking care of young Jack. It would make life a lot easier if his sister were to live in — Daisy smiled to herself. With luck all the pieces would fall into place, and just maybe her aunt would feel more settled in the country. It would be a shame to return to London too soon. There were people who needed her help, Dr Neville being one of them.

6

Daisy was up early next morning, but she was not the first down to breakfast. She entered the small dining room to find her uncle had finished his meal of eggs and bacon and was about to leave the table.

'I didn't expect to see you up so early, Uncle.'

Sidney wiped his lips on a clean white napkin. 'Ah, but I have a purpose for getting up from my bed this morning.'

Daisy sat down opposite him. 'That sounds interesting.'

'The landlord of the village pub has fishing tackle he wants to sell. I'm going to take a look at it and make him an offer.'

'Do you know anything about fishing, Uncle?'

'Not a thing, but I'm eager to learn. It would give me something to do and put food on the table. We have to be careful with the pennies now that I've retired from the business.' He stood up and stretched. 'That was an excellent breakfast. Everyone should have a good start to the day.' He headed for the door. 'If your aunt says anything, tell her I had to leave early or I might not get what I want.'

Daisy smiled and nodded as he left the room. She had never seen her uncle so enthusiastic about anything.

The door had hardly closed when it opened again to admit her aunt.

'Really, he's like an excited child,' Eleanora said crossly. 'He'll spend money on a fishing rod and it will be thrilling for five minutes. He'll change his mind when he spends hours on the river-bank and catches nothing other than a cold.'

'He might enjoy it, Aunt. And Hattie can cook the fish he brings home.'

Eleanora went to the sideboard and filled a bowl with porridge. 'I have so little appetite these days,' she said as she took her seat and reached for the sugar bowl. 'Pass the cream, please, Daisy.'

Daisy did as she asked and sat back, nibbling a slice of buttered toast as she watched her aunt spoon porridge laced with cream and sugar into her mouth.

'Thank goodness Hattie came with us,' Eleanora said, scraping the last morsels from the bowl. She licked the spoon with obvious enjoyment. 'She is such a good cook.'

'It was kind of you to take Linnet on. She's a bright girl and eager to learn.' Daisy eyed her aunt warily. So far so good. 'Do you intend to make her position permanent?'

'We have certain standards to keep up, and I can hardly expect Hattie to do all the work. She'd pack up and return to London in a blink of an eye.'

Encouraged, Daisy leaned forward, giving her aunt a persuasive smile. 'Then perhaps Linnet ought to be given a room of her own. There's a small one in the attic, next to Hattie's.'

Eleanora reached for a small brass bell and

rang it. 'If you say so, dear. I haven't been up there myself, but it does make sense to have the girl living in, and it will take some of the burden from Hattie.'

'That's a yes, then?'

'I said so, didn't I?' Eleanora was about to ring the bell again when Linnet burst into the room.

'You rang, missis?'

'You are supposed to knock,' Eleanora said firmly. 'And you address me as Mrs Marshall or ma'am.'

'Yes, ma'am.' Linnet placed a plate of crisp bacon and two fried eggs in front of Eleanora. 'Is there anything else, ma'am?'

'Yes, Linnet. My niece tells me that you will be happy to live in. There's a room next to Hattie's that you may use. Daisy will help you to make it comfortable.'

Linnet's cheeks flushed and her eyes shone with delight. 'Ta, ever so, missis. I mean, thank you, ma'am.'

'That's all. You may go.'

'Yes, ma'am.' Linnet gave Daisy a radiant smile as she hurried past her and almost ran from the room.

'She'll have to learn a few manners, but she'll do. One can't expect town polish in a backwater like Little Creek.' Eleanora picked up her knife and fork and began to attack the bacon with a determined look on her face.

'I was wondering . . . ' Daisy began tentatively.

'What, dear? Don't start a sentence and let it hang in the air.'

'Well, I know how kind-hearted you are, and

Linnet's younger brother had an accident yesterday. Dr Neville and I happened to be passing and we took him home. Jack had broken his arm and he was very brave when Dr Neville was treating him.' Warming to her subject Daisy leaned across the table. 'The family are so poor, Aunt. You can't imagine how they live. Their cottage is damp and in a dreadful state of disrepair. Mr and Mrs Fox are both ill with chest complaints and they have barely enough to feed them, let alone a sick child.'

Eleanora looked up from her plate, frowning. 'It's sad, but that's how the lower orders live, Daisy. There are plenty of poor people in London who are living in even worse conditions. We can't look after them all.'

'No, of course, not,' Daisy said hastily. 'But I was wondering if Jack might stay here for a week or two, just until his bones mend. Dr Neville thinks it would be a very good thing.'

'Does he indeed? Then perhaps Dr Neville ought to take the boy into his house and look after him. Hattie tells me that Creek Hall is huge. She had it from someone she met in the village whose sister used to work for the old doctor.'

'Nick can't afford the upkeep of the hall, Aunt. He thinks he might have to return to London, or find a practice elsewhere. He might even have to sell his old home.'

'That is a pity, but there's nothing we can do about it, dear.' Eleanora reached for a slice of toast, broke off a shard and dipped it in the egg yolk. She ate it with relish. 'You ought to have a

85

cooked breakfast, Daisy. You're all skin and bone as it is, and in this weather you need a bit of flesh on your bones.'

'I had a big meal at Creek Hall last evening, Aunt. Mrs Bee is an excellent cook.'

'I'm sure Hattie is the better of the two.'

'Oh, undoubtedly,' Daisy said tactfully. 'But what about young Jack? I can imagine Toby might have been like him when he was younger.'

Eleanora hesitated with the toast halfway to her lips, and Daisy knew she had scored a point in Jack's favour. Toby was her aunt's favourite — she had always known that, but it had never bothered her. Toby had a way with him that women of all ages found irresistible.

'How old is the boy?' Eleanora popped the toast into her mouth.

'He's about nine or maybe ten. I didn't ask, but all he needs is a comfortable bed and good food. He's very undernourished. I would hate to think of Toby suffering like that.'

'Your uncle and I have given our lives to rearing you and your brother. Never let it be said that I turned my back on a child in need. You may bring him here and he can stay until his broken bones knit together, but then he must return to his family. I want that clear from the start.'

'Yes, absolutely, Aunt. If it's all right with you I'll go and tell Dr Neville the good news and I'll leave it to him to persuade Mr and Mrs Fox that it's the best thing for their son.'

Eleanora eyed her speculatively. 'I suppose a doctor could earn a comfortable living, in the right place. It's a respectable profession.'

'Yes, Aunt.' Daisy knew better than to argue. She rose from the table. 'I'll set off for the hall. It's stopped snowing and the sun is shining. Perhaps a thaw has set in.'

'One can but hope.' Eleanora buttered another slice of toast. 'I must persuade your uncle to buy a pony and trap. Life would be much more pleasant if one could drive out once a week or so. I miss the shops and the bustle of London, and I doubt if I'll ever get used to living in the country.'

Daisy had no answer to this and she hurried from the room. She went to the kitchen where she found Hattie seated at the table, enjoying a cup of tea and a slice of toast, while Linnet washed the dishes in the stone sink.

'My aunt says that Linnet may have the small room next to yours, Hattie. I'll help her to get it ready, so it won't cause you any extra work.'

'I think it's a good idea. Linnet's a good worker and I'm not as young as I used to be.'

'Excellent.' Daisy tried not to sound too relieved. Hattie was a dear, but she could be awkward and vinegary when she chose. 'And the other thing is that my aunt has agreed to have your younger brother here until his arm heals, Linnet. Do you think your parents would agree?'

Linnet's plain face was transformed by a smile. 'Oh, miss, that would be too good to be true. Mum and Dad get sick every winter and it's Jack who suffers the most. Us older ones can look after ourselves, but Jack is only a nipper. But . . . ' she hesitated, frowning, 'they wouldn't

87

want charity from no one.'

'I guessed as much,' Daisy said quickly. 'That's why I'm going to walk to Creek Hall and ask Dr Neville to speak for me. I think your parents might listen to him.'

'Yes, they would. They respected the old doctor — we all did. The village won't be the same if Dr Neville goes away for good.'

'Who told you that, Linnet?'

'I'm sorry, miss. It's common knowledge that the old doctor was in trouble moneywise. Stands to reason that Dr Neville will be, too.'

'Is nothing private in Little Creek?'

Linnet chuckled and turned back to washing the dishes. 'No, miss. Not a thing.'

'Well then, perhaps you'd be good enough to take a message to Creek Hall when you've finished what you're doing? I'll write a note to the doctor, asking him to persuade your parents that it would be in everyone's best interests if Jack stayed with us, for a while at least. You could look after him and he'd feel quite at home with you living here as well.'

'It ain't right to take a child from his ma and pa,' Hattie said grimly. 'You shouldn't interfere in other folks' business, Miss Daisy.'

'Don't be such a wet blanket, Hattie. Having Jack here will lift all our spirits.' Daisy left the kitchen before Hattie had a chance to argue.

★ ★ ★

'They've arrived,' Daisy said, peering from the parlour window. 'Dr Neville has brought Jack.'

88

Eleanora rose from the chair by the fire, smoothing her skirts. 'I don't know why I agreed to this.' She followed Daisy into the hall and stood behind her as she opened the door. 'And I can't think why I allowed you to persuade me that the boy ought to have Toby's room.'

'We won't see much of my brother for the foreseeable future, and Jack will only be with us until his arm heals.' Daisy looked out into steadily falling rain. With the usual vagaries of the British climate, the temperature had risen and rain was falling steadily, turning the snow into slush.

'You'll drop the child,' Eleanora cried anxiously. 'Do be careful, Doctor.'

'Put me down, Doctor. I can walk,' Jack protested. 'I ain't a baby.'

Eleanora wagged a finger at Jack. 'You'll do as you're told, young man. We don't allow boys to be cheeky in our house.'

Daisy exchanged wry smiles with Nick as he stepped inside and put his wriggling burden down. 'Welcome to Creek Cottage, Jack. There's a fire in the front parlour, or would you rather go straight to your room and rest?'

'I don't want to go to bed,' Jack said angrily. 'If they're going to mollycoddle me I'd rather go home, Doctor.'

'Mrs Marshall is just thinking of your comfort, Jack.' Nick rested his hands on the boy's shoulders, turning him to face Daisy and her aunt. 'I suggest you thank the ladies for taking you in and making you welcome.'

Jack scowled, glaring at Eleanora with a sulky

frown. 'Ta ever so, missis.'

Daisy held her breath, but to her surprise
Eleanora's lips began to quiver and she started
to laugh. 'You do remind me of my nephew. Toby
hated being fussed over. You'll do, young man,
but you'll remember your manners while you're
under my roof.' She turned to Linnet, who was
hovering in the background. 'Bring your brother
a cup of cocoa and a slice of Hattie's seed cake.
I've never known a small boy who didn't have a
large appetite.'

Daisy was about to follow them into the
parlour, but her aunt forestalled her. 'No, Daisy.
I'll take this opportunity to get to know our
young guest. You have the advantage over me
there, so I suggest your take Dr Neville to the
kitchen and see that he has some refreshment to
keep out the damp.' She closed the door firmly.

'There,' Nick said, chuckling. 'You've been put
in your place, Daisy.'

'I know. It's always like this. Aunt Eleanora
can't get used to the idea that I'm a no longer a
child.'

'She seems to have taken to young Fox.'

'She said that he reminds her of my brother.
Toby can wrap Aunt Eleanora round his little
finger. Anyway, perhaps you'd like to come to the
kitchen and meet Hattie. She thinks she runs the
household, and she's not far wrong. My aunt
relies on her completely, so it's good that she has
Linnet to help out.'

'With the two girls living in and earning
money, even if it's not a high wage, the Fox
family should be able to survive the winter. They

aren't alone in their struggles either. There are others in the village, the squire's tenants in particular, who suffer equally.'

'You really care about the people of Little Creek, don't you?' Daisy said softly. 'I don't think you'd have the heart to walk away.'

'That's my dilemma, Daisy. My head tells me to sell up and move on, but my heart wants to continue the work begun by my father. It's not an easy decision to make.'

'I know you'll do what's right.' Daisy led the way to the kitchen, where the aroma of hot cocoa mingled with the savoury smell of the mutton stew simmering on the range.

'So you're the famous Dr Neville,' Hattie said without giving Daisy a chance to make introductions. 'This young girl speaks very high of you, sir.' She nodded in Linnet's direction. 'But she says you're going back to London.'

Nick held out his hand. 'You must be Hattie. I've heard so much about you from Miss Marshall. How do you do?'

Hattie's thin cheeks flushed scarlet and she shook his hand before bobbing a curtsey. 'Very well, thank you, Doctor.'

'Perhaps you'd like some tea or cocoa, Nick?' Daisy said hastily.

'Tea would be nice, if it's no trouble.'

Hattie bustled over to the range, pushing Linnet out of the way. 'Of course, Doctor. I'll make a fresh pot now and Linnet will bring it to you in the front parlour.'

'My aunt is getting to know Jack,' Daisy said, keeping a straight face with difficulty. It was obvious that Hattie wanted to make a good impression on the doctor. 'We'd best use the dining room.'

'There's no fire lit,' Hattie argued. 'The missis said to be economical with the coal and logs and only light the fire half an hour before dinner.'

'I could see to the fire for you, Doctor,' Linnet volunteered eagerly.

'Thank you, we'll manage.' Daisy backed towards the doorway. 'Tea for two in the dining room, please.' She ushered Nick out of the kitchen and closed the door. 'They're trying to kill you with kindness,' she added, giggling. 'I've never known Hattie to be so eager to please.'

'It's the profession, not me personally. The people of Little Creek had great respect for my father, which was well-earned because he worked tirelessly for their benefit.'

'He must have been a great man.'

'He was, and I know he wanted me to continue his work, but I really don't think it's going to be possible.'

Daisy took a seat next to him. 'I wish I could help.'

'There's just one avenue open to me now. It's one I didn't want to take, but I'll lose my home and the practice if I do nothing.'

'What is it? Can you talk about it?'

'I have an aged aunt, living in Canterbury. We used to visit her once a year on her birthday, and her anniversary is coming up next week. She's very wealthy and I'm her closest relative. She might lend me enough money to pay off the squire, and then I could stay and set up in practice.'

'You would still face the same problems, wouldn't you? If your patients are too poor to pay for your services you would be in the same position as your father.'

'I would have to ensure that I charged enough.'

'Did you ask for payment when you set Jack's arm?'

Nick shook his head. 'How could I? You saw how the family live, and Jack's father hasn't worked for years.'

'My point exactly. You might borrow money from your aunt, but it wouldn't be long before you were in exactly the same position as your father.'

A tap on the door preceded Linnet, who entered carrying a tray of tea and two large slices of seed cake. 'Mrs Cribb says she hopes you enjoy the cake, Doctor. And if you have a moment, could you look at her left shoulder? It pains her when she lifts anything heavy.'

'Yes, of course,' Nick said, smiling. 'I'll take a look at it before I go.'

Daisy waited until the door closed on Linnet. 'You see! You are too kind and obliging. People know that and they take advantage of your good nature.'

'I'll accept a cup of tea and a slice of that delicious-looking cake as payment.'

Daisy passed him his tea and cake. 'That will be your downfall, Dr Neville.'

'Making a fortune has never been my aim, but

a comfortable living and the upkeep of Creek Hall is something I have to consider. One day I hope I'll be in a position to marry and raise a family, and for that I need a steady income.'

Daisy was tempted to ask if he had anyone in mind, but that might lead to embarrassment on both sides and she hastily changed the subject. 'I thought I'd visit the village school tomorrow and ask if I might help Jack with his lessons at home, at least until he feels well enough to go back to school.'

'I'm sure Massey will be delighted. He's fairly new and I've only met him once, but he seems like a decent fellow.'

★　★　★

The sun was shining next morning and the thaw continued. The creek had swelled with snow melt and the crystal-clear water rushed past, tumbling small branches and pieces of flotsam over rocks in its haste to join the river and continue its journey out to sea. Daisy walked briskly, but she still had time to look around and marvel at nature. Already there were tight little buds on the trees, just waiting for spring to arrive and the warm kiss of the sun to burst into leaf. At the side of the lane, beneath the hedgerow, she saw a small patch of snowdrops and she was tempted to stop and pick them, but she was on a mission to persuade the schoolmaster to allow Jack to keep up with his studies at home. Jack had been showing signs of boredom, and it was astonishing how much difference good food and rest could make in such a short time.

As she approached the village Daisy was conscious of the interest she was creating. Some of the women she met greeted her with a smile and a nod, while others gave her sidelong glances and walked on. The Marshalls were still the subject of interest and speculation, as reported daily by Linnet. People had little to talk about and a new family in the village gave the gossips something new to discuss behind closed doors.

The school itself was situated opposite the village pub and the church, and the children had been allowed outside at break. The boys had found pockets of snow and were hurling snowballs at each other, while the girls played skipping games and chanted rhymes that were new to Daisy. She made her way between the different groups, narrowly avoiding being hit by a snowball thrown by a boy she recognised as being Danny, one of Jack's friends. He caught up with her as she was about to enter the building.

'Where's Jack, miss? Is he all right?'

'He's staying at Creek Cottage for a while,' Daisy said, smiling. 'He broke his arm, but Dr Neville set the bones and Jack has to be careful he doesn't injure it again.'

'When will he come back to school?'

'As soon as the doctor says it's all right. Now, where will I find Mr Massey?'

'He's right there, miss. Behind you.' Danny turned and raced back to join his rowdy friends.

Daisy turned to find herself facing a tall,

dark-haired young man, whose black jacket was worn at the cuffs and dusted with chalk. 'May I help you, miss?'

'You must be Mr Massey, the schoolmaster.'

'That's correct. I'm Elliot Massey. Might I ask your name?'

'I'm Daisy Marshall and I live at Creek Cottage. We only moved in recently, although it feels as if I've lived here for months.'

A slow smile lit his grey eyes. 'I know the feeling. How may I help you?'

'I was wondering if you could set some work for Jack Fox. I expect you know that he injured himself falling from a tree.'

'Yes, of course. I know that he's been taken in by the new people from London.'

'Mr and Mrs Marshall are my uncle and aunt, and Dr Neville thought it a good idea if Jack came to stay with us for a while. Jack's parents are unwell and his sisters are in service.'

'I am aware of the family history. It's impossible to do anything in Little Creek without everyone knowing.'

'You're not the first person to tell me that,' Daisy said, smiling. 'Anyway, if you think it a good idea perhaps I could help Jack with some work at home, so that when he returns he doesn't find himself far behind the other children.'

'Of course, and thank you. If only the parents of some of the other children thought the same as you my life would be so much easier. I try my best to make learning exciting and interesting, but it's impossible to get through to some of my

96

pupils. Young Jack shows promise but he's easily distracted.'

'If you would allow me to take a couple of books and a slate, I'll do my best.'

'I can do better than that, Miss Marshall. If you can wait until this afternoon, I'll bring the books after school.'

At that moment a bell rang and the children raced past them, bringing gusts of cold air with them.

'I can see that you're busy,' Daisy said hurriedly. 'I'm sure Jack would appreciate a visit from his teacher.'

Elliot leaned down to grab a small boy who was clutching a handful of snow. 'Take that outside, Benny. You don't bring snowballs into the classroom.'

The child shrugged and stomped out into the schoolyard where Daisy caught sight of him throwing what remained of the snow at a little girl, who started to cry.

'Thank you, Mr Massey. I'd better go now, but I'll tell Jack you're coming to see him.'

Daisy threaded her way through the crowd of rosy-cheeked children as they pushed and shoved in order to get inside out of the cold. She noticed that, although most were scrubbed clean, their clothes were patched and mended and their shoes down at heel. It was obvious that Little Creek was not a rich village, and she understood a little more of the dilemma that Nick Neville faced. She could only hope that his meeting with the aged aunt would prove fruitful.

The sun was still shining, but the temperature

was plummeting when Daisy set off towards home, but as she passed the pub she saw her uncle strolling on ahead with a fishing rod over his shoulder and a wicker basket clutched in his hand. She quickened her pace and caught up with him.

'You've bought the fishing tackle.'

'I tried it out yesterday. Perkins, the pub landlord, showed me how to cast and we spent a good two hours on the river-bank, until my poor feet and fingers were frozen, but now I'm off to try downstream. We'll have fish for supper tonight, Daisy.'

'I look forward to that.' Daisy fell into step beside him. 'You seem to have settled in to country living so easily, Uncle.'

'It's something I've dreamed of since I was a boy, my dear. Now I've got my chance and I'm grabbing it with both hands. I just hope your aunt can adjust, although I know she loves London and she'll miss the shops and the theatres.'

'It is a big change, Uncle.'

He turned his head to give her a searching glance. 'And what about you, Daisy? Are you happy here?'

She was about to answer when something further downstream caught her eye. She grabbed her uncle's arm. 'Look, on the river-bank. Oh heavens! I think it's a dead body.'

7

Daisy broke into a run. She could hear her uncle's heavy tread as he lumbered along behind her. He was calling out for her to stop, but although her heart was pounding and she was afraid of what she might find, she could not bring herself to hold back. The man was lying face down in the mud and the water was lapping round his ankles. Daisy came to a halt, holding her breath as she gazed down at his inert form. At first she thought he was dead, but a slight movement of his clenched fist was followed by a shuddering breath.

Sidney arrived at her side, puffing and gasping for air. 'Don't touch him, Daisy. He might have died of some terrible disease.'

'We can't just leave him like this, Uncle.' Daisy bent down and with a huge effort managed to turn the man on his back. Despite the mud that caked his face she could see that he was young, perhaps in his mid-twenties. 'We need to get him out of the water,' she said urgently. 'We don't know how long he's been lying here, but he's still breathing.'

Together they managed to pull him clear of the creek and Daisy took her hanky from her pocket to wipe the mud from his face. 'We need to get help, Uncle. He's too heavy for us to move.'

'You go, Daisy. You're quicker on your feet

than I am, and he might wake up and become violent. He could be a drunk who's fallen in the water on his way home. Go to the pub and tell Abel Perkins what's happened. He'll know the fellow, like as not.'

'All right. I'll be as quick as I can.'

Daisy picked up her skirts and raced back the way they had come. She burst into the pub and made her way between the tables to the bar where a portly man was polishing tankards with a grubby-looking cloth. 'Are you Mr Perkins?' she asked breathlessly.

'That's me, dearie.' He looked her up and down. 'We don't get many young ladies in here,' he added, chuckling. 'What can I do for you?'

'There's a man lying on the river-bank. He's unconscious and my uncle and I need help to move him.'

'Your uncle? You must be the young lady from London then?'

'I'm Daisy Marshall. Could you help us, please?'

'It's probably some vagrant who's lost his way in the dark. Dare say he was drunk. I dunno how many times we've fished a corpse out of the creek.' Abel lifted the hatch in the counter and beckoned to two men who were huddled round the fire. 'Give us a hand, lads. We've got another drowned rat.'

The men downed their pints and stood up. 'Who is it this time, Abel?'

'We'll find out shortly.' Abel opened the door and a gust of cold air drew smoke from the chimney into the taproom. 'Best wait here, miss.'

Daisy did not argue but she followed them anyway, and when they reached the casualty she was relieved to see that he was attempting to sit up.

'Well, I'll be damned,' Abel said, chuckling. 'Look who it is.'

'Can't tell for all that there mud.'

'It's that Jay Fox. I wonder what sort of trouble he's got hisself into this time.' Abel heaved Jay to his feet. 'Let's get you home, boy.'

'Wait a minute.' Daisy laid her hand on Abel's arm. 'His mother and father are unwell. You can't take him home in that state.'

'Don't interfere, Daisy,' Sidney said in a low voice. 'It's none of our business.'

'Maybe not.' Daisy turned to him angrily. 'But he obviously needs to see the doctor. If anything, he ought to be taken to Creek Hall. His sister is there and she'll know what to do.'

'Look here, miss. I can't go traipsing around the countryside because Jay Fox is in trouble again. This chap has been nothing but a worry to his family ever since he took his first breath.'

The elder and more vocal of the men from the bar nodded. 'That's true. He ran away to sea when he was just a boy. Spent some time in prison, so they say.'

Jay groaned and opened his eyes. 'What's going on?'

'He's all right.' Abel relaxed his hold and Jay's knees buckled beneath him. He sank to the ground, coughing. 'I've got a pub to run.' Abel slapped Sidney on the back. 'I'd leave the feller here and let him find his own way home, if I was

101

you, Sidney, my friend.' He strode off in the direction of the pub, followed more slowly by his two erstwhile customers.

Sidney helped Jay to his feet. 'Can you walk, young man?'

'You'd better come home with us,' Daisy said firmly. 'Your brother, Jack, is at our house and so is Linnet. You can clean up and dry your clothes before you go home.'

'Daisy, is this wise?' Sidney protested.

'What else can we do, Uncle? Anyway, Creek Cottage is nearer than the Foxes' home, and I'll send Linnet to fetch the doctor. I just hope he hasn't left for Canterbury.'

Jay shook his head. 'I'm all right. Thanks for your offer, but I'd best go home.'

Daisy stood aside. 'Let's see you walk then.'

He scrambled to his feet, stumbled and would have fallen if Sidney had not caught him.

'Daisy is right,' Sidney said reluctantly. 'We'll take you to our house, and you can go home when you've regained your strength.' He hooked one of Jay's arms around his shoulder and between them Daisy and her uncle helped Jay to Creek Cottage.

⋆　⋆　⋆

'Are we to have the whole Fox family dependent upon us?' Eleanora demanded angrily. 'Now you tell me that he has a bad reputation, and you have no idea how he came to be in this state.'

Sidney and Daisy exchanged anxious glances. 'Well, my love, we could hardly leave the poor fellow there. He would have died from exposure to the elements.'

'And Dr Neville said he must have been attacked and beaten. Jay has a slight concussion and needs to rest,' Daisy said earnestly. 'We couldn't take him home in such circumstances.'

'What is it about the Fox family?' Eleanora cried, throwing up her hands. 'Why have we become responsible for their offspring?'

Daisy glanced over her shoulder as Nick entered the room. 'Is he going to be all right?'

'He was lucky you found him when you did, but he'll be fine. Jay is tough and he'll recover, although I'm a bit worried about the concussion. Anyway, I'll take him back to Creek Hall, and his sister and Mrs Bee will look after him.'

'Thank the Lord,' Eleanora said wholeheartedly.

'What happened to him?' Daisy asked eagerly. 'Did he say?'

'I didn't ask too many questions. I'm not even sure he remembers, but I hope that will improve as he recovers. He suffered a bad beating and he spent some time in the water, so I need to keep an eye on him for the next few days at least.'

'Someone had better let his parents know.' Sidney gazed out of the window. 'Anyway, you don't need me now so I think I'll go fishing. Is that all right with you, Eleanora?'

'I suppose so,' she said, sighing. 'You go off and enjoy yourself, Sidney. I'll stay here and mind other people's children.'

'We'll be on our way, Mrs Marshall,' Nick said hastily.

Daisy followed him into the hall. 'He will be all right, won't he?'

'As I said, Jay is tough. We might have gone in different directions, but we're still friends, so you've no need to worry.'

'I thought he was dead when I first saw him.'

'You probably saved his life. If you hadn't found him when you did the outcome could have been very different. As it is I'm sure he'll make a full recovery.'

She smiled. 'I did what anyone else would have done.'

'Not everyone, it seems. Abel Perkins walked off and left a girl and an old man to manage on their own. I'm sure Jay will thank you both when he's fully recovered.'

'It was fortunate for Jay that you hadn't gone to see your aunt. I was afraid we might have missed you.'

'I had some things to do, so I decided to go tomorrow.' Nick met her worried gaze with a smile. 'Mrs Bee and Dove will take care of Jay while I'm gone, and I don't imagine he's in any real danger. At least, not now.'

'Perhaps we'd better rescue him from Hattie's ministrations,' Daisy said, chuckling. 'The last I saw of her she was making him a mustard footbath, which she swears by as a cure for just about anything.' She led the way to the kitchen where Jay was seated in a chair by the range with his bare feet soaking in a bowl of hot water laced with yellow mustard. His fair hair had been washed and it curled wildly around his head, giving him the look of a fallen angel. One eye was half closed and would be blackened by morning, but his good eye was an interesting shade of blue edged with long thick lashes that would make any female jealous. He was dressed in some old clothes that Toby had left behind when he decided they were not smart enough for a professional gentleman. The trouser legs were rolled up to keep them away from the mustard water, but the jacket sleeves were far too short, exposing Jay's bony wrists and muscular forearms.

'How are you feeling?' Daisy asked anxiously. 'Does your head hurt?'

He managed a lopsided grin. 'Not too much, thank you, miss.'

'He'll be fine,' Linnet said casually. 'Jay has a thick skull. If he fell on his head as a child we knew he would be all right.'

Hattie pursed her lips. 'He should be tucked up in bed with a hot-water bottle.'

'I'm all right,' Jay said abruptly. 'I wish everyone would stop fussing. I said, I'm fine.'

'I need to keep an eye on you, Jay.' Nick picked up a towel and tossed it at him. 'Dry your feet. I'm taking you to Creek Hall whether you like it or not.'

'I should go home, Nick. I've been away too long.'

'Your parents are far from well at the moment and they can't be expected to look after you. It's best if you come home with me. Mrs Bee will delight in fussing over you.'

Linnet picked up a towel and began to dry her brother's feet. 'You'll do as you're told for once, Jay Fox.'

'I wish you'd all leave me alone,' Jay said with a groan. 'I'm quite capable of looking after myself.'

'Well, you haven't been very successful, considering you've just been fished out of the river, half dead.' Hattie gave a disapproving sniff. 'Gallivanting around won't do you any good.'

'Don't worry, Mrs Cribb,' Nick said smoothly. 'Jay will be well cared for, and I'm sure you have enough on your hands with young Jack.'

Jack had been sitting quietly at the table, munching cake, but he looked up and grinned. 'It was worth breaking an arm to come here and be treated like a young gent. Mrs Cribb makes the best cake ever.'

Hattie puffed out her chest. 'Flattery will get you nowhere, young man.'

'You'd best be ready to see your teacher,' Daisy said hurriedly. 'Mr Massey is coming here after school with some books for you to study while your arm heals.'

Jack's mouth drooped at the corners and he pushed his plate away. 'I thought it was too good to be true. I don't like Mr Massey.'

'I thought he was charming,' Daisy said firmly. 'And you need to work hard in order to keep up with the rest of the class.'

'You'll have me to answer to now, Jack. I won't stand any nonsense.' Jay attempted to rise but subsided with a groan.

'Your brother will be around for a while yet.'

Nick helped Jay to his feet. 'I need to give you a more thorough examination, Jay. You might have cracked a couple of ribs.'

Jack pulled a face. 'I bet he's on the run from the coppers again.'

'Cheeky brat.' Jay made to cuff Jack round the head as he limped past, but missed. 'I'll get you next time, nipper.'

Jack poked out his tongue and was scolded by Hattie and Linnet in unison.

'Maybe you ought to come with us to Creek Hall,' Nick said severely. 'You need someone to keep you in order, young fellow.'

'I'll be good. Don't take me away from here. I never had such lovely grub, nor such a soft bed. Let me stay, please.'

'Of course you'll stay with us.' Daisy gave him an encouraging smile. 'I'm going to help you with your lessons.'

'Can I join the class, too, teacher?' Jay said, chuckling. 'My spelling ain't up to standard.'

Nick grabbed him by the arm. 'You'll behave yourself now you're home. I'd like to know what got you in this state in the first place.'

Jay's reply was lost as Nick propelled him out of the room and the door closed behind them. Daisy and Hattie exchanged worried glances.

'Don't worry about my brother,' Linnet said calmly. 'Jay might have got in with the wrong company at one time, but whatever happened to him I'm sure it wasn't his fault.'

'That's right,' Jack added. 'Jay's a good 'un.'

'Never mind all the chit-chat,' Hattie said

briskly. 'We've got work to do, Linnet. There's water to fetch, wood to chop, and make sure the fire doesn't go out in the front parlour. We don't want the schoolmaster to think we can't afford to live decently.'

Daisy took this as her cue to make herself scarce. 'Come with me, Jack. Let's see how far you've progressed with reading.'

★ ★ ★

Elliot Massey arrived promptly at five o'clock, bringing with him books and a slate for Jack to write on, together with a slate pencil.

'Good afternoon, Miss Marshall.' He took off his hat and long black coat and laid them on the hall stand.

'Thank you for coming, Mr Massey. Jack will be pleased to see you. He's in the front parlour.' Daisy opened the door and ushered him into the room. 'Please take a seat.'

Elliot placed the books and slate on a table in front of Jack and sat down next to him. 'How are you, my boy?'

Jack turned his head away and mumbled something unintelligible.

'I didn't hear what you said, boy. Speak up as I taught you in school.'

'I'm all right, thank you, sir.'

'That's better.' Elliot looked up at Daisy and smiled. 'He's looking well, and much cleaner than usual.'

Daisy chose to ignore his last remark. She noticed that Elliot had slicked his unruly hair into place with Macassar oil and his shoes had been polished to a mirror-like sheen. 'Jack has been working hard at his reading and spelling.'

'Well, I hope he realises what a lucky fellow he is to have been taken in by Miss Marshall and her family. I hope you're duly grateful, young man.'

Jack nodded, staring gloomily at the pile of books. 'Have I got to read all those, sir?'

'Perhaps not all of them, but I'll discuss your progress with Miss Marshall and allow her to decide. We want you to keep up with your classmates, don't we?'

'I suppose so.' Jack huddled in his chair, holding his injured arm and grimacing each time he moved it.

'Are you in pain,' Daisy asked anxiously. 'Perhaps you ought to go to your room and rest, Jack?'

'No, miss. I'm all right,' he said bravely. 'Dr Neville said I must be careful not to damage my arm, but I wasn't to let it stop me doing things. I want to be like Dr Neville when I grow up. He's kind and he's clever.'

Elliot recoiled as if Jack's childish admiration for another man had been intended as a slur on himself. 'Or you could be a teacher, like me. You have to work hard at your lessons if you wish to succeed, Jack.'

Jack shrugged. 'If you say so, sir.'

Daisy went to sit beside him. 'The main thing is to keep you occupied until your arm has healed, and then you can go back to school with your friends.'

'Well said, Miss Marshall.' Elliot beamed at her, his sallow cheeks tinged with pink. 'You obviously have a way with children.'

'I was a governess for a couple of years, Mr Massey. I was very fond of Master Timothy, but his parents thought he was old enough to go away to school, and I was no longer needed.'

'So you decided to come and live in the country?'

'Yes, for the time being, at least. I haven't quite made up my mind.'

'Oh, you must stay,' Elliot said earnestly. 'Someone like yourself could do so much for a village like Little Creek. I find the people here are sadly behind the times.'

'That isn't my impression, Mr Massey.' Daisy rose to her feet. 'Would you like a cup of tea? I'll go and ask Hattie to make up a tray.'

He half rose from his chair. 'Please don't go to any trouble on my behalf. I merely came to see Jack and make sure that he was all right.' He sank down again, flushed and obviously embarrassed. 'I didn't mean to cast aspersions on the care he is receiving here. I hope you didn't think . . . ?'

'No, of course not.' Daisy managed a smile. 'You can rest assured that Jack will be given the best of care and I'll make sure he does as much study as he can.'

'Yes, I'm sure you will.' Elliot stood up awkwardly. 'I'd better go now, but if you wish to talk to me about anything, or if you need my advice, please don't hesitate to contact me at the schoolhouse.'

'Thank you, I will. I'll show you out, Mr Massey.'

He hesitated, holding out his hand and then letting it drop to his side. 'Elliot, please. I hope we might be friends. There are so few people in the village with whom I have anything in common. It would be wonderful to have some intelligent conversation for a change.'

'Perhaps you haven't met the right people,' Daisy said more sharply than she had intended, but to her surprise Elliot seemed to take this as a compliment.

'You're right, of course,' he said eagerly. 'I must call on Squire Tattersall and introduce myself, and maybe that will lead to a more varied social life.' He shrugged on his coat and placed his top hat carefully on his smarmed-down hair. 'Perhaps I might call on you again, Miss Marshall? If I were fortunate enough to be invited to attend a soiree at Creek Manor, I would need a suitable companion.'

'A kind thought, Mr Massey.' Daisy opened the door. 'Who knows?'

He eyed her warily. 'Er, yes. Well, I hope to see you again soon. Good afternoon, Miss Marshall.'

She closed the door, heaving a sigh of relief. Perhaps the schoolmaster improved on further acquaintance, but she had no intention of finding out. She went into the parlour to find Jack drawing a picture on his slate. He jumped guiltily and attempted to rub it off but she took it from him with a smile of approval.

'You didn't tell me you were an artist, Jack.'

'It was meant to look like you, miss.'

111

'I can see that. It's very good, and I think I still have a paint box and some brushes. Perhaps you'd like to borrow them?'

'Really, miss?'

'Yes, of course. I wouldn't say so if I didn't mean it.'

'Do I have to read all these books?'

Daisy picked one at random and flipped through the pages. 'I think you might enjoy this one, Jack.' She handed him a well-thumbed copy of *Tom Brown's Schooldays*. 'We'll read this together, shall we?'

He nodded eagerly. 'I'd like that, but I can't manage long words.'

'That's what I'm here for. If you knew everything you wouldn't need to go to school, would you?'

'Do you think Dr Neville has read this book?'

'When we see him again you'll have to ask him.'

★ ★ ★

The winter days passed quickly, and Daisy was kept busy helping Jack to read and giving him simple sums to work out, which he did with his tongue held between his teeth as he concentrated on his slate. Sitting with him in the front parlour with the tea table for a desk, Daisy was reminded of the time she had spent with Master Timothy, and she wondered how the child was coping in boarding school. When it came to her broken romance with Julian, Daisy had gone through all the different stages of hurt, hope and then anger, and finally she had accepted the fact that she would never see him again. Julian Carrington was weak and she could never settle for someone so lacking in character.

Every day, weather permitting, Sidney went fishing with varying degrees of success, and sometimes they had trout for dinner or stuffed carp. Hattie objected to gutting and preparing fish for the table, but Linnet had acquired the knowledge from her father, and she took over in the kitchen when Sidney came home with a good catch.

Eleanora resented his continued absences, but a visit from Mrs Peabody, the vicar's wife, changed everything. Grace Peabody invited her to join a small group of local ladies, who pooled their efforts in an attempt to alleviate the poverty of many agricultural families in the area. Eleanora had not had the heart to refuse, but after the first meeting at the rectory she returned home filled with enthusiasm. Hattie and Linnet were given instructions to make beef tea, which would be given to invalids in the village, including Mr and Mrs Fox. Eleanora announced that she was now on a committee to raise money for repairs to the church roof, and had been asked to organise bazaars and to help with the village summer fête. For the next couple of days the cottage was filled with the savoury aroma of simmering calf's foot and baking cakes. Eleanora unpacked her best hats and tippets and, dressed in her finery, she accompanied Grace Peabody, distributing the calf's foot jelly to the sick and elderly.

With her uncle and aunt fully occupied, Daisy was free to concentrate on Jack. Three weeks after Jay's unexpected return, they wrapped up warmly and set off on foot for Creek Hall. Jack was eager to see his brother and Daisy wanted to speak to Nick and find out if he had managed to raise the sum needed to save his home. Not that it had anything to do with her, but she could understand why he was so desperate to hold on to the house that had been in his family for generations. Her own life had been turned upside down by recent events, and she could understand his desire to cling to the past. She herself was still coming to terms with the reality of living in a small village without all the amenities that she had enjoyed in London.

'We're here,' Jack cried, breaking her train of thought as he ran on ahead. 'Hurry up, Miss Daisy.'

His youthful enthusiasm made her smile, and as she followed him from the shelter of the trees she had an uninterrupted view of Creek Hall and the saltings. The old building looked serene and mellow in the morning light, and the rampaging weeds in the overgrown garden added a romantic touch to the scene. It would grow out of hand in the spring, and by summer the house would be surrounded by a wilderness if unchecked, but today it might have been an illustration from a book of fairy stories. The saltings shimmered with the sunlight glinting on the pools of water left by the ebbing tide, and wading birds fished in the shallows.

'There's Jay.' Jack pointed to the tall figure at

the side of the house. Jay had been chopping wood, but he stopped mid-swing. Jack broke into a run and hurled himself at his brother, who caught him deftly and swung him off his feet.

'Ouch!' Jack cried. 'That hurt.'

Daisy observed them from a safe distance. She did not know what to make of Jay Fox and she was wary of him. Whether or not he had a criminal past was not important, and Nick seemed to like him, but Jay was too sure of himself in her opinion.

He set Jack down with an apologetic smile. 'Sorry, nipper. I forgot you were a wounded soldier.'

'I see that you're better.' Daisy strolled up to them, and despite her misgivings she could not but be impressed by Jay's remarkable recovery. In clean clothes that fitted him perfectly, he was taller than she remembered, broad-shouldered and good-looking in a rugged and slightly disturbing way. His mop of blond curly hair framed his face, but his square jaw and strong features looked anything but angelic, just as the twinkle in his speedwell-blue eyes held a hint of mischief and self-mockery.

'I am back to my old self.' Jay bowed from the waist. 'I'm honoured that Miss Marshall has come to enquire about my health.'

'She came with me,' Jack said, puffing out his chest. 'Daisy is my friend and she knew I wanted to see you.'

'And I thought she came to see me.' Jay put his head on one side, his amused gaze a challenge.

'Is Dr Neville at home?' Daisy had the sudden urge to put Jay Fox in his place. He was obviously sure of himself when it came to dealing with women, but she was not so easily won over.

'Yes, I want to see him, too,' Jack added excitedly. 'He mended my arm, Jay. I can use it a bit now.' He shot a sideways glance at Daisy. 'But I'm not well enough to go back to school.'

'We'll see about that,' Daisy said, making an effort to look stern.

'He's in the stable, saddling up.' Jay jerked his head in the direction of the outbuildings at the rear of the house, and Jack raced off. 'You're not going to join them then, Miss Marshall?'

Daisy chose to ignore the inference that she had come to see Nick. 'You look as if you're fully recovered. Have you remembered what happened and how you came to be in such a state?'

He picked up the axe. 'Not entirely. It's a bit of a blur, but I'm recovered now.'

'I expect your parents will be pleased to see you.'

'They know I'm here. Nick called in to make sure they were all right and he told them.' He raised the axe and brought it down on the log, splitting it in two. 'I plan to go there today.'

Daisy glanced over his shoulder and saw Nick hurrying towards them with Jack close on his heels. The smile froze on her lips when she met his troubled gaze. 'Is anything wrong?'

He came to a halt. 'It's good to see you, Daisy, but I can't stop.'

'Where are you going?' Jay demanded,

throwing down the axe. 'What's the matter?'

'I've just received a letter from Squire Tattersall's solicitor. It's not good news, Jay.' Nick turned to Daisy with an apologetic smile. 'I'm sorry, Daisy. I have to leave right away.'

Jay laid his hand on Nick's arm. 'Why? What's so urgent?'

'I intend to have it out with the squire, face to face. That man is determined to get his hands on Creek Hall, no matter what, but he's reckoned without me.' Nick tossed a crumpled sheet of writing paper at Jay and it fluttered to the ground at Daisy's feet.

'Is there anything I can do to help?' She bent down to retrieve it but Jay snatched it from her as Nick strode back towards the stables.

Jay smoothed the paper and studied it for a long moment. 'The bastard,' he said angrily. He shot her a sideways glance. 'I suppose I should apologise for using such language in front of a lady, but I'm no gentleman, as you'll discover when you get to know me better.'

'What does it say?'

'That man should be shot.' He handed her the letter. 'Read this and see if you don't agree.'

8

Daisy studied the formal language used by the lawyer and she shook her head. 'I don't understand. What gives Squire Tattersall the right to send this sort of letter?'

'You're new here,' Jay said slowly. 'If you'd been born and bred in the village you'd know that the squire owns most of the land on both sides of the creek. The missing piece is Creek Hall and what's left of the estate, which isn't much. The old doctor was forced to sell it off piece by piece, so Nick told me last evening at dinner. The squire put up rents and refused to make any improvements on the properties, no doubt hoping that the tenants would move on.'

'But where would they go?'

'That's the point! The villagers have no choice. They either stay in damp, dilapidated housing or they're out on the streets, or in the workhouse. The squire doesn't care — he just wants the land and power.'

'And now he's demanding payment of this exorbitant sum or he'll send the bailiffs in and foreclose on a loan he made to Nick's father.' Daisy folded the piece of paper and handed it back to him. 'That's terrible.'

'I'm going with him. I've had many a run-in with the squire and I know how to handle him.' Jay ruffled Jack's hair. 'You stay with Miss Daisy and see her safely home.' He hurried after Nick and Jack followed him.

'Wait for me.' Daisy picked up her skirts and ran. She caught up with them in the stable yard where Nick was about to mount his horse.

'You can't do this on your own, Nick,' Jay protested. 'The squire will have you thrown out before you have a chance to put your case.'

'Jay's right,' Daisy said breathlessly. 'You might make matters worse.'

'The squire is determined to have Creek Hall and what's left of the estate,' Nick said angrily. 'How much worse can it be?'

Nick's distress was plain to see and Daisy laid her hand on his arm. 'Couldn't your aunt help?'

'Yes, but as you can see from the letter, which I assume you've both read, the squire has added interest on to the original loan. If only my father had confided in me I'd have left medical school and found work.'

'The old doctor must have been desperate,' Jay said, frowning thoughtfully. 'But Daisy is right, you can't go in there all guns blazing. That's something I might do, but it's not how you would normally act, Nick.'

'I have an idea.' Daisy stroked the horse's muzzle. 'I've listened to business talk amongst Mr Carrington's friends and acquaintances. They speak freely in front of a governess. I might as well have been invisible.'

Nick eyed her warily. 'What have you in mind?'

'Let's go indoors. I'm sure Jack wants to see his sister and Mrs Bee. We can talk over a cup of tea.'

'I appreciate your concern, but I have to go right away.'

'Listen to her, Nick,' Jay said urgently. 'You can't afford to make a mistake now — not with the fate of Creek Hall at stake.'

'Fifteen minutes,' Nick said grudgingly. 'I'll listen to what you have to say, Daisy, but time is short. According to this letter I have only days to come up with the extra money, and it's just not possible.' He beckoned to the stable boy. 'Hold the reins. I won't be long.'

Jay clapped him on the back. 'That's the ticket.'

Jack ran on ahead as they crossed the stable yard and entered the house through the scullery. Mrs Bee was in the middle of preparing the midday meal, but her face lit up when she saw them and she stopped what she was doing. 'Well, this is a surprise.'

Dove gave her brother a warm hug. 'Why aren't you in school, young man,' she said, smiling. 'What will Dad say when he finds out you've bunked off?'

'Mr Massey knows.' Jack turned to Daisy for confirmation and she nodded. 'Daisy is teaching me at home while my arm is bad, and Mr Massey comes to check on me, but I think he really comes to see Daisy. I think he's sweet on her.'

Daisy shook her head. 'Don't be silly, Jack. Mr Massey is very conscientious and he thinks you could go far, if you apply yourself to your books.'

'It looks to me as if you're ready to go back to classes,' Dove said primly. 'I'm sure Mr Massey has better things to do than to run round after you, Jack.'

Mrs Bee glanced anxiously at Nick. 'Is everything all right, Doctor? You look worried.'

'Everything is fine, Mrs Bee. We've got a few business things to talk about. Might we have some tea in the parlour?'

'Of course, Doctor.' Mrs Bee stared pointedly at Dove. 'I'll leave that to you.'

'Yes, Mrs Bee.' Dove turned to her brother with a stern look. 'You'd best sit at the table, Jack, and I'll give you a cup of milk and a biscuit.'

'Can I have a piece of cake?'

Daisy hesitated as she was about to follow the others from the room. 'May I have a piece of cake, Jack. Remember what Mr Massey says.' She did not stop to hear him repeat his request, but Dove's reaction to the mention of the schoolmaster's name had struck a chord. Perhaps Dove had feelings for Elliot Massey? Maybe the dull, over-zealous teacher had charms that she herself had not seen. Daisy hurried after Nick and Jay as they made their way to the parlour.

Nick waited until Daisy and Jay were seated and he went to stand with his back to the fire. 'I could lose all this before the week is out,' he said, gazing round the shabby, but comfortably furnished room.

Daisy followed his gaze, taking in the silver trophies on the mantelshelf, and the framed daguerreotypes of people she assumed must be Nick's parents, and of Nick himself as a child and a schoolboy. In one corner a cricket bat and stumps had been left and probably forgotten, half-hidden by a pile of medical books, the overspill from a crowded bookcase. The walls were barely visible beneath watercolours of the flat Essex countryside and oil paintings, mainly of dogs and horses. A portrait hanging above the fireplace caught Daisy's eye and Nick followed her gaze. The subject, a dark-haired young woman wearing a pale green gown, gazed down at them with a gentle smile in her hazel eyes.

'That's my mother when she was young,' Nick said proudly.

'She was beautiful.'

'Yes, and she loved Creek Hall. I owe it to my parents to keep the house in the family, and that's what I intend to do.'

'You won't get anywhere with the squire with polite talk,' Jay said thoughtfully. 'I could round up some of my crew and scare the old tyrant rigid.'

'Has your memory come back?' Daisy turned to give Jay a searching look. 'You said you didn't know how you came to be in such a state when we found you. Do you remember now?'

'We're not talking about me. We're supposed to be helping Nick.'

Nick gazed up at his mother's portrait. 'I'm not going to let that man take Creek Hall from me. Unless either of you has a better idea, I'm going to ride over to Creek Manor and demand to have it out with him, face to face.'

'Why do you think he wants to ruin your family, Nick?' Daisy said gently. 'Your father did so much good for the local people, and I suspect you would continue his work, given half a chance.'

'My maternal grandfather was rector here before Mr Peabody, and my mother was his only child. She kept house for him after her mother died and the squire paid court to her, but she rejected him in favour of my father. I don't think the squire ever got over it and I'm quite certain that's the reason why he's gone out of his way to ruin my family.'

'That's awful,' Daisy said earnestly. 'But if that's the case he's unlikely to accept any offer you might make.'

'She's right.' Jay fisted his hands. 'There's only one thing a man like him understands.'

'Violence isn't the answer,' Nick said hastily. 'And you'd end up in court. I don't know what shady business you've been involved in, Jay, but I don't want you taking risks on my behalf.'

Daisy held up her hand. 'Might I speak? I have an idea, but it means that you have to trust me, and you won't be riding over to Creek Manor today.'

★ ★ ★

Daisy was up half the night preparing her story so that the squire could not catch her out on even the smallest detail. It had been difficult to persuade Nick that her plan would work, and even harder to convince Jay, who was against it from the start. Next morning Daisy put on her green velvet travelling gown, a cast-off of Mrs

123

Carrington's, who had taken a dislike to the outfit when her husband had told her she looked like a peapod about to burst. Wrapped in Aunt Eleanora's fur-lined cape, Daisy waited anxiously for her transport to arrive. She felt a little bit like Cinderella about to attend the ball that would change her life for ever, only it was Nick's future that depended upon her plan taking shape.

Linnet rushed into the front parlour, her cheeks pink with excitement. 'He's here, miss. We're really going to do this.'

'Yes,' Daisy said firmly. 'We're going to teach the squire a lesson and save Creek Hall for the doctor.'

'I hope you know what you're doing.' Eleanora followed them into the hall. 'You shouldn't get involved in other people's problems, Daisy. From what I've heard, the squire is not a man to trifle with.'

'I know exactly what I'm doing, Aunt. Don't worry.' Daisy stepped outside into bright sunshine. The pale wintry sky was a celestial blue and Daisy was filled with hope as she climbed into the carriage.

Jay grinned at her from the driver's seat. 'Luckily the blacksmith is an old mate of mine. He's finished his work on this vehicle, but the owner isn't expecting it back until tomorrow.'

Linnet took her seat beside Daisy. 'This is the first time I've travelled in such style.'

Daisy smiled, remembering outings with Julian when they had taken Timothy to the Zoological Gardens or one of the London parks in the Carringtons' barouche. She glanced at her left hand and through the soft leather of her glove she could see the outline of the ring that Julian had given her. It was a bitter-sweet moment tinged with regret, but it was part of her plan.

'Drive on, Fox,' Daisy said, leaning back with a sigh. 'I could get used to this.'

'Let's hope my brother doesn't overturn the carriage.' Linnet tucked the travelling rug over Daisy's knees as well as her own. 'This is the most exciting thing that's ever happened in Little Creek.'

'If it works,' Daisy said grimly. 'I might be making a huge mistake, but it would be terrible if the doctor lost his home.'

'You like him, don't you, miss?'

'Hold on, ladies.' Jay flicked the whip over the horses' ears. 'Off we go.' He glanced over his shoulder. 'This is the first time I've ever driven a carriage, but I'm getting the hang of it.'

Daisy and Linnet exchanged worried looks as they clung to the sides.

★   ★   ★

Although the manor house was just across the water from the village they had to travel a couple of miles to the nearest bridge and it was close to midday when they finally arrived. Jay drew the horses to a halt. He tipped his hat so that the brim almost touched his nose and he pulled up his collar.

'I'm known here, so it's best that Molesworth doesn't recognise me.' He climbed down from the box to open the carriage door, and proffered his hand in such a professional manner that Daisy was tempted to giggle, although it was mostly nerves. Now they were here her scheme seemed hare-brained and even less likely to succeed. She was tempted to remain seated and instruct Jay to take them home, but Nick, unwilling as he had been to agree to her plan, was depending on her. Anyway, they had been seen. The heavy oak door opened and a footman appeared, followed by Molesworth, the stern-looking butler.

Daisy alighted with Jay's help and he winked at her. 'Don't let the old devil browbeat you. He'll try his best.'

'I'll bear that in mind.' Daisy held her head high as she walked up the steps with Linnet close behind.

'I was passing and I decided to call upon the squire. Is he at home?' Daisy said boldly. She took a gilt-edged visiting card from her reticule and handed it to the butler. It was one of Mrs Carrington's that Daisy had used when ordering items for her employer, and she waited, hardly daring to breathe.

'If you would care to wait, I'll see if the master is at home.' Molesworth ushered them into the entrance hall and the footman stood to attention while his superior walked off at a stately pace.

Daisy wondered if anyone ever hurried in the countryside. Inwardly she was quaking, but she managed to maintain an outward show of unconcern. Linnet was pale but she waited demurely at Daisy's side, saying nothing. There was a distinct chill in the air, which was not entirely due to the weather and Daisy could feel the figures in the portraits gazing down from their gilt frames. She could imagine their disapproval even though they had been dead and buried for a couple of centuries. A suit of armour at the far end of the hall looked even more menacing and she dared not look at the footman, who was eyeing her suspiciously. If the Carringtons' servants were anything to go by, those who worked below stairs had an uncanny knack of detecting a parvenu. She made a determined effort to remain calm and eventually Molesworth reappeared.

'Would you come this way, Mrs Carrington?' He glared at Linnet, who was about to follow Daisy. 'Wait there, if you please.'

'And what if I don't please?' Linnet said angrily. 'I'm here to look after my mistress.'

'It's all right.' Daisy gave her a reassuring smile. 'I won't be long.' She braced herself to follow the butler through a maze of gloomy oak-panelled corridors, and he ushered her into a room overlooking the rear of the building. The book-lined walls and leather-covered armchairs would not have been out of place in a gentlemen's club, and a large mahogany desk placed centrally was the dominant feature. A tall, well-built man dressed in tweeds rose from behind his desk.

'Will there be anything else, sir?'

'No, I'll ring when I need you, Molesworth.' Esmond Tattersall looked Daisy up and down as if she were an entry in a cattle show.

'Very good, sir.' The butler bowed out as if in the presence of royalty.

'Mrs Carrington?' The squire's weather-beaten features were set in a frown as he turned his attention to the deckle-edged card. 'Do I know you, ma'am?'

'I have to confess that I'm not Mrs Carrington,' Daisy said, smiling. 'But I hope to have that title very soon.' She peeled off her gloves and held out her left hand, displaying the diamond ring that Julian had given her as a pledge of his love. 'My fiancé is Julian Carrington, who is at present in Paris, having just taken up a post in the diplomatic corps.'

'I'm intrigued, but baffled. Take a seat, Miss, er . . .'

'Miss Marshall.' Daisy had thought long and hard before deciding to use her own name. She had been tempted to take on an alias, but it was probably safer to stick as near to the truth as possible. She sank down on the nearest chair, her knees giving way beneath her. 'What a delightful house you have, Squire.'

'Thank you, but I'm sure you didn't drop in to tell me that.'

Daisy smiled archly. 'No, of course not. I've been making enquiries in the district. My fiancé and I are looking for a country house, near the coast, where we can settle and bring up a family.' She turned her head away coyly, giving him a surreptitious glance beneath her lashes.

'And what has this to do with me, Miss Marshall?'

'I've heard that you are the biggest and most

128

important landowner in the area, and also a magistrate. You see, sir, I have done my research thoroughly. I'm hoping you might know of a suitable property that is up for sale, or likely to be so in the near future.'

'So you are looking to purchase rather than to rent?'

'We wish to buy, of course. My fiancé's family are very wealthy, and they want us to have a nice home. If we like a property we are prepared to take somewhere that needs a little love and attention, and that will be reflected in the price.'

Squire Tattersall sat down, staring at her as if he could see right through her deception. 'It sounds as if you have somewhere in mind. I'm not a fool, Miss Marshall. Are you speaking of Creek Hall? As far as I know it's the only property that fits in with your description.'

'It has been mentioned, sir.'

Squire Tattersall held the visiting card between his fingers, scrutinising it with a thoughtful frown. 'How do you come to be in this part of the country? It's a long way from Queen Square.'

'My uncle is a recently retired businessman. He bought a property in Little Creek because he wanted to take the air and follow less arduous pursuits. I am staying with him and my aunt for a while, and it would be convenient to live near them when I am married.'

'I see.' Squire Tattersall sat back in his chair, steepling his fingers. His shrewd brown eyes, set beneath bushy brows, seemed to bore into her soul. 'You wouldn't happen to be a friend of Dr Neville, would you?'

129

'I hardly know anyone in the village, Squire.'

'Creek Hall is all but derelict. Why would a young couple wish to burden themselves with somewhere that needs almost complete renovation?'

It was obvious that his suspicions were aroused and Daisy rose from her seat. 'I can see that I've wasted my time. Thank you for seeing me. I'll show myself out.'

Squire Tattersall leaped to his feet. 'Don't be so hasty. Sit down and we can discuss the matter further, or maybe you would like to stay to luncheon?' He reached for the bell pull.

Daisy shook her head. 'Thank you, but I have another property to see this afternoon. However, if you'd like to name your price I will have a word with my solicitor, and he will deal with matters from then on.'

'Do take a seat, my dear lady. I'm sure we can come to a mutually agreed arrangement, and it will be a pleasure to have you as a neighbour.' His eyes narrowed. 'But if your future husband is in the diplomatic service, won't he be away from home for long periods of time?'

'Of course, and that's why I wish to be close to my family.'

'I thought that wives usually accompanied their husbands on such missions.'

'I think that is a private matter, Squire. It need not concern you.' Daisy spoke hastily and for a moment she thought that she had made a dreadful mistake.

Twin spots of colour stood out above the squire's mutton-chop whiskers and his eyes flashed, but he twisted his lips into a smile. 'I like a woman with spirit. It will be a pleasure doing business with you, Miss Marshall.'

Daisy forced her lips into a smile and resumed her seat. 'Thank you, Squire. Now, how much are you asking for the Creek Hall estate?'

Squire Tattersall walked slowly round the desk and leaned against it, fixing Daisy with a hard stare. 'Well, you are direct, Miss Marshall. I think you and I are going to be good friends.'

'That depends upon how much you think the estate is worth, Squire,' Daisy said firmly. He was so close that she could feel the heat radiating from his body and the smoky scent of the Harris Tweed mingled with the heady odours of brandy and cigar smoke.

'I'm certain we can come to a mutually satisfactory arrangement. Are you sure you won't stay for luncheon?'

Daisy raised her left hand to brush an imaginary hair from her brow and the diamond ring flashed in a ray of sunlight that filtered through the panes of the lattice window. She needed to remind this domineering man that she was engaged to be married, although she had a feeling that such a consideration would carry little weight if he thought that she was fair game. She held his gaze, hoping that he could not hear her heart beating a tattoo against her ribcage, and she wished that she had insisted on having Linnet present, but the thought of saving Creek Hall was uppermost in her mind, and she leaned forward, forcing her lips into a smile. 'How much are you asking, Squire?'

'What happened?' Linnet demanded when they were shown out of the manor house.

'Not now,' Daisy said in a low voice. 'Wait until we're away from here. I wouldn't be surprised if the walls really do have ears. The squire seems to know everything that's going on in the area.

Jay was already standing to attention with the carriage door held open. 'Well, how did it go?' He helped Daisy into the carriage and then Linnet.

'I hope I never have to see that man again. He's a lecher and he disgusts me.'

'What did he do?' Linnet asked anxiously as she settled herself beside Daisy. 'Did he molest you, miss?'

'No, not physically, but he leered at me the whole time, and he was so condescending. He obviously thinks that all women are stupid and I'm not sure if he took me seriously. He seemed to think that I was offering myself as part of the bargain, but I made it clear that wasn't the case.'

'I'd have wiped the smug smile off his face,' Jay said angrily.

'And you'd end up in prison again.' Daisy met his angry gaze with a steady look. 'I've heard that you served time. It wouldn't be wise to get on the wrong side of the squire.'

'That was a long time ago,' Jay said casually. 'Anyway, we aren't talking about me. Did he say anything untoward? I won't stand for that.'

'It doesn't matter now — it's over as far as

I'm concerned. When I tell Nick how much it will take to pay back the debt his father incurred, and it's not as much as the interest that the wicked old devil was demanding, it will be up to Nick's solicitor to deal with Squire Tattersall. Whatever happens I have no wish to see the squire again.'

'Won't that be difficult, miss?' Linnet gazed at her, frowning. 'If the master does go ahead with the purchase, won't the squire be suspicious if you don't see him again?'

'I don't think a lady like Mrs Carrington would soil her hands with business matters. I'm relying on that fact, but in my opinion the squire is being greedy.'

'I hope you won't get into trouble with the squire, miss. If he discovers that you've tricked him he'll be furious.'

'There's no reason why he should find out,' Daisy said with more confidence than she was feeling. 'Don't worry about me, Linnet.'

'But I do, miss. You're one of us now, if you don't mind me saying so.'

'Not in the least. I'd be proud to be considered part of the village, and I'll do anything I can to save Creek Hall, within reason.'

'It's time someone stood up to the squire.' Jay climbed onto the driver's seat. 'Let's get away from here.'

'Yes, drive on, please, Jay.' Daisy sat back against the padded squabs. 'Nick will be waiting to hear what the squire said.'

★   ★   ★

133

'I should never have agreed to your plan in the first place,' Nick said angrily. 'I'm grateful to you for trying to help, Daisy, but I should have known how that man would react to a pretty face.'

'Just say the word and I'll knock some sense into the old goat.' Jay stopped pacing the floor, turning to Nick with an angry frown. 'I could have put a stop to it, but I let her go in on her own.'

'I wasn't allowed in with her,' Linnet added tearfully. 'We all know the squire's reputation with women.'

Daisy had been sitting quietly in the morning parlour at Creek Hall, but now she rose to her feet. 'Stop it, all of you. I chose to face the squire on my own, and nothing untoward happened. Yes, I was embarrassed, and to tell the truth I was a bit nervous at times, but he quoted a price for Creek Hall, and it's obvious that he's trying to extort money from you. I think your solicitor would be able to pin him down to a more reasonable repayment of the debt.'

'Thank you, Daisy. You've done splendidly, but Tattersall isn't the sort of man who would take kindly to being duped. I'll find a way to raise the interest he's put on my father's loan, and I'll deal with him myself. It was cowardly of me to let you go there in the first place.'

Jay shook his head. 'No one could accuse you of taking the easy way out. Daisy wanted to help and she did her best.'

'And I am truly grateful. It was a brave move,

Daisy, but the squire always seems to be one step ahead.'

'How will you raise the money?' she asked anxiously. 'What will you do?'

'I'll use the money my aunt gave me to pay off part of the loan, but I have no choice other than to return to London. I was offered a junior position in Harley Street before I left, and I'm seriously thinking of taking it up. I'll leave Mrs Bee in charge while I'm away.'

Linnet gazed at him in dismay. 'Who will take care of us in the village if you aren't here?'

'I'm sorry. It's not what I intended, and my father would be horrified if he knew, but I have no choice.'

'Are you really going back to London? I'm not afraid of the squire,' Daisy said earnestly. 'I'll carry on with the pretence if you're willing to accept his terms. Just say the word and I'll tell him so.'

9

Nick left for London next day, but Daisy chose to stay in Little Creek. She devoted herself to helping Jack with his lessons, and discovered that Mr Massey had been right: Jack was a bright boy and when he set his mind to studying he was an apt pupil. But he was young and as his arm healed he became bored and restless. Being confined to the house was not something he was accustomed to, and he admitted missing his friends. Despite the fact that he would have to be careful not to damage the arm again, Daisy thought it time he returned to school.

She brought up the subject on one of Elliot's frequent visits to the house and he agreed, reluctantly, although he suggested that perhaps another two or three weeks at home might speed up the healing process. Daisy suspected that this was because he would not have an excuse to call on her, but his open admiration was becoming embarrassing, as were the small tokens of appreciation that he brought with him. Sometimes it was a bunch of snowdrops or the first primroses, or it might be a book of poetry that he thought she would enjoy. When he suggested an outing to the fair that was visiting the area Daisy refused as tactfully as possible, but when Jay turned up at Creek Cottage with a similar proposition she accepted instantly.

It was a sunny day with a definite hint of

spring in the air, although there was a bite in the wind, demonstrating that winter had not entirely given up its icy grip. Not to be deterred, Daisy wrapped her shawl around the green velvet travelling gown she had worn when she visited the squire. 'Isn't that Nick's horse?' she asked as Jay handed her onto the driver's seat of the trap.

'Yes, it is. Nick asked me to see that the old fellow gets some exercise while he's away.' Jay shot her a sideways glance as he climbed up to sit beside her. 'That's the gown you wore to Creek Manor. That colour suits you. It complements your creamy complexion and emphasises your lovely eyes. I've always found dark-eyed women fascinating.'

Daisy stared at him in surprise. 'I suppose that's meant to be a compliment, or are you saying I'm like all the other women you've known with dark hair and eyes?'

Jay laughed and flicked the reins and the old horse ambled off towards the lane. 'I'm not a lady's man and never have been, but I can appreciate pretty things and I speak plainly. I might not be a gentleman, but I'm not an ignorant clod.'

'Who said you were?'

'I've been in prison, Daisy. I don't pretend to be better than I am.'

'What did you do?'

He chuckled. 'I never got on with my father. I felt that he hated me at times, and I fell in with a bad crowd.'

'But you didn't go to prison for being a naughty boy.'

Jay threw back his head and laughed. 'Naughty boy hardly describes me, Daisy. I got into fights, and I mixed with the wrong people. I'm not proud of my past.'

'You were arrested for being in a fight?'

'You might say that.' He stared ahead, his gaze fixed on the road.

'What happened?'

'There was a brawl outside a pub in Maldon. I can't remember what started it, but I joined in and I was the one who got caught. The squire was quick to make an example of me and I was sentenced to six months' hard labour. I suppose that seems shameful to a lady like you.'

'I'm not a lady. I was a governess until my employer's son was sent to boarding school.'

'You are a lady, and I'm someone you ought not to associate with.'

She turned to look at him, but he was intent on the road ahead. 'Why not? How do you earn your living now, and who had beaten you so badly when we found you face down in the mud?'

'You might say it was a difference of opinion between business associates.' He met her curious gaze with a careless smile. 'A disagreement between shipmasters.'

'You own a ship?'

'The *Lazy Jane* is a neat little schooner, and I'm her captain. The man who owns her gives us his instructions, and we carry them out. It's as simple as that.'

She shivered, experiencing a sudden chill, and she tucked her hands into the blanket that he had thoughtfully wrapped around her knees. 'Tell me about your ship.'

'She's small and fast, and the goods we trade in are much in demand locally.'

'Do you mean contraband? I thought smuggling had died out in the last century.'

'There are always men eager to make money in any way they can. I transport goods for the ship owner, and sometimes people. We land in the quiet inlets of the Blackwater or the River Crouch. I don't ask questions.'

'But something must have gone wrong for you to be beaten so viciously.'

'An altercation with a rival,' he said casually. 'They're a gang working out of Burnham-on-Crouch. They pose as fishermen, but it's a guise to cover up their criminal activities.'

'And what were you doing on the *Lazy Jane*?'

'It just so happens that we were minding our own business and making for shelter in a storm when we ran aground. They'd been after us since we sailed into the estuary, but I thought they'd given up. In hindsight I realise that wasn't the case.'

'But you were attacked near home.'

'It was pitch-dark and there was nothing to be done until morning, so I left my crew on board and set off to see my family. I had a pouch of money to give my mother, but I must have been followed. I was set upon and I don't remember anything until you found me in the water.'

'I suppose they stole the money.'

'They must have landed further upriver and the light of my lantern probably gave me away.

They knew I would be carrying money and they were determined to get their hands on it.'

'Is it worth risking your life for so little?'

'It's all I know, Daisy. I've been at sea since I was thirteen; that's nigh on ten years, and there's precious little for me to do on shore.'

'There must be some gainful employment you could undertake,' Daisy said, frowning.

'I'm a wanderer, Daisy. I don't know that I could ever settle down for long on land.'

'Never? You might change your mind one day.'

'Wait until you see the *Lazy Jane* and perhaps you'll understand. She's beached in a secluded spot and my crew are working on her, or at least that's what they're supposed to be doing. I'm going to check on them now.'

'I thought we were going to the fair.'

'We'll do that afterwards. I want you to see my boat. I trust you, Daisy. No one else knows of her whereabouts, or even how I earn my living.'

'Not even Nick?'

'He's the exception, but he doesn't know the exact location of my craft. I wouldn't put him in that position.'

'And yet you're willing to take me there? Why?'

His smile faded. 'I want you to see the boat, it's as simple as that.'

'Aren't you afraid that I might report you to the authorities?'

'Not at all. I don't think you give a damn for the rules.'

'I'm very law abiding.'

'But you didn't mind lying to the squire. You

were prepared to take him on at his own game. What do you think he would have done had he discovered your deception?'

'I try not to think about it. Anyway, I'm unlikely to meet the squire again. We don't move in the same circles.'

'Best keep it that way, too.' Jay clicked his tongue against his teeth. 'Walk on, Hero, old man. It's not too far now.'

Daisy held on to the side of the seat as the trap lurched forward, bouncing off the ruts in what was little more than a track. They were driving along the edge of the saltings and sunlight sparkled on the strips of water lying between the tussocky grass mounds. The whole area was alive with wildlife, and gulls soared above their heads, their plaintive cries filling the air. It was chilly but exhilarating, and Daisy felt a surge of anticipation as Jay guided Hero down a narrow track that opened out suddenly into a secluded strip of mud flat surrounded by trees. There, as he had said, was the *Lazy Jane*, with two seamen working to repair the damage caused when the boat was beached.

Jay drew Hero to a halt and leaped down from the driver's seat. He crossed the muddy foreshore to speak to his crew. Abandoned temporarily, Daisy watched curiously. Judging by the men's attitudes it was obvious that Jay was their leader, and a popular one at that. Their faces had brightened at the sight of him and they seemed eager to talk. Daisy climbed down from the driver's seat and stretched. The old trap was not the most luxurious form of travel and it was good to feel solid ground beneath her feet. She stroked Hero's muzzle and he rubbed his head against her shoulder in response.

After a brief conversation, Jay strolled back to join her. 'What do you think of my *Jane*?'

'She's very beautiful,' Daisy said truthfully. 'I'd love to see her under full sail.'

'Would you?' Jay studied her expression and smiled. 'I believe you mean it, Daisy.'

'Of course I do. I know nothing about boats, but it's obvious you care about her, almost as if she were a woman.'

'Boats and ships have personalities, just like people. *Jane* is a capricious little minx, and she's hard to handle, but with the wind in her sails she sets a fine course at a top speed. She's got us out of many a scrape in the past.'

'What sort of contraband do you bring ashore?'

He laughed, causing his mates to look up and grin. 'You've been reading too many penny dreadfuls, Daisy. It's not as exciting as it sounds.'

'But if you're caught you'll go to prison again.'

'Like everything it's a matter of being well prepared, plus a large amount of luck.'

Daisy glanced over his shoulder at the men who had resumed their work. 'Are you satisfied with what they've done so far?'

'Yes, they're good lads, and they haven't had any bother.'

'Do you really enjoy living like this?' Daisy looked him in the eye. 'Don't you sometimes wish that you had a more peaceful existence?'

'No. I love every minute of it.'

'Even after the beating you took?'

'If I hadn't ended up face down in the mud I might never have met you, Daisy.'

She turned away, aware that she was blushing. 'You might have died in that icy water.'

'I'm still here and that's all that matters.' Jay patted Hero's neck. 'I'm done here. Shall we go to the fair?'

★ ★ ★

It took over an hour to drive to the fairground and Jay handed Hero's reins to a small ragged boy, who promised to watch over the horse and trap, although Daisy suspected that the child would pocket the money Jay had given him and disappear the moment their backs were turned. Jay, on the other hand, appeared to be supremely confident and carefree as he guided her through the crowds of people, who were there to enjoy themselves. All around them there was the sound of chatter, laughter and throaty music from a Dutch organ. Stall holders shouted their wares and children raced around shrieking with excitement. Daisy wondered why they were not in school, but it was none of her business — today she was determined to forget her problems and delight in her new-found freedom, even if it was only temporary.

Jay was an amusing companion and they wandered round the fairground, visiting each stall in turn. They tossed wooden hoops in an attempt to win the rather ugly ornaments, and shied balls at coconuts. They ate mutton pies as they strolled, something that Aunt Eleanora would have condemned as dreadfully bad form, had she seen Daisy munching food in public. It felt like a small rebellion against the rules of polite society and added piquancy to the ginger beer that Daisy sipped from a bottle that she shared with Jay. It was gloriously common and totally delightful. She even allowed Jay to hold her hand as they sat on hard wooden seats, watching acrobats and jugglers perform in a makeshift circus ring. When it was over they were just leaving when they were confronted by none other than Squire Tattersall. There was no escape.

'Miss Marshall. This is a pleasant surprise.' Tattersall's eyes narrowed to slits as he looked Jay up and down. 'What are you doing here, Fox? I told you never to show your face round here again.'

'I do what I please, Squire. I'm a free man.'

'Put one foot wrong and I'll send you down again.'

'Everyone deserves a second chance, Squire.' Daisy met Tattersall's cynical gaze with a defiant stare. 'Fox is simply here to protect me.'

'And who'll protect you from him? What would your diplomat fiancé think if you knew you were gallivanting round the countryside with a felon?'

Daisy could feel Jay's muscles tense as he stood close by her side. 'You're right, Squire,' she said, smiling. 'He would be very annoyed, but I was so looking forward to visiting a fair. Having lived all my life in London I'm just getting to know the pleasures of residing in the country-side. How fortunate you are to have all this on your doorstep. Although I've heard that you own most of the land in this part of Essex. You are lord of all you survey.'

The flattery worked and Tattersall puffed out his chest. Turning his back on Jay he proffered his arm to Daisy. 'I had you down as a minx, Miss Marshall, and now I can see my first impression was correct. You will allow me to see you safely home.'

Daisy thought quickly. The last thing she needed was for the squire to discover that she was living in a small cottage with her aunt and uncle. It would destroy the image she had taken such pains to create. 'Thank you, Squire, but I have an appointment at Creek Hall. I contacted the housekeeper and asked if I might view the property. I wouldn't want to take you out of your way. Fox will drive me there.'

'Then I'll walk you to your carriage.' Tattersall grasped her hand and was about to tuck it in the crook of his arm when a commotion broke out close to them and a fight ensued. 'What the devil? Where are the police when you need them?' He released Daisy and strode towards the mêlée.

'Quick,' Daisy gasped. 'Let's go.'

Jay took her hand and plunged into the crowd that had gathered to watch the scrap. They raced across the grass, like a couple of children running away from an irate schoolmaster, and when they reached the trap the boy was still holding Hero's reins.

'Good fellow,' Jay said, pressing a silver sixpence into the astonished child's hand. 'That's for being trustworthy.' Jay lifted Daisy onto the driver's seat and sprung up beside her. 'Walk on, Hero. We're going home.'

'Do you think the squire believed me?' Daisy asked anxiously.

'Not a chance. He's no fool, and he'll be on the lookout for me now. I should have kept my mouth shut.'

'Does he know that about the *Lazy Jane?*'

'If the authorities knew where we'd beached they would have impounded her by now,' Jay said evasively. He shot her a sideways glance. 'I'll need to disappear for a while, Daisy.'

'Where will you go?'

'*Jane* is almost seaworthy. It's time I rejoined my crew. Life ashore isn't for the likes of me.'

'I'm sorry,' Daisy said with genuine regret. 'It seems wrong that your past mistakes don't allow you to have a normal life. Your parents will be sad and so will Jack.'

'You're right about Jack, but he's young and he'll get over it. As to my dad, he'll be glad to see the back of me, and Mum just goes along with whatever he says.'

'I'm sure your parents love you.'

He chuckled. 'You'd never know it. Anyway, I'm a man now, Daisy. I don't need to be tied to my mother's apron strings. But I will miss you.'

'Isn't there another way? I mean, you could find work and prove that you can live a normal life.'

His derisive laughter echoed off the bare

146

branches of the trees as they drove through a small spinney. 'What is normal, Daisy? Farmworkers striving to bring up families on starvation wages? Fishermen unable to make a living in winter due to bad weather? Able-bodied men unable to find work of any kind? The workhouses are full of people like these, and I don't want to end up like that. I'm not clever like Nick — I haven't got the brains to be a doctor or a lawyer, so I do what I can in order to survive.'

'You'll never get anywhere if you think like that,' Daisy said angrily. 'What sort of example are you setting for Jack? He thinks the world of you.'

'And what do you think of me, Daisy? What is your honest opinion?'

'I think you could do whatever you set your mind on, Jay. You just need to decide what it is you want.' She had expected him to argue, but he looked away and they travelled on in silence. Daisy was tempted to apologise for being too outspoken, but she was convinced that she was in the right. One day his luck would run out and the law would catch up with Jay and the *Lazy Jane*. If Nick were here he would almost certainly agree with her, and maybe Jay would listen to his childhood friend, but Nick was in London attempting to save Creek Hall. Why was life so complicated?

They parted outside Creek Cottage. The sun had plummeted below the horizon, it was bitterly cold and it would soon be dark. Jay leaped to the ground, but Daisy climbed down before he had a chance to help her. She needed to distance herself from this complicated and dangerously exciting man.

'Thank you for taking me to see the boat, and the fair.' She was suddenly conscious of his nearness, and she dropped her gaze.

'I won't see you for a long time and I don't want to part on bad terms.'

She raised her eyes slowly, but his face was in deep shadow and she could not read his expression. He was standing very close and the scent of him filled her nostrils as he leaned forward to kiss her long and hard on the lips.

'That was goodbye. I would stay if I could, but my presence would bring trouble to you and my family. Tattersall is not a man to be ignored. I have to go right away.' He brushed her lips again with a gentle kiss. 'Be good to Nick. He's a sound chap and I think he loves you, Daisy.'

He climbed up onto the driver's seat and urged Hero into a trot, leaving Daisy staring after him, too stunned to speak and shocked by her reaction to his brief embrace. He was gone, swallowed up by the gathering gloom, leaving her alone and enveloped in silence apart from the gurgling sound of water tumbling over the stones in the creek, and the mournful cry of a barn owl.

*   *   *

Daisy was helping Hattie to prepare breakfast next morning when Linnet walked into the kitchen, having slept at home on her day off.

'He's gone,' she said brusquely. 'Jay packed his bag and left last night. Not a word to Mum and

148

Dad, just a hug for me and he said he had no choice.' She glared at Daisy. 'I know you were with him yesterday. Why did he leave so suddenly?'

Hattie stopped carving a ham and waved the knife at her. 'You don't speak to Miss Marshall in that tone, Linnet. You forget yourself.'

'I'm sorry, miss, but he's my brother and I want to know why he left without saying goodbye.'

'Not another word from you, young lady, or you'll be on your way, too,' Hattie said angrily.

'No, it's all right, Hattie.' Daisy met Linnet's angry gaze with an attempt at a smile. 'You're right in a way, but it wasn't because of me that Jay left. We were enjoying ourselves at the fair when we bumped into Squire Tattersall and he recognised Jay.'

'What does that mean?' Hattie demanded. 'Am I missing something here?'

'Jay was in trouble with the law when he was younger,' Daisy said in a low voice.

'He went to prison,' Linnet added, shaking her head. 'Jay was the wild one, but he's a good man. It was all a mistake.'

'A likely story.' Hattie shrugged. 'They all say that.'

'I believe him.' Daisy turned to Linnet. 'It was unfortunate that the squire recognised Jay and he remembered sentencing him. Jay thought it best for all of us, including you and Jack, if he made himself scarce for a while. I'm sorry, Linnet.'

'I don't know why you're apologising to her,'

Hattie said crossly. 'She's better off without him, if you ask me.'

Linnet opened her mouth as if to reply but at that moment the door opened and Eleanora burst into the kitchen. 'Why are you all standing round gossiping? Where's my breakfast?' She fixed Daisy with an uncompromising look. 'I want a word with you, young lady.'

Daisy followed her aunt to the parlour. 'What have I done now, Aunt?'

'Hattie and Linnet are paid to do the work, Daisy. It isn't proper for a young lady to spend so much time with the servants, and I'm not happy about you consorting with that Fox fellow. Grace Peabody told me that he's been in prison. Were you aware of that?'

'Yes, Aunt. I know, and I haven't been consorting with him. He took me to the fair yesterday, that's all.'

'That is quite enough to set tongues wagging. I haven't been here long, but Grace has told me how things are done in Little Creek, and mixing with riff-raff is definitely out of the question — unless you want to be the subject of gossip.'

'Yes, Aunt.'

'Don't look so smug, Daisy. I know that expression and it means that you intend to do whatever you want. Am I correct?'

'I won't be seeing any more of Jay Fox. He's gone away.'

Eleanora sank down in her usual place at the breakfast table. 'Thank heaven for small mercies. I don't mind you being on friendly terms with the young doctor. Nick is your brother's friend and we know he comes from a good family, but I still think you could do better. I believe Squire Tattersall is a widower. You could do worse, Daisy.'

Daisy went to the sideboard and took out clean napkins. 'The squire is very unpopular, Aunt.' She laid the linen on each place setting.

'He's a very wealthy man and owns half the county, so I believe. He is just the sort of person you ought to be encouraging, and certainly not one of the Fox family or that mealy-mouthed schoolmaster. I can't abide the man.' She looked round, frowning. 'Where is Jack? He should be up and about like a normal child. It's high time he returned to school anyway.'

'I've had a word with Mr Massey, although he suggested that Jack ought to remain off school for another couple of weeks.'

'Poppycock. The man's a fool and I'll tell him so when I next see him. You'd better wake the boy, Daisy. Tell him to come downstairs immediately or there'll be no breakfast for him.'

'Yes, Aunt.' Daisy went upstairs to her brother's room, where Jack was snuggled beneath the covers, fast asleep. She gave him a gentle shake. 'Jack, wake up. It's time for breakfast.'

He groaned and opened one eye. 'Go away.'

His rosy cheeks and the curve of his thick golden eyelashes reminded her of young Timothy Carrington, and she sighed. That part of her life was over and done with, and she might never see Jay Fox again, but the memory of his kiss lingered. Even more shocking was the realisation that Jay's brief embrace had left her shaken and wanting more. She tickled Jack and he began to giggle.

'Get up, Master Fox, or I'll call Linnet. She won't be so gentle with you.'

Jack sat up, rubbing his eyes. 'All right. I'm coming.'

'Wash first, then get dressed. Do I have to treat you like a baby and do it for you?'

Jack's blue eyes widened in horror. 'No. I'll do it myself. I promise.'

Daisy went to the door and opened it. 'If you're not downstairs in five minutes you'll have your sister to deal with.'

Jack rushed over to the washstand and tipped water into the basin. He ducked his whole head in the bowl, coming up and shaking his head like a wet dog as he felt for the towel. 'See,' he said breathlessly. 'I'll be quick.'

Daisy was still laughing when she reached the morning parlour. 'That boy will end up as prime minister one day, Aunt.'

Eleanora reached for a slice of toast and buttered it. 'More likely he'll end up in prison like his brother. I've been in their hovel, Daisy. I've met Jack's parents and the father is a shiftless creature, too lazy to work and support his family. The mother is a pathetic soul, brow-beaten, I dare say, and sickly. Grace and I have tried to show them how to improve their living conditions, but they don't seem able to better themselves.'

'Mr Fox used to be gamekeeper at Creek Hall until the late Doctor Neville could no longer afford to keep on the outdoor servants. From what I saw of the cottage it's beyond patching up. It needs a lot of work to make it habitable and that's the squire's responsibility. He owns most of the village now.'

'Oh, well. I expect he has his reasons.'

'I think he has an ulterior motive, Aunt. I don't know why he would want to evict the villagers from their homes, but that seems to be his aim. He wants to purchase Creek Hall, and he's making it almost impossible for Nick to hold on to his home.'

'From what I've heard, the squire is an astute businessman. He must know what he's doing. It's none of our business, Daisy. You'd do best to keep out of matters that don't concern you.'

'I care what happens to the people here.' Daisy sliced the top off her boiled egg. 'That sounds like Jack coming downstairs. He'll fall and break his other arm if he's not careful.'

Jack rushed into the room, smoothing his wet hair into place. 'I did it in four minutes, Daisy.'

She smiled. 'Yes, you did. Well done.'

'You're still late for breakfast, young man,' Eleanora said severely. 'Sit down and eat your porridge before it gets cold. We mustn't waste good food.'

Jack took a seat next to Daisy and began to eat, spooning the porridge into his mouth, oblivious to the frowning looks from Eleanora.

'Manners, Jack. Don't gobble,' she said sternly.

Daisy finished her egg and wiped her lips on her napkin. 'I might visit the school this morning, Aunt. Jack can come with me, and if Mr Massey is agreeable, he could join his classmates.'

'I'd like that,' Jack mumbled.

'Don't speak with your mouth full,' Eleanora said automatically. 'Yes, an excellent idea, Daisy.' She was about to rise from the table when a noise outside made her turn to stare out of the window. 'Good gracious, there's a very elegant carriage outside. Go and see who it is, Daisy.'

'Yes, Aunt.' Daisy stood up and went out into the hall just as someone hammered on the door. There was no sign of Linnet and the person outside seemed impatient. 'All right,' she said loudly. 'I'm coming.' She opened the door and his large presence blotted out the early spring sunshine.

10

'So it's true.' Squire Tattersall looked Daisy up and down. 'The wealthy Miss Marshall lives in a farm worker's cottage. My informant was correct.'

Daisy met his sarcastic smile with a defiant stare. 'I believe I told you that I was visiting my aunt and uncle. This is their house, Squire.'

'They might own the property for now, but I am the freeholder and when their lease expires, as it does before the year is out, the price for renewal will be very costly.'

'I know nothing of this, sir,' Daisy said slowly. 'Is this the reason for your visit today?'

'Certainly not. I have a land agent who deals with such matters. Are you going to invite me in? Or are you going to keep me standing on the doorstep?'

Daisy sensed trouble and she was trying to think of an excuse to bar him from the cottage when her aunt emerged from the dining room.

'Who is it, Daisy?' Eleanora peered over Daisy's shoulder. 'Who is this gentleman?'

Squire Tattersall doffed his top hat. 'Good morning, ma'am. If your niece will not oblige I must introduce myself. Esmond Tattersall, at your service.'

'Oh, good heavens! Where are your manners, Daisy?' Eleanora pushed her aside. 'Please come in, Squire Tattersall.'

'Delighted, ma'am.'

His presence filled the entrance hall and suddenly the cottage seemed very small and humble compared to the manor house. Daisy eyed him warily. Squire Tattersall had seen through her attempt to deceive him, although why he had come here in person was a mystery. She held her breath, waiting for him to reveal all to her aunt, but he was all smiles.

'Please come into the parlour,' Eleanora said hastily. 'I hope that girl has lit a fire. It's so hard to get good servants these days, Squire.'

He bowed and smiled. 'Indeed it is, ma'am. I don't want to cause you any inconvenience.'

'You aren't. I mean, it's no trouble at all. Daisy, ring for Linnet. Tell her to bring tea to the parlour. Or would you prefer coffee, Squire? I'm afraid my husband is not here at the moment. He left early to go fishing. He's quite obsessed with the sport these days.'

'He must try the lake at the manor some time, Mrs Marshall. I keep it well stocked.'

'Oh, too kind.' Eleanora rushed into the parlour. 'Tea and coffee, Daisy. See if there's any cake left, or biscuits if that boy hasn't eaten them all.' She motioned the squire to take a seat by the fire and Daisy took the opportunity to escape. If the squire was going to denounce her she would prefer to answer questions after the wretched man had gone back to his grand house. She hurried to the kitchen to relay the message, which sent Linnet into a panic and annoyed Hattie.

'Who does he think he is? Calling at this early

156

hour and the rooms not yet swept and dusted. I never heard of such a thing. People in London have better manners.'

'What business has the squire here?' Linnet's hand trembled as she set a tray with the best china. 'Trouble follows that man like his own shadow.'

Daisy had heard enough. 'I'm going to take Jack to school. Hopefully the squire will have gone by the time I return.'

★　★　★

The smell of chalk, ink and musty books enveloped Daisy as she ushered Jack into the classroom where Elliot was about to begin the first lesson. The children turned their heads to stare at them and Jack's friends called out to him but were immediately silenced by a word of warning from their teacher.

'Jack would like to attend class, Mr Massey,' Daisy said, smiling. 'His arm is healing well, but he does need to be careful and he mustn't indulge in rough games in the playground.'

'Of course.' Elliot beamed at her. 'He will stay in under my supervision at break and practise his reading.'

'I think you'll find he's improved immensely,' Daisy said quietly. She could hear sniggers coming from some of Jack's classmates and Elliot rapped on his desk with a wooden ruler.

'Children, open your primers at page twenty-three, where we left off yesterday. Read on and I'll test you later.' He glanced down at a small child who held her slate up for his inspection. 'Very good, Ida, but a dog has four legs, not five.'

'That's his tail, sir,' Ida lisped.

'Yes. Well done. Sit down now and your sister Letty will show you how to write the word dog.' Elliot turned to Daisy with an ingratiating smile. 'You have such a talent for teaching, Miss Marshall. I wonder if you would be interested in helping with some of the younger ones. I really need an assistant.'

Daisy glanced round at the children and was tempted to accept, but she had no intention of encouraging Elliot's tentative advances. He had betrayed his feelings for her in looks rather than words, and it was time to let him down gently. He was a good man, but not for her. She smiled and shook her head. 'Thank you, Mr Massey, but I'm afraid I have too much to do at home to consider taking up such a challenge.' A sudden memory of something that Dove had said occurred to her in a flash of inspiration. 'But I think I know someone who would make an excellent assistant.'

Elliot's face fell and he swallowed hard. For a moment she thought he was going to cry and she hoped the children had not noticed. From experience she knew that the young could sense weakness in someone of authority and play on it for all their worth. She did not wish to add to Elliot's distress.

'I'm so sorry, Miss Marshall. Might you reconsider your decision when you have had more time to think about it?'

'I'm afraid not, Mr Massey. I really must go

now, but I'll have a word with the young lady in question. I think she would be so right for the school, but that would be for you both to decide.' Daisy laid her hand briefly on his chalky sleeve, smiled and hurried from the classroom before he could think of anything to delay her.

Outside in the deserted playground she took deep breaths of the cold, clean air. It was all so different here from living in the city. London seemed further away than ever, but she still missed the bustle of the busy streets and the feeling of being at the heart of things. Out here they lived in a small world, seemingly ruled by Squire Tattersall. It had been a shock to learn that he held the lease on her aunt and uncle's cottage, and now he knew the truth he would realise that she did not have two pennies to rub together, let alone the funds to purchase Creek Hall. She ought to go home and rescue Aunt Eleanora, but her aunt was capable of looking after herself, and she would not stand for any nonsense from the squire. In fact, he was likely to come off worst in any argument. Aunt Eleanora had more than twenty-five years' experience of brow-beating her husband and bending him to her will, which would stand her in good stead when dealing with the squire. Daisy smiled as she thought of her uncle, who had found peace at last. Fishing had taken over his life and he could spend hours wading in ice-cold water or huddled on the river-bank, enjoying the freedom away from the business world and an overbearing wife.

Daisy wrapped her cape tightly around her to

159

combat the chill wind from the east and she set off on foot for Creek Hall, where she hoped to find Dove. The lane ran parallel with the creek, and when she came to the shallows where she and her uncle had found Jay, she wondered whether he and his crew had managed to refloat the *Lazy Jane*. Jay's sudden departure had upset Jack and Linnet, and Daisy could understand why they were so fond of their wayward elder brother. Life would never be dull with a man like Jay Fox, but neither would it be safe nor settled. He was a born wanderer and an adventurer, but that only added to his attractiveness. She sighed and quickened her pace.

Born and bred in the city, Daisy found life in the countryside a challenge, but living in London she had barely noticed the seasons changing. Now each day she noticed something that brought hope of spring, whether it was a patch of snowdrops at the foot of the hedgerow, or the buds on the trees waiting to burst forth into leaf. It was as if the world renewed itself by magic, and today was no different. The wood close to Creek Hall was carpeted in the bright golden flowers of lesser celandine and winter aconite. The birds seemed to realise that winter was gradually losing its grip and the saltmarsh was teeming with life. Daisy slowed down as she approached the mellow house, which seemed so much a part of the landscape that it might have grown from the clay soil rather than having been built brick by brick all those years ago. She could understand Nick's devotion to his old home and she experienced a surge of anger towards Squire

Tattersall, whose greed was consuming the county that she had come to love, even in such a short space of time.

Daisy entered the kitchen and was enveloped in a warm fug of cooking smells and the scent of herbs, which hung in bunches from the rafters. Mrs Bee and Dove were seated at the pine table, cleaning the silver, but they stopped what they were doing and looked up, smiling a welcome.

Mrs Bee put down the polishing cloth she had been using so energetically. 'Put the kettle on, Dove. We'll have a break and enjoy a chat with our visitor.'

Daisy took off her bonnet and cape and laid them on a chair. 'Thank you. That would be lovely. It's beautiful outside but very chilly.'

'It's brought the roses to your cheeks,' Mrs Bee said approvingly. 'As you can see we're busy cleaning the silver, not that there's much of it left. The old master sold off some of the more ornate pieces, but we keep what's left nice, ready for the doctor when he chooses to visit.'

'Have you heard from him recently?' Daisy pulled up a chair and sat down, rubbing her hands together in an attempt to stop them tingling. In her eagerness to escape from the squire she had left her gloves at home.

'No, not yet, but it's not long since he went up to London. I expect he's busy at that big hospital.'

'Yes,' Daisy said vaguely. 'You're probably right.' She hoped her disappointment did not show. It would have been nice to have had a letter, however brief, but Nick was probably caught up in the excitement of starting a new job. Creek Hall must seem like another world, and maybe he had forgotten her already.

'I don't suppose Jay will get in touch either,' Dove said sadly. 'I'm used to my brother's absences, but it worries Mum and makes Dad angry. They think he should stay at home and support the family.'

'Quite right.' Mrs Bee nodded. 'The young should look after the old.'

Dove put the kettle on the range and bustled about, setting a tray with cups and saucers from the large pine dresser. She glanced over her shoulder. 'How is Jack? I keep meaning to come and see him, but there's always something to do here.'

Mrs Bee sighed heavily. 'We do our best to keep the house spick and span, Miss Marshall, but it's not easy with just the two of us.'

'I'm sure you do an excellent job,' Daisy said hurriedly. 'And Jack is very well. In fact I just left him at school. Mr Massey is going to keep him in at break so that he doesn't join in the boys' rough games.'

Dove pulled a face. 'Jack won't like that. He can be a little monkey, but he's a good boy at heart.'

'Mr Massey is looking for someone to help with the younger children in class,' Daisy said vaguely. 'I took the liberty of saying I knew someone who would be suitable for the position, and I thought that you might be interested. Does that appeal to you, Dove?'

'I don't know about that.' Dove glanced anxiously at Mrs Bee. 'I love it here, even though I haven't been paid, except in the occasional basket of food that I've taken to Mum and Dad.'

Mrs Bee shook her head. 'You see how it is, Miss Marshall. I haven't been paid either, not for months.'

'But how have you managed?' Daisy stared at her aghast. 'Dr Neville can't expect you to stay on under such circumstances.'

'We've been living off the produce from the kitchen garden, and we have plenty of eggs from the hens. Farmer Clarke gives us butter, cheese and milk in return for allowing him to pasture his herd of cows in Ten Acre field, and Dove takes eggs to Miller Jones in return for flour.'

'But you can't carry on like this. It isn't fair. Have you thought of finding another position, Mrs Bee?'

'Master Nick gave me what he could to buy fuel and paraffin for the lamps, and he's promised to send money from London when he gets paid.' Mrs Bee stared down at her gnarled hands. 'I'm too old to change now, and if I left, where would I go? I've no family and no home other than Creek Hall.'

'I'm so sorry,' Daisy said earnestly. 'I had hoped to help, but the squire saw through my attempt to save the situation, and I might even have made matters worse.'

'I'm sure you did your best, miss.' Mrs Bee turned her head to glare at Dove. 'Where's that tea? I'm parched.'

Dove brought the pot to the table. 'Luckily the

water was almost boiling, but that's the last of the tea leaves.'

'This is ridiculous,' Daisy said angrily. 'Nick can't expect you two to exist on so little.'

'I suppose I'd be paid if I worked at the school.' Dove poured the tea and Mrs Bee added the milk before passing a cup to Daisy.

'I would imagine so. I didn't ask, but surely he wouldn't expect anyone to work for nothing, unlike Dr Neville. I'll have words with Nick when I see him next.'

'Please don't,' Mrs Bee said anxiously. 'I don't want him to think I've complained. I'm lucky to live in such a lovely house.'

'Something must be done.' Daisy sipped her tea. 'If I had any money I'd be glad to help, but I've only what's left of my wages from the Carringtons, and it's not very much.'

'I'll go and see Mr Massey,' Dove said, taking her place at the table. 'I love children, so it wouldn't be a hardship to help out at the school.'

'You can't leave me all on my own in this big house. Years ago we had plenty of kitchen staff, not to mention maidservants and a housekeeper.'

Daisy gazed at Mrs Bee in surprise. 'I thought that the late Dr Neville didn't make much money from the practice.'

'Mrs Neville inherited quite a substantial sum of money from a rich relative, but it all went on the upkeep of the house.' Mrs Bee looked round the large kitchen as if seeing ghosts from the past. 'She was such a sweet lady — so considerate and kind — it was sad that she died so young.'

'What happened to her?' Daisy asked, unable to contain her curiosity.

'She had several stillborn babes and she died in childbirth when Master Nick was six.'

'What about the rest of her family? I'm just trying to think of people who might be willing to help Nick now.'

'She was an only child and there are no close relatives still living, just a distant aunt.'

'That's such a sad tale,' Daisy said, wiping a tear from her eye. 'Poor Nick, his family seems to be ill-fated.'

'I've looked after Master Nick since his poor mother passed away. I don't know what else to do.'

'This old house means so much, not only to Nick but to you as well, and probably the whole village.' Daisy finished her tea and stood up. 'There must be something that can be done, and I won't rest until I have the solution. I'd best be getting home to see how my aunt has fared with the squire. Thank you for the tea.'

Dove sprang to her feet. 'Would you mind if I go with Daisy, Mrs Bee? I'll call in at the school and see what Mr Massey says. Even if the work pays very little, at least I can help with the housekeeping.'

'What about your family, Dove?' Mrs Bee's bottom lip trembled as if she were holding back tears. 'Maybe you ought to be at home looking after them instead of living here with me.'

'I'll make sure they're all right, and Linnet is keeping an eye on them, too. But you've been good to me and I won't leave you to cope on

165

your own. That wouldn't be at all fair.'

'Wrap up warm then, dear,' Mrs Bee said, beaming. 'The vegetable stew will be ready for you when you come home.'

★　★　★

Daisy let herself into Creek Cottage half expecting to find Squire Tattersall waiting for her in the parlour, but there was an unusual silence in the house, and she found her aunt in the parlour seated by the fire, mending a sock. Eleanora looked up and smiled. 'What a charming man the squire is, Daisy. I think you were being very unfair in your description of him.'

'He holds the lease on this cottage, Aunt. It's due for renewal later this year and he's more or less threatened us with eviction.'

'Nonsense, dear. I'm sure you misunderstood him, and anyway your uncle will sort all that out. As to the squire, he was merely giving us a courtesy call and he's invited all of us to dine at Creek Manor on Saturday evening. He's even sending a carriage to take us there in style.'

Daisy stared at her in amazement. 'He wants us to dine with him?'

'That's what I said. He couldn't have been more charming, and I'm looking forward to it immensely. Hattie is going through the trunks to find my smartest gown and you must wear something that will show you to your best advantage. I know you don't want to think about it, but such a match would be most advantageous.'

166

Daisy was too horrified by the idea of spending a whole evening at Creek Manor to argue, and there was little point anyway. She could see that her aunt was thrilled by the invitation and it was obvious that the squire had managed to charm her, although to what purpose Daisy could not imagine. The prospect of a whole evening spent in his company was enough to make her want to catch the first train back to London. However, the more she thought about it she managed to convince herself that this might prove just the opportunity she needed. If she used all her powers of persuasion she might be able to convince the squire to renew the lease on Creek Cottage. Her aunt had seen a good side to him, although her experience with Esmond Tattersall bore no relation to Daisy's first impression of the all-powerful squire. She would have to tread carefully.

★   ★   ★

On Saturday evening the avenue leading up to the manor house was lit by flaming torches, giving the old place a fairy-tale appearance, but to Daisy it seemed like the residence of an ogre, who was waiting to devour them. Such fancies belonged to childhood, but it took all her courage to make her climb down from the luxurious vehicle and cross the paved area to the front entrance. A liveried footman held the door open but she waited dutifully for her aunt and uncle and followed them into the house.

The oak-panelled entrance hall was lit by

dozens of expensive wax candles and a blaze roared up the chimney in the huge and ornate fireplace. Stern faced as before, Molesworth showed them to the drawing room, which in daylight must have had a view of the deer park, but this evening the heavy velvet curtains were drawn against the cold night.

Esmond Tattersall was standing with his back to the fire. He approached Eleanora with his hands outstretched and a smile on his face.

'My dear Mrs Marshall, how elegant you look. It's so kind of you to grace my humble abode.'

Eleanora blushed and fluttered her eyelashes. 'How kind of you to invite us, Squire Tattersall.'

'Esmond, please. We don't stand on ceremony here.' He bowed over her hand before turning to Sidney.

'It's good of you to come, sir.'

Sidney harrumphed and cleared his throat. 'Er — thank you. This is a very fine house, Squire.'

'Yes, it is rather. Please take a seat and make yourselves comfortable.' He moved to the sofa and sat down. 'Sit here, Miss Marshall, and we can converse without shouting across the room.' He patted the space beside him, but to Daisy's intense relief her aunt chose to sit next to the squire.

'You have a beautiful home,' Eleanora said, smiling. 'I don't think I've ever seen a finer house.'

Squire Tattersall signalled to his butler. 'We'll have a glass of sherry wine before dinner, and afterwards we'll play a hand or two of cards. I take it that you can all play whist?'

Eleanora glanced anxiously at her husband. 'I'm not very good at card games.'

'My wife speaks the truth,' Sidney said apologetically. 'I prefer poker myself, but that's neither here nor there.'

'I don't play cards,' Daisy said firmly.

'A pity, but perhaps we can remedy that in time.' Esmond moved closer to Eleanora, leaving a small space at his other side. 'Come and sit by me, Miss Marshall. I will be a thorn between two roses.'

Daisy was tempted to refuse, but it would have been bad manners to snub their host so she went to sit beside him.

'Er, you mentioned fishing, Squire,' Sidney said casually. 'You said you have a lake in the grounds.'

'Indeed I have and it's well stocked. You are welcome to try your hand at fishing there whenever you wish. My gamekeeper will be pleased to accompany you and show you the best places to cast your line.'

'How generous of you, Squire.' Eleanora took a glass of sherry from the silver tray proffered by Molesworth. 'This is so delightful, don't you think so, Daisy?'

Daisy took a large mouthful of her drink and swallowed hard. She could feel the warming effect of the alcohol as it reached her stomach. Perhaps, given enough wine, she might make it through the evening, but if the squire continued to inch closer, pushing her even further into the corner of the sofa, she would forget that she was a lady and slap his smiling face. She gazed down in horror as he walked his fingers across the folds of her skirt and laid his hand on her knee.

'If you don't mind, I think I'll sit in a chair,' she said, leaping to her feet. 'I find it rather warm in here.'

The evening dragged on, relieved only by a delicious meal served in the huge banqueting hall where the long refectory table would have seated thirty people in comfort. It seemed strange to be the only guests present, but the squire made up for lack of company with a monologue listing all his achievements, which were all money orientated and designed to show how he had restored the failing fortunes of his family. Daisy was tempted to rise to her feet and tell him what she thought of a landlord who allowed his properties to fall into disrepair while charging exorbitant rents to his tenants. Somehow she managed to restrain herself, but she could see that her aunt was impressed and Uncle Sidney nodded in agreement at some of the squire's comments on running an estate like a business. In Daisy's opinion the squire was boasting like a small boy who was out to impress, though as far as she was concerned, he failed.

'We will forgo the brandy and cigars as there is no hostess to entertain the ladies,' Squire Tattersall announced at the end of the meal. 'Instead I suggest a tour of the old house. It dates back to the fifteenth century in parts, and has had quite a history, although I won't bore you with details.' He rose to his feet and walked round the table to proffer his arm to Daisy. 'Will

170

you allow me to escort you, Miss Marshall?'

She looked anxiously at her aunt, who, being the senior woman present, should have been the one to receive such attention from her host, but Eleanora seemed happy with the arrangement and she smiled, nodding her assent. Reluctantly, Daisy rose to her feet, wishing wholeheartedly that the evening would soon come to an end. The squire had been giving her covert looks during the meal and had smiled ingratiatingly when he caught her eye. It was embarrassing to have a middle-aged man making eyes at her like a love-struck youth. There was no way out now and she managed a shadow of a smile as she laid her hand on his arm.

'We will follow you,' Eleanora said eagerly. 'But we might not be able to keep up with you young people.'

This remark was so ludicrous that Daisy was tempted to giggle. Esmond Tattersall was fifty if he was a day, and at least five years her aunt's senior.

'Hold on there, Eleanora, old girl.' Sidney jumped to his feet. 'We can keep up with the best of 'em.'

'Oh, hush, Sidney. You know what I meant.' Eleanora dug him in the ribs as he took her by the arm.

The squire signalled to Molesworth, who was standing to attention in front of the carved oak buffet. 'We'll have coffee in the drawing room after I've shown my guests round.' He picked up a silver candlestick. 'Follow me, my good people.'

Creek Manor was a rabbit warren of narrow corridors and passageways, and Daisy lost her bearings completely as the squire led them from one room to another. Her aunt and uncle were doing their best to keep up with them, but when they reached the long gallery at the top of the house, Eleanora and Sidney were lagging behind, staring at suits of armour and a sword collection strung out along the wall. Daisy found herself alone with the squire at the far end of the room.

He slipped his arm around her shoulders as he pointed to a portrait of a man in Elizabethan costume. 'That is my ancestor. He was a privateer and earned the thanks and a huge fortune from the Queen herself.'

'That's very interesting, Squire. But I thought your ancestors were mine owners.' Daisy tried to edge away, but his grip on her tightened.

'They were, but you're the only person who has dared to question me. I like that.' He lowered his voice. 'My first wife was a brainless fool, and barren — but you are a woman of spirit. You attempted to deceive me and failed, and I respect you for trying, although it would take a very clever female to get the better of me.'

Daisy twisted round to face him, but in the dim light she could not see his face clearly. 'I'm not sure what you're saying, Squire. But if you think I would be interested in someone like you, you're sadly mistaken.'

'I enjoy a challenge, and you are a pauper. Don't worry, my dear. I know all about you now and your kind-hearted but foolish aunt and uncle. I could make them homeless if I chose to do so, and you, too.'

Daisy pulled away, glaring at him. 'Are you threatening me, Squire?'

'Believe it or not — and I find it hard to understand myself — I find you very appealing. I'm hoping to achieve a knighthood, or maybe even a baronetcy in the near future and I'm in desperate need of an heir. I need someone to inherit the fortune I've made, besides which, having a young and attractive wife would be a definite advantage in public life. I intend to go into politics.'

'Daisy, come and look at this painting.' Eleanora's voice echoed eerily off the wainscoted walls.

Daisy could have cried with relief. 'My aunt wants me, sir.'

Tattersall caught her by the wrist. 'You haven't given me an answer, woman. I'm asking you to marry me. You won't get another chance like this. Give me an answer now.'

'I hardly know you,' Daisy protested. 'Let me go this instant or I'll call out and my uncle will want to know why.'

'Don't be a fool. I'm offering you all this.' He released her, making a gesture with his open arms. 'You would share my good name and my wealth.'

'I want neither,' Daisy said stoutly.

'You're just saying that. I know that young ladies like to keep a gentleman in suspense.'

'Daisy, do come and look at this lovely painting.' Aunt Eleanor's voice echoed up and down the long gallery, as if the subjects of the

173

portraits were mocking her.

'You couldn't be more wrong, Squire. Please believe me when I say that I do not wish to marry you.'

'You'll change your mind,' he called after her as she walked away. 'I always get what I want.'

11

Eleanora chattered volubly during the carriage ride home, but Daisy said little. She could think of nothing other than the squire's insulting behaviour, and his assumption that she would be honoured by his proposal. The mere thought of an intimate relationship with him made her feel physically sick, and the fact that he had tried to blackmail her with the threat of evicting her aunt and uncle from their home made matters even worse. Oblivious to the fact that neither her husband nor her niece seemed to share her enjoyment of the evening's entertainment, Eleanora continue to extol the virtues of Squire Tattersall and the grandeur of his house. Sidney answered in monosyllables when forced to respond, and Daisy closed her eyes, feigning sleep.

When she eventually lay down in her bed Daisy could not sleep. She found herself thinking of Julian and comparing his romantic proposal with the one she had received that evening from Squire Tattersall. She wondered if Julian ever thought of her now, or perhaps he was too busy establishing himself in his new profession. His rejection still hurt, but the pain had eased and perhaps it was more bruised pride than a broken heart. As they were unlikely to meet again she might never know her true feelings, and her dislike of Esmond Tattersall and anger at the way he had treated her was uppermost in her mind. The clock in the hall below struck midnight and sleep still evaded her. She decided to get up and go downstairs. A cup of cocoa might help her to relax, and she reached for her wrap.

She managed to avoid the fifth step from the bottom, which creaked loudly when trodden on in a certain place, and she tiptoed to the kitchen. The warmth from the range had permeated the whole room and Hattie had banked up the fire. All she would have to do first thing next morning was to riddle the embers and they would burst into flame. Daisy moved the kettle to the hob while she went in search of the cocoa tin, sugar and the milk jug, which was in its usual place on the marble slab in the larder. She had just settled down to sip the hot drink when she heard a noise outside. Someone was banging on the scullery door. She sat for a moment, hoping that whoever it was would go away, but the knocking became more insistent and she rose to her feet. She went to the door and hesitated, afraid of who might be demanding admittance at this ungodly hour, but curiosity got the better of her and she opened the back door.

A boy she recognised as Alfie Green, one of Jack's friends, was pale-faced in the moonlight, and shivering violently.

'What's the matter?' Daisy asked anxiously.

'Ma's sick, and the doctor's gone away.'

'You're cold. Come inside and get warm.' Daisy ushered him into the kitchen. 'I'm sorry to hear that your mother is ill, but why do you think I can help?'

'You knew what to do when Jack broke his arm, and you saved Jay Fox when he was drownded.'

Daisy shook her head. 'He wasn't drowned, and I really didn't do anything for Jack other than immobilise his arm.'

'But Ma's going to die, miss. There's no one who can help me.'

'Where's your father? Isn't he at home?'

'He's dead drunk, miss. He's no good to man nor beast.'

Daisy stared at Alfie in dismay. Her medical knowledge was scant — really little more than common sense — but she could see that the boy was trembling violently and alarmingly pale. She was wondering what to do when the door opened and Linnet peered into the kitchen.

'I heard the noise,' she said, staring at Alfie. 'What's going on?'

'He says his mother is ill and his father is too drunk to be of any use.' Daisy poured the remainder of the cocoa into a clean cup and handed it to Alfie. 'Drink this. It will warm you up.'

'I got to get back to Ma. Will you come, miss? Please.'

Daisy turned to Linnet. 'I'm not a nurse. She might be really ill.'

'Mabel Green is in the family way for the fifth time,' Linnet said in a low voice. 'If it's the baby coming why didn't you go for the midwife, Alfie?'

'She not there. I dunno where she is.'

Linnet patted him on the back. 'Never mind,

love. I'll see if I can find Annie Maggs.' She met Daisy's worried glance with a smile. 'I think I might know where she is, but it would help if you could go home with Alfie. Just keep Mabel comfortable while I fetch the midwife.'

Daisy stared at them in horror. She had never seen a woman in labour, let alone been present at a birth, but the boy was clearly terrified and Linnet seemed confident she could get help. Daisy managed a smile. 'Of course I'll go with you, Alfie. I'll get dressed and then we'll set off.'

'Me, too.' Linnet followed Daisy out into the hall. 'Don't worry, miss. I know where Annie might be. I just hope she's sober.'

★ ★ ★

The Greens' cottage was small and cramped, quite similar to the one rented by the Fox family. A single tallow candle burned with a dull flame, filling the room with the overpowering smell of rancid animal fat. Alfie's brothers sat huddled on the flagstone floor, the eldest boy holding their baby sister in his arms. From upstairs low moans developed into high-pitched screams, and the two smaller boys buried their heads in their hands, sobbing loudly. The baby, who looked to be about a year old, started to wail, and Alfie wiped his nose on his sleeve, stifling a sob.

'She's upstairs, miss,' he said unnecessarily.

'Where's your dad?' Daisy asked warily. 'You said he was dead drunk.'

'He's out in the yard, miss. Fell flat on his face on his way back from the privy. We couldn't move him, so we left him there.'

The screams from above were getting louder and Daisy headed for the stairs. 'We'll worry about your dad later. You stay here and look after the young ones. I'll see what I can do for your ma.' Daisy hoped she sounded more confident than she felt, but she went upstairs anyway.

Mabel Green was lying on a bare mattress, the double bed being the only furniture in the room apart from a chest of drawers. The stub of a wax candle shed a feeble, flickering light on the woman's distorted body as she writhed in agony. Plucking up all her courage, Daisy went to stand at the bedside. 'I'm Daisy Marshall, Mrs Green. I've come to sit with you until the midwife arrives.'

Mabel opened her eyes and she reached out to grasp Daisy's hand. 'Are you an angel?'

Daisy shook her head. 'No, I'm afraid not, but I'll see if I can make you more comfortable. Just tell me what to do.'

Mabel closed her eyes and her grip on Daisy's hand tightened until Daisy was certain her bones would break. A low moan turned into a scream, and Daisy was tempted to run away, but seeing the woman's pain and distress she forced herself to be calm. She stroked Mabel's matted hair back from her forehead, murmuring words of encouragement, and she flexed her fingers when Mabel's grip slackened and she was able to pull her hand free.

'Don't worry, Mrs Green, the midwife is on her way. She'll help you.'

'She'll be drunk at this time of night,' Mabel

muttered. 'You must stay, miss. You'll have to help birth my baby.'

'Of course I'll stay,' Daisy said, trying to sound confident. 'Can I fetch you something to drink. A glass of water, perhaps?'

'Or a tot of gin.' Mabel uttered a throaty laugh. 'Send Alfie for a mug of water — my throat is parched — but don't leave me.' She grabbed Daisy by the hand as she turned to leave the room. 'Call out for him. Alfie's a good boy, he'll do as you say.'

Daisy did as she asked and after a minute or two Alfie came clattering up the stairs with a tin mug, although he had slopped most of the water on the floor in his haste.

'Is she going to die, miss?' he asked nervously.

'Of course not,' Daisy said with more confidence than she was feeling. 'Go downstairs and try to keep the little ones from fretting. I'm sure Mrs Maggs will be here soon.'

He glanced anxiously at his mother, but a low moan from her made him take flight. Daisy closed the door behind him, as Mabel's screams grew louder. Her pains seemed to be getting closer together, and although Daisy knew nothing about childbirth, Mabel was able to give her instructions in between contractions.

The candle burned down even further and still there was no sign of the midwife. Mabel was growing weaker and Daisy was close to panicking, but somehow she managed to keep an outward show of calm. And then, just as she was beginning to think that Mabel could bear it no longer, everything happened so quickly that

Daisy had no time to be afraid. The tiny, red-faced baby entered the world in a rush, just as Linnet arrived, although there was no sign of the midwife.

'What do I do now?' Daisy asked breathlessly.

Linnet handed her a pair of scissors and Mabel, miraculously alert although weak and exhausted, talked Daisy through the process of cutting the umbilical cord and tying it off.

'You've done well, miss. Better than old Annie Maggs when she's had a skinful.' Mabel lay back on the pillow, holding the baby in her arms.

'I couldn't have done it,' Linnet whispered. 'I'd have run away.'

Daisy felt her knees trembling but she managed a smile. 'You've got a lovely baby girl, Mrs Green. What are you going to call her?'

'If you don't mind, miss, I'd like to call her after you. What did you say your name was?'

'It's Daisy, and I'd be honoured to have the little mite named after me.' Daisy was deeply touched and she smiled through tears of exhaustion. 'We'll make you comfortable and then perhaps you can get some sleep.' Daisy glanced round the room. 'Is there a cradle for the baby?'

Linnet drew her aside. 'We'll leave the little one with her ma while I take a drawer from the chest. It's only the rich people who can afford cradles and the like.'

A vision of the nursery in Queen Square flashed through Daisy's mind and she felt her cheeks redden with embarrassment. She had not meant to sound patronising, but she was only just beginning to understand the gulf between those who had and those who had not. The Greens were definitely from the latter group, and another mouth to feed would only add to their problems. She acknowledged Linnet's advice with a nod and, having made Mabel comfortable, Daisy went downstairs to comfort the children.

Alfie was alone in room, seated cross-legged on the floor in front of the hearth where the log fire had burned down to little more than ash. He leaped to his feet when he saw Daisy.

'Is Ma dead? It's gone so quiet.'

Daisy wrapped her arms around him. 'Your mum is fine and so is your new sister. I was hoping to make a pot of tea for your mother, or perhaps some hot milk.'

Alfie shook his head. 'There ain't no tea, miss. No milk neither. I gave the last of it to the young 'uns before they went to bed.' He jerked his head to the space under the stairs where the children lay top to toe on a thin mattress, covered by an equally thin and threadbare blanket.

'Is your dad still outside?' Daisy struggled to contain a feeling of anger that roiled in her stomach. If the children's father had enough money to get himself so drunk, he could have spent it on necessities for his family.

'Yes, miss. I left him there, the drunken old bastard.'

'I'd better go and take a look at him.' It was not something Daisy wanted to do, and it would serve him right if she left him to freeze, but her conscience would not let her rest until she was satisfied that the children's father would live to support them.

'Wait a minute,' Alfie said hastily. 'It's pitch-dark outside. There should be just enough oil left in the lamp to light the way.' He picked up an ancient lantern and struck a match on the hearth. There was not much of the wick left, but it gave out sufficient glow to light their way in the tiny back yard. As Alfie had said, his father lay prostrate on the ground with frost forming all around him. Daisy bent down to feel the pulse in his neck, as Toby had once shown her how to do.

'What's his name, Alfie?'

'It's Joe.' Danny prodded his father's side with the toe of his boot. 'Wake up, Dad.'

Daisy used all her strength to turn Joe onto his back. She slapped his cheeks. 'Open your eyes, Joe.'

He groaned and curled up in a ball, muttering something unintelligible.

Daisy took the lantern from Alfie and held it high enough to cast its beam around the tiny yard. 'We need some water. Where is the pump?'

'It's in the back lane, miss. We share it with the rest of the cottages.'

'Fetch some water.' Daisy handed him the lamp. 'I'll stay here and try to wake him up.'

Alfie hurried off and she watched the lantern bobbing up and down as he walked. She shook Joe and slapped his cheeks, calling his name, but he was very drunk and unresponsive. She waited until Alfie returned with the bucket of ice-cold water.

'Give it to me and stand back, Alfie.'

His eyes gleamed in the lamplight. 'Let me do it, miss.'

'No, you'd only get into trouble when he sobers up. I'm going to enjoy this.' Daisy took the heavy bucket and tipped the contents over Joe's head.

He coughed and, swearing loudly, he struggled to a sitting position.

She dropped the bucket and stood arms akimbo, glaring at him as he tried to stand. 'You have a baby daughter, Mr Green. Mother and baby are fine, no thanks to you.'

Joe scrambled to his feet and stood there, swaying and cursing as he shook the water from his hair. Daisy turned her back on him and returned to the house. Her stomach heaved at the stench from the candle and a pile of rotting vegetable peelings in the tiny scullery, but she managed a smile for Alfie.

'Go to bed now. You've done more than enough tonight.'

'Will Ma be all right, miss?'

'She just needs rest and good food, and I'll do my best to see that she gets both. It's very late, so I can't do anything now, but I promise I'll be back in the morning.' Acting on impulse, she leaned over and dropped a kiss on Alfie's matted hair. She looked up as Linnet came downstairs carrying a pile of bloodstained towels. 'I'm going home. Are you coming with me?'

Linnet nodded. 'Yes, but what about this washing?'

'We'll take it home with us.'

'Hattie will complain.'

'She'll grumble even more when I raid the larder for food for these poor children, but somebody has to help them, and it doesn't look as if he's going to be much help.' Daisy jerked her head in Joe's direction as he lurched into the room and slumped down on his chair by the embers of the fire. Daisy turned to Alfie, who was staring nervously at his father. 'If your dad lays a finger on you I'll . . . ' she hesitated, eyeing Joe warily as he raised his shaggy head to glare at her.

'You'll do what?' he demanded angrily. 'Interfering bitch.'

Daisy thought quickly. 'I'll tell Squire Tattersall and we'll see what he has to say.'

Joe's expression changed subtly and he responded with a grunt.

'Would you really tell the squire?' Linnet asked as they left the cottage and headed for home.

'No, of course not, although it would serve Joe right if I did, but it had the desired effect. Most people in Little Creek seem to be scared of Squire Tattersall.'

'Except Dr Neville and Jay.'

'Yes,' Daisy said thoughtfully. 'Except those two.'

★   ★   ★

After a few hours' sleep, Daisy was up and dressed, and went downstairs to the kitchen to find Linnet and Hattie having an argument about the Greens' washing.

'Once we start that sort of thing we'll have half

185

the village thinking they can bring their dirty clothes here for us to see to,' Hattie said crossly.

Daisy sent Linnet a warning look. Hattie could be very stubborn and needed to be handled carefully. 'The poor woman only gave birth last night. She needs our help.'

'Yes, and that wastrel of a husband was dead drunk,' Linnet added. 'He's a real toper, Mrs Cribb.'

'And I agree with you in general, Hattie,' Daisy said earnestly. 'But surely we can make an exception this time.'

Hattie sighed and picked up a saucepan. 'I suppose it won't hurt, just this once. But you'll have to light the fire under the copper, Linnet, and see to the bedding. I'll make some porridge for the little ones, but he's not to have a mouthful.'

Linnet picked up the soiled sheets and hurried to the wash house while Daisy raided the larder for supplies.

'And you must have some breakfast, too, Daisy,' Hattie said firmly. 'Heaven knows what your aunt and uncle will say when they know you were out half the night delivering a baby. It's not the sort of thing an unmarried young lady like yourself should see.' She added a generous helping of sugar to the mixture. 'Poor little mites, having a drunken father. Men like that deserve to be tossed into prison and the key thrown away.'

'That wouldn't do the family much good,' Daisy said with a wry smile. 'At least he keeps a roof over their heads.'

'For how long?' Hattie demanded. 'If he's as bad as you say he'll drink all his wages, and his wife and the nippers will end up in the workhouse. I've seen it happen before, Daisy, and there's nothing you can do about it.' She stood with arms akimbo, her lips pursed. 'You can take one of the loaves I baked this morning, but . . .'

'Make sure that brute doesn't get any.' Daisy chuckled and kissed Hattie's plump cheek. 'You don't fool me, Hattie Cribb. You've got a heart as soft as butter, and I will make certain that the children and their mother are fed first. Anyway, I don't think there'll be much left for Joe, and he probably feels too poorly to eat anyway.'

'I hope so,' Hattie said fervently. 'But I don't know what the missis will say when she finds out what's been going on. She won't like it, Daisy. I'll tell you that for nothing.'

★   ★   ★

Hattie was right. Eleanora was not amused and she told Daisy so at breakfast. 'We can't feed the whole village,' she said crossly. 'I'll do my bit with the local ladies, and some beef tea and a few cakes are not going to put us in the poorhouse, but you must stop giving food away, and I forbid you to go out in the middle of the night to deliver babies. I never heard of such a thing, Daisy.'

'I'm sorry, Aunt Eleanora,' Daisy said patiently.

'But the boy was desperate and he's Jack's

friend. I didn't know what else to do.'

'That's another thing.' Eleanora wiped her lips on a table napkin. 'It's high time young Jack went home to his parents.'

Daisy knew this was true, but she was fond of Jack and she would miss him. 'Yes, Aunt.'

'I mean it, Daisy. I'm not a mean woman but we aren't made of money. Now that your uncle has retired from the business we have to be careful with our expenditure.'

'I didn't realise that money was tight.' Daisy's appetite suddenly deserted her and she pushed her plate away. 'I'm a burden on you both and I should look for another position.'

'I didn't mean that,' Eleanora said hastily. 'You are family, my dear. Money doesn't come into it.'

'I'm a grown woman, Aunt. I need to earn my own living.'

'Nonsense, Daisy. You are an attractive young lady. I saw the way the squire was ogling you, and he's a great catch. If you married him you would want for nothing and, speaking selfishly, we would be assured of having the lease renewed. Your uncle apparently knew about the lease, because he handles all our financial affairs. He was confident that we could get it renewed cheaply.'

'And you would if I agreed to marry the squire.' Daisy met her aunt's gaze with a straight look. 'I love you both, but that's asking too much.' She rose to her feet. 'I think it's time I returned to London, Aunt Eleanora. I'll stay with Toby while I look for work.'

'You can't do that, Daisy. You can't live in

bachelors' quarters even if you are sharing rooms with your brother. It's not the done thing, my dear.'

'I can't see that it would matter to anyone but you and Uncle Sidney, and you know I wouldn't do anything to disgrace the family name. No, Aunt, my mind is made up. I need to get a job and London is the place I know best. Perhaps I can train as a nurse, or even a doctor. I seem to have a leaning for that sort of work.'

Eleanora uttered a faint shriek. 'A doctor? Heaven help us — women can't be doctors, Daisy. It's against nature and I don't really approve of nursing, although it is a little more respectable now, thanks to Miss Nightingale, but there are no women doctors.'

'I think you're wrong there, Aunt. There's Elizabeth Blackwell, who qualified as a doctor in America. I read about her in the newspaper when she visited London a few years ago. Times are changing and we have to change with them or be left behind.'

'I think you'd be heading for a dreadful disappointment, Daisy. Consider the squire's offer. You would be a lady with a beautiful home and a carriage at your disposal.'

'I'd rather die than marry that man. Everything you say makes me even more determined to make my own way in life. I'm sorry, Aunt, I love you and Uncle Sidney dearly, but I am not going to be swayed in this. I'm going back to London.'

12

It was an easy decision to make in the circumstances, but there were things that Daisy had to do before she left Little Creek. The first was to ensure that Jack's parents were well enough to take care of him at home. Later that morning, accompanied by Linnet, Daisy called on the Fox family. She was pleasantly surprised to find Mary Fox up and about, and doing her chores in an effort to make the dilapidated cottage into a comfortable home. There was no sign of Lemuel, which was a relief as his glowering presence made Daisy feel ill at ease.

'Of course I want my boy home,' Mary said eagerly. 'I'm much better now, thanks to the medicine that Dr Neville gave me before he went up to London. I hope he comes back soon because we need him here.'

'Miss Marshall is going to London to train as a nurse.' Linnet beamed at Daisy. 'She'll come back to Little Creek and look after us all.'

'I don't know about that,' Daisy said hastily. 'I might not get accepted as a probationer.'

Linnet shook her head. 'There's no doubt in my mind, miss. You're clever and you've got learning. I can read and write and add up sums, but that's an end to it. Jay is the clever one in our family, even if he did go wrong.'

'We don't talk about him, even when your pa isn't around, Linnet.' Mary shot an anxious glance over her shoulder, as if expecting to see her husband standing behind her. 'You know how he disgraced the family, even though I have to say he's a good boy at heart.'

'It was that Squire Tattersall who put him in prison, Ma,' Linnet said darkly. 'He's a bad man and he'll be the ruin of all of us.' She shot a sideways glance at Daisy. 'You'll be safe from the old devil in London, miss.'

'What do you mean by that?' Mary demanded. 'Watch your tongue, my girl.'

'It's all right, Mrs Fox,' Daisy said hastily. 'The squire has been making his presence felt and I want to put distance between him and me. It's as simple as that.'

'Forgive me for saying so, but you don't want to get mixed up with that person.' Mary clasped Daisy's hand. 'Go to London, and keep away from the squire. He's ruined many a young life in his time.'

'I'll be leaving later today.' Daisy nodded and forced a smile. 'That's why Jack must come home, Mrs Fox. His arm is healing nicely and he needs to be here with you. I'll miss him, though.'

A slow smile lit Mary's blue eyes, reminding Daisy forcibly of Jay. 'My Jack is a good boy, and I'm grateful to you for looking after him while me and his dad were poorly.'

'Where is pa?' Linnet asked anxiously. 'He hasn't gone off sermonising again, has he?'

Mary cleared her throat nervously. 'My Lemuel is a lay preacher, Miss Marshall. He goes round the villages spreading the word of God, when he's well enough to face the walk. He's

191

sincere in what he believes, but he does get carried away sometimes.'

Linnet pulled a face. 'You could say that, Ma. The truth is that Pa thinks we're all sinners, especially the brother whose name I'm not supposed to mention.' She leaned over to kiss her mother on the forehead. 'I'd best get back to Creek Cottage. Hattie will be cross if I stay out too long.'

'Come again soon, dear.' Mary raised her hand to stroke her daughter's hair. 'Your father misses you and Dove, even if he doesn't know how to show his feelings.'

'I must go, too.' Daisy backed towards the door. 'Please tell Jack that I'll come and see him when I return from London.' She let herself out into the early spring sunshine and took a deep breath of fresh air. The fusty smell of the cottage would linger on her clothes for some time, but it was not for want of effort on Mrs Fox's part, and Daisy wished with all her heart that she could do something to make life better for the people of Little Creek. She had only been invited into a couple of the cottages, but it was obvious that Squire Tattersall was a bad landlord and he had no sympathy for his tenants or their families.

'Are you coming back to Creek Cottage, miss?'

Linnet's voice broke into her thoughts and Daisy turned to her with a start. 'I'm sorry. I was miles away. I think I'll go for a short walk and say goodbye to Little Creek.'

'When are you leaving, miss? If you don't mind me asking.'

'There's a train at two o'clock. Now I've made up my mind I don't want to wait around.'

'You'll need me to help you pack.'

'I won't take too much with me this time. After all, I might be unsuccessful and have to return in a day or two. Anyway, whatever happens, it will be good to see my brother again.'

'I'd better not waste any more time or I'll be in trouble.' Linnet hurried off in the direction of Creek Cottage, leaving Daisy to walk on at a more leisurely pace.

She had no particular plan, but it was a fine day and the birds were singing as if they knew that spring was not far off. She followed the creek as it wound its way through the wood, and as she emerged from a thicket of brambles and hawthorn bushes she came across a sight that brought her to a halt. Up to their knees in the fast-moving water, her uncle and Lemuel Fox were standing midstream, casting their lines. She wondered if Lemuel would tell his wife that he had been fishing instead of preaching to his flock, and she stifled a giggle. She was about to retreat when she trod on a fallen branch, which snapped, sending a sound like a pistol shot echoing across the water.

'Who's there?' Lemuel demanded angrily. 'You've frightened off the fish.'

Daisy emerged from the cover of the bushes. 'I'm sorry. I didn't see you until too late.'

'What are you doing here, Daisy?' Sidney demanded, reeling in his line. 'Is something wrong?'

'Not at all, but I'm glad I came across you.'

Daisy moved to the water's edge, balancing precariously on the slippery bank. 'I've decided to return to London and look for work.'

Sidney waded towards her. 'This is very sudden, my dear.' He gave her a searching look. 'Has this anything to do with our visit to the manor house? I noticed how quiet you were on the way home, and quite honestly I didn't like the way the squire treated you. I would have said something, but your aunt told me to be quiet.'

Daisy eyed Lemuel warily, although he did not seem to be listening. 'It has in a way, Uncle.' She lowered her voice, just in case Lemuel was more interested than he appeared to be. 'You'll hardly credit it, but the squire proposed to me. He made it clear that if I didn't comply he would refuse to renew the lease on Creek Cottage, or he would make the terms prohibitive.'

'The bounder. I'll have it out with him man to man. This has nothing to do with you, Daisy. I won't stand by and see you treated like this.'

'Please don't get involved, Uncle. Squire Tattersall is a nasty man and he holds the lease on Creek Cottage. I don't know why, but he seems to be hell-bent on evicting people from their homes.'

Sidney shook his head. 'Maybe it's because he doesn't want to pay for repairs to their cottages. Perhaps he'd rather raze them to the ground, but whatever his motives he's not the sort of husband I'd wish for you, my dear.'

'I'll be safe from him in London, although I've grown to love it here, even in such a short time.'

'You must do what's best for you, Daisy. We'll

194

miss you, but I wouldn't trust myself if the squire came calling on you — I'd throttle the swine.'

The idea of her meek and mild uncle doing anything violent made Daisy want to laugh and cry at the same time. She patted him on the shoulder. 'I wouldn't want you to do that, Uncle.'

He was about to reply when a call from Lemuel made him turn round to see the former gamekeeper landing a large fish.

'They're biting again, Mr Marshall. Best cast your line, sir.'

Daisy backed away. 'I'll leave you to it, Uncle, but I'll say goodbye now, because I might not see you again before I leave.'

'You're going so soon, Daisy?'

'I think it's for the best. You mustn't suffer on my behalf, and I hate that man. I'd rather enter a nunnery than marry someone like him.' Daisy leaned over to kiss Sidney on the cheek. 'Take care of yourself and Aunt Eleanora. I love you, Uncle.'

She hurried off, not wanting him to see the tears that threatened to spill from her eyes, but instead of heading back to the cottage she found herself walking in the direction of the cove where she had last seen Jay's vessel. She was not sure what she hoped to find, but she had a sudden urge to see if the *Lazy Jane* really had sailed, or if the ship was still at anchor, and as the cove widened out she broke into a run. But there was no sign of Jay's craft or any other vessel and she came to a sudden halt. Perhaps it was as well that he had sailed away; there could be no hope of a settled future for her with someone like Jay Fox. He was a free spirit, and she doubted if any woman would be able to tie him down. She knew that she was allowing mere physical attraction to overcome common sense, or perhaps she had simply been in the mood to be charmed by a dashing young man, who refused to conform to the rules of society. She might never know the answer to that particular conundrum. She turned away slowly and began the long walk home.

★   ★   ★

Later that day, after a relatively comfortable journey by rail and a cab from the station, Daisy arrived outside her brother's lodgings in Mount Street, not far from the London Hospital. She knocked on the door of the three-storey terraced house, but when there was no response she decided to walk to the hospital. It had started to rain and she wished she had thought to bring an umbrella, but she put her head down and broke into a run, arriving in the vestibule soaked to the skin and breathless.

'May I help you, miss?' A uniformed desk clerk looked her up and down.

'I — I've come to — '

'Probationer nurses over there,' he said impatiently.

'No, you don't understand.'

'Take a seat, please, miss. You'll be dealt with as soon as possible, and maybe if you'd come earlier you wouldn't be in such a state.' He pointed to a row of seats where a group of fresh-faced young women were seated.

Daisy gave up all attempts to explain and went to sit next to a dark-haired girl, who looked up and smiled at her.

'Are you hoping to enrol on the nursing course?'

'No . . . well, yes, maybe.' Daisy glanced at the other applicants, all of whom looked to be calm and self-controlled, despite what they might be feeling inwardly.

'I was inspired by Miss Nightingale.' The girl held out her hand. 'Minnie Cole from Hertfordshire.'

Daisy shook hands. 'Daisy Marshall, lately from Essex, although I grew up not far from here. My brother is a doctor.'

'And you wish to train as a nurse. How exciting.'

'Miss Cole. Come this way, please.' An efficient-looking nurse beckoned to Minnie, who jumped to her feet.

'Wish me luck, Daisy. Wouldn't it be fun if we were both accepted for training?' She hurried off after the nurse and they disappeared into a side room.

Moments later another nurse, this time much younger and less formidable, stopped in front of Daisy. 'What name is it?'

'Daisy Marshall.'

'I don't seem to have you on my list.'

'I won't be on it, because I've only just arrived from the country.'

A flicker of sympathy crossed the nurse's

pretty face. 'We've all started that way, Daisy. But there's no need to be nervous. I can see that your clothes are soaking too. I'll put you in next, or you might end up as a patient on the women's ward.' She chuckled and glided off to speak to the other applicants, who gave Daisy resentful glances, but did not dare challenge the nurse's decision. Daisy decided to go along with the interview. After all, she needed to work and earn enough money to pay for her keep. Her dream of becoming a doctor would have to be put aside, but maybe one day women would be accepted into medical school. In any event she needed to find Toby or she might end up sleeping in a dosshouse.

After what seemed like a very long wait, Minnie Cole emerged from the room, smiling broadly. 'I've been accepted. Good luck, Daisy.'

'Thank you.' Daisy managed a smile but she could see the stern nursing sister advancing on her and she knew that she must come to a decision quickly.

'I've been told you haven't filled in an application form, Miss Marshall.'

Daisy rose to her feet, fighting down a sudden feeling of panic. 'Maybe I ought to do so now and try again later.'

The nurse looked her up and down with a critical eye. 'No matter. You're here now. Come this way.'

Somewhat reluctantly Daisy followed her into a tiny office furnished with a single desk, and two chairs.

'I am Sister Johnson, in charge of the student

nurses.' She sat down, motioning Daisy to follow suit. 'Fill in this form giving your personal details.' She indicated an inkstand and pen. 'And you'll need a character reference. Have you been in employment before?'

'Yes, I was a governess.' Daisy wrote her name and her brother's address on the sheet of paper, and brief details of her education at the private school before handing it back.

Miss Johnson read it, raising an eyebrow as she looked up at Daisy. 'And why did you leave your employment?'

'My charge was sent to boarding school and I was no longer needed.'

'Why did you not apply for another such position?'

'I've spent the last two months in the country, living with my aunt and uncle in a small village near the coast. I've seen great poverty and how the lack of proper medical treatment affects people. It made me realise that I could do something to help.'

'Very laudable, but it sounds to me as if the residents need a good doctor. Presumably there is a local midwife?'

'Yes, an old drunken woman who is totally unreliable, and because of that I was put in the position of helping a woman to give birth even though I had absolutely no experience in the matter.'

'And how did you feel about that?'

'Terrified, but somehow a healthy baby was delivered and is now thriving. The good people of Little Creek suffer enough at the hands of a ruthless landlord, and the very least they should have is someone to take care of them when they fall ill.'

Sister Johnson made a note on the piece of paper. She looked up, her piercing grey eyes holding Daisy's gaze. 'Can you give me the name of someone who will give you a reference?'

Daisy thought quickly. She did not want anything to do with the Carrington family and she had no wish to see Julian again. 'My brother is a doctor here, Sister. He will vouch for me.'

'Toby Marshall is your brother?'

For a moment Daisy thought that she had made a huge mistake. Surely Sister Johnson was too old for Toby to have toyed with her affections? But then a slow smile transformed the sister's stern features.

'I've known Toby since he was a first-year medical student. He's come a long way. I suppose you know Nick Neville, too?'

Daisy felt the blood rush to her cheeks. 'Yes, he's a good friend of the family.'

'I'm old enough to remember Nick's father. Now, there was a brilliant doctor. He could have made a fortune in a prestigious Harley Street practice, but he chose to return home to his native village. It was London's loss.'

'So I believe, although I never met him.' Daisy studied the document in front of her and filled in the necessary details before handing it back to Sister Johnson.

'I see that you've had a good education, Miss Marshall. You are exactly the sort of young lady we need.'

Daisy cleared her throat nervously. 'To be perfectly frank I came to London on the off chance of finding work.'

Sister Johnson gave her a searching look. 'Perhaps you'd like to think it over before you commit yourself to nursing? If you want a more formal training you might try St Thomas' Hospital, but here you would have to start as a probationer and, I warn you, it's hard work with long hours and low pay.'

Daisy considered her options. She had rushed back to London with only a vague plan of how she would find the money for her board and keep until she received her first wage. Her uncle had pressed a small purse into her hand before she left, but the contents would not go far. Here at least was the chance to become independent while obtaining her qualification as a nurse. All these thoughts flashed through her mind as she faced Sister Johnson.

'I would be happy to accept the place you offer, Sister.'

'If you are prepared to start on Monday, I'm happy to recommend you to Matron and the Board of Governors.'

'Thank you, Sister Johnson. I'll work hard and prove myself to be a good student.'

'I'm sure you will, Miss Marshall. It's Friday now, so I'll expect you to be here at seven o'clock on Monday morning.'

Daisy rose from her seat. 'Thank you again.' She left the room feeling slightly dazed by the unexpected turn of events, and when she reached the waiting area she was accosted by Minnie Cole.

'How did you get on, Daisy?'

'I start on Monday morning,' Daisy said slowly. 'I still can't believe it.'

Minnie gave her a hug. 'I'm so excited, and I'm glad that you were accepted, too. I tried for a place at St Thomas' but they didn't have any vacancies, so I came here. Anyway, enough of me. Where are you going to stay? Have you a room nearby?'

'I've only just arrived in London. I was hoping to lodge with my brother.'

'I have a room in Mrs Wood's boarding house in Fieldgate Street. She's a bit of a dragon, but the rooms are clean and very respectable. My pa is vicar of Little Threlfall and he sends me as much money each month as he can afford, but it doesn't go very far. I was hoping to find someone to share the rent with me, but I didn't want just anyone. Would you be interested, Daisy?'

★　★　★

Mrs Wood's establishment was a four-storey terraced house in a busy back street. It was an area that Daisy knew well from her childhood, and it might not have been as salubrious as Queen Square, but she was used to the hustle and bustle of the East End. It was a huge contrast to the quiet rural setting of Little Creek, but she had little time to think about anything when she was with Minnie, who chattered

202

constantly and bubbled over with enthusiasm. She was still talking when the door was opened by a small, plump woman whose smile did not quite reach her eyes.

'So were you successful in your application for employment, Miss Cole?'

'Yes, indeed, Mrs Wood, and I was wondering if you would allow my friend Miss Marshall to share my room. She is also a probationer nurse at the London.'

'A respectable calling.' Mrs Wood stepped aside and ushered them into the wainscoted entrance hall. 'You are most welcome to join our happy little household, Miss Marshall. The rent is five shillings a week, including breakfast but dinner is extra. You will be supplied with clean linen once a fortnight.'

'Thank you. I'd be pleased to share with Miss Cole.'

Mrs Wood held out a plump hand. 'A month's rent in advance, if you please.'

Daisy took her purse from her reticule and counted out the coins, placing them in Mrs Wood's outstretched palm. The purse was significantly lighter when she replaced it, and she knew she would have to be very careful with her money if she were to survive until pay day.

'Miss Cole will show you to your room, and I expect you to read the house rules and know them off by heart. They are for the benefit of all, as I'm sure you will agree.' Mrs Wood folded her arms and watched them as they ascended the stairs.

'She's not so bad, if you keep on her right

side,' Minnie whispered when they reached the third floor. 'This way, our room is at the front, looking down onto Fieldgate Street.

Daisy was pleasantly surprised. Their room was large enough for two iron bedsteads, covered in bright patchwork quilts, two chests of drawers and a small table situated in the window with a view of the street below.

'We have to share a washstand,' Minnie said hastily. 'And we have to fetch water from the pump in the back yard. That's where you'll find the privy.' She perched on the edge of her bed. 'You'd best read the rules before we go downstairs again, in case she quizzes you on them.'

Daisy studied the neatly printed list, which hung on the inside of their door. There were set hours for everything from when to use the pump in the back yard to meal times. All the young ladies in the house must be in by ten o'clock at night, unless they were on duty at the hospital. No gentlemen visitors were allowed, with the exception of close relatives, and even then they must be entertained in the communal sitting room on the ground floor, situated next to Mrs Wood's accommodation. An evening meal would be provided for an additional ninepence a day, but they had to be booked in advance, and food must not be consumed in the bedrooms. This was followed in block capitals by the word RATS, presumably as a warning of what might happen if the last commandment was broken. Daisy felt quite exhausted by the time she had finished absorbing the dos and don'ts of living in

Mrs Wood's lodging house.

'You'll get used to it,' Minnie said cheerfully. 'Come on, I'll give you a tour of the rooms we're allowed to inhabit.'

Minnie led the way, pointing out the rooms that were occupied by the other lady lodgers, and ending in the front parlour. With its horsehair sofa and uncomfortable-looking chairs adorned with spotless white antimacassars, it was not the sort of place in which to relax, and the looming presence of a large aspidistra standing like a sentinel in the window made Daisy feel distinctly ill at ease. Added to all this was a collection of Toby jugs, grinning at them from shelves in the alcove on one side of the chimney breast, and vacant-looking pot dogs gazing blindly at each other from either end of the mantelshelf. Cheap china fairings in the shape of shepherds and shepherdesses, chubby children with rosy cheeks and fat little cherubs were arranged on small tables dotted around like an obstacle course. Even with all the bric-a-brac the room felt cold and unwelcoming, and a shiver ran down Daisy's spine — this place was so different from her aunt's cosy parlour in Creek Cottage.

'I'd be afraid to move in case I knocked one of those ugly china ornaments over,' she said in a stage whisper.

Minnie giggled. 'I'm sure that Mrs Wood has a spyhole concealed behind one of those hideous paintings, and I suspect she has an ear trumpet glued to the wall when any of the girls entertain their gentlemen friends. I know for a fact that Ivy Price passes her sweetheart off as her brother, and heaven help her if Mrs Wood finds out. But,' she concluded in a fair imitation of Mrs Wood's voice, 'it's all for your own good, ladies. This is your home from home and you may consider me to be your surrogate mama.'

'I suppose she means well,' Daisy said in a low voice. Not that she believed that Mrs Wood would be eavesdropping on their conversation, but she thought it best to be careful.

'One would hope so.' Minnie pulled a face. 'Anyway, I'm starving. I must eat soon or I'll faint from lack of nourishment.'

'How do you manage for food?'

'I've only been in London for a week. Sometimes I go out with Ivy, who shares a room with Flora Mackenzie on the second floor. They work in an office in the City, and we go to the pie and eel shop round the corner, or we buy ham rolls and coffee from a stall in Whitechapel Road. I haven't met the two older ladies who have a room next to them — they keep to themselves mostly — and there's a couple of theatrical girls who share an attic room on the top floor. They're appearing at the Pavilion Theatre, but they sleep most of the day and they return in the small hours. I think Mrs Wood only allows that because they give her free tickets for the shows.'

'It sounds as if it's never dull here,' Daisy said, chuckling.

'It's been quite lively so far.' Minnie's smile faded. 'But you need to be careful when you speak to Gladys, Mrs Wood's daughter. She's only fifteen, but she's a little sneak and she likes to cause trouble. I think she goes through my things, although I can't prove it.'

'Is there a key?' Daisy asked anxiously. 'I haven't brought much with me, but I don't like the thought of someone poking around amongst my belongings.'

Minnie shook her head. 'No, Mrs Wood won't allow us to lock our door. She says it must be kept unlocked so that the maid can get in to clean, although I think that's just an excuse because you could make a fur coat from the dust balls under my bed.'

'Well, I'm sure we can sort something out. In the meantime, what about something to eat? I'm really hungry and very thirsty.'

'Then we'd better get to Old Joe's coffee stall while it's still quite quiet. He sells out quickly when he gets a rush on.'

'But we're not allowed to eat in our room.'

'It's all right as long as Mrs Wood doesn't find out. You could opt for supper here, but take my tip and avoid her food at all costs. When you smell what's cooking you'll know what I mean.' Minnie opened the door. 'And if you do bring food into the house make sure that Gladys doesn't see what you're carrying or she'll run to her mother and peach on you.'

'I'll be careful,' Daisy said with a sigh. 'Gladys sounds like a menace.'

'If you think she's bad you haven't met the beast of Fieldgate Street.'

'Good heavens. What could that be?'

Minnie shook her head. 'Don't ask. You'll find out soon enough.'

Daisy followed her new friend from the room, closing the door carefully behind her. First she must eat and then she would concentrate on finding Toby, even if it meant posting a note through the door of his lodging house. It would be so good to see him again, and in all probability he would be in contact with Nick.

She hurried after Minnie, who had raced on ahead and, as she turned the bend in the stairs Daisy saw someone loitering in the passage leading to the basement stairs, but at the sound of her footsteps the watcher vanished into the dim region at the back of the house.

'Someone was spying on you,' Daisy said breathlessly as she caught up with Minnie.

'That would be Gladys, of course. The young wretch.' Minnie tossed her head. 'She'll be there again when we return. I'm certain she keeps a note of the time we spend indoors, and I wouldn't be surprised to receive a bill for being in the house longer than necessary or wearing out the stair carpet. Mrs Wood is very keen on making a bit extra, as you'll find out.' Her expression changed subtly. 'Don't look now, but Ivy is coming and she's got that strange fellow with her. I don't know what she sees in him.'

Unable to resist temptation, Daisy glanced over her shoulder and her hand flew to cover her mouth. 'Oh, no! I thought I'd seen the last of him.'

13

'Do you know him?' Minnie asked in a whisper.

'Yes, unfortunately I do.' Daisy painted a smile on her face as the couple approached. 'It's Jonah Sawkins. He used to work for my uncle.' Her first instinct was to run, but Jonah had seen her and he quickened his pace, limping towards them with his odd shuffling gait.

'Well, I never! Fancy seeing you here, Miss Daisy.' Jonah came to a halt and patted Ivy's hand as it rested in the crook of his arm. 'Might I introduce you to my friend Miss Price?'

'How do you do, Miss Price?' Daisy eyed the young woman critically. Even Ivy's best friend could not honestly describe her as pretty, but surely she could do better than Jonah Sawkins? There was, as Aunt Eleanora always said 'no accounting for taste'. Maybe Jonah had hidden depths, although she could not think of one redeeming quality.

'Pleased to meet you, miss.' Ivy seized Daisy's hand and shook it. 'Are you going to lodge here, too?'

'Yes, she is, Ivy.' Minnie pushed past Jonah, who was leering at her in a way that was all too familiar to Daisy. 'Come on, Daisy,' Minnie added, wrapping her shawl more tightly around her shoulders. 'We haven't time to stand around and gossip. Come on, Ivy.' She marched off in the direction of Whitechapel Road with a reluctant Ivy in tow.

Daisy was about to follow when Jonah barred her way. 'I've done well since your uncle retired. I'm manager now, in total charge of the shop.'

'That's good,' Daisy said vaguely. 'I'm sure you'll make a success of whatever you do.'

'You should have been nicer to me,' Jonah hissed as she attempted to dodge him. 'You could still be living in your old home. I'd have treated you like a lady.'

'Never,' Daisy said firmly. 'Let me pass, Jonah.'

'Don't think I've forgiven you for the way you treated me, Daisy Marshall.' Jonah stood aside, his face contorted in a spiteful grin.

Daisy chose to ignore his last remark, although she could feel him staring at her as she hurried after Minnie, who had parted from Ivy at the corner of the street. 'Ivy needs to be careful,' Daisy said breathlessly. 'Jonah isn't the sort of man to treat a girl well.'

'I don't know what she sees in him. I had to walk on or I might have said something I would regret.'

'He was my uncle's assistant, and he's not a nice man.'

'Well, you'd better warn her. She won't listen to me.'

'I will, at the first opportunity. Anyway, there are more important things in life than Jonah Sawkins, and I'm very hungry.'

'So am I. Let's hope old Joe hasn't sold all his pies or ham rolls.'

'Where will we eat, if we can't take food back

to the lodging house?'

Minnie shot her a mischievous look. 'There's always St Mary's churchyard, unless of course it's raining, and then we have to smuggle the food in and make sure we don't leave any crumbs. Mrs Wood is terrified of rats and mice, and for that reason she relies on the beast of Fieldgate Street.'

'Who is he?'

'Rex is a cat, Mrs Wood's pride and joy, and he's the terror of the local vermin. You'll meet the brute sooner or later, and if you'll take my advice you'll pet him, even if he hisses at you, and smile if he scratches you. To be honest, he's a hateful creature, but Mrs Wood adores him.' Minnie came to a halt at a coffee stall on the corner of Fieldgate Street and Whitechapel Road. 'What have you got for me today, Joe?'

★ ★ ★

Despite a brief shower, they drank their coffee standing close to the stall and, having returned the mugs, they walked the short distance to the churchyard of St Mary Matfelon, where they sat on a slightly damp bench and ate ham rolls and hard-boiled eggs. It was almost dark by the time they arrived back at Mrs Wood's lodging house and Ivy let them in, but she did not look pleased. Her pale face was marred by a sulky pout and her sandy eyebrows were drawn together in a frown.

'What's the matter with you?' Minnie demanded as she stepped over the threshold.

211

'It's her.' Ivy pointed a finger at Daisy. 'He went on and on about her after you'd gone.'

Daisy entered the hall, closing the door behind her. 'Jonah isn't a nice person. Maybe it's the life he led before he came to live and work in the shop, but you could do better.'

'You're just jealous.' Ivy headed for the stairs, but she came to a halt, rounding on Daisy. 'I'll never get a husband. If a cripple like Jonah throws me over for someone else, what hope is there for a dull little thing like me?'

Daisy shook her head. 'Don't say things like that, Ivy. You'll meet someone who really appreciates you.'

'I thought Jonah did until you came along.'

'Believe me, you don't want to get too involved with Jonah Sawkins. He's mean and you can't trust him.'

'That's what you say, but I don't believe you.' Ivy picked up her skirts and took the stairs two at a time.

'I never liked him,' Minnie said, shrugging. 'She'll have to learn the hard way, Daisy. Don't waste your breath on her.'

Daisy took off her damp mantle and untied the strings of her bonnet. 'What do we do now? Are we allowed to use the parlour?'

'Oh, Lord, yes. Mrs Wood lights a fire at exactly half-past four in the afternoon.'

'That seems very reasonable.'

Minnie pulled a face. 'It saves on coal and kindling because we aren't allowed to have a fire in our rooms, no matter how cold it gets, so we huddle round the hearth in the front room. It also means that she can keep an eye on us, and there's little or no chance of anyone smuggling a gentleman friend into the house.'

Even as the words left Minnie's lips, the parlour door opened and Mrs Wood emerged, bristling with importance.

'Miss Marshall, you have a visitor. He assures me that he is your brother.'

Toby appeared in the doorway behind her, grinning broadly. 'My sister will vouch for me, ma'am.'

Mrs Wood stepped aside as Daisy rushed across the hall to fling her arms around her brother. 'How did you know I was here?'

'Sister Johnson,' he said cheerfully. 'She told me you were looking for me and that you'd gone off with Miss Cole.' He shot an apologetic glance in Minnie's direction. 'I'm afraid I persuaded her to give me your address. I hope you don't mind.'

Mrs Wood sniffed disdainfully. 'That wouldn't have happened had I been in charge.'

'Well, I'm very glad she did,' Daisy said wholeheartedly. 'I stopped by your lodgings first and when you weren't there I went straight to the hospital.'

'And applied for a job as probationer nurse,' Toby added, chuckling. 'I must say you don't waste time, Daisy old thing.'

'Give me your mantle and bonnet, Daisy, and I'll take them upstairs,' Minnie said firmly. 'I'm sure you and your brother would like some time for a private chat.' She emphasised the last words, fixing Mrs Wood with a meaningful stare.

'I'm not a one to intrude in family matters,'

Mrs Wood said, bridling. 'Perhaps the good doctor would like a cup of tea?'

Minnie turned away, winking at Daisy as she took to the stairs. 'You're honoured, Dr Marshall.'

'That's enough of your cheek, Miss Cole.' Mrs Wood turned on her heel and marched off in the direction of the back stairs.

Daisy hurried her brother into the parlour and closed the door. 'It's so good to see you, Toby.' She shivered, gazing at the desultory flames licking around a few pieces of coal in the grate. 'Mrs Wood doesn't believe in spoiling her lodgers.'

'What's going on, Daisy? I thought you were happy in Little Creek.' Toby stood with his back to the fire. 'Why did you return to London so soon?'

She lowered herself gingerly onto the horsehair sofa, which proved to be just as uncomfortable as its appearance suggested. 'It's a long story.'

Toby's blue eyes twinkled mischievously. 'Start at the beginning. I've always suspected that was the best way.'

'I'll tell you, but I don't want you to get angry.'

He sat down next to her. 'Go on. What happened?'

Daisy took a deep breath. It was not easy to put her experience with Squire Tattersall into words without incensing her brother, but she managed to give him a shortened version of the events that had led her to hurry back to London.

'I'd have sorted the squire out, had I been at

214

home,' Toby said furiously. 'How dare he treat you like that and threaten our family? I've a good mind to get the next train to Little Creek.'

'You mustn't do that. Our uncle and aunt are in a difficult situation because the lease on the cottage is due to expire before too long, and the squire owns the land on which it is built. Anyway I've lived off their charity for long enough. I need to earn my own living.'

'That's ridiculous. No one would expect that of you, and they love you as if you were their own child.'

'I know, which makes it even more important that I don't do anything to jeopardise their future. The squire will find some other unfortunate woman to marry him, and I suppose in some ways he is a good catch. He's rich and powerful and that would be enough for some women.'

'But not for you?'

She smiled reluctantly. 'No, definitely not for me.'

'Perhaps you have someone in mind?' Toby put his head on one side. 'Would Nick have anything to do with your decision to take up nursing?'

'No, not really. Although I can see how badly the people of Little Creek need a doctor, or even a qualified nurse and midwife. It was quite by chance that I arrived at the hospital looking for you and found myself amongst the applicants for nurse probationer.'

'At least I'll be able to keep an eye on you,' Toby said, grinning.

'That's funny, coming from someone who was constantly being reprimanded for flouting the rules in the medical school.'

'Rules are made to be broken. That's always been my excuse, but it doesn't apply to young ladies like yourself. I'll spread the word that you are my sister and must be treated with the greatest respect.'

Daisy rolled her eyes and was about to comment when the door opened and the largest tabby cat that she had ever seen prowled into the room, his tail held erect and twitching irritably. Mrs Wood came in next, carrying a tea tray, which she placed on a small table in the window.

'You'll have to move up, Miss Marshall. You're sitting in Rex's place.'

Daisy took one look at the cat, who was preparing to spring, and she did not argue. Rex leaped with the grace of a tiger, landing beside her and he proceeded to turn in tight circles until he sank down with an almost human sigh.

'You may stroke him, Miss Marshall.'

It was an order rather than a request and Daisy raised her hand slowly, touching the thick fur as lightly as she could. Rex turned his head, glaring at her with malevolent yellow eyes and hissed. She withdrew her hand quickly. 'I don't think he likes me.'

'Rex takes time to get used to new faces. He'll be fine when he gets to know you. Rex is a good judge of character.'

Daisy could sense Toby's amusement and she did not dare raise her eyes to meet his, focusing instead on the slices of cake laid out on a china plate. 'That looks delicious, Mrs Wood.'

'Don't expect this every evening,' Mrs Wood said grimly, but her expression changed as she turned to Toby. 'I have the miseries in my back, Doctor. Perhaps you could give me something to ease the pain?'

'I'm afraid I can't prescribe outside the hospital, Mrs Wood. But if you would like to attend the outpatient department, I'm sure someone better qualified than I would be able to help you.'

'Well, you're not much use then, are you?' Mrs Wood slammed out of the room, taking the plate of cake with her.

Daisy looked at Toby and they doubled up with laughter. They were still convulsed when Minnie rushed into the room.

'What did you say to Mrs Wood? She's fuming.'

Toby wiped his eyes on a slightly grubby hanky. 'She took exception to being told that I can't treat her privately and she must attend the hospital outpatient department.'

'Trust her to want something for nothing.' Minnie sat down to pour the tea. 'Did I see cake on the plate she had in her hand?'

'She took it away.' Daisy glanced anxiously at Rex. 'I wish she'd left the cake and taken her cat with her.'

Minnie handed her a cup of tea. 'Don't touch the brute. He's vicious, but if you want to stay in Mrs Wood's good books you'd better pretend to like him.'

'I prefer dogs, myself,' Toby said casually.

'Anyway, Daisy, you're going to join us in the hospital. I hope you're prepared for hard work. You'll see things that will be very distressing.'

'I'll do my best,' Daisy said stoutly. 'I can't say fairer than that.'

'We'll help each other.' Minnie was about to take a seat next to Daisy on the sofa, but Rex chose that moment to stretch and his claws were out. Minnie moved to a chair by the fire. 'That animal thinks he owns the place.'

'You girls must come round to my lodgings.' Toby stared into his cup. 'This tea looks like dishwater. As I was saying, you'll find it more pleasant spending an evening with us.'

'Who are you lodging with?' Daisy inched away from Rex, who was threatening to take up the entire sofa.

'With Nick at the moment, although he's moving to Harley Street in a day or two.'

'It's a long way to Harley Street.'

'Yes, that's why he's going to live above the shop, so to speak. He's saving every penny in an attempt to raise the money to pay off the squire, although at the rate he's going it will take him twenty years or more.'

Daisy shook her head. 'Squire Tattersall has a lot to answer for.'

Toby placed his cup and saucer back on the tray. 'That was truly the worst tea I've ever tasted.' He rose to his feet. 'It's good to see you, Daisy, but I have to go now because I'm on duty again in half an hour.'

She jumped up and gave him a hug. 'Perhaps we can all meet up for a meal somewhere cheap.'

'I suppose that includes Nick?'

'I'd like to see him.'

'Of course, and he'll be keen to see you, too, Daisy. He's always talking about you and the way you tried to help him.'

'Anyone would have done the same.'

Toby kissed her on the forehead. 'No, they wouldn't, Daisy. Your attempt to fool the squire was a mad idea in the first place, but if Nick finds out what it's cost you personally he'll be devastated.'

'You mustn't tell him because it's over and done with. I want you to promise that you won't say a word.'

'All right, if it means so much to you, I promise.'

'It's all so exciting,' Minnie said dreamily. 'I enjoyed reading *Lady Audley's Secret*, but this is better by far. I wonder what will happen next, Daisy.'

'Who knows? This is real life, Minnie.'

'And I have to get back to work.' Toby opened the door. 'I'm on duty this weekend, but I'll no doubt see you at the hospital on Monday, Daisy. We can arrange something then, after I've had a chance to speak to Nick. Although I wouldn't be surprised if he comes round to see you as soon as he knows that you're in London.' He stepped aside as Rex leaped off the sofa, but the cat walked past him and ambled out of the room in a leisurely fashion.

★　★　★

Later that evening, Daisy and Minnie were huddled round the embers of the fire in the parlour when they heard someone rapping on the front door.

'I wonder if that's your gentleman friend,' Minnie said eagerly. 'Best hurry, Daisy. If Mrs Wood gets there first he'll be turned away with a flea in his ear.'

Daisy sprang to her feet and she could hear Nick's voice as she opened the door. 'It's all right, Mrs Wood. Dr Neville is an old friend.'

'No gentlemen callers after nine o'clock.' Mrs Wood slammed the door in Nick's face.

'There was no need for that,' Daisy said angrily. She pushed past the irate landlady and wrenched the door open. 'Nick, wait.' She stepped out onto the rain-soaked pavement. 'I'm so sorry.'

He retraced his steps. 'Your landlady is a fierce woman.'

'I heard your voice but she forestalled me.'

'Never mind that, Daisy. I'm just glad to see you.'

'Miss Marshall, kindly shut the door.' Mrs Wood's stentorian tones made Daisy turn her head.

'Just give me a minute, Mrs Wood.'

'I'll go,' Nick said hastily. 'Are you free tomorrow, Daisy?'

'Step inside, Miss Marshall. I don't want the neighbours to see you making a show of yourself.'

Daisy chose to ignore her. 'Yes, Nick. I hadn't planned to do anything in particular.'

'I'll call for you at ten o'clock. We can talk in private then.' Nick tipped his hat to Mrs Wood, who was glaring at him over Daisy's shoulder. 'Good evening, ma'am.' He winked at Daisy and strolled off into the darkness.

Daisy stepped back inside, closed the door and spun round to face Mrs Wood. 'That was very rude. Surely you could see that Dr Neville is a respectable person?'

'He's a man,' Mrs Wood snapped. 'They're all the same. You need to watch your step, young woman, or you'll find yourself in trouble. You know what I mean.'

'There's no need to worry, ma'am. My nursing career comes first and foremost.' Daisy was seething inwardly, but she needed a roof over her head, and at least Mrs Wood's establishment was reasonably comfortable and cheap, even if the fearsome landlady was stingy when it came to home comforts. She shook the rain from her hair as she returned to the parlour, and was surprised to find that Minnie had company. Ivy was seated on the sofa next to a pretty young woman with flame-red hair and green eyes.

Minnie looked up, frowning. 'Did she send your gentleman friend away?'

'Yes, but I called him back and apologised.'

'She won't like that,' Ivy said nervously. 'She'll take it out on the rest of us if you make her mad, Daisy. She likes Jonah, but only because he flatters her and goes out of his way to be charming.'

The red-haired young woman rose to her feet,

holding out her hand. 'They've forgotten their manners. I'm Flora Mackenzie and I've heard all about you from our dear Gladys, the sneak from hell.'

'How do you do?' Daisy shook her hand. 'Is Gladys really that bad?'

'I expect the girls have told you that Gladys will go through your things when you are out. She'll report any slight misdemeanour to her mother, and she'll tell whoppers just to make trouble.' Flora sank back on the sofa and produced a tobacco pouch from her skirt pocket. She proceeded to roll a cigarette. 'Don't look at me like that, Ivy. I know it's not a ladylike thing to do, but I never was a lady, despite what my poor papa thinks.'

Ivy leaned towards Daisy. 'Flora's father is a vicar,' she said in a low voice. 'He's very strict.'

Daisy watched in awe as Flora struck a match and lit the cigarette, exhaling plumes of blue smoke into the air. 'That's why I came to live here. It's handy for work and Papa doesn't have a say in what I do.'

'Mrs Wood will be furious if she smells tobacco smoke.' Ivy glanced nervously at the door, as if expecting Mrs Wood to burst in at any moment.

'She won't come in while I'm here,' Flora said confidently. 'She knows that I'll give as good as I get, and one day I'm going to throttle that spawn of the devil, Gladys. You'd best be careful, Daisy. Don't leave any of your valuables about or she'll steal them and blame the cat.'

'I've never heard of a cat stealing anything

other than food.' Daisy looked from one to the other, suspecting that this was a joke, but they were all nodding in agreement.

'Rex is capable of anything,' Ivy said in a low voice. 'I think Gladys trained him to fetch things for her, like a dog, and she listens at keyholes.'

'That's true.' Minnie nodded emphatically. 'The cat stole one of my hankies. I caught him taking it downstairs, and he didn't want to give it back.'

'Perhaps he has a cold,' Flora said, laughing. 'Does anyone else want a smoke?' She offered her pouch to each in turn but they all shook their heads. 'Suit yourselves. You don't know what you're missing.'

Daisy looked round at their faces, rosy in the firelight, and she stifled a yawn. 'I'm afraid I'll have to go to bed. It's been a long day and I'm exhausted.'

'I'll come with you.' Minnie scrambled to her feet. 'We're only allowed one candle for each room and I don't fancy groping my way upstairs in the dark, especially when Rex sleeps on the stairs. He lies in wait and leaps out to scratch anyone who happens to be passing, except Mrs Wood and Gladys, of course.'

'I'm tired, too,' Ivy said warily. 'I don't suppose you are, Flora.'

'Indeed I'm not. I'm just waiting for my gentleman friend to tap on the window and then I'm off out for the rest of the evening.'

'But the door will be locked,' Ivy said anxiously. 'You won't be able to get in.'

'Don't worry. I persuaded the new maid to

223

leave the area door unlocked.'

'You mean you bribed her.' Ivy shook her head. 'You'll never get to heaven, Flora.'

'I don't care — I think it would be terribly boring.' Flora stretched out on the sofa. 'Good night, ladies. Go to your cold beds and think of me enjoying a drink or two in a nice warm pub, with someone playing jolly tunes on a piano and everyone having a good time.'

Minnie picked up a chamber candlestick and lit the wick with a spill from the fire. 'You're braver than I am. I'd be too scared to stay out like that.'

'It'll end in tears,' Ivy said grimly. 'Don't wake me when you get in.'

'Good night,' Daisy added, 'and good luck, Flora.' She followed the wavering light of the candle as Minnie made her way through the darkness to the staircase.

★　★　★

Breakfast next morning was served in the dining room at eight o'clock on the dot. A steaming tureen filled with sticky grey porridge was placed in the centre of the table, and left for those who took their places on time to eat piping hot.

'We're the first,' Minnie said, ladling the unappetising mixture onto her plate.

The young maidservant placed a plate of bread, smeared with butter in front of Daisy. 'No, miss. The two school teachers were up at six. They were taking some of their pupils to Box Hill and they won't be back until late this evening.'

Minnie glanced round the table. 'I don't suppose there's any jam today, Aggie?'

'No, miss. It's Saturday, you only get jam on Sunday and Wednesday.'

'I was just hoping that Cook was feeling generous.'

Aggie grinned and bit her lip. 'I'm sure I don't know about that, miss.'

'I don't suppose Flora will be taking breakfast,' Daisy said, helping herself to porridge.

Minnie filled Daisy's cup with tea. 'She and Ivy will have gone to work — they only have one day off a week — and it looks as if they missed breakfast.'

'Flora must have an iron constitution if she can stay out so late and then get up early next morning.' Daisy stared down at the grey mess on her plate. 'I think I'll just have a slice of bread.'

'The dancers stay in bed all day, so you won't see them until this evening.' Minnie spooned the porridge into her mouth and swallowed it in one gulp.

'Do they come down any earlier on Sunday? I'd like to meet them.'

'They don't take breakfast, miss,' Aggie said solemnly. 'They eat like sparrows on account of their figures.'

Minnie looked up, frowning. 'Hadn't you better get on, Aggie? You'll be in trouble with Cook if she catches you chatting to us.'

Aggie's thin cheeks flushed pink. 'Yes, miss. I forgot me place. Don't tell the mistress.'

'Of course we won't,' Daisy said hastily. 'It was

my fault for asking questions.'

'Ta, miss.' Aggie bobbed a curtsey and rushed from the room.

Daisy pushed her plate away. 'I really can't face this. It's awful.'

'But it's filling, and it comes with the price of the room. You'll get used to it, Daisy.' Minnie licked her spoon and dropped it back in the empty bowl. She reached for a slice of bread. 'If you've got any sense you'll fill up on this and then you can get by until the evening.'

'But you don't have supper here.'

'The school mistresses are the only ones who eat in at night. I think they must be used to dreadful food at the private school for young ladies, but I'd rather exist on watercress and boiled eggs from Old Joe's stall than risk eating Cook's evening meals. You'll do the same if you've got any sense.'

'Do we get meals provided at the hospital when we're on duty?'

'Yes, but I doubt if they're any better than Cook's offerings. At least, that's what I've been told by some of the more senior probationers. Maybe you ought to have asked your nice doctor friend to take you out to luncheon instead of a walk in the park, or whatever he has in mind.' Minnie put her head on one side, giving Daisy a knowing look. 'You're blushing.'

Daisy pushed her plate away and stood up. 'I am not. It's the steam from the porridge that's made my cheeks flush. Nick is just a friend.'

'I believe you,' Minnie said, giggling.

'I'm going to be too busy to think about

romance.' Daisy picked up her cup and drank the tea down to the dregs.

14

'So why did you decide to return to London?' Nick held the umbrella tilted to protect Daisy's bonnet from the sudden shower. 'Toby was very vague about it when I asked him that question.'

'It seemed like the right thing to do,' Daisy said evasively.

'But I thought you were happy living with your aunt and uncle in Little Creek.'

'And I was, but they aren't so well off now, and I need to earn my own living.' She shot him a sideways glance. 'If I were a man I'd train to be a doctor, but I realise it's virtually impossible for a woman to get qualified.'

'Things are changing slowly. One day I'm sure we'll have women doctors or even surgeons.'

'In the meantime I have to start somewhere.'

'So you're serious about becoming a probationer at the London?'

'Does that surprise you?'

'No, not at all. I think you would do well whichever path you took.'

'Actually it was pure chance that led me to walk into the waiting area of the hospital when the interviews were taking place. I was looking for Toby, but the nurse thought I was applying for a position as probationer.'

'You could have refused.'

'Yes, but I didn't. I think I saw it as a challenge.'

Nick stopped outside a teashop and opened the door. 'Let's get out of the rain, and we can talk in comfort.' He followed her into the steamy atmosphere redolent with the smell of hot coffee, tea and freshly baked buns. It was crowded with office workers and shoppers but they found a table near the window and they sat down.

Nick gave the friendly waitress an order for a pot of tea for two and toasted teacakes, and when she had bustled off, he relaxed visibly. 'It's so good to see you again, Daisy. I thought it might be several months before we met again.'

'Well, I'm here now and I intend to make the most of it. I'll work hard and study at night.'

A wry smile curved Nick's generous lips. 'You might find you're too tired to read medical books after a long day on the wards, but I can see that you're determined.'

Daisy sat back as the waitress delivered their order. Without thinking Daisy picked up the teapot and filled their cups, passing one to Nick. 'That's enough about me. Tell me about your practice in Harley Street.'

'It's not my practice. I don't know what Toby has been telling you, but I'm a very junior partner. It's interesting, but the only difference between our patients and those at the hospital is that ours are wealthy enough to pay handsomely for their treatment. It's not what I saw myself doing when I was studying medicine.'

Daisy eyed him curiously. 'You almost sound as if you wish you were back at your father's old practice in Little Creek.'

'I do, Daisy. That's exactly how I feel. If I

didn't have this debt hanging over me I would go home and carry on exactly as my father did, but until I've paid Tattersall the money he claims I owe him, I'll have to remain in London.'

'That man has a lot to answer for,' Daisy said bitterly. She sensed that Nick was staring at her and she looked up from stirring her tea. 'What?'

'I knew there was more behind your sudden departure from home.' He leaned across the table. 'And it has something to do with Tattersall. Don't deny it, because I can see it's true by your expression. You would make a terrible poker player, Daisy.'

'It seems that I made quite an impression on Squire Tattersall when I tried to convince him that I was heiress to a fortune.'

Nick's eyes narrowed. 'Go on.'

'He invited my aunt and uncle and myself to dine at the manor house, and he asked me to marry him. Totally out of the blue, I might add. I couldn't have been more shocked or surprised.' Daisy selected a teacake and cut it in half, avoiding meeting Nick's gaze.

'You put him in his place, I hope.'

'Yes, of course.'

'That's not all, though. I can tell. There's something else.'

'He won't take no for an answer, and he threatened to evict my aunt and uncle from Creek Cottage if I didn't reconsider his offer. Apparently the squire owns the freehold and the lease is due to expire later this year. Uncle Sidney didn't realise the property was leasehold when he arranged to move to the country.'

'This is all my fault,' Nick said angrily. 'I put you in this position, Daisy.'

She reached out to lay her hand on his as it rested on the table top. 'No, I won't allow that, Nick. It was my decision to get involved, and the problem of the lease would have come up sooner or later.'

'Even so, I feel responsible for involving you with that man. It's time someone put a stop to his cavalier treatment of his tenants.'

'And rightly so,' Daisy said vehemently. 'He's threatened the Fox family with eviction, too.'

'It's said in the village that Tattersall has a personal grudge against Lemuel Fox, although I don't know the details and I don't ask because it's none of my business.'

'It's a small village. I dare say rumours spread like wildfire, even if they're based on very little fact.' Daisy sipped her tea thoughtfully. There was one person who would know how Lemuel had fallen foul of the squire: Mrs Bee was a fount of knowledge when it came to anything that had happened in Little Creek.

'That's true. Anyway, enough about the village and the squire. I'm very glad you're in London, Daisy, whatever the reason. I hope we'll be able to see more of each other, although I have to say I don't get much free time. My superior is a hard taskmaster, and he expects me to be on call day and at night.'

'But it's only temporary,' Daisy said firmly. 'You're not going to remain in Harley Street for ever.'

'Certainly not. As soon as I've saved enough

231

money I'll be handing in my notice and heading back to Little Creek.'

'The villagers need a doctor badly.'

Nick's eyes twinkled. 'And a qualified nurse?'

She returned the smile. 'I suppose so. I haven't had time to think about what I'll do when I finish my training.'

'I'll need a nurse to help me run my practice, if I can run it at a profit. My father barely made a living, as I've discovered to my cost.'

'Who knows what will happen?' Daisy made an effort to sound casual. 'Anyway, I won't return to the village for a while yet. I'm hoping that the squire will take the hint when he discovers that I've returned to London. If he really wants to find a wife I'm sure there are plenty of young women far more eligible than I.'

'But none so pretty or charming.' Nick reached for a teacake. 'Do have another. These are delicious, although not as good as the ones that Mrs Bee makes.'

A sudden commotion outside in the street made all the customers stop talking and some of them rushed to the window. A woman screamed.

Nick leaped to his feet, gazing over the heads of the curious onlookers. 'There's been an accident. I'd better see if I can help. Stay here, Daisy.' He put his hand in his pocket and left a pile of coins on a side plate before shrugging on his overcoat as he hurried into the street. Daisy had no intention of sitting there idly and she followed him outside to see if she could help. But the sight that met her eyes made her gasp with horror. A man and woman had been in collision with an omnibus. It looked as if they had both been trampled by the horses and the man was pinned beneath one of the wheels. The woman was screaming and crying, but the man was ominously silent. Nick was on his knees examining the woman while the driver tried to calm the frightened animals.

'Stand back, everyone. Give the doctor space.' Daisy was shocked to hear herself speak so authoritatively, and to her surprise the crowd obeyed her. 'Somebody run to the hospital and get help.' She went down on her knees beside the woman. 'You'll be all right. My friend is a doctor.'

'Keep her as quiet and still as possible, Daisy,' Nick said in a low voice. 'I need to take a look at the other casualty.'

Daisy slipped her arm around the sobbing woman's shoulders. She did not have to be a doctor to see that the poor creature's right leg was broken and bleeding, and there was a nasty gash on her forehead. Daisy took her hanky from her pocket to staunch the head wound. 'Try to keep still. We'll get you to the hospital as quickly as possible.'

'My husband,' the woman gasped. 'Is he all right?'

Daisy glance at Nick, who was bent over the inert male figure. 'The doctor is looking after him now. I'm sure he'll be fine.'

'Is he dead? I can't see him moving.'

'He's unconscious, but you mustn't worry. He's in good hands.' Daisy tightened her hold on the woman's trembling body. 'Can you tell me your name?'

'It's Hilda. Hilda Begg and that's my husband, Stanley. We was on our way home when it happened. Is he all right? We've got to get home to the children.'

'You need to go to the hospital, Hilda,' Daisy said gently.

'But I left Judy in charge of the little 'uns. She's only nine and she's not very strong.'

'Try not to worry.' Daisy mopped a trickle of blood from Hilda's forehead. 'I'm sure we can get someone to look after your children until you're well enough to go home.'

The bus driver had managed to quieten the frightened horses and he handed the reins to a passer-by. 'She run in front of the bus, miss.' He leaned over the casualty, pushing his cap to the back of his head. 'You could have killed us all, you silly bitch.'

'That's enough of that,' Daisy said severely. 'This poor woman is badly hurt. It doesn't matter whose fault it was. We must get her and her husband to hospital.'

'It's a wonder I ain't lying there, too.' The bus driver turned to Nick. 'Is he a goner, mister?'

Nick rose to his feet as a policeman pushed his way through the crowd. 'Give your details to the constable.'

'But it weren't my fault,' the driver protested as the policeman approached. 'She run out, Constable. There weren't nothing I could do.'

'All right, mister. You can make a statement later, but you'd best take care of your horses.' The young constable glanced at the two casualties. 'The ambulance is coming. It's lucky this happened so near the hospital. Move back, everyone. This ain't a peep show.'

The horse-drawn ambulance arrived and the unconscious man was laid on a stretcher and lifted carefully inside, followed by Hilda, who had momentary respite when she fainted from the pain.

'I'll go with them,' Nick said hastily. 'I'm sorry to abandon you, Daisy.'

'It's all right. Do what you can for them.' Daisy stood back as Nick climbed onto the box beside the driver, who flicked the reins and urged the horses to a brisk walk.

'Are you hurt, love?' An elderly woman stepped off the pavement to peer into Daisy's face.

'No. I wasn't involved in the accident.' Daisy wiped her hand across her forehead.

'You're bleeding, my dear.'

'No. It was the poor woman who was injured.' Daisy gazed down at the bloodied hanky still clasped in her hand.

'You're very pale. You ain't going to swoon, are you, love?'

'No, I'm all right, thank you.' Daisy stepped back onto the pavement as the traffic began to move again and the crowd dispersed. The normal sounds of the street erupted in a cacophony, almost deafening her, and it seemed that the tragedy that had befallen the Begg family was already forgotten. She hesitated, undecided what to do next. She could return to her lodgings, but Hilda's stricken face haunted her thoughts and Daisy knew she would not rest until she knew that the poor woman was on the road to recovery. Hilda had mentioned that her eldest was only nine, and there were younger children who would be in need of care. Daisy could only hope that they had relatives who would look after them, but the whole family would be in dire financial straits if Mr Begg's injuries proved fatal. Daisy set off for the short walk to the London Hospital.

There was no sign of Hilda or her husband when Daisy arrived, and none of the busy nurses could give her any information. She waited for half an hour and was on the point of leaving when Nick emerged from a side room.

Daisy could tell by his expression that the news was not good. He walked slowly over to her, shaking his head. 'There was nothing anyone could do to save the husband,' he said in a low voice. 'Mrs Begg is being prepared for theatre.'

'But she'll be all right, won't she?'

'It's a bad fracture, Daisy. I'm afraid it will take a long time to heal, and she might be left with a permanent limp. I don't know how she earns her living, but this could be enough to send her to the workhouse.'

'Oh, no. Poor woman. Can I see her?'

'She's been given a hefty dose of laudanum. I think it's best to leave it for a while. You'll probably see her on the ward on Monday.'

'Yes, I suppose you're right,' Daisy said reluctantly. 'But there are children at home, waiting for their parents to return. Will anyone check on the family?'

'We have enough trouble treating our patients, let alone their offspring.' Nick patted her on the shoulder. 'We take care of the sick. That's the best we can do, Daisy.'

She nodded. 'Yes, I see that.'

'I'm not really supposed to be here,' Nick added gently. 'Why don't you take a seat while I hand over the patient to the houseman on duty? Then we can decide where we'll go from here. I have the whole day off, so you can choose what you would like to do.'

She caught him by the sleeve as he was about to walk away. 'Has anyone told Mrs Begg that her husband has passed away?'

Nick shook his head. 'Not yet, but someone will have to break it to her when she's in a fit state to take the news.'

Daisy absorbed this in silence, but she could not put the accident from her mind, nor the plight of Hilda and her family. Nick was right, of course: there was nothing she could do. She could only hope that perhaps Hilda had relatives or a kind neighbour who could help them through this terrible time. Daisy settled down to wait for Nick to hand the poor woman over to the hospital doctors.

* * *

The Begg family were constantly on her mind despite the fact that Nick did his best to entertain her. He took her on the underground train to Baker Street, which was an experience in itself. The gas-lit wooden carriages were hot and dusty and the windows had to be kept closed to keep out the smoke. Daisy was nervous at first, but then she began to enjoy the experience, although it was a relief to leave the train and emerge from the station into the relatively fresh air at Baker Street.

'As it's reasonably fine in between showers, I thought it would be nice to visit the Zoological Gardens, Daisy.'

'I went there once when my aunt and uncle took me as a treat on my tenth birthday.'

'And I thought we'd go to Harley Street first. I want you to see where I live and work.'

'It will be nice to see a consultant's house. Is it very grand?'

'Wait and see.'

★　★　★

The consultant's house in Harley Street was in the middle of an elegant terrace. Nick showed Daisy round the beautifully appointed consulting rooms, and his small apartment, which was on the fourth floor, just below the servants' rooms in the attics. They did not stay long, even though the family were not at home, and after a quick lunch in a small café they walked to the Zoological Gardens. After everything that had happened in the last few months it was good to relax and enjoy the sights. Even so, the terrible accident that morning was never far from Daisy's thoughts.

It was late evening when they parted outside Mrs Wood's lodging house, having enjoyed a tasty supper at Ye Olde Cheshire Cheese in Wine Office Court.

Nick raised her hand to his lips. 'We must do this again, Daisy.'

'I'd like that, but you're supposed to be saving your money.'

'Maybe it will be a ham roll from Old Joe's barrow next time, but I've really enjoyed today.'

'Apart from that terrible accident this morning.' Daisy spoke more sharply than she had intended.

'Yes, of course. I wasn't forgetting that, but you'll come across similar tragedies all the time when you're a nurse. It's probably the most difficult thing to accept, but we can't always save our patients.'

She drew her hand away, attempting to smile and failing. If she allowed herself to dwell on the fate of the Begg family she knew she would cry. 'Yes, you're right, of course. Anyway, thank you for today, Nick. I've really enjoyed myself.'

'I did, too. I hope to see you again very soon, although it won't be so easy now I'll be living in Harley Street.'

'It can't be helped, and I dare say I'll be working long hours, too.'

Nick backed away as the door opened. 'Good night, Daisy.'

'Good night, Nick.' She stepped inside, nodding to Aggie, who stared at her bleary-eyed with fatigue. 'It's late. You should be in bed.'

'I can't, not until the last person gets in, and them dancers keep all hours.'

'Where is Mrs Wood?'

'She'll be sitting by the fire in her parlour with a glass of gin, I expect.'

Daisy knew she was on dangerous ground if she criticised her landlady. Aggie was a nice young girl, but she was almost certain to repeat any comments against Mrs Wood and that would cause trouble. 'I hope you get to bed soon, Aggie. I'm going straight to my room, so you needn't worry about me.'

'Good night, miss.' Aggie turned away and trudged towards the basement stairs, the flame of her candle guttering in the draught.

Daisy lit another candle and took it upstairs to her room. There was no sign of Minnie, which meant she could undress, wash and get into bed without having to go through everything that had happened that day.

★　★　★

On Monday morning Daisy and Minnie walked to the hospital, arriving early for their first day as probationer nurses, and after a stern talk from Matron herself and a bracing lecture from Sister Tutor, they were assigned to their first duties. Daisy found herself in the sluice emptying and washing bedpans. It was not quite what she was expecting, but she applied herself to the task and earned a nod of approval from Sister Johnson when she had finished. Daisy was then assigned to a qualified nurse with instructions to follow her every move and to learn from observation. As this was mostly a question of cleaning everything in sight with carbolic soap it was not difficult to emulate, and Daisy took a hand at wiping down metal bed frames and the side lockers. She earned a rebuke from Nurse Patterson for chatting to the patients, who were feeling well enough to talk, and was reduced to simply giving those who were alert a sympathetic smile. But when she came to the ward where patients were recovering from operations she was dismayed to find Hilda Begg in a state of near hysteria.

'Is she in pain, Nurse? Can we give her something to make her feel better?'

Nurse Patterson turned on her, frowning. 'It's not our place to prescribe medication, Miss Marshall. I believe the patient has been informed of her husband's demise.'

'The poor thing,' Daisy longed to comfort Hilda, but a withering look from Nurse Patterson was enough to make her hold back.

'The patient will be given a sedative if she continues to disrupt the ward.' Nurse Patterson marched over to Hilda's bedside, glaring down at her. 'Now, now, Mrs Begg. You're upsetting the rest of the ward. Please calm yourself.'

Hilda buried her head in the pillow and her shoulders shook. Nurse Patterson strolled back to join Daisy. 'You just have to be firm with the patients, Miss Marshall. Now where were we?'

Daisy pointed to a patient in the nearby bed and Nurse Patterson leaned over the inert body, shaking her head. 'This one's trials are over. Fetch a porter, Miss Marshall, and then you must help me strip and remake the bed.' Nurse Patterson drew the curtains.

With the senior nurse out of sight, Daisy stopped by Hilda's bed. 'Mrs Begg, it's me, Daisy. I was at the scene of the accident yesterday.'

Hilda turned her heard to peer at Daisy with bloodshot eyes. 'My Stanley is dead.'

'I know, and I'm so very sorry.' Daisy glanced anxiously over her shoulder, hoping that Nurse Patterson could not hear them. 'Is there anything I can do to help?'

'Not unless you can look after my nippers. I dunno what poor Judy must be thinking.'

'Hasn't anyone told her you're here?'

Hilda shook her head and succumbed to a fresh bout of sobbing. Daisy laid a hand on her arm. 'I'm on duty until eight o'clock, but if you'll give me your address I'll go and make sure that the children are all right.'

'You will? Why would a lady like you care what happens to my kids?'

'I'd hope that someone would do the same for me if I were in your position.'

'There's not many as would go out of their way for someone like me.'

'I can't stop and talk because Sister might be listening. I have to go now but when I come back you must tell me where to find your children.'

Nurse Patterson stuck her head out between the folds of the curtains. 'Miss Marshall, I told you to find a porter.'

'Yes, Nurse. I'm just going.' Daisy hurried out of the ward, but now she was even more determined to seek out Hilda's children and to do anything she could to help them.

15

Green Dragon Yard had obviously seen better days. Dimly lit by a couple of gaslights, the cobblestones glistened with an oily sheen after the last sharp shower. The tall terraced houses had a dilapidated appearance with many of the windows boarded up or broken, water dripped from broken guttering. There were few signs of habitation, apart from the flickering light of the odd candle in an upstairs window, and the occasional banging of a door. On the other side of the street there was a hotchpotch of two-storey cottages squashed between work-shops. Billboards advertising the services of cabinet makers and cobblers lay drunkenly on the narrow pavements, and feral dogs fought over scraps of food in the gutters. It was not the sort of place for a young woman to walk unaccompanied in the daytime, let alone at night, but Daisy was determined to find Hilda's children.

She had come straight from work, even though it was getting late, and she made her way through the detritus that littered the narrow pavement, almost treading on a tabby cat. It spat and hissed before disappearing through a hole in one of the front doors. She found the house number that Hilda had given her and knocked, but it was some time before anyone answered. Daisy had a feeling that she was being watched and she glanced round anxiously, wondering if there was anyone lurking in the shadows, but the noise of traffic from Whitechapel Road would have drowned out any sound of approaching footsteps. She held her breath and knocked again.

This time she was answered by a small voice. 'Who's there?'

'Is that Judy?'

'I don't speak to strangers.' The child's voice quavered and sounded on the verge of tears.

'Are there any grown-ups in the house, Judy?'

'It's just me and me sister, Molly, and the two little 'uns; Pip and Nate.'

'Please open the door. I have a message from your mother.'

There was a scuffle and the sound of younger children crying and the door opened just an inch. A large brown eye underlined by a bruise-like shadow peered nervously at Daisy. 'Who are you?'

'My name is Daisy Marshall and I'm a nurse at the London Hospital.' The moment the words left her lips Daisy knew she had made her first mistake. A loud howl was followed by sobbing.

'Ma's in hospital?'

'Let me in, please, Judy. Your mother is in hospital because she broke her leg, but she's on the mend and she asked me to come and make sure that you are all right.'

This seemed to convince Judy and she opened the door just wide enough for Daisy to slip into the narrow hallway. The first thing that hit her was the stench of damp and the overpowering smell of an overflowing privy. It was too dark to see very much, but Judy was standing with her arm around a smaller girl and two younger children, still in petticoats, were hiding behind them.

'You ain't going to take us to the workhouse,' Judy said fiercely. 'My pa will be home soon and he'll tell you that for nothing.'

Daisy glanced into the darkness of the hall beyond them. It was colder in the house than outside. 'Can we go into the living room?' she asked tentatively. 'I came to make sure you are all right. Have you had anything to eat?'

'Ma went out to get what we needed, but she didn't come back. Pa will be home before long.'

This was going to be much more difficult than Daisy had first thought as she entered the living room. She peered into the shadowy recesses, but she could see very little in the dim light of a single candle. She could feel the damp rising from the floor and ash spilled from the grate. It must have been a day or two since the fire had been giving out warmth, and one thing was clear, this was not a fit place for anyone to live, let alone young children.

Daisy laid her hand on Judy's shoulder. 'When did you last have something to eat?'

'Ma never come home, and neither did Pa.' Judy's voice broke on a sob and the younger children began to wail.

'Your mother is getting better, but she needs to stay in hospital for a bit longer.' Daisy thought quickly. She could not leave the children here, but she knew instinctively that they would not be welcomed by Mrs Wood, even for one night. She sat down at the table and lifted the youngest child on to her knee. 'Have you any relatives who could look after you?'

Judy shook her head. 'No, miss.'

'Is there anyone else living in this house?'

'No, miss. The landlord wants the house for hisself and we got to get out, too. Pa was going to find us somewhere to live. Where is he, miss?'

'I'm afraid your pa had an accident, too. He can't come home.'

Judy's small face puckered but she did not cry. 'He's a goner, ain't he?'

'I'm afraid so, dear.'

Judy's eyes welled with tears and her lips quivered, but she did not cry. 'Ma always said we'd end up in the workhouse. I sell matches by day but I can't do that and look after the little 'uns.' Judy ruffled her sister's curls before bending down to pick up the younger child. 'We ain't got nothing to eat, so we'd best go there now and get it over.'

'There must be another way,' Daisy said desperately. 'Your mother is frantic with worry, and I promised I would do what I can to help.' She thought quickly. It was too late to take the children away from this awful place this evening, but they were in desperate need of food and warmth. 'I'll find you somewhere safe to stay until your ma comes out of hospital, Judy, but I can't do that until tomorrow.'

'No, miss.' Judy sank down on a wooden chair as if her knees had buckled beneath her, and the child in her arms began to snivel.

'But what I can do is get you some food and some candles, and a bag of coal. Will you be all right here for a while?'

'Yes, miss.' Judy's hand shot out to grasp Daisy's wrist. 'You will come back, won't you?'

'Yes, I promise I will, and I'll bring you something to eat and drink. I know where there's a shop that stays open until very late and it's not far from here, so I'll be as quick as I can.' Daisy patted Judy's hand. 'Don't be afraid. Everything will be all right. You're a very brave girl, Judy.'

Daisy left the house and set off for the shop in Whitechapel Road where she knew the owner, who had been one of her uncle's former customers. She walked briskly, ignoring the salacious remarks from men who openly propositioned her. In this mood she would have taken on anyone who tried to prevent her from getting sustenance for the children. She breathed a sigh of relief when she found the shop was still open and Mr Gittins greeted her like an old friend. She explained her mission and he insisted on sending his son to carry her purchases, including a bag of coal and some kindling. When it came to payment she found she was sixpence short, but he refused to take back any of her purchases.

'It's my contribution to the family,' Gittins said, shaking his head. 'I know Hilda well and she's as honest as the day is long, and a hard worker. Unlike that husband of hers. She's better off without him, in my opinion. He was a wastrel and a drunk, and that's why the family are in such a sorry state.'

'Thank you, Mr Gittins. I'm very grateful.'

'Your uncle did me many a good turn in the past, Daisy. Give him my regards when you next see him.'

'I most certainly will.' Daisy left the shop trailed by young Bob, who hefted the coal onto his shoulder as if it had been a sack of feathers. When they arrived at the Beggs' house he carried it inside and set it down by the empty grate.

'Shall I get a blaze going for you, miss? I'm good at lighting fires.'

Daisy placed her purchases on the table. 'Yes, Bob. Thank you.' She lit two candles and began to unpack the food with the children already seated at the table, their eyes wide open and their small fingers twitching with eagerness to snatch the smallest crumb. Judy sliced and buttered the bread and shaved off pieces of cheese, making sure that each of the children had their fair share, while Daisy filled cups with milk from the jug she had borrowed from Mr Gittins.

Bob stood back, admiring the fire he had managed to get going so that flames roared up the chimney. 'I done a good job, even if I says so meself.'

'Yes, that's excellent.' Daisy handed him the empty jug. 'Would you be kind enough to take this back to the shop? And thank you for your trouble. I'd give you a tip but I haven't got a penny left. Next time I see you I'll make up for it.'

Bob touched his cap. 'Don't worry, miss. Glad to help. I'd best get going or Pa will wonder what's happened to me.'

'Yes, of course,' Daisy said hastily. 'And thank him again. The children look better already.'

Daisy sat with the children long after Bob had left. The way the food was disappearing was a testament to how little they had eaten for a day or more, and the poverty in which they were living was all too obvious. The light from the newly lit candles and the cheerful crackling of the fire only succeeded in making the surroundings look even more desolate. The bare boards were rotten in places and stained, despite Hilda's obvious attempts to scrub them clean. A bedstead in one corner of the room seemed to suffice for all the family and the bedding looked as though it needed a good wash. As the room heated up Daisy became aware of a foul stench and she discovered an overflowing chamber pot that had been pushed under the bed. She took it out into the back yard to dispose of the contents and rinsed it under the pump before hurrying back indoors to check on the children, but she need not have worried. Judy was in the process of putting the little ones into their tattered nightgowns, although giving them a wash seemed out of the question and hardly relevant considering the general state of the room. Daisy helped Judy to put the small children to bed, and she stoked the fire. 'I think it's time you got some sleep, Judy,' she said gently.

'Will you stay, miss?'

'I can't, I'm afraid. I have to be up early to go to work at the hospital, but I'll see your mother first thing, and I'll tell her what a wonderful daughter she has. I know she'll be proud of you, Judy.'

'But what will we do tomorrow? The landlord is going to throw us out.'

'Try not to worry. I'll think of something and I'll find somewhere for you to stay while your ma is in hospital. You'll have to trust me, Judy.'

'Yes, miss.'

'I've made the fire safe, so there's no need for you to touch it. I want you to lock the front door after me, and don't open it to anyone until I return tomorrow. I'll get here as soon as I can, so you feed the little ones with what's left of the bread and butter, and I'll bring more food.'

★　★　★

Daisy hardly slept that night for worrying about the four children she had been compelled to leave in the deserted, unsanitary house. Minnie came in late, but Daisy pretended to be asleep. Minnie was a lovely person but she was inclined to idle chatter and Daisy was not in a mood to listen. Eventually Minnie climbed into the bed next to Daisy's and was asleep within minutes, but Daisy was still wide awake. The clock in the entrance hall struck the hours and chimed the quarters with monotonous regularity and, just as Daisy was falling asleep, she heard the clatter of feet on the stairs and muffled laughter as the dancers from the Pavilion Theatre returned to their room. She heard the clock strike three, and the next thing she knew someone was shaking her and calling her name.

'Wake up, Daisy. You'll be late for work if you don't get up now.'

Still half asleep, Daisy sat up and swung her legs over the side of the bed. The floorboards were cold beneath her feet, but the chill had a bracing effect and she was now fully conscious.

'I had a wonderful time last evening,' Minnie said gleefully. 'I went to the Gaiety Theatre with Flora and Ivy and we had dinner in the restaurant, where I met the most charming man. His name is Giles Coleman and he works in the City. He treated us all to champagne and he wants to see me again. Isn't that exciting?'

'Yes, very.' Daisy poured what was left of the water into the bowl and had a quick wash. 'I'm glad for you, Minnie. You deserve someone who will treat you well.'

Minnie blushed a delicate shade of pink. 'Oh, I don't know about that. Pa always tells me I talk too much, and I haven't a sensible thought in my head.'

'That's not true. You were accepted to train as a nurse at the London. That should make your father proud.'

'I hope so,' Minnie sighed, shaking her head. 'Anyway, enough about me. Did you find Hilda's children?'

'Yes, I did, and they're in desperate need of somewhere to stay while their mother is in hospital. I promised to help, but I don't know who would take them in.'

'I'm afraid I can't help you there. I don't know many people in London. I suppose it would be easier if you were at home in Essex.'

251

Daisy laced her stays as tightly as possible and slipped her dress over her head. 'I think you might have the solution there, Minnie,' she said thoughtfully. 'But I would have to take them to Little Creek and I don't know if I could get time off.'

'You could try asking Sister Tutor.' Minnie checked her appearance in the tiny mirror placed on the top of the chest of drawers. 'I'm going down to breakfast. I can't go a whole morning without eating, even though I had a splendid dinner last night. Giles is very generous. He insisted on paying for everything. I think I have a rich beau, Daisy. Isn't that splendid?'

'Yes, splendid indeed.' Daisy scraped her hair into a tight knot at the nape of her neck and secured it with half a dozen pins as if daring a single lock to escape.

'Come on. Hurry up.' Minnie held the door open. 'I hate cold porridge.'

'I'm coming.' Daisy followed her downstairs to the dining room, but even before she had reached the door she had made her mind up. The children would be safe in Little Creek and she knew exactly where to take them. Mrs Bee and Dove would take care of them and Dove would make sure that Judy attended school. She had always suspected that Dove had a soft spot for Elliot Massey, and that it was mutual. Even if she hadn't taken up the position of his assistant teacher at the school, this would give them the opportunity of seeing more of each other. But first Daisy would have to get permission from Hilda, and then she would have to face Sister Johnson. It was going to be a busy morning.

★ ★ ★

Hilda was tearful but in the end she acknowledged that the welfare of her children was the most important thing, and her convalescence was likely to be a long one. 'Are you sure that these people will be kind to my little ones, Nurse?'

'I wouldn't have suggested it if I didn't know them personally, and Creek Hall is an ideal place for children. They'll get fresh air and good food, and the village school is excellent. Besides which, Mrs Boynton is one of the kindest people you could wish to meet.'

'But the gent who owns the house might not be happy to have my nippers foisted on him.'

'Dr Neville is a friend of mine and I know he'd agree with me. In fact, I'll go and see him first to get his permission, but I know he won't object.'

Hilda dashed tears from her eyes. 'Why would you do this for me? We were strangers before the accident.'

'You're someone in need of help. That's what nursing is all about, Hilda. The surgeons can fix your bones, but a broken heart is another matter. If your children were taken into the workhouse it would be the worst thing that could happen, apart of course from losing your husband.'

'I'll miss him, of course, but my old man was no good as a provider. He could charm the birds from the trees if he put his mind to it, but a good husband he weren't, nor a good father neither.' Hilda reached out to grasp Daisy's hand. 'Take care of my nippers and I'll be grateful to you for evermore. I can't say truer than that.'

Daisy gave her an encouraging pat. 'Leave it to me, Hilda. I won't see you for a day or so, but if Sister Johnson gives me leave of absence I'll take the children to Creek Hall today.'

'And if she don't?'

'I'll go anyway, but don't worry, I'm sure I can persuade her to let me do the right thing.'

★ ★ ★

Despite the fact that she arrived in Harley Street during surgery hours, Nick had Daisy shown into his consulting room.

'What is it, Daisy? What's happened?' He gave her a searching look. 'You'd better sit down and tell me.'

'It's to do with that dreadful accident on Saturday. I saw Hilda on the ward after her operation, and she was in a terrible state worrying about her children, so I said I'd check on them for her.'

'That was good of you.'

'I felt it was the least I could do so I went to Green Dragon Street and found them living in the most horrible conditions imaginable. The eldest is only nine or ten and she was trying to look after the little ones. I think they would have starved to death if they'd been left alone much longer.'

Nick perched on the edge of his desk. 'Have they no one to look after them?'

'Not a soul. The landlord has evicted the rest of the tenants so they're completely on their own and he's threatening to throw them out.'

'So how can I help?'

'I hardly slept last night for worrying about them, but it was Minnie who suggested that I take them home to Little Creek. The only problem is that my aunt and uncle are too old to look after such young children . . . '

'And you thought of Mrs Bee. I know the way your mind works, Daisy, and I agree wholeheartedly. There's precious little for her to do while I'm in London and I hadn't the heart to sack Dove, knowing what a help she is to Mrs Bee.'

'So you don't mind?'

'Of course not.' He moved round the desk to take a seat, reached for pen and paper and began to write. 'I would come with you, if it were possible, but sadly I have appointments booked all day. However, take this note to Mrs Bee and I know she'll do her best by the children.' He opened a drawer and took out a leather pouch. 'I was going give her this money for housekeeping on my next visit home, but perhaps you could do it for me.'

'Yes, of course I will.'

He eyed her curiously. 'How did Sister Tutor react when you asked for leave of absence?'

'She wasn't at all happy. She said I shouldn't get involved in patients' affairs, but when I told her of the children's plight she said I could have two days off.'

'She must think a lot of you to agree to such a thing.'

'I was expecting her to refuse, but then I would have had to resign. I can't leave those poor children alone in that terrible place. I'm going there now and I just hope their landlord isn't around.'

'Have you seen Toby yet? I know he's been on night duty for nearly a month, but I'm sure he'd go with you if you managed to wake him.'

'I knocked on his door before I came here, but there was no response. Toby always did sleep heavily.'

'Have you enough money for the railway tickets?'

Daisy bit her lip. She hated asking for a loan, but these were exceptional circumstances. 'Actually, I'm afraid I was going to impose on your good nature.'

'Nonsense. That's what friends are for. Take what you need from the pouch. I'll make up the difference next time I return home.'

'Thank you, Nick. You're a true friend.' Daisy rose to her feet. 'I'm sorry I interrupted your consultations.'

'I've always got time for you, Daisy.' He pushed back his chair and stood up. 'But I'd like to take you out to tea on Sunday, if you're free.'

'I'd like that, although a picnic in Hyde Park would be nice, and it would cost less.'

'Has anyone ever told you what a remarkable person you are, Daisy?'

'Yes, often,' she said, laughing. 'Only Jonah Sawkins doesn't count, and anyway he's got his sights set on Ivy, poor girl.'

Nick opened the door and followed her into the waiting room. 'Do I know the fellow?'

'No,' she said firmly. 'And you don't want to.' She was suddenly aware that two elegantly dressed ladies, seated on gilded chairs amongst potted palms, were staring curiously at them. 'Thank you, Doctor,' Daisy added in a more formal tone. 'I'll recommend you to all my friends and acquaintances. Good morning.' She managed to keep a straight face until she stepped out onto the pavement, and she was still giggling as she climbed into the hansom cab and instructed the driver to take her to Green Dragon Street.

★　★　★

Despite the fact that the children were terrified by the great iron beast of a steam engine when it roared into the station, the rest of the journey to Little Creek was reasonably easy. The little ones slept for most of the time and Judy gazed out of the window, crying out excitedly at the sight of green fields dotted with woolly white sheep and cows placidly munching the grass. It had not occurred to Daisy that a child born and bred in the city might never have seen farm animals, but Judy was clearly enchanted by everything she saw. As luck would have it Grace Peabody was travelling on the same train and she pounced on Daisy, demanding to know everything from the time Daisy had left Creek Cottage until the moment she spotted her handing out buns to the children.

'Well, Daisy, I'm proud of you for acting in such a Christian manner. My husband will doubtless use this story in his sermon on Sunday. I hope we'll see you in the congregation.' Grace sat down suddenly as the train slowed and came to a halt.

'I'm afraid I only have permission to stay overnight and then I must return to my duties,' Daisy said hastily. 'But I'm sure that Dove will bring the little ones to Sunday school as soon as they've settled in.'

'I suppose Dove Fox is a steady young person, unlike her elder brother, and Mrs Boynton is a good woman. I know she'll do her duty as far as the children are concerned. Their mother must be very grateful to you for going to so much trouble.'

Daisy glanced out of the window. 'We're here.' She felt her spirits lift as she gazed at the neatly kept station with its flowerbed surrounded by small rocks painted white. Daffodils swayed in the breeze and the trees behind the stationmaster's house were bursting into leaf. She had always thought of herself as a city girl, but she realised with a sense of surprise that she had missed the countryside even though she had only been gone for such a short time.

'My husband is meeting me with the pony and trap.' Grace rose from her seat. 'We could take you to Creek Hall. The babies look far too tired to walk all that way.'

'That would be very kind,' Daisy said reluctantly. She had been looking forward to a

258

walk along the river-bank and through the wood, but she had to admit that Pip and Nate, the two youngest, would never manage such a long trek.

'Right then. I'll go on ahead and tell John that we have a mission of mercy.' Grace bustled out of the compartment, the plumes on her bonnet quivering with intent, and as Daisy martialled the children she could see Grace marching purposefully along the platform.

It was a tight squash to get everyone seated safely in the trap, and luckily the children had only one small bag containing their worldly possession. Daisy had also travelled light, safe in the knowledge that she had several changes of clothes at home in Creek Cottage, and soon they were tootling through the country lanes at a brisk pace. The vicar offered to drop them off at the cottage, but Grace insisted that they carry on to Creek Hall, although Daisy suspected that this was due to curiosity rather than kindness. According to Mrs Bee the vicar had tried many times to persuade the late Dr Neville to attend church, but had never succeeded. Daisy suspected that Grace Peabody wanted to inspect the home of the man who had been beloved by everyone in the village, even though he had refused to conform. But if that was the case then Grace was doomed to disappointment as they were greeted at the gates by Mrs Bee and Dove.

'We received a telegram from the master,' Mrs Bee said by way of explanation. 'It said you were bringing the little mites here, Daisy.'

'So we thought we'd walk to the station to meet you,' Dove added hastily. 'The poor little souls look worn out. Let's get them indoors.'

Daisy could have kissed them both. It was a relief to find that Nick had forewarned his housekeeper and that they were expected. There was no need for lengthy explanations and Mrs Bee had picked up two-year-old Nate and Dove scooped Pip into her arms, leaving Daisy to take care of Molly and Judy.

'Thank you so much, Mr and Mrs Peabody,' Daisy said hurriedly. 'It was so kind of you to give us a lift.'

'Perhaps we ought to see the children safely settled?' Grace gave her husband a meaningful look, but he shook his head.

'I can see that they are in good hands, my dear. I think we'd best get home. I have parishioners to visit this afternoon.' He flicked the reins. 'Good day, ladies.'

Mrs Bee acknowledged him with a smile and Dove bobbed a curtsey. Daisy could hear Grace protesting as the horse plodded forward, breaking into a trot as it seemed to realise it was on the homeward journey.

'I'll leave the explanations to you, Dove.' With Nate clasped in her arms, Mrs Bee set off along the gravelled carriage sweep, heading towards the house.

'What's the matter?' Daisy asked anxiously. 'Is anything wrong?'

'There's a reason why Mrs Bee didn't want the Peabodys to come up to the house.' Dove quickened her pace.

Daisy smiled down at Judy. 'If you and Molly run after that nice lady I'm sure she'll find you something nice to eat.'

'You want to talk to her in private,' Judy said, sighing. 'It's always the same with grown-ups.'

'Maybe I do, but I can assure you that Mrs Bee is a marvellous cook and she makes delicious cakes.'

Judy grabbed her sister's hand and broke into a run.

'Now then,' Daisy said when the girls were out of earshot. 'What's going on? Why didn't Mrs Bee invite the vicar and his wife into the house?'

16

'It's Jay,' Dove said in a low voice. 'He turned up late last night.'

'Why would he risk coming ashore? He only just got away last time.'

'You can ask him yourself.'

'Why did he come here, of all places?'

'He can't go home because Pa would throw him out or turn him over to the authorities.' Dove hurried on and Daisy had to run in an effort to keep up with her.

'What has Jay done that is so terrible?' Daisy demanded as she caught up with her outside the scullery door. 'I don't understand why your father is so unwilling to help his eldest son. I'm sure that Jay isn't bad at heart.' She turned with a start as the door opened and Jay stepped outside into the spring sunshine.

'At last,' he said, chuckling. 'Someone who believes in me. It's good to see you again, Daisy.'

'I'll take this little one into the kitchen.' Dove pushed past her brother, giving him a warning look. 'Don't cause trouble, Jay. We've had enough of that in our family.' She carried Pip inside and closed the door.

Jay stood with his thumbs hooked into his belt, his head on one side as he gazed at Daisy with an irresistible twinkle in his eyes. 'Are you collecting orphans, Daisy? I've just seen Mrs Bee with two little girls and a young child, and my sister has another in her arms.'

'Their father was killed in a collision with an omnibus and their mother is in hospital. I promised to see that her children were cared for until she's well enough to look after them.'

'I seem to have missed something. This couldn't have happened in Little Creek. The most dangerous vehicle is the brewer's dray, and that doesn't go fast enough to catch a snail.'

Daisy stifled a giggle. 'You always manage to turn everything into a joke.'

'I'm serious now, and I'm sorry for the children, but I'm still confused. Where were you when this happened?'

'I've just started as a probationer nurse at the London Hospital, and I witnessed the accident. Hilda — that's the children's mother — had to be admitted to one of the wards and she was frantic with worry. I promised to help if I could.'

'So you decided to bring them here?'

'When I found the children living in appalling conditions with no one to care for them I didn't have much choice. They're here with Nick's permission, of course.' Daisy met his amused look with a frown. 'Why am I explaining myself? More to the point, why are you here? If you're in trouble with the authorities you could get Mrs Bee and Dove into trouble.'

'I was going to steer clear of Little Creek, but I had a brush with the squire and he's threatened to evict my family from their cottage.'

'He also owns the freehold on Creek Cottage and the lease will come up for renewal before the year is out. He's threatening not to renew it and it's obvious that the squire wants my aunt and uncle out, too,' Daisy said with feeling. 'That man is pure evil.'

Jay's smiled faded. 'I agree, and something needs to be done.'

'He's a magistrate. He does what he likes.'

'No one is above the law, not even Tattersall, and I intend to bring him down, one way or another.'

'I don't see what you can do. Get on the wrong side of him and he'll have you up before him on some trumped-up charge.'

'I'll work something out, don't worry.'

'I wish I could stay to help, but I have to return to the hospital tomorrow.'

'Has Nick got anything to do with your decision to stay in London?'

The question, asked outright, brought a blush to her cheeks. 'No, certainly not. I'd been thinking about taking up nursing, and I decided it was the right time. Although I suppose it might have appeared that I was running away.'

'I don't believe you've ever run from anything in your life, Daisy. But I still think there's something you're not telling me.'

'The situation was beyond my control.' Daisy hesitated. If she told him the truth it might make him even more determined to take on the powerful squire, but as she met his intense gaze she knew she could not lie. 'I thought I could help Nick, but taking on the squire was a big mistake.'

'How so?'

'Apparently he admires bold women, or so he

told me when I accompanied Aunt Eleanora and Uncle Sidney to dinner at Creek Manor. The squire asked me to marry him.'

'The devil he did.'

'You needn't look so surprised. I think he showed admirable good taste.'

'You know I didn't mean it like that. Anyway, I hope you put him in his place.'

'He said he wouldn't renew the lease on Creek Cottage if I refused his offer, and I'm afraid I panicked.'

'The old bastard!' Jay shook his head. 'I apologise for swearing, but that man is unbelievable. He's done his best to ruin my family and now he's turned on your aunt and uncle. It's time he had his comeuppance.'

'I couldn't agree more,' Daisy said earnestly. 'But you have so much to lose, Jay. If you cross him he'll make an example of you.'

'I'm already an outlaw.' Jay's lips twisted in a wry smile.

'If there's anything I can do to help, just say so.'

Jay was about to answer when the door opened. 'Don't listen to my brother's ramblings,' Dove said, frowning. 'He's leaving soon, anyway.'

'Are you?' Daisy gave him a questioning look. 'What are you going to do?'

'I intend to bring Tattersall to his knees and have him begging for mercy.'

'You're all talk, Jay.' Dove laid her hand on Daisy's arm. 'Come in and leave my mad brother to continue on the road to ruin. He might think he can outwit the squire, but he'll soon find out that it's not so easy.'

'Do be careful, Jay,' Daisy said earnestly.

He clutched his hand to his heart, smiling. 'Does that mean you care about me, Daisy?'

'If you want my honest opinion, I think you ought to get as far away from here as you possibly can. The squire has money, position and power on his side, and if you take him on you'll be the one to come off worst.'

'That is going to change. He's done enough damage to the people of Little Creek. It ends now.'

Jay strode off across the courtyard and disappeared into one of the stables.

Daisy was about to follow him, but Dove caught her by the sleeve. 'Let him go, because nothing you can say or do will stop Jay when he's made his mind up.'

'But he's heading for trouble, Dove. Don't you care?'

'Of course I do, but I know from experience that you have to leave him to his own devices. He'll do exactly as he wants anyway.'

★   ★   ★

Daisy stayed for an hour, but by that time she was satisfied that the children would settle in well and that Mrs Bee and Dove could cope with their antics. Daisy said goodbye to the children although she promised to visit them again before she returned to London. She was reluctant to leave, but she wanted to see her aunt and uncle, although she suspected that they already knew of

266

her arrival. It would have been an irresistible piece of gossip for Grace to pass on, and was probably all round the village by now.

It was a glorious spring afternoon and Daisy set off to walk to Creek Cottage. The recent showers followed by warm sunshine had brought a touch of spring to the woods with buds bursting open and tiny leaves unfurling like ladies' fans. The white blossom of the blackthorn looked like bridal lace as it adorned the hedgerows; birds were nesting, and small animals scuttled about in the leaf mould. Daisy was even more conscious of the difference between living in the city and life in the country, and although she would never have thought it possible she knew that this was where she truly belonged. However, she had a job to do and she would have to return to the dirt, smoke and crowded streets of London in the morning.

She arrived at Creek Cottage to find her aunt peering out of the window. Daisy chuckled to herself — she had been correct in her assumption that Grace Peabody would have spread the news of Daisy Marshall's unexpected return home accompanied by four children. She opened the gate in the picket fence and was halfway up the path when the front door opened and her aunt emerged from the house, arms widespread in welcome.

'My dear girl, how lovely to see you. Grace told us that you had come back from London with several small children, but why didn't you bring them here?' She hustled Daisy into the house. 'I'm sure we're used to looking after the waifs and strays you bring home.'

'I knew you would want to help,' Daisy said tactfully. 'But the two youngest children are little more than babies and their mother will be incapacitated for months. Her husband was killed in the accident and she has no one to look after her children. They were facing the workhouse.'

'Oh, how dreadful.' Eleanora bustled into the parlour where, despite the relative warmth outside, a fire burned in the grate. 'Anyway, tell me everything from the moment you left us. Your uncle and I have really missed you.' She rang the bell, but Daisy suspected that Linnet must have been loitering in the hallway as she appeared immediately.

'You rang, ma'am?'

'Yes, Linnet. Bring tea and cake, if there is any. If I'd known earlier that you were coming home I'd have asked Hattie to bake your favourite chocolate cake, Daisy.'

'That's quite all right, Aunt.' Daisy turned to Linnet and smiled. 'How are things with your family?'

'The same as usual, thank you, miss.' Linnet bobbed a curtsey and retreated to the kitchen.

Even with the door closed Daisy could hear her calling to Hattie. 'Miss Daisy has come home, Hattie. Put the kettle on.'

Eleanora resumed her seat by the window. 'Are you staying long, Daisy?'

'No, Aunt. I'm sorry but I have to return to London tomorrow. I've been taken on as a probationer nurse at the London Hospital, and I had to ask permission to bring the Begg family to Little Creek. I expect Grace has told you what happened.'

'Yes, she did. A terrible accident, but it was lucky for the children that you took them under your wing. You're a good girl, Daisy, and you deserve to have the best in life. You could live in luxury if you change your mind and accept the squire's proposal.'

'Would you really see me married to a man who tried to blackmail me into accepting his offer of marriage?'

'Well, if you put it like that, then no, of course not. But I don't believe he would stoop so low. In fact, I think he must have said that in the heat of the moment. After all, he isn't getting any younger and he needs an heir. You are a beautiful and talented young lady and if he receives a knighthood, you would become Lady Tattersall.'

Daisy gazed at her aunt in dismay. 'I'm not that easily bought.'

'I didn't mean that, my dear. You take me too literally. I wish your uncle were here to persuade you.'

'Where is he?'

'Fishing, of course. I hardly see him these days. Not that I'm complaining. I find I have plenty to do with running the house and helping Grace with her good works.'

'I'm so glad you've settled in so well, Aunt Eleanora.' Daisy tried to sound positive, but it was obvious that her aunt and uncle had not taken the squire's threats seriously. Then there was Jay, who said he was prepared to risk everything in an attempt to stop the squire from evicting his family. Daisy went to sit by the fire, staring into the flames as they licked around the glossy black coals. Perhaps her desire to get away from the squire's advances had led her to act selfishly, leaving the people who had raised her so lovingly to face losing their home.

The rattle of teacups announced Linnet's arrival with the tray and she placed it on the small table in front of Eleanora.

'Thank you, Linnet. That will be all for now.

'Yes, ma'am.' Linnet slipped silently from the room.

'Come and sit by me, Daisy. You can pour, because my hands are a bit rheumaticky today, but they'll improve with the good weather. I want to hear every detail of your time in London.'

★ ★ ★

When her aunt retired upstairs to take her afternoon nap, Daisy took the opportunity of going for a walk along the river-bank. She hoped to have a few words with her uncle in private, if he could be distracted from fishing for long enough to have a sensible conversation. Aunt Eleanora seemed oblivious to the threat of losing Creek Cottage and Daisy needed to find out if her uncle was similarly deluded. Despite his previous bravado, Daisy knew that both he and her aunt were in awe of Squire Tattersall — that had been obvious from the outset — but Daisy could see him for what he was: a posturing bully,

270

drunk with his own power, and so full of himself that he thought he could buy the affection of any woman he chose.

She walked slowly along the bank, enjoying the warm spring sunshine and the peace and tranquillity of the scenery. Maybe she had made a mistake by going away too soon? Perhaps she should have faced the squire again, making it clear that she could never marry a man she did not love. She was not a coward, but running away never solved any problem, and she had left her aunt and uncle to face the consequences of her refusal to consider the squire's proposal. Jay had come home and was prepared to risk everything in order to save his family, although why the squire should have singled him out for particularly harsh treatment was a mystery. Daisy was beginning to think that there was more to the story than Jay had been prepared to disclose. She came to a sudden halt. There was someone she needed to speak to, and she headed back to the village.

Mary Fox was on her hands and knees scrubbing the front step. She sat back on her heels and smiled up at Daisy.

'This is a surprise, miss. I thought you was in London.'

'I'm here on a short visit, Mrs Fox.' Daisy glanced into the dark interior of the cottage. 'Is your husband at home?'

'He went fishing with your uncle. My Lemuel misses his work as gamekeeper, and going out with Mr Marshall makes him feel useful again. We get fish for supper nearly every day, which is a great help in these hard times.'

'Might I have a word with you?' Daisy asked tentatively. 'In private.'

Mary dropped the scrubbing brush into the bucket and scrambled to her feet. 'Of course. Is anything wrong? It's not Jack again, is it?'

'No, it's nothing to do with Jack.' Daisy stepped over the threshold and, once again, was almost overpowered by the smell of mould and damp.

'I'd offer you a cup of tea, but I haven't had time to go to the shop.'

Daisy knew this was a lie, but she smiled and shook her head. 'I had tea with my aunt, thank you, anyway.'

Mary wiped her hands on her apron, gazing anxiously around the room. 'Won't you take a seat, miss?'

Daisy pulled up a chair and sat down at the scrubbed pine table. She was struck once again by Mary's desperate attempts to make her home as neat and clean as possible, and she cleared her throat, searching for the right words. 'I hope you don't think I'm being impertinent, Mrs Fox, but I know that the squire has threatened you with eviction.'

'Has my Linnet been gossiping? I'll have something to say to her if she has.'

'No, it wasn't Linnet. I'm only asking you because the squire is also making life difficult for my aunt and uncle. They didn't realise that the squire owns the freehold to Creek Cottage, and there's some doubt as to whether he will allow them to renew the lease.'

'I heard something of the sort.' Mary subsided onto a chair opposite Daisy. 'You know what a place this is for gossip, but it wasn't Linnet who told me.'

'Then you probably know why the squire is being so difficult.'

Mary stared down at her clasped hands. 'Yes, miss.'

'I'm going to ask you something you may not wish to answer, but I have a very good reason for the question.'

'Yes, miss.' Mary raised her head to give Daisy a questioning look.

Daisy leaned forward. 'I know that the squire sent your son to prison for some minor offence.'

Mary jumped to her feet. 'We don't speak about it in this house.'

'But Jay is your son. Surely you want to help him?'

'It's all in the past. My Lemuel insists on it being that way. Please don't ask me anything else.'

'I don't understand,' Daisy said slowly. 'Jay's been punished for the crime he committed. Why can't you forgive him?'

'Who says I don't forgive him? It ain't my choice, miss. He's suffering for my sins, not his. My boy made a mistake, but he's paid for it.'

'I'm sorry, I don't understand.'

'No, and it's best that way. I'm asking you to leave now, please. You're very welcome here but I don't want my boy's name mentioned again.'

'I apologise if I've upset you, Mrs Fox.' Daisy left the cottage, walking slowly towards home.

She was even more mystified after her brief conversation with Jay's mother. Mary Fox was hiding some deep dark secret and Daisy had a feeling that the squire might have the answer. There was only one action that she could take now, and it was something she should have done at the outset.

★ ★ ★

Next morning, instead of catching the train to London, Daisy walked to Creek Hall, having told her aunt that she wanted to make sure that the Begg children were not causing Mrs Bee too much trouble. She knew that they would be well cared for, but it was a relief to see Judy and Molly enjoying the fresh air and sunshine as they explored the overgrown grounds. Judy bounded up to her and gave her a hug and Molly managed a shy smile.

'Where are the little ones?' Daisy took them by the hand. 'Have they been good for Mrs Bee?'

'Pip cried for our ma when Dove put him to bed, but she sung him a song and he fell asleep. Nate was tired out so he was no trouble at all.' Judy puffed out her chest. 'I'm good with the little 'uns. I've looked after them while Ma was out at work, so I know what to do.'

'I help,' Molly added shyly.

'I'm sure you do.' Daisy opened the scullery door and the smell of baking wafted out from the kitchen. Judy and Molly raced on ahead, but Daisy stopped to speak to Mrs Bee, who emerged from the linen cupboard carrying some drying cloths and a pile of dusters.

'You needn't worry about the little ones, miss. They've settled in as if they've always lived with us. Dove is a natural when it comes to children.'

'I knew they would love it here,' Daisy said, smiling. 'I hope it's not too much work for you.'

'It's good to have nippers about the place again. It's a big old house for just Dove and me.'

'I've come to ask another favour.' Daisy lowered her voice. 'I need to go somewhere and I wondered if Billy, the stable boy at Creek Hall, could drive me there in Dr Neville's trap.'

'You're going to call on the squire.' Mrs Bee nodded with approval. 'It's time someone stood up to the old devil. He's been making mischief round here for far too long.'

'How did you know that?'

Mrs Bee chuckled. 'I'm a witch. Didn't Master Nick tell you that?'

'He thinks the world of you, Mrs Bee.'

'I used to tease him when he was a little boy. If he was naughty I'd tell him the witch would come and turn him into a frog. He thought I was talking about myself, but it did the trick. Although I have to say he was a good boy, most of the time, anyway.'

'So is it all right if I take Billy and the trap?'

'You go, my dear. Do whatever it is you have to do with my blessing.'

★ ★ ★

Hero was getting old and Billy was not an expert when it came to handling the reins, but eventually they arrived at Creek Manor. Daisy had been silently rehearsing what she would say to the squire, but as Billy drew the horse to a halt outside the front entrance Daisy began to have second thoughts. Her previous meetings with Esmond Tattersall had ended badly, and there was no guarantee of a successful outcome now.

'Shall you get down, miss?' Billy asked anxiously. 'Do you want me to help you?'

'No, thank you,' Daisy said stiffly. 'I can manage perfectly well.' She cocked her head on one side. 'Do you hear that?'

Billy craned his neck. 'Someone's coming and they're riding hell for leather, if you'll excuse the expression, miss.'

The words had barely left his lips when a horseman rounded the corner of the building at a breakneck speed. He reined in the animal, coming to a halt in a cloud of dust and flying gravel.

'Daisy. What in the devil's name are you doing here?'

'I could say the same for you, Jay Fox. Are you mad?'

'I don't know what you think you can achieve, but I'm telling you it's a waste of time.' Jay leaned over to grab Hero's bridle. 'Turn back, Billy. Get Miss Marshall away from here as quickly as you can.'

Billy heaved at the reins but the startled horse reared and whinnied in fright. Daisy turned her head at the sound of shouts and running footsteps.

'What have you done, Jay?' she cried anxiously. 'Did you steal that animal?'

'I borrowed it,' Jay said, grinning. 'You have to get away, Daisy. The squire isn't in a friendly mood, and I can't stay to protect you.'

Billy struggled to gain control of the frightened horse. 'The poor beast can't go fast, miss. He'll drop dead if I try to make him.'

'Miss Marshall, I want a word with you.'

The sound of Esmond Tattersall's voice booming across the carriage sweep made Daisy glance over her shoulder. She knew by the look on his face that her mission was futile.

Jay manoeuvred his mount to the side of the trap. 'Stand up and I'll lift you onto the saddle.'

'I can't.'

'Do you want to spend the rest of the day fighting off Tattersall? Because he's coming down the steps as I speak.' Jay leaned over and grabbed her round the waist.

With a little help from Billy, Daisy found herself sharing the saddle with Jay, and suddenly they were off at speed and it was all she could do to catch her breath. She clung to the horse's mane as they approached the gates but two groundsmen appeared as if from nowhere and started to close them. Jay urged the animal on and Daisy closed her eyes, fearing the worst.

'It's all right. We're through.'

'I do believe you're enjoying this,' Daisy said angrily. 'Put me down, Jay. I'm not going far like this.'

He glanced over his shoulder. 'Tattersall is mounting up and he obviously intends to give chase. We'll beat him even with two of us on this beast. It's his personal favourite.'

'Have you lost your mind?' Daisy gasped breathlessly. 'Horse theft is a serious crime. Set me down and go on alone.'

'Hold on. We'll soon lose them.'

It took Daisy all her efforts simply to stay on the horse despite the fact that Jay's arms were around her, but he was using the reins to guide the animal across fields and along narrow bridal paths. She had to duck her head constantly to avoid overhanging branches and she gave up trying to speak as the wind robbed her of breath. They rode through a thickly wooded area and suddenly they were out in the open and she recognised the cove where she had last seen Jay's ship. And there was the *Lazy Jane* at anchor, bobbing gently up and down on the outgoing tide.

Jay drew the horse to a halt and leaped to the ground, and Daisy did not argue when he lifted her from the saddle. Her knees felt weak and every muscle in her body ached.

She slapped him on the arm. 'You fool,' she cried angrily. 'What do you think you're doing?'

He held the reins, patting the horse's neck. 'I saved you from yourself, Daisy Marshall. Did you think you could get the better of Tattersall? Or were you going to appeal to his better nature? Because I can tell you he has none.'

'You've put paid to any chance I had of coming to an amicable arrangement with him. You've stolen this poor horse and you've abducted me. These aren't the actions of a sane man.'

'You are free to go.' Jay encompassed the wide sweep of the cove with open arms. 'You can ride the horse back to Creek Manor, if you so wish. Or you can sail away to freedom with me.'

'You are completely mad,' Daisy said angrily. 'You've just ruined any chance you might have had to clear your name.'

'Don't you think I'm used to being in the wrong? I grew up knowing that my father hated me, and my mother considered me an embarrassment. I've just discovered why, thanks to Tattersall.'

'I don't understand,' Daisy said slowly. 'What did he say to you, Jay?'

17

'He took great pleasure in telling me that he's my father,' Jay said bitterly. 'I was conceived out of wedlock and Lemuel Fox only married my mother out of pity.'

'Oh, Jay. I'm so sorry, but he might be lying.'

'I believe he was telling the truth, and it explains a lot. I can understand now why the man I've always thought of as my father hates the sight of me, and my mother feels shame every time she looks at me.'

'I doubt if that's true,' Daisy said earnestly. 'I'm sure your mother loves you just as much as her other children.'

'She has to keep on the old man's right side. He might preach peace and goodwill, but he has a fierce temper.'

'I think you should go home and talk to your mother. Give her a chance to put things right.'

'No, it's too late for that. My ship's waiting to take me far away from here.' Jay seized both her hands, his eyes shining. 'Come with me, Daisy. We'll sail the world together.'

'I've run away once, and I realise it's not the answer. Please speak to your mother before you do anything rash.'

'She'll be better off without me. At least she might get some peace of mind if I'm far away. When you see her again, tell her I love her, and always will.' He glanced over her shoulder at the sound of plashing oars. 'They've come for me.'

She turned to see one of Jay's crew rowing towards the shore. 'You don't have to go like this. I thought you were going to stand up to the squire.'

'I've decided he's not worth the trouble. Are you going to take a chance and come with me?'

'I think you're making a mistake.' They were standing so close together that she could feel his breath warm on her cheek and she could see a pulse throbbing at his temple. She found herself gazing into his blue eyes, a prisoner of raging emotions that she could not explain. She tried to move away but he caught her in his arms and kissed her until her lips parted and she lost herself in a dizzying flood of emotion. She closed her eyes and allowed herself to melt into the moment, and then suddenly she was free again as Jay released her from his passionate embrace.

'Come with me, Daisy. We were meant to be together.'

The inclination to throw everything away and the desire to be with him was almost overwhelming, but she knew in her heart that it could never be. No matter what the temptation, she could not betray the trust of the people who had loved and looked after her for most of her life. She was on the brink of entering a profession where she could do some good and she could not simply walk away from her old life.

'No, not like this, Jay.' She backed away, keeping him at a safe distance. 'It would end in disaster for both of us.'

'I love you, Daisy, and you feel something for

281

me, I know you do.'

'Of course I do, but . . . '

'But not enough to take a chance with me.'

'I don't want to live like a criminal on the run from the law, Jay. I think you ought to stay and face up to the past. If you go now you'll have allowed the squire to ruin your life as well as those of your mother and Lemuel.'

His eyes darkened. 'What would you do if you were me?'

She met his bleak look with an attempt at a smile. 'I'd do my best to prove that I was the heir to the Tattersall estate and fortune. Think what a difference the money would make to your family.'

'You're forgetting that I was born out of wedlock. I'm a bastard and there's an end to it.'

'Now you're wallowing in self-pity,' Daisy said angrily.

'You have no notion of what my life has been like, Daisy. You have a loving family and you haven't experienced the harsh reality of being poor.'

The surge of passion she had felt for him turned to ice in her veins. She wanted to shake some sense into him, but part of her longed to throw her arms around him and comfort him as if he were a small child. She knew she must not weaken. 'Go then,' she said angrily. 'Run away to sea like a spoilt little boy. Break your mother's heart and make your sisters and your brother unhappy. I don't care what you do.'

She seized the horse's bridle and led the sweating animal to the edge of the wood, where she used a fallen tree trunk as a mounting block.

The desire to get away overcame her fear as a novice rider. She clicked her tongue and flicked the reins. 'Walk on.'

Despite her anger she could not resist glancing over her shoulder and she saw Jay standing in the shallows, staring after her. She rode on, struggling with a feeling of failure and disappointment, but it was for Jay that she suffered and not herself. He was playing into the squire's hands and committing himself to the life of an outlaw. Despite Lemuel's treatment of him, Daisy could not believe that he really hated his stepson. Jay was the innocent victim in all this, and he seemed hell-bent on destroying himself. She sighed and guided the horse in the direction of Creek Hall. Billy could take care of the animal when he arrived back at the stables, and it was up to Squire Tattersall to have his horse collected. She had no intention of facing him again.

★ ★ ★

It was mid-afternoon by the time Daisy arrived at Creek Hall. Having left the squire's horse in Billy's capable hands, she made her way to the kitchen where Mrs Bee plied her with cups of tea and biscuits, still warm from the oven. Judy claimed that these were all her own work and Daisy sampled one, declaring it to be delicious. Puffing out her chest, Judy wrapped two of the biscuits in a piece of butter muslin.

'Will you take these to Ma, please, Daisy? Tell her that I made them all by myself.' Judy shot a wary glance at Dove. 'I did, didn't I?'

Dove smiled cheerfully. 'You did the hard work, Judy. You'll be a very good cook one day.'

'And you're never too young to learn.' Mrs Bee ruffled Judy's fair hair, which Daisy noticed had been washed and brushed until it shone like silk. In fact all the children had been bathed and their clothes were clean and neatly ironed, and despite the enforced separation from their mother, they seemed happy. Molly had drawn a picture of a butterfly, which she added to her sister's offering, while Pip and Nate sat cross-legged on the floor, munching biscuits and dropping crumbs everywhere.

Mrs Bee filled Daisy's teacup for the second time. 'So did you accomplish what you'd set out to do, miss?'

'Unfortunately I didn't have the chance to speak to the squire,' Daisy said evasively. She had no intention of telling Dove that her brother had fled the country, and had no intention of returning. 'I'll have to try again.'

'I saw you come riding into the stable yard.' Dove eyed her curiously. 'I don't recognise that horse. It looks like a proper thoroughbred, although I'm no expert.'

'It's on loan. The owner will send someone to collect it today or tomorrow.'

'It just seems a little strange that you had to borrow someone's horse when Billy could have brought you home.' Mrs Bee and Dove exchanged meaningful glances.

'I really must go now.' Daisy rose to her feet. Any further explanation would involve Jay and she was not very good at lying. 'I'll have to

284

return to London later today. I'll take the gifts to your mum, Judy, and I'll tell her how good you are all being.'

'Will you ask her to get better quickly?' Judy's eyes filled with tears. 'Perhaps she can come here when she's well enough. I want to show her the garden and everything.'

'We'll have to see.' Daisy knew it was an unsatisfactory answer, but bringing children to Creek Hall in an emergency was one thing — whether Nick would take their mother in was another matter. Hilda was bound to have her own ideas on what she considered to be proper. 'Goodbye. I'll come again when I have time off from the hospital.'

Mrs Bee saw her to the door. 'Is everything all right, miss? You look worried.'

'I'm just tired, Mrs Bee. I'm not used to all this exercise and east coast air is so bracing.'

'Get some rest, dear. And give my love to the doctor when you see him next. Tell him he's sadly missed.' She stood in the doorway, waving each time Daisy turned her head. She knew she had not satisfied Mrs Bee's curiosity, but leaving her wondering was better than telling her exactly what had happened that day. Daisy trudged home, each step an effort. Somehow the prospect of returning to London next day was not as exciting as perhaps it ought to be.

* * *

The scent of wood smoke mingled with the fruity smell of damp river mud and leaf mould

285

as Daisy approached Creek Cottage. Her heart sank when she saw a carriage outside the house and she recognised the footman, who was chatting to the coachman. She had barely reached the front door when it opened and Squire Tattersall greeted her with a false smile.

'This is fortunate indeed, Mrs Marshall,' he said, turning to Eleanora. 'Just as I was about to leave, the young lady in question walks up the path. Come in, my dear. I want to have a word with you.'

Eleanora stood by the parlour door, clasping her hands to her bosom. 'The squire has come to call on you, Daisy,' she said pointedly.

'I'd like a few words with your niece in private, if you don't mind, Mrs Marshall.' Tattersall fixed Daisy with a hard stare. 'We have some business to discuss.'

'Oh! I — well, I never did. I mean it's not right for a young lady to be alone with a gentleman. Daisy has her reputation to consider, Squire.'

'A few minutes, Mrs Marshall. I am a magistrate, a man of the law, so I doubt if anyone, even the vicar's wife, would find that unreasonable.'

Daisy could see that her aunt was at a loss for words and she stepped over the threshold, closing the door to escape the prying eyes of the squire's servants. 'It's all right, Aunt. As the squire said, it will be a very brief conversation.' She pushed past him, giving her aunt an encouraging smile as she entered the parlour.

Tattersall strode in after her and slammed the

286

door. 'Now then, Miss Marshall. Explain yourself.'

Daisy faced him, her head held high. 'If you want your horse, it's being cared for at Creek Hall.'

'That animal cost me fifty guineas.'

'I can assure you that the animal is being well looked after.'

'More to the point, where is that Fox fellow? Is he your lover?'

'How dare you suggest such a thing?' Daisy said angrily. 'I won't allow you to speak to me like that in my own home.'

'It won't be your home for much longer if you continue to behave like this.'

'You are the one at fault here, Squire Tattersall. Your argument is with your son. I can't help you there.'

'His mother was a temptress, and he's a bastard with no claim on my estate.'

'His mother must have been very young when you seduced her. You are the one who ought to be ashamed.'

'She was pleased enough to oblige me and I saw to it that she left with enough money to rid herself of the child. It was her choice to keep him.'

Daisy stared at him in disgust. 'As far as I can see you've done nothing for Jay other than send him to prison for some minor offence, and now you want to make his mother suffer even more. What sort of man are you?'

'They were both taken care of when she married that psalm-singing gamekeeper, no

287

doubt using my money as a dowry.'

'Then you can't be certain that Jay is your son.'

'He was supposed to be a seven-month baby, but I know better. Anyway, this has nothing to do with you. You've twisted the conversation round to make me out to be the villain of the piece, when I am the one who has been wronged.'

'You've turned Jay into a fugitive and you've threatened his family, and mine. How dare you stand there and say that you've been badly treated?'

He threw back his head and laughed. 'You really are a woman after my own heart.' His expression darkened. 'But you use your beauty to torment a man, and then you walk away. I offered you marriage and you refused. You've hurt and humiliated me, so why should I not do the same to you?'

'Because that's just the way you are, Squire. For one thing I hardly know you, and what I have learned about you doesn't bode well.'

'Then you need to get to know me better, my dear.' Tattersall moved a little closer. 'I could say I was smitten by your undoubted charms, but I can see you would be hard to convince.'

'You are right in that, sir. You've never once mentioned love or even affection, and you have no respect for anyone's feelings other than your own. You seem to think you can use your wealth and position to get whatever you desire. Well, sir, it isn't so. I wouldn't marry you if you were literally the last man on earth.'

There was a moment of complete silence. Daisy held her breath, waiting for the storm to break over her head, but to her surprise the squire shrugged and opened the door.

'Come in, Mrs Marshall. I have no doubt that you were standing outside with your ear to the keyhole.'

Eleanora fluttered into the room, her cheeks suspiciously pink. 'I did no such thing, sir. But you were shouting so loudly that I'm sure that you could be heard in the kitchen.'

'The squire was just leaving, Aunt,' Daisy said firmly. 'We have nothing more to say to each other.'

Esmond Tattersall picked up his top hat, cane and gloves. 'There's one thing you'll learn about me, Miss Marshall. I never give up. If I want something badly enough I will persevere until I win.' He sauntered out of the room, leaving Daisy and her aunt staring at each other. They both jumped at the sound of the front door being slammed with some force.

'Oh, my goodness!' Eleanora sank down on the nearest chair. 'My heart is beating so fast I can hardly breathe. What was all that about, Daisy?'

'I thought you had heard most of it, Aunt.'

'Not everything, dear.'

'Well, you mustn't worry. The squire is all bluff and hot air.'

'It didn't sound like that, Daisy. What will we do if he refuses to renew the lease? We'll be homeless.'

'I think Uncle Sidney ought to consult a

solicitor to see if anything can be done, but I have to return to London today. I promised Sister Johnson that I would only take two days off.'

'Really, Daisy? Do you have to do this? Why can't you remain at home until you meet some nice young man and get married, like any other well-brought-up young lady?'

Daisy leaned over to kiss her aunt's soft cheek. 'Because I want to be useful, and I don't intend to marry for money. Squire Tattersall thinks he can do what he likes and get away with it — well, it's time he learned that's not the case. He only wants me because I'm a challenge.'

'I suppose you're right, but money and position can make life a lot more comfortable, my dear girl.'

'I'll bear that in mind,' Daisy said, smiling.

'Will you stay for luncheon at least? I know Hattie has made a rabbit pie especially for you.'

'Yes, of course I will, but first there's something I have to do. I have an urgent errand in the village.'

★　★　★

Daisy had seen her uncle and Lemuel walking downstream with their fishing gear so she knew this was as good a time as any to find Mary on her own. Daisy's last meeting with Jay's mother had gone badly, but this time she hoped they might have a more honest conversation. She quickened her pace and arrived at the cottage just as Mary was about to leave.

'Might I have a minute or two of your time, Mrs Fox?'

Mary glanced up and down the lane, as if expecting her husband to appear. She nodded reluctantly. 'I have a cleaning job at the church, so I can't stay long.'

Daisy followed her into the cottage. 'I'm leaving for London this afternoon, but I needed to speak to you.'

'If it's about Jay, I don't want to know.'

'It does concern him, and you, too. He went to see the squire.'

Mary's cheeks paled to ashen and she sat down as if her knees had given way beneath her. 'Why would he do a thing like that?'

'He was trying to make things better for you, but I'm afraid it had the opposite effect. The squire told him everything.'

'Everything?'

'Jay knows that Lemuel isn't his father. Squire Tattersall said that you and he were lovers and that he is the father of your eldest child.'

Mary's blue eyes, so like those of her son, filled with tears. 'We were not lovers. I was a chambermaid at the manor house and he forced himself on me, not once but several times. I was too frightened to tell anyone.'

'And then you discovered that you were in the family way.'

'I told him and he called me a whore. He said I couldn't prove that he was the father, but then I grew desperate and threatened to tell his father, who was an old man with failing health.'

'He said he gave you money.'

291

'He wanted me to get rid of the baby, but I had been walking out with Lemuel for quite a while, and when he asked me to marry him I saw a way out.' Mary buried her face in her apron and her thin shoulders shook. 'I was desperate.'

'I can understand that,' Daisy said gently. 'So you didn't tell Lemuel.'

Mary raised her head to look Daisy in the eye. 'I didn't have the courage to admit what I'd done. I let him think that he was the father, but when Jay was born it was obvious that he wasn't a seven-month baby and I'd lied.'

'What happened then, Mary?'

'Lemuel was furious. He dragged me from my bed and beat me until I was almost unconscious, and I feared he was going to kill my child. I pleaded with him and he stormed out of the cottage. He didn't return for two days and when he came back he was a different man. The Lemuel I knew had gone for ever, and I found I was married to a stranger. He said he would acknowledge the baby as his son, but my beautiful little boy was the spawn of the devil and must be treated as such. It's broken my heart to see Jay treated so badly, but there was nothing I could do about it.'

'How can you live with a man like Lemuel?'

'What else could I do? I had no family to support me and a baby to bring up. As time went by I had my other children to feed, although I lost three babies to diphtheria, but I had to protect my girls and Jack. We all have to live with the consequences of our actions, Daisy. I just wish I had had the courage to tell Jay the truth before the squire filled his head with poison.'

Daisy put her arms around Mary and gave her a hug. 'Jay loves you, and he wouldn't hear a word against you. Of that I'm certain.'

'How do you know all this?' Mary wiped her eyes on her apron. 'When did you see my boy?'

Daisy pulled up a chair and sat down beside her.

' . . . So you see,' she said when she had finished relating the events of earlier that day, 'Jay refused to believe that you were in any way to blame. One of the last things he said to me was that he loved you and always will. That won't change.'

'He loves you, too,' Mary said slowly. 'Do you love him?'

'All I know is that I care for him deeply. I want him to be safe and happy. Maybe that's love, but I let him go. Maybe that was a mistake.'

Mary patted her hand. 'You're a good girl, Daisy. Follow your heart.'

★   ★   ★

It was early evening by the time Daisy arrived at Mrs Wood's lodging house. Aggie answered the door and her plain face broke into a smile when she saw Daisy.

'It's good to see you, miss. I thought you wasn't coming back.'

'I told Miss Cole that I was only going to be two days.'

'It were that Gladys, miss. She told her ma that you'd gone for good, but Miss Cole insisted that you was coming back.' She held her hand out to take Daisy's small valise. 'I'll carry it upstairs for you. I'm afraid you're too late for supper. It were terrible anyway. The lady lodgers are in the parlour.'

Aggie headed for the staircase and bounded up it like a gazelle, narrowly avoiding a collision with the two dancers as they thundered downstairs, their capes flying and their high-pitched laughter echoing round the entrance hall.

'We're late, as usual.' The girl with the red hair brushed past Daisy, leaving a waft of cheap scent in her wake.

'Good evening.' Daisy stepped out of the way.

'Is it, love?' The younger of the two rolled her eyes. 'We sleep all day and come out when it's dark. We're like them creepy things what fly around and get tangled in your hair.'

'Bats.' The redhead propelled her friend towards the front door.

'I ain't bats, Flossie. Don't say such things.'

'I never said you was, you stupid cow, Ethel. Bats fly around at night — don't you know nothing? Anyway, we'll have more problems than a few flying creatures if we mess up our routine like we did at rehearsal.' She reached out to open the front door and shoved a grumbling Ethel out into the gathering gloom.

Slightly breathless after this whirlwind encounter, Daisy took off her cape and hung it on the hall stand before heading to the parlour, where she found the cat, Rex, ensconced on the sofa like an eastern potentate with his harem consigned to less comfortable seats. Minnie and Ivy shared a chair and the two older ladies sat at the tea table in the window, playing cards.

Ivy looked up and smiled. 'So you've come back.'

'Are the children all right?' Minnie asked anxiously.

'They seem to have settled in well, and they have two of the kindest people I know taking care of them.' Daisy glanced hopefully at the space beside Rex, but he was staring at her with a hostile look in his yellow eyes, and it was obvious that none of the others had dared to challenge his supremacy. She was about to pull up a chair when the door opened and Flora peered into the room.

'Oh, there you are, Daisy. I wasn't sure if you'd returned. There's a handsome fellow at the door who says he's your brother?'

'Toby! Did you ask him in?'

Flora shrugged. 'It would be more than my life's worth, darling. You know the rules.'

'I hope you didn't send him away.' Daisy pushed past her and flew across the hall to wrench the door open. 'Toby!' She could have cried with relief when she saw him standing on the pavement. His look of bafflement was replaced by a broad grin.

'What's going on, Daisy? I had the door slammed in my face.'

'Mrs Wood doesn't allow gentlemen callers, so I can't ask you in.'

'Never mind that. Have you eaten? Because I'm starving and I was going to the pie and eel shop when I suddenly thought of you.'

'I'm not sure how to take that,' Daisy said, giggling. 'Just give me a minute and I'll fetch my cape. I've only just arrived back from Little Creek.' She closed the door and when she opened it again she was dressed for outdoors.

Toby proffered his arm. 'I wondered why I didn't see you on the wards. What possessed you to take time off to go home? Is anyone ill or dying?'

'Let's eat first. I didn't realise how hungry I was until you mentioned eel pie.'

'I know just the place.'

★ ★ ★

Later, replete after eating eel pie and mash, served with the tasty liquor, Daisy related the latest events to take place at Little Creek. Toby listened in silence, shaking his head when she came to the way the squire had treated her.

'He's a tyrant, Daisy. Well done for standing up to him.' He gave her a speculative look. 'But what about Jay? Are you in love with the fellow?'

'I don't know. Honestly, Toby, my feelings are so confused. When he's away I can be rational and sensible, but when I'm with him it's quite different.'

'Best avoided then, if you ask me.' Toby leaned back against the steamy wall. 'I always thought you and Nick might make a go of it.'

She smiled. 'Did you now? I didn't think you were interested in anything unless it concerned you personally.'

'I'm hurt, Daisy. You know I love you, even if I don't always show my feelings.'

'Of course I do, and the feeling is mutual. But one thing has become clear to me, and that is I need to prove to myself that I can do something worthwhile. I'd become used to the idea that the only future for me was as someone's wife. Julian put paid to that when he decided that marriage wasn't for him, at least not with me.'

'I'm sorry.' Toby reached out to lay his hand on her arm. 'But he wasn't worthy of you. I never liked the chap.'

'It seems like another life,' Daisy said, sighing. 'But one thing is for certain, Toby. I am going to concentrate on learning everything I can about nursing.'

'It's a pity that women like you aren't allowed to study medicine. You'd make a good doctor. If I've managed to qualify you most certainly could.'

'I have to prove to Sister Johnson that I'm capable of qualifying as a nurse, and I'll have to work twice as hard to make up for taking time off, but it was important to get Hilda's children settled into a caring home.'

'The poor woman's troubles aren't over yet, I'm afraid. The surgeon in charge is keeping a close eye on her. If the wound doesn't show signs of healing soon it will mean amputation.'

'That's terrible news.' Daisy stared into her empty teacup. 'How will she support her children? If she can't find some sort of employment it will mean the workhouse for the whole family.'

'Daisy, you can't take the woes of the whole world on your shoulders. I'm afraid that's one thing you'll learn when you work in a hospital. There's suffering all around, but you can only do your best.'

She managed a weak smile. 'I'll bear that in mind.'

'Enough of sad talk. If we hurry we will just catch the show at the Pavilion. What do you say to an evening's entertainment, Daisy?'

18

After the show Daisy and Toby strolled back to Fieldgate Street, arms linked and in perfect harmony with each other. It was dark now, but there was a hint of approaching summer in the air, and the cold winds and April showers were fading into a distant memory. Daisy was feeling at peace with the world until they reached Fieldgate Street, where she saw Ivy struggling to free herself from Jonah Sawkins' clumsy attempts at an embrace. Daisy broke into a run.

'Let her go,' she cried angrily.

'Mind your own business, Miss High and Mighty.' Jonah attempted to drag Ivy away but she was doing her best to fight free.

Toby strode up to them. 'Don't speak to my sister like that, Sawkins.'

'You ain't nothing to me now, Master Toby.' Jonah tightened his hold on Ivy. 'I remember when you was a snotty-nosed nipper.'

'Let me go,' Ivy pleaded. 'I told you I wasn't having any of it, Jonah, but you wouldn't listen.'

'You heard the lady.' Toby moved closer, hands fisted. 'Let her go or I might forget that you're a cripple and sock you on the jaw.'

'You just try it.' Jonah released Ivy so suddenly that she stumbled and fell against Daisy. He made vague punching motions in Toby's direction.

'On second thoughts, you're not worth the

trouble.' Toby turned away. 'Get back to the hole you crawled out of, Sawkins, and don't bother this young lady again.'

'Young she may be, but she ain't no lady.' Jonah spat on the ground at Ivy's feet and sidled off towards Whitechapel Road.

Daisy slipped her arm around Ivy's shoulders. 'Are you all right? You're trembling. Did he hurt you?'

'He tried to put his hand up my skirt,' Ivy whispered. 'He called me a whore and said I owed him a favour for all the drinks he'd bought me. But I only had a glass of cider and I told him I don't like public houses, but he insisted on taking me to one.'

'I wish I had thrashed him,' Toby said angrily. 'It's time someone put that little worm in his place.'

'Forget him, Toby.' Daisy guided Ivy to the front door and knocked. 'I'll look after Ivy. Thanks for the meal and the show. It'll be my treat next time.'

'I'll hold you to that,' Toby said, grinning. 'Maybe we could all go out on Sunday. I'm not on duty and the weather is improving. How about a trip to Victoria Park and a spot of tea?'

'That would be lovely, Dr Marshall.' Ivy spoke before Daisy had a chance to answer.

'It's Toby, and it would be my pleasure,' Toby said, doffing his hat. 'Good night, ladies. I'll see you on Sunday. Maybe we can persuade Nick to join us. You'd like that, wouldn't you, Daisy?'

'Yes, of course, but I'll have to check whether or not I'm on duty that afternoon.'

Toby kissed her on the cheek and strolled off, whistling a tune from the show.

Daisy smiled and shook her head. Toby would never change. He would always be a boy at heart, despite the responsible position he held, and that was part of his charm. She stood back as the door opened and Ivy pushed past Aggie, who stared at her in astonishment.

'What's got into her? Miss Price is usually so polite and nice.'

'She's had a bit of a fright, but a cup of tea would go down well, if you'd be so kind, Aggie.' Daisy stepped inside and closed the door. She did not think that Jonah would return, but there was no telling with someone like him.

'Cook's been at the sherry and she's asleep with her cap over one eye, so she won't know what I'm doing. I was going to make some cocoa for meself — perhaps Miss Price would prefer that.'

'I'm sure she would. Thank you, Aggie.'

'Perhaps you'd like some too, miss. You always speak to me like I was worth something, whereas the others treat me like I was a nobody.'

'You are someone to be reckoned with, Aggie. We all depend on you for so many things.'

Aggie stared at her blankly. 'I dunno what, miss.'

'Well, for one thing, you warn us when Gladys has been making mischief, and you never grumble if we ask you to do anything. I haven't been here long, but already I rely on you.'

Aggie seemed to grow an inch or two in front of Daisy's eyes. She puffed out her chest and smiled. 'I'm somebody now.'

'You always were,' Daisy said, smiling. 'And now I'd better go and make sure Ivy is all right.' Stopping first to hang her cape and bonnet on the hall stand, Daisy made her way to the parlour where she found Ivy relating the events of the evening in great detail to Minnie.

'Well, you are a muggins,' Minnie said casually. 'What did you expect from a fellow like that? It's obvious he's after one thing only, but you couldn't see it. Anyway, he's as ugly as sin. I wouldn't go out with him even if he had lots of money.'

'I felt sorry for him.' Ivy's bottom lip trembled. 'And I'm not pretty like you and Daisy.' She brightened suddenly. 'But Dr Marshall is taking us to Victoria Park on Sunday, so he must think I'm all right.'

Minnie sent an enquiring look to Daisy. 'Your brother asked her out?'

'Toby volunteered to take both of us for a stroll in Victoria Park.' Daisy lowered her voice as Aggie bustled in with a tray of steaming cocoa. 'I think he was sorry for Ivy. She did have a nasty experience tonight.'

'Maybe I should endure something similar and Dr Marshall would ask me out. He's so good-looking, all the probationer nurses are in love with him.'

'Really?' Daisy stared at her in surprise. 'I thought you had a rich gentleman friend.'

Minnie shrugged. 'He was only interested in one thing, Daisy. I told him I wasn't that sort of girl and he bowed politely and walked away. I won't be seeing him again.'

'Then perhaps you'd like to come with us on Sunday?'

'Yes, indeed. I'll make sure I'm not on the roster.'

★   ★   ★

Daisy had been on duty since very early on Sunday morning, but she had managed to get the afternoon off. She had arranged to meet the others in the park, although it was never possible to guarantee that she would get away on time. It was just as well she had not asked Minnie to wait for her as there had been two emergency admissions and, as usual, the cleaning up fell to the probationer nurse. Daisy was getting accustomed to mopping up all kinds of things that in the past would have made her retreat hastily. Matron was a stickler for disinfectant and Daisy's hands were reddened and sore from contact with harsh soap and hot water. The smell of carbolic clung to everything, including her clothes and hair.

Even though she was in a hurry to leave she made time to visit Hilda on the ward, and she answered all the questions that the anxious mother had thought up since their last conversation. Although Daisy had described Creek Hall and its grounds in detail, and the area of marshland with its abundance of wildlife, Hilda wanted to hear it all again. She had been born and raised in the East End and she knew nothing of the countryside and had never seen the sea. She listened enthralled as if Daisy was telling her a tale from *The Arabian Nights*, and of course she wanted to know how each of her four children was coping with her absence. Daisy was careful to stress that they were happy and well cared for, but naturally they missed their mother and were waiting eagerly for Hilda to return to them.

Finally off duty, Daisy put on her bonnet and fastened the ribbons under her chin. She checked her appearance in the small cracked mirror that one of the nurses had hidden in the china cupboard and left the changing room, exchanging cheery words with the porter who was on duty in the reception area. She stepped outside the main doors and came face to face with someone she had thought never to see again.

'Julian!'

'I've been waiting here for over an hour, Daisy. I couldn't believe it when that crippled fellow told me that you were working here as a menial.'

'You went to the shop?'

'How else was I supposed to find you?'

'I gave Jonah strict instructions not to reveal my whereabouts to you or anyone in your family. I suppose this was his way of getting back at me.'

'I don't understand.'

'Why would I want to see you again after the way you treated me, Julian? If you've come to apologise, you've left it too late.' Daisy was about to walk away but he caught her by the wrist.

'I know I behaved badly. I am truly sorry.'

304

Julian's handsome face was a mask of contrition. 'I suppose I panicked — it was all too much for me.'

'What do you mean by that?' Daisy demanded angrily.

'I knew my parents would object to our engagement, and I was afraid that our union might jeopardise my prospects in the diplomatic service. I know it was wrong as well as stupid, but that's how I felt.'

She met his desperate gaze and was surprised to realise that she felt nothing for him, not even pity. 'I was very hurt at the time, but I've changed, too. I know what I want to do in life and it doesn't involve you. I don't want to see you again, Julian.'

He released her and took a step backwards, staring at her in disbelief. 'You don't mean that?'

'Yes, I do.'

'But you love me. We were going to be married.'

'You were the one who finished with me, Julian. You didn't even have the decency to tell me to my face.'

'I wrote you a letter, didn't I? I practically grovelled.'

'If that's what you call it.' Daisy made an attempt to walk past him but he barred her way.

'Is there someone else? My mother said you were a scheming minx.'

'Please get out of my way. I have to be somewhere.'

'You're meeting a gentleman friend. Is he richer than me?'

'Don't be ridiculous. What I do is none of your business.'

'Then return the ring I bought you. It cost me all the money I had at the time.'

'Gladly, but I don't have it on me. I'll send it to you at Queen Square.'

'No, don't do that. I don't want Mama and Papa to find out that I've seen you again.'

'So nothing has really changed, has it, Julian? You're still a little boy afraid to stand up to your parents. What do you think would have happened had I fallen into your arms and agreed to marry you now?'

'You would have given me courage, Daisy.' Julian's lips trembled and he dropped his gaze. 'You have more strength of character than I have. I admit that humbly and freely. I need you, Daisy.'

'I'll leave the ring with Jonah Sawkins, but you'd better collect it quickly or he'll have taken it to the nearest pawnshop. I'm meeting my friends, so I can't stay here and talk, but I wish you good fortune, Julian. Goodbye.' Daisy raised her hand to hail a cab. She had intended to walk, but it was a long way and she was tired. Ignoring Julian's pleas for her to stay and talk, she climbed into the hansom cab. 'Victoria Park, please, cabby.'

The unexpected encounter with Julian had upset her more than she cared to admit, even to herself. He had been her first love and the life they had planned together had seemed perfect, but she knew now how wrong she had been. She had taken Julian at face value and might have married him in total ignorance of the fact that he was selfish and shallow, only to discover his faults when it was too late. But she had loved him, and the pain he had caused her was not yet forgotten, although she had buried it deep within her heart. Perhaps the scars would remain, but she had said her piece and as far as she was concerned that was the end of a sad affair.

It was good to see smiling faces when she found Toby and the girls in the tearoom in the park, and Nick was with them. He rose from his seat and pulled up a chair for her.

'We didn't think you were coming, Daisy.'

'I was delayed at the hospital,' Daisy said truthfully.

'I suppose you were chatting to Hilda.' Minnie reached for the teapot and filled a cup, which she passed to Daisy. 'You look pale, love. Have a cup of tea and a currant bun. Ivy's eaten two, but then she's a little piggy.'

'I am not,' Ivy protested, giggling. 'I didn't have any dinner.'

'Have as many cakes are you like, Ivy,' Toby said cheerfully. 'My rich friend the Harley Street specialist is treating us.'

'My pleasure.' Nick smiled as he laid some coins on the table before rising to his feet. 'Would you care for a walk by the lake, Daisy?'

She put down her teacup. 'That would be nice. It's such a lovely day and the greenery reminds me of Little Creek.'

'Don't worry about me,' Toby said lazily. 'I'll look after the two ladies. I don't often get the chance to enjoy such charming company.'

Minnie shot him a sideways glance. 'Come now, Doctor. I heard that you're very popular with the nurses.'

'I have heard it said.' Toby leaned across the table, fixing Minnie with his most charming smile. 'And what about you, Nurse Minnie?'

'Probationer nurse,' Minnie said primly. 'I'm not so easily impressed, Doctor. Handsome is as handsome does, so my mama always says.'

Daisy slipped her hand into the crook of Nick's arm as they left the tearoom. 'I think Minnie can hold her own with my brother. Toby won't find her as easy to impress as poor little Ivy.'

'Ivy told me how that fellow Sawkins treated her. I'm glad you don't have to deal with him now.'

'I can handle Jonah.' Daisy fell into step beside him. 'It's such a lovely day, let's talk about something else.'

'Don't change the subject. Toby told me about your encounter with Sawkins. I think you should keep well away from him.'

'I intend to, don't worry.'

He came to a sudden halt as they reached the lake. 'But I do worry about you. I can't help it. I feel responsible for everything that has happened since you tried to help me pay my father's debts.'

She avoided his intense gaze and stared down into the green water where fronds of weed waved as if in a breeze. 'That's ridiculous. It was my idea to trick the squire into believing that I was an heiress, and now I look back on it

I realise how foolish I was.'

'No, I won't have that, Daisy. You went out of your way to help a friend. We are still friends, aren't we?'

The anxious note in his voice made her look up. 'Of course we are. Why would you think differently?'

'The others are coming. Let's walk on before they catch up with us.'

'What's the matter, Nick?' She had to quicken her pace in order to keep up with him. 'There's something on your mind, I can tell.'

'Yes, there is. I don't think Toby broke any confidences when he told me that the squire had proposed to you.'

'I dealt with that. He won't bother me again.'

He shook his head. 'I'm not so sure. Tattersall is a man who hates to be crossed. He won't give up easily.'

'I suppose I should be flattered by his advances, but there's nothing on earth that would persuade me to marry him.'

'I'm glad, but . . . ' he paused. 'But what about Jay?'

'Jay comes and goes as he pleases, but if I choose to be his friend I think that's my business.'

'I'm sorry. I didn't mean to offend you, it's just that I care about you, Daisy, and I'm stuck in Harley Street until I've saved enough to pay off Tattersall, but Jay isn't for you. Please believe me. I grew up with him and I know him all too well.'

'What do you mean by that?'

'He's wild and he thinks only of himself. He doesn't seem to care that he's upset his entire family.'

'You don't know then,' Daisy said slowly. 'Didn't you ever suspect that there was something strange about the way Jay's father treated him?'

'I thought it odd, but then people are strange. Perhaps Lemuel was jealous of the affection his wife showed the child.'

'Or maybe it's because he isn't Jay's natural father.' Daisy had the satisfaction of seeing Nick's expression change from one of disbelief to consternation. 'Mrs Fox was a servant in the squire's house when she was very young,' she added pointedly. 'Do I have to spell it out for you?'

'Are you saying that Squire Tattersall is Jay's father?'

'Yes, I am, and it came from the squire himself.'

'How do you know this?'

'Jay was at Creek Hall when I arrived with Hilda's children. He'd heard that his parents were about to lose their home, and he was furious. I was afraid he would do something rash so I went to see Mrs Fox, but she wouldn't tell me anything.'

'You should leave that family to sort out their own problems.'

'Is that all you can say? Lemuel Fox worked for your father for years and now he's fallen on hard times, made even harder by the squire's vindictive treatment.'

'You can't take that man on, Daisy. He's too rich and powerful.'

'I know that all too well. He's still holding the threat of eviction over my aunt and uncle, and I decided that it was time I stood up for the people who were too afraid to speak for themselves. I persuaded Billy to drive me to Creek Manor.'

'I'll have words to say to that boy when I go home.'

'Billy didn't have much choice. Anyway, when I arrived at the manor house I was too late. Jay had already spoken to the squire, and Jay left in a fury after a terrible row. He stole the squire's favourite horse, and I arrived in time to see him being pursued by a small army of estate workers and grooms.'

'I hope you told Billy to take you home.'

'Everything happened so quickly. Jay took me on the horse and it was a wild ride, ending up at the cove where the *Lazy Jane* was moored.'

'So Jay ran away to sea, leaving you to sort out the tangled web of lies and deceit that had been built up around him. How typical.'

'It's easy for you to stand there and criticise his actions. You know who you are and everyone loved and respected your father. How dare you set yourself up in judgement against someone who was supposed to be your friend?'

'Don't let Jay fool you into thinking he cares about you, Daisy. He's selfish, as I said before, and if you allow yourself to fall for him he'll ruin your life.'

'I'm disappointed in you, Nick. I thought you

311

would be more loyal and understanding.'

'I'm just trying to protect you, Daisy.'

'I can look after myself and I don't need you to act as my conscience.' Daisy turned away at the sound of voices. 'Here come the others. Don't spoil their day out. Try to look as if you're enjoying yourself.' She greeted them with an attempt at a smile.

'You two look serious,' Toby said cheerfully. 'We can't have that. This is our afternoon off and we won't get another for heaven knows how long. Let's do a couple of turns of the lake and maybe take a boat out, and I'll treat us all to ice cream.'

Daisy silenced Nick with a warning look. 'That sounds lovely.'

The rest of the afternoon passed off pleasantly enough, but Daisy was still angry with Nick and he treated her with a hint of reserve. Their argument over Jay had left her feeling ill at ease in Nick's company. Perhaps she did not know him as well as she had thought, but at least it had had the effect of taking her mind off Julian's sudden reappearance, albeit temporarily.

When Daisy returned to the lodging house she left Minnie and Ivy heading for the parlour, still chatting about the lovely time they had had in 'Vicky Park' and giggling like a pair of schoolgirls. Daisy made an excuse of needing to change her shoes and she went straight to her room, where she unlocked her jewel case and took out Julian's ring. The diamond sparkled in the early evening sunlight that filtered through the haze of city grime and bird droppings on the windowpanes. It was a pretty thing and the most expensive piece of jewellery she had ever possessed, but it held no sentimental value now. She wrapped it in a handkerchief and tucked it into her reticule. Tomorrow morning, first thing, she would take it to the shop and leave it with Jonah, making him promise to keep it for Julian Carrington. Ordinarily she would not have entrusted him with anything of value, but she knew Jonah well enough to be certain that he would not do anything to offend a possible client, and if there was one thing that Jonah Sawkins respected it was money and the Carrington name.

Daisy sat on her bed and sorted through the textbooks that Sister Johnson had given her. Her unexpected falling out with Nick had upset her more than she had imagined possible, but, if anything, it had made her even more determined to follow a career in medicine. The men in her life all seemed to have feet of clay, and at the first sign of trouble they crumbled to dust before her eyes. Nick's possessive attitude was the biggest disappointment of all. She selected a book on general ward hygiene and skimmed through the index, but the silence in the room was unnerving. It was oddly quiet without Minnie's constant chatter, but she was probably relating the events of the afternoon to anyone who was prepared to listen. On the way home Minnie and Ivy had been making plans for another such Sunday outing, and Daisy suspected that they were both sweet on Toby. She sighed and turned back to her selected book.

Next morning Daisy was assigned to the outpatient department. She was sent to fetch the patients and take them to the appropriate cubicles where the doctor examined them while she stood by ready to assist. The clinic had gone smoothly enough and she went to find the last person in the waiting area, but it was Nick who rose to his feet, clutching a large bunch of violets.

'Are you ill?' Daisy asked warily.

'No, I came to apologise for my behaviour yesterday. I realise it was unforgiveable, Daisy. You are your own woman and I am a clumsy fellow who can't put his feelings into words.' He held out the flowers. 'Would you accept these with my apologies?'

She could feel everyone staring at them and she hurried him into an empty cubicle. 'There was no need for this, Nick, but the flowers are lovely. Thank you.' She took them from him and buried her face in their soft purple petals, the scent reminded her of the woods near Creek Hall.

'Am I forgiven?'

'Yes, of course. Perhaps I was a bit hasty, but let's forget it, shall we?'

'Gladly. I'll try to curb my tongue in future.'

She smiled. 'I think you might find that rather difficult.'

'I'm going to be very busy for the next two or three weeks, but perhaps we could go to the theatre some time, or I could take you to dinner.'

'I'd like that, but I intend to spend much of my spare time studying. I want to get my qualifications as soon as possible.'

'I have to go now, Daisy. I put off a very wealthy patient to come here and I'll be in trouble with my employer if I don't get back within the hour.' He kissed her briefly on the cheek. 'I'll see you very soon.'

'I hope so, Nick.' She opened the curtains and stood for a moment, watching him as he walked purposefully towards the main doors. She sniffed the violets again and their scent was intoxicating. She found a small glass and filled it with water, arranging the flowers carefully to show them off at their best, but the sound of Sister Johnson bellowing her name brought her back to the present. She left the violets on a shelf and went to answer her superior's summons.

Later, when she was allowed to take a break for lunch, Daisy retrieved the flowers and took them to Hilda, who seemed to have been improving slowly, but Daisy was concerned to find her lying down with her face to the wall.

'What's the matter? Are you in pain?' Daisy placed the violets on the bedside locker.

Hilda turned a tear-stained face to her. 'They say I got to have me leg amputated. It's not healing properly.'

19

Daisy clutched Hilda's hand. 'I'm so sorry, Hilda, but if the doctors say that, you know it must be for the best, hard as it might seem.'

'But how will I earn me living? I'll be a cripple and me and the nippers will have no choice but to go to the workhouse.'

'I won't allow that to happen,' Daisy said firmly. 'The children are safe and happy in the country, and when you're well enough to travel I'm sure we can arrange for you to join them.'

Hilda shook her head, tears spilling down her cheeks. 'But what then? Who's going to support us, and what work can a one-legged woman do?'

'Please don't upset yourself, Hilda.' Daisy leaned over to brush a lock of hair from Hilda's damp forehead. 'Everything will be all right, I promise you that. We'll find a way somehow.'

She looked round to see Minnie approaching followed by a more senior nurse.

'Good afternoon, Mrs Begg. I've come to give you something to calm your nerves,' Minnie said with a bright smile. She shot a wary look at her superior.

'Help the patient to a sitting position, Nurse. You can't pour the medication down her throat while she's supine.' The senior nurse's fingers twitched impatiently.

'I'll help you, Nurse Cole,' Daisy said hastily, and together they managed to get Hilda propped up on the pillow and able to drink the mixture.

She pulled a face. 'That tastes blooming horrible.'

'We'll be taking you to theatre in a few minutes,' Minnie said gently. 'You mustn't worry, Hilda, you're in good hands.'

'There's no time to chat, Nurse Cole.'

The senior nurse marched off with Minnie following at a slower pace, and Daisy stayed with Hilda until the medicine took effect and her eyes closed.

'I'll try to be here when you come round,' Daisy whispered. 'It will be all right, Hilda. I promise.' But as Daisy left the ward she knew that life for Hilda would be far from easy.

She managed to snatch a brief conversation with Minnie at their afternoon break, and she learned that Hilda's operation had been successful — her right leg having been amputated below the knee. Daisy forgot about food and hurried back to Hilda's ward. She reached her bedside just as Hilda opened her eyes.

'You're going to be fine,' Daisy said gently. 'The operation went well.'

'I can still feel me toes.' Hilda focused her eyes on Daisy's face. 'Did they save me leg?'

'Don't worry about that now.' Daisy looked up as a senior nurse appeared at her side. 'I'm just going, Sister.'

A faint smile creased the older woman's stern features. 'Don't worry, Nurse Marshall. Stay as long as you like. Mrs Begg has come through the operation very satisfactorily.' She walked away to

317

speak to another patient, who was calling for her attention.

Daisy gazed down at Hilda's ashen face. If life had been hard for the Begg family before the tragic accident, it was not going to be any easier in the foreseeable future, but if there was anything that could be done to help them she would do her very best to see that they were not condemned to the dreaded workhouse.

★　★　★

For the next couple of months Daisy concentrated all her efforts on work and study. She saw very little of Nick, and although she bumped into Toby almost daily in the hospital he was working long hours with little time to socialise, much to Minnie's disappointment. Hilda recovered slowly and at the beginning of June she was able to walk with the aid of crutches, but what seemed to terrify her most was the prospect of being discharged from hospital. Daisy tried to visit her daily, and she made an effort to sound hopeful, but quite what Hilda would do was another matter. It was unseasonably hot and the hospital wards were filled to capacity with diseases caused by overcrowding and poverty. Beds were needed desperately and Hilda was due to be discharged, although she still had nowhere to go.

Daisy had thought about asking Mrs Wood if Hilda could stay in Fieldgate Street for a while, but the only rooms as yet unoccupied were on the top floor and Hilda would never be able to negotiate the stairs. The alternative would be, if it were possible, to take her to Creek Hall, where at least she would be well cared for and she would be reunited with her children. Daisy mentioned this to Toby when they met one afternoon in the outpatient department.

'I don't know,' he said, shaking his head. 'Nick's had word from Mrs Bee that there's an outbreak of cholera in the village. I saw him last evening and he told me that he'd given up his position in Harley Street and he was leaving today for Little Creek.'

Daisy stared at him in dismay. 'Cholera! But Dr Snow proved that horrible disease was passed on by contaminated water. Surely that can't be true in the country?'

'I only know what Nick told me, Daisy. He obviously thought it serious enough to go there as a matter of urgency.'

'In that case I need to make sure that Aunt Eleanora and Uncle Sidney are keeping well,' Daisy said anxiously.

'They have Hattie and Linnet to take care of them.' Toby gave her a searching look. 'You aren't thinking of following Nick to Little Creek, are you?'

'It might be a false alarm,' Daisy said slowly. 'Perhaps it's an isolated case. As a matter of fact I was going to ask permission to take Hilda to Creek Hall. The poor woman is desperate to see her children, and terrified that they will all end up in the workhouse.'

'I'm sorry for her, but I don't see what you

can do about it, Daisy.'

'I haven't got a plan, I just feel responsible for her in some way. If Sister Johnson allows me to take Hilda to Creek Hall I could go and see Aunt Eleanora and Uncle Sidney. I'd like to make sure they're all right.'

Toby threw up his hands. 'I know that look, Daisy. You'll go whatever happens. I'm not certain if it's the village you love or the village doctor, but I think you need to find out.'

'You're talking nonsense. I owe it to our aunt and uncle to make sure that they're safe and well, and I do care about the people who live in the village.'

'And what do you say about Nick?'

'He's a friend, and if there is a serious problem he's going to need my help. I've made my mind up, Toby. I'll leave as soon as I can make the necessary arrangements.'

Sister Johnson had not been encouraging when Daisy asked for time off, explaining that she intended to take Hilda Begg to recuperate in the country where she would be with her children. Then, seeing that this argument was getting her nowhere, Daisy mentioned the outbreak of cholera, expressing her concern for her aunt and uncle. Anxiety made her eloquent and Sister Johnson agreed that she could take Mrs Begg to Creek Hall, but if Daisy chose to remain in Essex she would lose her place as a probationer nurse. The prospect brought Daisy close to tears, and as if to prove that she had a heart, Sister Johnson gave Daisy three days' compassionate leave.

With their bags packed and Hilda seated on a chair in the waiting area, Daisy was about to step outside to hail a cab when a familiar carriage pulled up at the main entrance of the hospital. She recognised the coachman and the footman who leaped down from the box to open the door, but it was too late to turn and run. The woman who alighted from the luxurious equipage was none other than Agnes Carrington, who possessed the eyesight of a hawk, and she had spotted Daisy even before her feet touched the ground. She sailed towards her with her full skirts swaying like a bell. She was smartly dressed in a lavender silk gown, and her bonnet was trimmed with pink roses, which matched the spots of colour in her otherwise pale cheeks. Her expression was anything but friendly.

'So, I've caught you, young woman. Mr Sawkins said I would find you waiting for payment.' In a dramatic gesture she tossed a leather pouch at Daisy's feet. 'There are your thirty pieces of silver, you Jezebel.'

'I think it was Judas who received the money, Mrs Carrington. But I really don't know what you're talking about.' Daisy glanced over her shoulder, anxious to see if any of the hospital staff were listening, but to her relief they were all too busy to take any notice.

'You always did act the innocent. I thought that my son was safe from your wiles, but it seems that you won't leave him alone.'

A cold shiver ran down Daisy's spine.

Someone had been telling lies about her, and if it was not Julian, there was only one other person it could be. 'I can't imagine what Jonah Sawkins told you, or how you came to be in contact with that man, but you've obviously been fed a pack of lies.'

'Mr Sawkins brought me the ring that you'd tried to sell him.'

'I did no such thing,' Daisy protested. 'I gave him the ring to pass on to Julian. It was obviously a mistake to trust Jonah, but I wanted nothing more to do with your son and I told him so.'

'That's not the way Mr Sawkins put it, Miss Marshall. He said you'd sent him to Queen Square to beg Julian to see you, and when he refused you instructed Mr Sawkins to sell the ring.'

'That's not how it was, but I can see that whatever I say you'll choose to believe someone like Jonah. Did you think to ask Julian?'

'My son has returned to Paris, thank goodness. He's far away from your scheming, which is why I came here today. Take the money and leave my son alone.'

The temptation to throw the money at Mrs Carrington was almost overwhelming, but Daisy knew that it would do nothing to change her former employer's opinion of her. For reasons best known to himself, Jonah had put the final seal on her involvement with the Carrington family, but she was not going to allow him to win. Instead, she bent down and picked up the purse.

'I will take this, because the ring was mine to sell, had I so wished. Jonah Sawkins was supposed to return it to your son, but I have a purpose for this money and I know where it will do the most good.' Daisy held her head high as she walked to the edge of the kerb where a growler had just dropped off a fare.

'I have a crippled lady I need to take to Bishopsgate Station, Cabby. Would you wait for a few minutes please?'

He tipped his hat and grunted assent, and Daisy retraced her steps, walking past Agnes Carrington without a backward glance. She wanted nothing more to do with that family. Julian had proved himself to be weak and feckless — she was well rid of him. There were more important matters to hand and one of them was Hilda.

★   ★   ★

With Daisy's help and a pair of wooden crutches, Hilda managed to cope with the journey to Little Creek, although it was clear to Daisy that she was in a great deal of pain. Earlier that morning Daisy had sent a telegram to Creek Hall, giving the time of their arrival, and Billy was waiting for them at the station with the horse and trap. Hilda was pale with fatigue and lines of suffering were etched on her face, but she did not complain even when Daisy and Billy had a struggle to get her onto the trap. Not a word passed her lips when the vehicle bounced over the ruts in the country lanes, but her knuckles whitened as she clutched the wooden side rails and she closed her eyes.

Daisy had hoped that Nick might be at home when they finally arrived at Creek Hall, but it was Dove who came hurrying to greet them and Mrs Bee was standing in the doorway with a welcoming smile.

'Where are my babies?' Hilda demanded weakly.

'Judy and Molly are at school in the village,' Dove said in a matter-of-fact voice. 'And the two little ones are taking a nap. Mrs Bee thought it best to keep your arrival a surprise.'

'The girls shouldn't be in school,' Hilda protested. 'They might catch the disease.'

'We're trying to carry on as usual,' Dove said hastily. 'The doctor said it was all right for them to attend classes. Mr Massey, the schoolmaster, is a very capable person and so far none of the children have been taken ill.' Dove hooked one of Hilda's arms around her shoulders. 'Lean on me, Mrs Begg. Billy will take the other side and Daisy will hold your crutches. We'll get you indoors and make you comfortable.'

Daisy followed them into the house. 'Are there many cases of cholera locally, Dove?'

'My father is very ill and Ma is nursing him, but your aunt and uncle are well, and Mrs Marshall said that Jack can stay with them for as long as it takes Pa to recover.'

'Most of those affected live in the cottages owned by the squire,' Mrs Bee said angrily. 'Dr Neville says the creek has been contaminated by overflowing privies. Thankfully our supply comes direct from a spring.'

'Where is the doctor? I need to see him,' Daisy said urgently.

'He's doing his rounds in the village.' Mrs Bee eyed Hilda warily. 'I've put you in one of the downstairs rooms, Mrs Begg. I haven't had time to give it a proper spring clean, but I dare say you'll be comfortable enough.'

Hilda nodded tiredly. 'I'm very grateful to you, I'm sure, but I don't intend to impose on you or the good doctor any longer than necessary.'

'Come and sit down, my dear.' Mrs Bee's tone softened and she ushered Hilda into the kitchen. 'A cup of tea and something to eat will perk you up, and then the little ones will wake up and find their mama here.' She guided Hilda to a chair at the table.

'What will they think when they see me like this?' Hilda's voice shook with suppressed emotion.

'They'll be so delighted to have their ma home they won't even notice,' Mrs Bee said firmly. 'Is that right, Miss Marshall?'

'Yes, indeed.' Daisy gave Hilda an encouraging smile. 'They love you no matter what.'

'Put the kettle on, Dove.' Mrs Bee reached for a knife and began slicing a loaf still warm from the oven. 'Now then, Hilda. We must build you up.' She buttered the bread and finished it off with a large dollop of plum jam.

Daisy could see that Mrs Bee had everything under control and she knew that Hilda was in good hands. Despite Dove's assurances that her aunt and uncle had escaped the dreaded disease,

Daisy wanted to check on them for herself, and it was just possible that she might cross paths with Nick. Work and study had kept them apart even after his apology, and the bunch of violets on Hilda's bedside locker had long since died, but Daisy had kept several of the flowers pressed between the pages of one of her weightier textbooks.

'I'm leaving for a while, Hilda,' Daisy said, backing towards the doorway. 'But I'll come back later to see how you're getting on.'

'Will you be sleeping at Creek Cottage, miss?' Mrs Bee turned to her with a smile. 'I can always make up a bed for you here.'

'Thank you, but I'll stay with my aunt and uncle tonight.' Daisy left before Mrs Bee had a chance to question her further. She really had no idea how long she might spend in Little Creek, although she was prepared to assist Nick in any way possible if he needed her help, but that would be up to him.

She set off through the wood, heading for Creek Cottage, and yet again she found herself wondering at the beauty of nature. The summer foliage was fresh and green and the damp earth smelled rich and plummy, like the best fruitcake. The air was fresh and balmy compared to the city stench she had left behind, and it seemed impossible to imagine that there could be some deadly disease lurking in the bubbling waters of the creek. Even so, as she walked along the river-bank, she could see traces of effluent muddying the water, and unhealthy flotsam. Dr John Snow had traced the Soho cholera epidemic of 1854 to a pump in Broad Street, and she wondered what he would make of the polluted creek. She made up her mind to ask Nick for his opinion, although it seemed unlikely that he would have ignored the state of the water that was used for every purpose in the village.

She grew more and more anxious as she neared Creek Cottage and she quickened her pace to a run. Cholera could strike quickly and when there was no immediate sign of life she convinced herself to expect the worst. Her frantic knocking on the door was answered by a healthy-looking Linnet, who beamed at her in delight.

'Mrs Marshall will be so pleased to see you, and Jack will come home after school. He's been staying here because Pa is sick.'

'Yes, I heard,' Daisy said breathlessly. 'I've just come from Creek Hall, and Dove told me that your father has been taken ill. How is he?'

'I don't know. I haven't been there today. Ma told me to keep away in case I caught the sickness. She said you can get it from the bad air.'

'I don't think that's so, but I'll call in later, if you like.'

'Yes, please, miss. I heard that the doctor is back so I hope he'll have been to see Pa, although I doubt if they can afford to pay him.'

'I don't think that would make any difference. Dr Neville is more concerned for his patients than he is with making a fortune.'

'Daisy? Is that you?' Eleanora emerged from the parlour. 'I thought I heard your voice.' She bustled towards Daisy, enveloping her in a hug. 'You shouldn't have come, dear. There's sickness in the village.'

'I know, Aunt, that's why I'm here. I wanted to make sure that you and Uncle Sidney are all right.'

Eleanora looked past Daisy, frowning. 'You didn't bring any luggage, dear. Does that mean you're not stopping?'

'I had to go to Creek Hall first and I left my valise there. It was too heavy to carry so Billy is going to drop it off for me.'

'So you'll be staying for a while — how lovely. Linnet will bring us tea.' Eleanora hustled Daisy into the parlour. 'I think about you all the time. I wonder how you're getting along and I envy you being back in London. At least I do sometimes, until I remember what it was like in the hot weather and the dreadful smells, and the peasoupers in the winter.' Eleanora took her usual seat by the fireplace, only now there was a vase of flowers on the hearth instead of a coal scuttle.

Daisy stifled a sigh of relief. Everything seemed reassuringly normal. 'London is the same as ever, Aunt.'

'Yes, I suppose so, but what brings you home so unexpectedly?'

'You'll remember that I told you about the poor woman who was so badly injured in the street, and I brought her children to Creek Hall? Anyway, Mrs Begg has been discharged from hospital after having part of her leg amputated, and she wanted to be near her children. I left her

328

with Dove and Mrs Bee to fuss over her. Also I was worried about you and Uncle Sidney. I wanted to make sure you are both well.'

'As you can see, I'm perfectly fine and so is your uncle, although I do wish he'd keep away from that Lemuel Fox. He visits the cottage every day and I'm afraid he'll catch the disease.'

'I'm sure that Dr Neville wouldn't allow it if he thought there was any risk involved.'

'I certainly hope so. Anyway, how long are you staying, dear? I do hope you aren't travelling back tomorrow.'

'I have three days off, thanks to Sister Tutor, but if things are really bad here I might stay on and help Dr Neville.'

'Linnet told me that he'd returned in order to treat the sick. He's such a good man. You could do worse, Daisy. Although I still think you might have given the squire more of a chance. He can't be all bad, especially if he's taken a fancy to you. I mean a good wife might have a positive influence on the man.'

Daisy shook her head. 'If I have anything to say to the squire it will be to tell him what I think of a landlord who allows his tenants to live in squalor. The outbreak of cholera could be laid directly at his feet.'

'I don't know about that, dear.' Eleanora looked up and beamed at Linnet, who arrived with a laden tea tray. 'Hattie must have known you were coming, Daisy. I think that's your favourite cake.'

★　★　★

329

Having listened to her aunt's detailed account of everything that had happened in the village since her previous visit Daisy managed to get away at last, and she set off to check on Lemuel Fox. Not that she liked the man, but his daughters were loyal to him and Daisy felt sorry for Mary, who had suffered first at the hands of the squire, and then years of bullying from the man who was supposed to love and care for her. But first, and even more importantly, Daisy went to the carpenter's workshop, which was a lean-to attached to his cottage. The sound of sawing and hammering led her straight to his door and the smell of sawdust and wood chips filled the air. The door was open and Fred Shipway was finishing off a pine coffin.

He looked up. 'You're that Marshall girl from London, ain't you?'

'Yes, Mr Shipway.'

'Thought so.' He nodded and went back to sanding off the rough edges. 'Can't take too much time over this one,' he added. 'Got several more to make.'

'Has the cholera taken many?' Daisy asked anxiously.

He grinned. 'Good for business, you might say — if the families was able to pay the going rate. As it is I'm barely making anything on each one.'

Daisy did not know how to respond to this. Making a profit from the misery of others seemed wrong, but the carpenter had to live and feed his family, and if she remembered rightly his son Danny was one of Jack's young friends.

'Yes, it's a very difficult time for everyone,' she said tactfully.

He gave her a calculating look. 'Have you come here to watch me work?'

'No. I'm sorry, I should have said at the outset, but I can see that you're very busy.'

'If it ain't a coffin you're after, then what is it?'

'I was wondering if you could help a lady who was crippled by an accident earlier this year.'

'What was you thinking of, miss? I don't make Bath chairs.'

'The lady has had part of her right leg amputated, Mr Shipway. I was wondering if you could fashion a peg leg, which would enable her to become more mobile?'

Fred straightened up, wiping sweat from his brow with the back of his hand. 'Well now, I've been asked to make some strange objects, but never a peg leg.'

'Is it possible?'

'I suppose so, but I'd have to see the lady first and take a look at her injured limb.'

'Mrs Begg is staying at Creek Hall for the time being. Maybe you could visit her when you have a moment.'

A suspicious frown deepened the furrows on his brow. 'It ain't a charity case, is it?'

Daisy opened her reticule and took out the pouch that Mrs Carrington had thrown at her. She had earmarked the money for the sole purpose of helping Hilda and her children, and she took out a half-crown. 'This is a deposit, Mr Shipway.'

'Accepted, Miss Marshall. I'll pay the lady a

visit first thing in the morning, but I can't promise to be quick with the work. Folk are dropping like flies from the sickness and I can barely keep up with orders as it is.'

'There's no hurry.' Daisy dropped the coin into his outstretched hand. 'Her wound needs to heal, but the hope of being able to move reasonably freely in the future will surely help her to recover more quickly.'

'You'd need to ask the doctor about that, miss. He called in less than half an hour ago to tell me that there was another coffin needed.'

'Do you know where he went?'

'He said something about visiting Lemuel Fox, but I told him not to bother. That family is cursed.'

'Why do you say that?' Daisy demanded angrily.

'She brought the wrath of the squire down on the village. If he gets his way Little Creek will be a ghost village.'

Daisy had no answer for this. It seemed that Mary was still suffering from the squire's abuse, and the misfortunes that had befallen her family were considered in some way to be a punishment for her wickedness, when in fact she was the innocent victim.

'I have to go now, Mr Shipway.' Daisy managed to keep an outward display of calm, but as she left the workshop she was inwardly fuming. Squire Tattersall had caused so much misery in his lifetime, and it was possible that the outbreak of cholera could also be laid at the door of the neglectful landlord. Spurred on by anger she set off to find Nick.

She arrived at the Fox family's cottage just as Nick was about to leave. He looked tired and drawn and he blinked dazedly as he stepped out into the sunlight.

'Daisy. What are you doing here?'

'I brought Hilda to be with her children. I hope you don't mind, because she had nowhere else to go.'

He shook his head. 'No, of course not. There's plenty of room at Creek Hall, but you should have stayed in London. Didn't you know there is an outbreak of cholera in this area?'

'Yes, I knew, and that's another reason for coming. I wanted to make sure that my aunt and uncle were all right, and I thought you might need some help. I know I'm not fully qualified but I've learned a lot in the last few months, at least enough to be of some assistance, if only in making beds and general hygiene.'

'I know I'm tired — I've been up all night — but are you telling me that you've given up your place at the hospital?'

'Not exactly. Well, it depends on you, Nick. Have you anyone else to help you?'

'No. It's true I'm single-handedly trying to stem a possible epidemic, but that doesn't mean you have to give up everything you've worked towards.'

'We'll argue about this later, but you look as though you need to go home and have a rest.'

'I can't, not yet.' Nick lowered his voice. 'Lemuel is fading fast, Daisy. There's nothing more I can do for him.'

'Is Mary all right?'

'She shows no sign of the disease, at least not yet. She's a strong woman.'

'What about the girls and Jack? Shouldn't they be allowed to come and say goodbye to their father? Or at least be given the choice.'

'Mary doesn't want to risk them catching the sickness, even though I told her it's unlikely. Although to be honest, by the time they get here it may be too late.'

'Have you any other patients to see?'

'Not yet, but that could change.'

'Then go home, Nick. I can't tell you what to do but I think Dove deserves to know that her father is dying. She's a grown woman and she can make up her own mind.'

He nodded dully. 'I expect you're right.'

'And you are dead on your feet, Doctor. As your senior nurse I insist that you get some food and rest. I'll stay with Mary.'

'Doctor! Thank God you're still here.' Mary Fox appeared in the doorway, white-faced and trembling. 'Come quickly.'

20

Lemuel's death had come as a shock to his family. He had been a strong man, used to working outdoors and seemingly indestructible. The disease had overtaken and overwhelmed him with terrifying suddenness, and Daisy knew that her uncle would miss his fishing companion. Although the two men had been quite different in character they had become good friends. Mary was obviously shaken by her husband's unexpected demise, but Daisy could not help wondering whether it had come as a blessed release from an unhappy marriage. But now there were the girls to consider and Jack. How Jay would feel was another matter. Daisy broke the news to Linnet and Jack, leaving Nick to tell Dove when he returned home to snatch a meal and a brief rest. Linnet was visibly upset, but she put her own feelings aside to comfort her younger brother.

It had been a long and exhausting day, and late that evening Daisy was alone in the parlour, studying one of the nursing textbooks she had brought with her. She was disturbed by someone tapping on the door and she dragged herself away from the chapter on ward hygiene. 'Come in.'

'Might I have a word with you, miss?' Linnet stood in the doorway, a pale shadow of her usual cheerful self.

Daisy put her book down. 'Of course. Come in and sit down. You look exhausted.'

'I've just been to our cottage. I wanted to make sure that Ma was all right.'

'She's a brave woman.'

'Yes, she is, but she's worried about Jack. I told her that he was taking Pa's death as well as could be expected but she wants him to come home.'

'I can understand that, but is the cottage a safe place for him to be? I heard that the outbreak started with overflowing effluent from the shared privies in that area.'

'I don't know about that, miss. I haven't got any medical knowledge. Not like you.'

'I'll go and see your mother, if it would help, but I think Jack should stay here until the danger is past.'

'I agree.' Linnet stared down at her tightly clasped hands. 'Ma wants to see Jay, but after the last set-to with our dad, Jay swore he'd never cross the threshold again.'

'He isn't in trouble with the law now, is he?'

'No. At least, I don't think so. He might have been a bit wild as a youth, but he was never guilty of serious crime. The squire sent him to prison supposedly as a warning to others, but if you believe that you'll believe anything.'

'I find it hard to understand how that man could treat his own flesh and blood in such a way.' Daisy shot an anxious glance in Linnet's direction. 'I hope I haven't said the wrong thing.'

'Ma told me what happened to her when she was a young girl in the squire's service, but I

336

don't know why that man is set on ruining our family. You'd think he'd done enough damage already, and if anything he'd want to make amends.'

'I agree, but the only person who could answer that is the squire himself,' Daisy said slowly. 'But perhaps Jay will come home when he finds out that his mother needs him.'

'I'll ask the local fishermen if they know where he might be found, and I'll try to get a message to him.'

'I think that's the best thing to do.'

'Is there anything I can get for you, miss? I was going to turn in early, if you don't need me again.'

'You go and get some rest, Linnet. I'll be going to bed soon anyway. It's been a very tiring day, and I've a feeling tomorrow is going to be even busier.'

Linnet hesitated in the doorway. 'You're not going to leave us again, are you, miss?'

'Not while this disease is rife. Dr Neville can't do it all on his own.' Daisy settled down to write a letter to Minnie, explaining that she was going to remain in Little Creek until the cholera outbreak was over. She penned another more formal letter to Nurse Johnson, explaining her situation and then another, much briefer note to Toby, asking him to pay her half of the rent on Minnie's room until such time as she was able to return to London. She left the correspondence on the salver in the hall with the money for postage. That done she went to bed, her conscience appeased.

Next day there were more cases and the most notable were Charity and Patience Harker, the daughters of Colonel Harker from Four Winds, a large property on the edge of the village. The colonel and his lady were stationed in Poona, although expected home very soon, but Mrs Jones, their housekeeper, was apparently distraught. She sent a message with the coachman, begging Nick to visit the sick girls.

Seated beside Nick in the trap, Daisy accompanied him to the Harkers' imposing house on the headland. The interior was even more impressive than the exterior, and Daisy looked around in awe at the elegant furnishings and priceless antiques as she followed Nick and the housekeeper upstairs to the sickroom. Nick examined each of the girls in turn, but even to Daisy's eyes it was obvious that they were very ill.

'What will we do?' Mrs Jones wept openly. 'If anything happens to the young ladies I'll be held responsible.'

'They ought to be in an isolation hospital, but the nearest is St Mary's in Colchester,' Nick said thoughtfully. 'I think the journey might be too much for the young ladies.'

Daisy drew him aside. 'Nick, this may be the answer you're looking for.'

He stared at her, frowning. 'What do you mean?'

'You wanted to turn Creek Hall into a cottage hospital, but you lacked the funds. This might be the ideal opportunity, and it could save the girls' lives.'

'But Creek Hall isn't set up to receive patients, especially ones who are critically ill.'

'You have plenty of rooms, and I'm sure that Mrs Bee and Dove would be willing to make them ready to receive patients.'

He shook his head. 'But a hospital, even a small one, needs nursing staff. You know how much hard work goes into running a hospital ward.'

'Yes, I do, and I might not be fully qualified, but I know how a ward is run and I'd be prepared to move in, if necessary.' Daisy thought quickly. 'Then there's Mary Fox, she might be glad of the work and she's had experience nursing her husband.'

'I understand what you're saying, Daisy, but it isn't as simple as that. The house has to be kept spotlessly clean and Mrs Bee couldn't manage to feed everyone on her own.'

'I'm sure Hilda could help Mrs Bee in the kitchen as well as keeping an eye on the children, and she would work even harder than an able-bodied person. Besides which, there must be women in the village who would do the more menial tasks and be glad of the income.' Daisy glanced round at the expensively furnished bedroom, and the dressing table laden with cut-glass trinket pots and a silver-backed brush and comb set. 'I'm certain that the colonel would pay handsomely for his daughters' care.'

Mrs Jones cleared her throat noisily. 'I couldn't help overhearing, sir. I handle the housekeeping while the mistress is away, but I know she and the colonel wouldn't count the cost when it comes to their daughters' welfare. I've done my best to look after them, Doctor, but I simply can't cope with them in this state.'

'Of course not, Mrs Jones. You've done your best, but the ladies need constant nursing.'

'I'm most grateful, sir.'

Nick packed his stethoscope into his medical bag. 'There's one thing that puzzles me, Mrs Jones. The source of the infection seems to be fairly obvious in the light of Dr Snow's findings, but have you any idea how the young ladies might have come in contact with the disease? They seem to lead a sheltered life here at Four Winds.'

'They do normally, Doctor, but they're wayward girls. It was a particularly hot day in the middle of last week and I warned them against paddling in the creek, but they ignored me. Soaked, they were, when they returned home. I wouldn't be surprised to discover they'd been dousing themselves with the water. They're saying in the village that it's the miasma from the creek that's causing the illness.'

'Well, we won't worry about that for now,' Nick said hastily. 'If you agree, I'll have beds ready for the young ladies at Creek Hall, where they'll have the best treatment we can offer.'

'That will be a relief, Doctor. I'll have the carriage ready to bring them to you as soon as I receive the word.'

'Thank you, ma'am. I'm going home now to make the necessary arrangements.'

'I'll come with you, Nick,' Daisy said as they ascended the sweeping staircase to the entrance hall. 'I can help Dove to get their rooms ready.'

'If you remain here to help fight the disease you'll lose your place at the London. I can't ask you to make such a sacrifice.'

Daisy caught hold of his arm as they reached the foot of the stairs. 'This is more important. I know so many of the people in the village and I care what happens to them. You need help and I'm prepared to do what I can.'

A tired smile lit his eyes. 'I can see that to argue would be futile.'

'Yes, it would.' She followed him outside onto the gravelled carriage sweep and the warm summer sunshine caressed her cheeks. The air was fresh and filled with the scent of flowers and the briny tang of the sea. On such a lovely day it seemed incredible that the threat of a dreaded disease was hanging over the village like a thunder cloud.

The Harkers' groom had been walking Hero, but at the sight of the doctor he brought the trap round to the front door.

'The head gardener's two nippers are poorly, Doctor. Will you take a look at them afore you go?'

'I'll stop at their cottage on the way.' Nick helped Daisy onto the driver's seat and climbed up beside her. 'Let's hope it's some childish ailment and not cholera. Walk on, Hero.'

'I've been reading up on the disease,' Daisy said, holding on to her bonnet as Hero lurched forward. 'If we can keep people from passing it on through poor hygiene and ignorance, maybe we can prevent it from spreading.'

They stopped at the head gardener's cottage, but Nick returned quickly and took the reins from Daisy.

'There's nothing wrong with those two that a dose of castor oil won't cure. The little monkeys have been eating unripe fruit from the hothouse. They'll survive, thank goodness. Walk on, Hero.'

⋆   ⋆   ⋆

Daisy and Dove worked hard to get a room ready for their first patients. They removed the Holland covers, and took the rugs downstairs to hang on the washing line, using wicker carpet beaters to send clouds of dust into the air. Despite the seriousness of the situation they turned the task into a competition to see who could finish first and ended up helpless with laughter at each other's efforts. A word, accompanied by a disapproving frown, from Mrs Bee sent them hurrying back to the pleasant upstairs bedroom that overlooked the saltings, where they swept and polished the floor and changed the bed linen. The rugs were replaced and the room was ready just as the Harkers' carriage drew up outside. Nick and the Harkers' coachman carried the sick girls upstairs to their light and airy room, where Daisy and Dove attended to all their immediate needs and made them as comfortable as possible.

Later that afternoon Mary arrived, ready to do anything that was required of her, and Nick brought home three more very poorly patients. Everyone worked together, including Hilda, who took charge of the children, keeping them well away from the sickrooms. She also helped Mrs Bee by preparing vegetables for the evening meal and they worked in perfect unison. Daisy suspected this was due to the fact that Mrs Bee was clearly in charge, and Hilda was content to take orders and obey them to the letter. Kind and generous she might be, but Mrs Bee was queen in the kitchen and not about to abdicate.

Daisy sent Billy with a note to her aunt explaining her absence. He returned later with her luggage and a response from Aunt Eleanora expressing her fears that Daisy would succumb to the disease. Daisy chose to ignore the note. There was nothing she could say that would make the situation any easier to bear, and she was too busy looking after their existing patients to worry about anything other than their progress.

Sadly, one of the older men passed away during the night, but his wife survived and next morning the Harker sisters were showing hopeful signs of recovery. Daisy had taken turns with Dove to watch over their patients during the long hours of darkness, giving Mary time to catch up with some much-needed sleep.

* * *

During the next few weeks there was a steady flow of patients admitted to Creek Hall Hospital, as it was now known in the village, and many simply turned up at the door demanding to see the doctor with a variety of ailments and minor injuries. Nick treated everyone, taking a fee from those who could afford to pay, but Daisy suspected that he let most people off or accepted garden produce and the odd chicken or rabbit in return for treatment. Charity and Patience recovered slowly and Mrs Jones paid the bill for their care promptly, a benefit that Nick said would not have happened had the colonel been at home. The gentry, he added, were notorious for keeping tradesmen waiting for months, if not years, for their money, and that included medical fees. But the news that both the Harker girls were recovering well had circulated and Nick had urgent requests for treatment from people who were more than able to pay. He was too busy to keep the accounts, but Daisy discovered that she had a head for figures and she kept a detailed ledger, noting down each remittance and their day-to-day expenditure. At the end of the first two months the books balanced. They were not making a fortune, but they could pay the staff, and she had even managed to put a little aside for repayments to the squire.

Gradually, aided by Dove and a couple of women from the village, Daisy managed to get all twenty bedrooms ready for the inevitable influx of patients. The suffering were admitted, treated and many recovered. The tragedy was that equally as many succumbed, and the village graveyard was filled to capacity. The vicar did his best to comfort the bereaved, and Mrs Peabody organised Eleanora and the other ladies on her committee to make calf's foot jelly and other nourishing foods for those who were recuperating. Elliot Massey's mother was one of those who died, and Linnet spent most of her time at the school, taking lessons in Elliot's absence and assisting him when he returned. Daisy suspected that a romance was blooming, despite the sad situation that had brought Linnet and Elliot together.

As the weeks went by Daisy was too busy to think about returning to her position at the London Hospital, and in any case she doubted whether she had a place now. The occasional letter from Minnie brightened up the dull days when nothing seemed to go right, or the cholera claimed yet another victim, but as the weather cooled the cases were fewer, and there was hope that the epidemic might be coming to an end. Daisy continued to visit her aunt and uncle whenever possible, and they remained in good health, as did Hattie and Linnet. Jack was still living with Eleanora and Sidney, and they encouraged Mary to call on them whenever she could snatch an hour or two of free time. She lived in at Creek Hall as her old home was uninhabitable. Heavy rains in August had flooded the cottage, turning the packed earth floor into a sea of mud, which was inevitably contaminated by the overflow from the privies. Most of the families in the terrace had no alternative but to stay in their homes and try to make the best of it, but Nick was appalled. He did his best to seek a solution through official channels, but the properties all belonged to

Squire Tattersall, and he refused to do anything, claiming it was an Act of God, and the tenants must sort it out for themselves.

* * *

On a chilly late October morning, Daisy had her hair covered by one of Dove's mobcaps and her plain linsey-woolsey dress was protected by an apron that came up to her chin. It was her turn to empty the chamber pots into the outside privy, and she was rinsing them at the pump when a tall man came striding into the stable yard. She had never met Colonel Harker, but this person fitted the description that Mary had given her.

'You, girl!' he shouted, pointing his cane at her. 'Where is everyone? What sort of establishment is this when no one answers the door?'

Daisy wiped her hands on her pinafore. 'I apologise for that, sir. We are very busy at this time in the morning.'

'It doesn't say much for your organisation, young lady. Where is your superior?'

'I am Daisy Marshall and I'm in charge while Dr Neville is out on a call. Might I ask your name?'

'You aren't from round here or you would know that I am Colonel Harker. My wife and I came to thank Dr Neville for saving our daughters' lives.'

'How do you do, sir? Perhaps you would like to come indoors and wait for Dr Neville to return?'

'I'll see what my wife says. She isn't used to being kept waiting, and she most certainly won't want to walk through the stable yard.'

'I'll go through and open the front door, Colonel.' Daisy abandoned her task and crossed the cobbled yard to enter the house through the back entrance. She had not taken to the colonel, and if his wife was of a similar disposition she did not think she would like her either. Snatching off the mobcap, Daisy patted her hair in place as she ran through the house to open the door. Much as she disliked the way the colonel had spoken to her, she knew that she could not afford to offend a wealthy client, and it was well known in the village that Mrs Harker was the one with the money. She had inherited a fortune from a distant relative who owned a cotton mill in Lancashire, while the colonel came from a relatively poor family and had only his army pay. Daisy shrugged off her apron and dropped it onto a chair as she hurried to open the door before the colonel had a chance to hammer on the knocker.

Mrs Harker greeted her with a warm smile as she stepped over the threshold, followed by the colonel, who appeared to be more subdued when in his wife's company.

'My husband tells me that you are Miss Marshall.' She grasped Daisy's hand and held it to her cheek. 'My girls have spoken so warmly of you that I feel I know you already.' She glanced over her shoulder and her tone changed. 'Roland, close the door. You're letting in the cold air and there are sick people here.' She tucked

347

her gloved hand in the crook of Daisy's arm. 'We've come to thank you for saving our daughters' lives and to make a donation to this little hospital, which is so badly needed by the people of Little Creek.'

Daisy could hardly believe her ears. She led their prospective benefactress to the drawing room where a log fire blazed up the chimney. 'Dr Neville might be a while. He had two visits to make, and I never know how long they'll take.'

Mrs Harker settled herself gracefully on the sofa and began to peel off her gloves. 'Do sit down, Roland. You're making the place untidy.'

Daisy kept a straight face with difficulty. She wondered how the colonel's men would react if they could hear the way his petite and attractive wife spoke to him. She treated him as if he were a small boy, and maybe that's what he was beneath the bluster.

'Very well, my dear, but perhaps we ought to go home and return at a more convenient time.'

'Certainly not. I want to talk to Miss Marshall.'

'I'll take a stroll in the grounds.' Colonel Harker marched out of the room, closing the door with enough force to emphasise his bad mood.

'My husband is at a loss when it comes to drawing-room manners,' Mrs Harker said, smiling. 'He is much more at ease on the parade ground. But tell me about yourself, Miss Marshall. What is a young lady like you doing in a backwater like Little Creek?'

'Much the same as yourself, I imagine, ma'am. I grew up in London, but I've come to love the village and its surroundings. I've seen your beautiful home, so I imagine you love it here, too.'

'Yes, I do. When my husband retires from the army it is my ambition to live the rest of my days in Four Winds. Which is why I think it's important for Dr Neville to keep this hospital open for the continuing benefit of all the village, rich and poor.' She opened her reticule and took out a slip of paper, which she handed to Daisy. 'I think this will help.'

Daisy scanned the banker's draft and she could hardly believe her eyes. 'This is most generous, Mrs Harker. Dr Neville will be delighted, and I can't thank you enough.'

They chatted for a while, but there was no sign of Nick, and the colonel kept peering through the window and tapping on the glass, waving his pocket watch at his wife. After several such interruptions Mrs Harker decided it was time to leave, but she promised to set up a committee amongst her wealthy friends and acquaintances in order to raise funds to support the hospital. Daisy was overcome by the sudden turn of events and she could barely wait to pass on the good news to Nick. There was, she calculated, enough money to pay off the interest demanded by the squire, with enough left over to keep the hospital running for the next few months.

★　★　★

It was mid-afternoon when Nick finally arrived, but he looked so pale and tired that Daisy insisted he must eat before she gave him the good news. Mrs Bee ladled soup into a bowl and Hilda sliced bread from one of the loaves she had helped to bake. Nick sat at the kitchen table and was not allowed to move until he had finished his meal, ending with a slice of apple pie made from windfalls that had been collected by the children. Although the orchard was neglected and overgrown, the trees had produced a bumper crop and Judy had helped her mother to peel and core the fruit. Daisy was quietly proud of the way they all worked together, and Hilda's prosthesis would soon be finished and she would learn to walk again. The outbreak of cholera had been brutal, although in a strange way it had created an extended family that supported each other. The end of the terrible epidemic was in sight, but it was not over yet.

Nick had managed to escape the clutches of the women who were doing their best to look after him and he joined Daisy in the drawing room.

'You said you have good news. I certainly need something to brighten my day. There was another death in the village. I couldn't do anything to save the old fellow. He lived in the terrace that the squire refuses to renovate, despite the fact that the cottages are virtually uninhabitable.'

'The squire has a lot to answer for.' Daisy took the banker's draft from the mantelshelf and handed it to him. 'Mrs Harker gave us this. She wanted to do something to show how much she appreciated the treatment her daughters received.'

Nick sat down, staring at the piece of paper as if he could not believe his eyes. 'But this is a huge amount.'

'I know, and you'll be able to pay off the squire with some to spare.'

'It should go on improving our facilities here,' Nick said doubtfully. 'But it would be wonderful to pay off that bloodsucker.'

'Mrs Harker is going to raise money for the hospital, and we have a few well-off patrons who pay their way. I think you ought to settle with the squire and be done with it.'

'You're right, of course, and it will give me great pleasure to cash this and throw the money in his face.'

'I wish I could be there to see his reaction,' Daisy said, laughing.

Nick eyed her seriously. 'Then come with me. We'll show him that we're in this together and he can forget any ideas of trying to bully you into doing what he wants.'

'I'd love to, but he might take it out on my aunt and uncle. Their lease is due to expire shortly.'

'I knew Mrs Marshall's aunt, Miss Featherstone, and she was a very capable woman. I can't imagine that she would have left her cottage to her niece knowing that the lease was about to expire. I think your uncle ought to demand to see the document.'

'I'm sure he's done that already. My uncle ran

the family business for years, so I'm certain that he'll have gone into everything very carefully.'

'I do hope so, because the squire will stop at nothing to get what he wants. He's driving his tenants out of their homes for no better reason other than they spoil his view, and I suspect that's why he wants Creek Cottage.'

'That man is an out-and-out villain.'

Nick tucked the banker's draft into his breast pocket. 'So you'll come with me to Creek Manor? Or are you afraid to face him, Daisy?'

21

A bitter east wind rampaged over the saltings, churning the waters of the creek into a boiling cauldron. Frost sparkled on the grass and coated the remaining leaves on the trees with silver. Birds pecked hungrily at the berries and rosehips in the hedgerows, seemingly oblivious to the sound of Hero's hoofs on the hard ground or the rumble of the vehicle's wheels as the trap bounced over ruts in the frozen mud. Daisy sat beside Nick on the driver's seat, wrapped up against the cold in her fur-lined cape. Mrs Bee had insisted on giving her a hot brick wrapped in a towel, but after twenty minutes it had grown cold and she placed it in the well beneath her feet. She was not looking forward to meeting the squire again. He had not bothered her during the cholera outbreak, but she suspected that was more from cowardice than any finer feelings on his part. Of one thing she was certain — the squire did not like to be crossed and he did not give up easily.

'We're almost there.' Nick gave her a sideways glance. 'Are you all right, Daisy?'

'Yes,' she lied. 'I'm here to support you against the squire.'

'We'll stand together. He's a bully and he needs to be shown that he can't always get what he wants.'

'I just wish that he would do something for Jay. It's breaking his mother's heart to think she might never see him again.'

'I suppose miracles do happen occasionally.' Nick reined in as they approached the closed gates and a man rushed out of the gatehouse.

'What's your business here, mister?'

'I'm Dr Neville . . . ' Nick had barely uttered the words when the gatekeeper pulled back the bolts and motioned him to drive on.

'You was sent for two hours ago,' the man said grimly. 'Let's hope you're not too late. I can't afford to lose me job.'

'What did he mean?' Daisy asked urgently.

'I don't know. I'm not Squire Tattersall's doctor. He wouldn't put his trust in someone from Little Creek.' He flicked the reins. 'Walk on, Hero.'

As if to add to the sense of urgency, the main door was already open as they drew up at the foot of the steps and Molesworth rushed out to meet them.

'We sent for Dr Phipps.'

'I don't know anything about that,' Nick said calmly. 'I am a doctor, but I came to see the squire on a private matter.'

Molesworth beckoned to a stable boy, who had appeared from the back of the house. 'Take the doctor's trap to the stables. You'd better come with me, Doctor.' He shot a suspicious glance at Daisy. 'The squire won't want to see you.'

'Miss Marshall is my nurse. If the squire is unwell we both need to see him.'

'Be it on your own head.' Molesworth marched into the house and led them up the elaborately carved oak staircase to the first floor. He came to a halt outside a door. 'This is the squire's bedchamber. Perhaps you'd best wait here, miss?'

Daisy held her head high. 'I'm a trained nurse.' It was a slight exaggeration, but she felt that she had learned more during the height of the cholera epidemic than she would have done in a year at the London Hospital. Dealing with self-assertive underlings had been part of her day-to-day experiences, and she was not going to be intimidated by the squire's butler. She followed Nick into the bedroom and shut the door in Molesworth's face.

The windows were closed and the curtains drawn, allowing in only a chink of daylight, but the smell in the room was enough to convince Daisy that the squire had fallen victim to the dreaded disease.

Nick strode over to the window and pulled back the curtains, allowing light to flood the room. The tapestry bed curtains hung limply from the four-poster and the heavy mahogany furniture glowed dully in the cold light. A fire burned in the grate, but it did little to heat the large room and the chilly atmosphere made Daisy shiver.

Nick examined the squire, who seemed to have shrunk in size. His cheeks were ashen and his eyes were clouded with suffering, but even so, Daisy felt no pity for the man whose cavalier treatment of his tenants had been the cause of the outbreak in the first place. It seemed like poetic justice that the arch tormentor was now suffering a similar fate to those who were far below him in the social scale.

'Will he live?' she asked in a whisper.

Nick put his stethoscope back in his medical bag. 'It's only a matter of time.'

'I'm not dead yet.' Esmond Tattersall's voice was loud and strong, despite his physical condition.

'You have cholera, Squire,' Nick said calmly. 'You need proper nursing care. I suggest you try to contact your own doctor.'

'She can do it.' Esmond raised his arm with difficulty and he pointed a shaking finger at Daisy. 'She owes me that.'

'I owe you nothing,' Daisy said coldly. 'You've done your best to ruin the village and you've made my relations' lives intolerable with your threats of eviction.'

'I'll renew their lease if they can find the money to pay for it.'

'Money won't do you any good where you're going.' Daisy's last shred of sympathy for the desperately sick man snapped, and she backed away from the bed. The stench in the room had made her feel sick, even though she had treated many patients with the disease, but this time it was personal. The man she detested was dying, but she felt no pity, and that shamed her. As a nurse she ought to be able to set her own feelings aside, but Esmond Tattersall had destroyed lives and refused to acknowledge his own son. He was past redemption.

'You could receive the necessary treatment at Creek Hall, if you wish.' Nick placed his bag on a chair at the bedside. 'Or you could wait for your own doctor to examine you.'

'Why are you here, Neville? You can't have known about this.' Esmond indicated his emaciated body with a feeble wave of his hand.

'I came to pay off the interest on the loan you gave my father. It's blood money, but I can repay you in full.'

'Leave it on the table. I'll take what I'm due.'

Daisy turned away. 'I can't bear to look at you. Anyone else in your situation would be shamed into refusing the money.'

'Money can't shame me, but it can buy me what I want.' Esmond raised himself weakly on one elbow. 'I will renew the lease on Creek Cottage, but only if you stay here and nurse me back to good health.'

'I can't do that,' Daisy said, horrified. 'I'm needed at Creek Hall.'

'You'll do as I ask, or your aunt and uncle will lose their home.'

Daisy turned to Nick. 'He can't do this, can he?'

'I'm afraid he could, if he was so minded.'

'But you need me at Creek Hall. I have patients there who rely on me.'

Nick drew her aside. 'We haven't had any new cases this week. Do what you must, Daisy. I'll respect your decision.'

She returned to the squire's beside, gazing down at him with contempt. 'I will stay here and look after you, but in return I want you to sign the lease on Creek Cottage over to my aunt and uncle.'

A faint smile deepened the creases on Esmond Tattersall's face. 'You have my word.'

'There's another condition,' Daisy said firmly. 'You will formally acknowledge Jay Fox as your son.'

'Never!'

'Then I'll return to Creek Hall with Dr Neville and you can take your chances.'

There was a moment of complete silence before Esmond sighed and nodded. 'Very well. I agree to your terms.'

'I want it in writing.' Daisy stood firm, meeting his gaze with steel in her heart.

'You can take my word as a gentleman.'

'You are no gentleman, Squire.' Daisy moved swiftly to a small escritoire at the far end of the room, and as she had hoped, found pen and paper. She sat down and drafted the document releasing the freehold of Creek Cottage to her aunt and uncle. When she was satisfied with the wording, she took it over to the squire's bedside and read it to him. He added a barely legible signature, and fell back on the pillows with a groan.

'You'll stay now until the end.' Esmond's voice tailed off and he closed his eyes.

'Yes, I will. I'll keep my part of the bargain.' Daisy turned to Nick and found him watching her with a worried frown. 'I'll be fine.'

'Are you sure about this, Daisy?'

'I am, but I'd be grateful if you would deliver this to my uncle on your way home.' She handed him the folded sheet of paper. 'He'll know what to do.'

'Very well, although I'm not happy about this.'

'There's one other thing you could do for me,' Daisy said in a low voice. 'Ask Mary to come here to keep me company. Tell her I'd be very much obliged if she could bring herself to do this for me.'

Nick eyed her suspiciously. 'What are you up to?'

She gave him an angelic smile. 'Nothing for you to worry about, Doctor.'

★ ★ ★

Molesworth made it clear that he suspected Daisy's motives for agreeing to nurse his master, but Mrs Ralston, the squire's housekeeper, was more amenable. She had a bedroom made up so that Daisy would be near the squire at all times, and she saw to it that trays of food were sent up to the sickroom to tempt Daisy's appetite. It was hard to treat the squire like an ordinary patient, but Daisy somehow managed to put the past behind her and even if she could not be sympathetic, she dealt with his symptoms in a professional manner and, to her surprise, he responded with gratitude. The disease stripped the sufferers of their dignity as well as being debilitating and painful, but Esmond was not a man to give up easily.

On the third morning Daisy had managed to snatch a few hours' sleep after tending to the squire's needs during the night, but she was awakened at first light by someone shaking her shoulder. She opened her eyes, staring blearily into Mary's worried face.

'I came as soon as I could.'

Daisy sat up in bed, shivering and reaching for her wrap. It was bitterly cold in her room and particles of ice had formed on the inside of her window. 'The squire is failing fast, Mary.'

'What do I care? That man ruined my life. I came here to help you, not him.'

'I want to see justice done, and this might be his only chance to save his soul, if such a thing is possible.'

Mary glanced round the room. 'Should I light the fire? It doesn't look as if the maid is going to oblige.'

Daisy slipped her wrap around her shoulders. 'Yes, please do. I'd better go and check on my patient. I'll explain everything when I get a moment.' She fastened the voluminous garment with a sash and left the room, padding barefoot on the thick carpet as she entered the squire's bedchamber. She pulled back the curtains, allowing the pale dawn light to filter into the room. The squire's breathing was stertorous and when she drew nearer to the bed she could tell by the blueness of his skin that the end was very near. For a moment she felt a surge of pity, but she quelled the emotion, falling back on the months of experience she had endured with the killer disease. This was not the time to be sentimental. She made him as comfortable as possible before ringing for a servant. When the flustered maid put her head round the door as if

360

afraid to enter the room, Daisy sent her to fetch Mr Peabody, the vicar. The maid fled, calling for Mrs Ralston in a panic, but Daisy had a plan.

'Can you hear me, Squire?' She plumped up his pillows, giving him a gentle shake.

He opened his eyes and was immediately alert. 'What do you want, woman?'

'You know that the end is very near.'

A wry smile curved his lips. 'I'm going to meet my maker. This isn't how I planned to get you into my bedroom, Daisy.'

'I'm giving you a chance to right a wrong you did to a much better woman than I will ever be.'

'I don't know what you're talking about.'

'Yes, you do, and Mary is here now. Will you do the right thing by her and her son — your son?'

'Do I have a choice?' he asked weakly. 'You have taken my place as the one who is in command, Daisy. I knew you were a woman after my own heart.'

She nodded. 'I've sent for the vicar.'

'So be it. I suppose I could do one good thing before I die.'

'I'll go and tell Mary. She'll argue, but I want you to promise one more thing.'

'You would harass a dying man?' His brown eyes glinted with amusement even though it was obvious his strength was failing.

'Make Jay your heir. As I see it you have no one closer to you than your only son.'

'And what do you get out of this? Are you aiming to become mistress of Creek Manor?

What would you do if I insisted on marrying you instead?'

'I'll walk away and leave you. I'm not doing this for myself, strange as it may seem to you.'

He closed his eyes. 'Leave me in peace, you harpy. Do what you will.'

★ ★ ★

Mary listened in silence, but her eyes widened and filled with tears when Daisy finished speaking. 'I can't,' she whispered. 'It's not right. He's a dying man; he doesn't know what he's doing.'

'He's more sensible at this moment than at any time since I've known him. I think he really wants to make reparation to you and to Jay. Would you deny your son the chance to inherit all this?'

'I can't speak for Jay. I don't even know where he is.'

'I know him well enough to say that he would want what's best for you, and if you marry the squire now, as you should have done all those years ago, then you will become mistress of Creek Manor.'

'But it seems wrong to take advantage of a dying man.'

'He didn't stop to question his conscience before he took advantage of you, Mary. Allow him to atone for the wrong he did you and the child you bore him.' Daisy rose from the chair by the fire. 'The vicar should arrive soon, but you must do what you feel is right. I'm not saying any more. It's up to you.'

Daisy returned to the squire's bedside and sat with him until Mr Peabody rushed into the room. 'I am sorry I took so long, Squire.' He glanced at the inert figure in the bed and then at Daisy. 'Am I too late?'

'No, you're not. Get on with your job, Parson.' The squire's voice was strong and there was no suggestion of confusion in his eyes as he glared up at the clergyman. 'Where is she, Daisy? Fetch the mother of my son and let me do one decent thing before I die.'

'What is this?' John Peabody glanced anxiously at Daisy. 'Am I hearing correctly? The squire wishes to marry you?'

Daisy moved towards the doorway. 'Not me, Vicar. The lady in question was wronged by the squire many years ago. He wishes to make amends.'

The Reverend John Peabody stared at Tattersall as if seeing a total stranger. 'You do?'

'Oh, get on with it. I'm sound in mind, if not in body. I know I did the girl a disservice, and I'm prepared to make up for it now.' He beckoned to Daisy. 'Write down my dying wishes. I leave everything to Jay Tattersall, my true-born son, and fetch the woman I'm to wed.'

Daisy settled herself back at the escritoire and it only took a matter of minutes to write the simple will, leaving everything to Jay. When it was signed and witnessed by herself and Mr Peabody, Daisy went to fetch Mary.

'I don't think I can go through with it.' Mary

363

paced the floor, wringing her hands. 'It's not right.'

'I can't force you,' Daisy said gently. 'But think of Jay and the injustice he's had to put up with all his life.'

Mary stopped short and took a deep breath. 'Yes, you're right. He suffered because Lemuel couldn't forgive me, even though I was the innocent party, and he took it out on Jay. I will do it.'

Daisy sent for Mrs Ralston and Molesworth, who acted as witnesses to the bedside marriage of Esmond Tattersall and Mary Fox. Molesworth was visibly shocked, but Mrs Ralston threw her arms around the new Mrs Tattersall and wept.

'I'm so happy for you, Mary.'

Daisy looked from one to the other in surprise. 'Do you know each other?'

'We were in service here at the same time,' Mrs Ralston said, wiping her eyes on a spotless white handkerchief. 'Mary was the pretty one, which was unlucky for her. Sometimes there are advantages in being plain and homely.'

'You weren't plain,' Mary protested. 'You were the clever one, Ida.'

'Stop cackling like old hens.' Esmond attempted to sit up, but he lacked the strength. 'Get them out of here, Daisy. I've done my duty. Now leave me to die in peace.'

Molesworth eyed his new mistress warily. 'Might I suggest we retire to Mrs Ralston's parlour, ma'am.'

'I'd better get back to Creek Hall,' Mary said hurriedly. 'I have work to do.'

'You're the mistress of Creek Manor now.' Daisy gave her a hug. 'You'll never have to work again.'

Mary's eyes widened. 'But what will I do all day?'

Mr Peabody cleared his throat noisily. 'My dear lady, I'm sure that Mrs Peabody would be only too happy to offer you help and advice. You will be most welcome on her committees. There are certain obligations and responsibilities that go with the position of lady of the manor.'

'I don't think I can do all those things.' Mary sent a pleading glance in Daisy's direction. 'I'm still the same person.'

Daisy slipped her arm around Mary's shoulders. 'I've seen how you've coped with dire circumstances that would terrify an ordinary woman. You'll have your family to help you and we'll find Jay and bring him home.'

A groan from the bed brought Daisy back to reality and she shooed everyone from the room, including the vicar, who protested that he ought to sit with the dying man.

'Get the sanctimonious old goat out of here,' Esmond said feebly. 'You'll stay, Daisy.'

She closed the door and went to stand at his bedside. 'You've done the right thing, Squire.'

His eyelids fluttered and closed. 'Hold my hand.'

★　★　★

The squire's funeral took place within days and the entire village turned out to see their landlord

365

interred in the graveyard, although there seemed to be very few genuine mourners, if any. Mary arrived at the church surrounded by her family. She had refused to stay at the manor house, preferring to remain at Creek Hall until the will had gone through probate. Daisy could understand her reluctance to accept the change in her fortune, but she knew that Mary would never be happy living in the place that held mixed memories, unless Jay returned to take up his rightful position. The squire's death seemed to have signalled the end of the cholera epidemic and no new cases had occurred.

Despite the recent losses and hard times, life in the village slowly returned to normal. Eleanora and Sidney now owned the leasehold on their cottage and Daisy was happy to see them both settled and free to enjoy living in the country. She moved back to Creek Cottage and Jack went to live at Creek Hall with his mother and sister. Hilda had been fitted with her wooden leg, as she called the contraption made for her by Fred Shipway. She had managed at first using a crutch and then a stick, and now she could walk, albeit with a slight limp, and get about unaided. She proved to be an able cook and Mrs Bee said she was invaluable now that they were feeding in-patients, although there were fewer rooms occupied since the end of the recent outbreak.

Daisy walked to Creek Hall daily, but there was not as much for her to do now and she was wondering whether she would be allowed to finish her training at the London. She brought

366

up the subject one morning after she had assisted Nick in his morning routine.

'I'm thinking of returning to London, Nick.'

He met her anxious look with a frown. 'Do you miss London so much?'

She shook her head. 'Not really. It's just that there isn't very much for me to do here. You don't need me now.'

'We have three in-patients and I do two surgeries a day. Of course you're needed.'

'But I'm not fully trained, Nick. I ought to get my qualifications.'

'So you're leaving me without a nurse?'

'I didn't say that. It's just that if I did decide to settle here in Little Creek I could be of more use if I was fully qualified.'

He shrugged and turned away. 'It's up to you entirely, Daisy. If you feel you need to return to London it's entirely your decision. You must do what you think is best.'

22

It had not been an easy decision, and if Nick had asked her to stay Daisy knew she would not have left the place she had come to love. But he had been adamant that she must make up her own mind, and he had been cool towards her, which made her feel guilty and angry at the same time. After all they had gone through together during the outbreak of cholera, she would have expected him to show some regret that she had chosen to return to her studies. He had not even been at the station to see her off, and it was Aunt Eleanora who had cried and kissed her goodbye, while Uncle Sidney had made sympathetic noises, patted her on the back and wished her well. Despite her disability, Hilda and the younger children had walked all the way from Creek Hall together with Dove and Linnet, but there was no sign of Nick and that made Daisy angry. There might once have been a hint of a romance between them, but their relationship during the cholera outbreak had been purely professional, and he had no right to make her feel guilty for wanting to continue with her studies. Jay would have wished her well, had he been there to wave her off. Jay would have understood.

★ ★ ★

It was late afternoon when Daisy arrived at the lodging house in Fieldgate Street and she received such a warm welcome from Minnie that it made up a little for Nick's apparent indifference and ingratitude. Minnie was openly overjoyed to have her roommate returned to her, and even Flora Mackenzie had shown a degree of pleasure when Daisy walked into the parlour. But Rex was his usual grumpy self and he leaped at her with claws outstretched and fangs bared when she climbed the stairs to her old room. Minnie joined her and they sat on their beds while Daisy related the horrors of the cholera outbreak, ending with the squire's dramatic change of heart on his deathbed.

Minnie's hand flew to cover her mouth. 'Oh, my! Who would have thought it? But Mary won in the end — how marvellous.'

'It would be if only Jay would come home. He isn't aware of what's happened, and I don't know how to set about finding him. The *Lazy Jane* could be anywhere by now, and he swore never to return to Creek Manor.'

'But it's different now,' Minnie insisted. 'Jay is the lord of the manor. It really is like something from a novel by Mrs Gaskell.'

'But the happy ending is yet to be written,' Daisy said drily. 'His mother needs him.'

'Then let's hope he decides to visit her at Christmas. It's only a matter of weeks away.' Minnie blushed rosily. 'Christmas will be special this year.'

'Why so?'

Minnie leaned across the gap between the

beds to grasp Daisy's hands. 'It's supposed to be a secret, but I have to tell you.'

'Tell me what? Go on, Minnie. I can't stand the suspense.'

'I've been seeing Toby quite a lot since you went away.'

'I asked him to pay my half of the rent. I hope he did.'

'That was why he came in the first place, but then he asked me out to dinner.'

'Are you telling me that you and Toby are stepping out?'

Minnie's colour deepened. 'He's asked me to marry him. I know it's quite sudden, but we're in love and we plan to announce our engagement at Christmas. My parents don't know yet and I'm a bit nervous because they're quite old-fashioned and they'll say we haven't known each other long enough.'

Daisy had a sudden vision of Mrs Carrington's contemptuous attitude when they had last met outside the London Hospital. 'Don't take any notice of other people, Minnie,' she said earnestly. 'If you and Toby love each other that's all that matters.'

Minnie's eyes darkened. 'I'm so sorry, Daisy. I can see you're upset. I didn't mean to remind you about your broken engagement.'

'I'm not upset and I'm delighted for you and Toby. I can't think of anyone I'd rather have for a sister-in-law.'

'Thank you. I knew you'd be on our side. Anyway, Julian Carrington wasn't good enough for you.'

'That's what I think,' Daisy said, chuckling. 'I didn't tell you at the time, but he had the nerve to turn up at the hospital and he wanted us to get together again. When I refused he demanded that I return his ring.'

'The bounder! I hope you told him off.'

'I made my feelings very clear, and I won't be seeing him again. But that's enough about Julian. I'm more interested in you and my brother. I can't wait to see him.'

'He's calling for me this evening. We're going to see a show at the Pavilion Theatre. The girls from upstairs are much in demand these days. You must come with us, Daisy.'

'I'm tired — it's been a long day. Maybe tomorrow, if you're both off duty?'

'That would be lovely.' Minnie jumped up from her bed. 'He'll be here any minute now. You must come down and give him a surprise. He wasn't expecting to see you today.'

'Yes, of course I will, and then I must have an early night. I'll need all my wits about me when I face Sister Tutor tomorrow, and I'm not looking forward to that interview.'

★   ★   ★

Sister Johnson was surprisingly helpful. She accepted the fact that Daisy had had little choice other than to stay in the country and do what she could during the cholera outbreak, and she seemed quite impressed.

'In the normal course of things I wouldn't allow a student to take such a long time off, but in your case it was unavoidable, and you will have gained knowledge first-hand of nursing a terrible disease. Under the circumstances I'll allow you to rejoin your colleagues on the wards. You're a good student and I'm sure you'll soon catch up.'

'Thank you, Sister. I'll work twice as hard.'

'I'm sure you will. You may start today. The wards are always very full at this time of the year.'

Daisy slipped back into the routine the moment she put on her starched grey uniform dress, white cap and apron. She worked tirelessly, finding it much easier than the arduous work at Creek Hall during the worst of the epidemic. That evening, back in her room, she made copious notes as she studied her textbook, but she found herself nodding off and she made herself ready for bed. She was exhausted, but when she stretched out on the thin mattress she could feel the metal base and she longed for her comfortable bed in Creek Cottage. The sound of horse-drawn traffic in the street below filtered through the badly fitting window, adding to the noisy tramp of booted feet and roars of laughter, as men rolled out of the public house further along the road. The older ladies had gone to their room, which was directly above hers, and Daisy could hear them walking around, their bare feet padding on uncarpeted floorboards, and the dull chatter of their voices. All this was strange to her ears after a long absence, and she could imagine how a child must feel when sent away to boarding school for the first time. It came as something of a shock to realise that home for her was now Little Creek. She might be a Londoner born and bred, and she loved the city, but her past and present had come together and she found herself pining for the quiet of the countryside, the soft rippling of the creek as the water rushed over the pebbles, and the occasional sharp cry of a fox somewhere deep in the woods. She closed her eyes and dreamed of the *Lazy Jane*, floating at anchor on the sunlit waters of the inlet.

* * *

For the next weeks Daisy worked harder than she had ever done before. The long hours on the wards were followed by evenings occupied with her studies. She spent as much of her precious free time as she could with Toby and Minnie, who were obviously very much in love. Daisy was delighted for her brother, but the pair were so wrapped up in each other that she often declined their invitations to accompany them for a meal or to the theatre. She wrote once a week to her aunt and uncle, keeping them up to date with her progress, and although she penned several letters to Nick, his replies were infrequent and brief. She knew that he must be extremely busy and that made her feel guilty. Perhaps she ought to have remained at his side and worked for the good of the people she had come to know so well. In London the crowds that thronged the streets were a faceless mass, whereas in Little Creek she knew everyone, if only by sight, and certainly by reputation. Mrs Bee and Hilda had kept her up to date with the gossip and, as the days went by, she felt the gap between herself and her adopted home widening into a huge gulf.

The other occupants of Mrs Wood's lodging house seemed to sense Daisy's inner turmoil and they went out of their way to comfort her. The two older ladies invited her to share their tea and biscuits whenever she came across them in the parlour, and Ivy was always ready to chat about anything and everything. She was a different person now that she was free from Jonah Sawkins' attentions. He had not bothered her since Daisy had sent him away, although Ivy said she had seen him walking out with the barmaid from the Old Three Tuns, who towered over him and made him walk to heel like a well-trained puppy. Perhaps, Ivy suggested with obvious relish, Jonah secretly liked dominant women with muscular forearms like a navvy and a reputation for throwing drunks bodily from a pub. Despite the unfavourable description of Jonah's latest conquest, Daisy could not imagine what any decent woman could see in him, but it was a relief to know that he was no longer a threat to Ivy, who definitely deserved better.

★   ★   ★

Winter was closing in, with freezing temperature and peasouper fogs, and there was a threat of snow in the air. Heavy clouds hovered just above the rooftops, trapping the smoke from thousands of chimneys and filling the air with noxious fumes.

Daisy was in the outpatient department one morning when a young seaman was brought in on a stretcher. He was suffering from severe burns to his face and torso and was in a great deal of pain. Toby was on duty and he gave the patient a hefty dose of laudanum before beginning the examination.

'Can you tell me your name?' Toby asked gently.

The young man muttered something unintelligible and Daisy had to lean closer in an attempt to understand him. 'I think he's saying Benny and something about a ship.'

'How did this happen to you, Benny?' Toby leaned closer. 'I can't understand what he's saying, Daisy. Can you?'

'No, I didn't get a word of that.' She held Benny's hand. 'We'll take care of you.'

'Find out if anyone came with him, Daisy.'

'Yes, Doctor.' Daisy left the cubicle and walked out into the main reception area, threading her way through crowds of people of all ages, some in rags and others reasonably well dressed. She stopped one of the porters.

'Do you know if there was anyone with the injured seaman?'

'One of his shipmates came with the poor fellow.' The porter jerked his head in the direction of a man who was standing by the door, looking as if he would rather be anywhere than in a hospital.

'Thank you, Smith.' Daisy left him and made

her way towards the man, who looked disturbingly familiar. She had a sudden memory of a sunny day in a secluded creek off the River Crouch.

He turned his head at the sound of her approaching footsteps and a look of recognition crossed his weathered features.

'What ship are you from?' Daisy asked breathlessly, but she already knew the answer.

'The *Lazy Jane*, miss. I've seen you before.'

Daisy glanced anxiously over her shoulder to see if anyone was listening. 'Is the captain on board?'

'He might be. It depends who's asking.'

'I must see him. I have some important news for him.'

'He won't come ashore, miss. I could pass on a message.'

'No,' Daisy said firmly. 'I must tell him in person.' She quelled the excitement rising within her. She must remain professional despite the temptation to do something rash. 'Your shipmate is very ill. We'll do what we can for him, but his burns are very serious.'

The man shook his head. 'Poor Benny. He was always a clumsy devil, but he didn't deserve to suffer like this.'

'Can you tell me his full name, and if he has any family who need to be informed.'

'He's Benjamin Sykes and he supports his widowed mother. The old lady won't be able to manage if he don't send her money.'

'We'll do what we can for him and there's always a glimmer of hope. Please tell the captain that, and ask him to come to the hospital. I'm on duty this evening until ten o'clock. If he asks for Probationer Nurse Marshall someone will tell him where to find me. I have something of great importance to tell him.'

'I'll pass the message on, miss. But we're due to sail at midnight. And the captain won't want to miss the tide.'

Daisy caught him by the arm as he was about to leave. 'Why has he brought the *Lazy Jane* to London if he's afraid to come ashore?'

'I can't tell you that.' He hesitated. 'I'm Guppy, in case we meet again, miss. Clem Guppy.'

Daisy smiled and nodded. 'I trust we will see each other in happier circumstances should we meet again, Clem.'

He tipped his cap. 'I'll pass your message on to the captain, miss.'

She waited until he had left the building before hurrying back to the cubicle where Toby was doing his best to treat the severe burns.

'You took your time, Daisy. Did you find anyone who knows this fellow?'

'Yes, this poor chap is Benjamin Sykes and he comes from a ship moored in the Upper Pool. It's sailing at midnight.'

'Well, this is one crew member who won't be going with them.' Toby gave her a searching look. 'You're very flushed, Daisy. Are you all right?'

'Yes, I'm perfectly fine. I should be used to seeing such terrible injuries but it's always upsetting, especially in someone so young, and apparently he supports his widowed mother.'

'That's sad, but you can't take on the woes of the world, Daisy. Go and get yourself a cup of tea and something to eat. I'll manage here, although there's very little I can do other than clean him up and give him large doses of laudanum.'

★　★　★

Daisy was on edge for the rest of the day, hoping that Jay would contact her, even if it was just a message passed on by Guppy. She was kept busy in the outpatient department and then on the female ward, where Toby found her late that evening. She was in the tiny kitchen washing the dregs of cocoa from the cups she had collected from the patients' bedside lockers.

'We couldn't save him,' he said tersely. 'He slipped away peacefully enough.'

Daisy turned her head away so that he would not see the tears that had sprung to her eyes. She had not known Benjamin Sykes personally, but he was very young to die and she could not help wondering who would break the sad news to his mother. 'Was anyone with him at the last, Toby?'

'A shipmate of his turned up at the very end. A chap called Guppy. I think you spoke to him this morning.'

'Did he leave any message for me?'

'Why would he? What's going on, Daisy? Why are you so upset about the fate of a stranger?'

'I'm tired, Toby. I'm just about to finish my shift and I'm going back to Fieldgate Street and straight to bed.'

He leaned over and kissed her on the forehead. 'You do look exhausted. I'd walk you home, but I'm on duty for another two hours.'

'Don't worry about me. I just need a good night's sleep and then I'll be fine.' Daisy rinsed the last of the cups and wiped it before placing it in the cupboard with the neat rows of clean crockery. 'I'm off then. I'll see you in the morning.' She went before Toby had the chance to question her further, and having wrapped herself up against the bitter cold she left the hospital.

It had started to snow. The heavy clouds that had hung over the city all day had fulfilled their promise and large flakes were tumbling down from the dark sky. Daisy pulled the hood of her cloak over her head and was about to walk off towards Fieldgate Street when a man stepped out of the shadows.

'Daisy.'

She knew that voice and she came to a halt, hardly daring to breathe. 'Jay?'

He took her by the arm. 'You told Guppy that you needed to see me urgently. Is there anything wrong?'

She pulled free from his tight grasp. 'You gave me a fright, jumping out like that.'

'I'm sorry, but I wouldn't have come ashore but for your message.'

'Are the police after you?'

'When are they not?' Jay smiled as he tucked her hand into the crook of his arm. 'We took a chance by coming upriver to London, and I have to catch the tide.' He quickened his pace. 'I'd love to stay and talk, but I have to get back on board.'

'Don't go so fast. I can't keep up.'

'If I had a horse to hand I'd scoop you onto the saddle as I did when we were last together.'

'Don't remind me of that mad ride. You caused me a lot of trouble, Jay.'

'I'm sorry. Truly I am. I wouldn't do anything to hurt you, Daisy.'

She glanced up at his face, but they were in an ill-lit side street and she could not see his expression. The snow was falling faster now, settling on the pavement and the cobblestones like icing on a cake. 'Where are you taking me? I have to get back to my lodgings.'

'You said you had something important to tell me.' Jay raised his hand to hail a passing hansom cab. 'Irongate Stairs, cabby.' Jay hoisted Daisy onto the seat before she had a chance to argue and climbed in to sit beside her. He closed the doors and banged on the roof. The cab lurched forward, leaving Daisy little alternative but to sit tight.

'So you've kidnapped me again,' she said breathlessly. 'What now?'

'Don't worry, I'll pay the cabby to take you back to wherever it is you're lodging.' He turned to give her a searching look. 'Why are you back in London, anyway? Guppy said you're a nurse. Is it true?'

'I'm a probationer, but I spent the entire summer in Little Creek looking after the victims of cholera.'

His expression changed subtly. 'I did hear

something about sickness being rife in the village.'

'And you didn't think to check that your family were all right?'

'How could I? I'm a wanted man, thanks to the squire.'

'Are you still involved with free trade, or whatever you call smuggling in your circles?'

'We have to earn our living, but it's getting harder and harder. To hear the old fellows talk they could make a fortune from silk or spirits, but with the Government lowering the tax on imported goods there's not much incentive, and the revenue men are better organised.' He hesitated, turning his head away. 'That's enough about me. I was worried when I heard of the cholera outbreak. Are my mother and sisters all right? And young Jack, of course.'

'They escaped the disease but Lemuel wasn't so fortunate.'

'He's dead?'

'I'm afraid so.'

'He hated me and the feeling was mutual.'

'The squire also passed away. Quite recently, as it happened. In fact he was the last to succumb to cholera.'

'I'm glad. I won't pretend differently. The old devil deserved to suffer, if only for the way he treated my mother.'

'This is what I want to tell you, Jay.' Daisy clung to the sides of the cab as it rattled over the slippery cobblestones. The snow was swirling around the vehicle, enveloping them in a cold white cloud and an eerie silence, deadening the

381

sound of the horse's hoofs and the rumble of the wheels.

'I'm listening, although I doubt if anything you could tell me about that man would come as a surprise. You didn't give in and marry him after all, did you?'

'No, but your mother did. After all these years the squire behaved like a gentleman.'

'So she owns the manor house? She deserves nothing less.'

'No, Jay. The squire made a new will on his deathbed, acknowledging you as his son and he left everything to you. You're a very wealthy man now.'

'That can't be true.'

'It is, I promise you. I was there at the end.'

'Then I have you to thank. Ma would never be bold enough to stand up to the squire.'

'I helped, of course, but she said her piece and the squire decided to do the right thing, probably for the first time in his whole life.'

'I still can't believe it. My whole life has been ruled by that man's actions. It doesn't seem possible that I might be free from his influence.'

'I don't understand,' Daisy said slowly. 'I thought you'd served your time.'

'It's not as simple as that.' Jay stared at her, frowning. 'So he's dead and buried. I don't think I'll believe it until I see his tombstone.'

'The whole village turned out to watch his funeral, and it wasn't because they loved him. I think it's sad that he's remembered only for the bad things he did. Now you'll have a chance to make amends.'

'I'm a seafarer — a wanderer — and I don't know if I could settle to a life on shore, especially one of responsibility and privilege. Maybe leaving everything to me was his way of keeping me tied to him for ever.'

'What you do now is up to you, but think of your mother. She refuses to move into the manor house until you return and take up your rightful position. Do you really want her to spend the rest of the winter in that damp cottage, or helping out at Creek Hall, when she could live in comparative luxury?'

'You make it sound so easy, but it's far from simple.' Jay peered into the snowstorm. 'At least this will make our departure easier, provided we don't collide with any other vessel.'

'Don't say things like that.' Daisy settled back against the shabby leather squabs, but she was growing anxious. 'Maybe I should get another cab, while the roads are still passable. I've never seen snow settle so quickly.'

'We're nearly there, and, as I said, I'll pay the cabby to see you safely home.' Jay turned to her with a wicked grin. 'Or you could come with me. I know you've been longing for a voyage on the *Lazy Jane*.'

This made her smile. 'In the summer, maybe, but I've seen the North Sea at its worst and I think I'd prefer to be on dry land in the winter months.'

She had tried to make light of her predicament, but Daisy grew increasingly anxious as their progress slowed down with the horse picking its way carefully through the deepening snow. When they finally came to a halt at the head of Irongate Stairs, Jay paid the cabby.

'I'll give you double to take the young lady back to Whitechapel.'

The cabby peered down through the open roof window, shaking his head. 'Sorry, guv. I live nearby and I ain't risking a return journey. Got to get the animal stabled and meself home.'

'I'll give you three times the cost then.'

'You can see for yourself that there's no traffic about. Sorry, guv.'

Jay lifted Daisy to the ground and her booted feet sank into a good four inches of freezing snow. 'There must be someone willing to take a chance,' Daisy said desperately. 'I can't stay here on the docks.'

The cabby looked down from his perch high above them. 'I'd take you home with me, dear. But the missis might object.' He chuckled and flicked the reins, encouraging his horse to plod forward.

Jay hitched his arm around Daisy's shoulders. 'Look down there. Guppy's waiting at Irongate Wharf. You'll have to come with me whether you like it or not.'

'I can't, Jay. I'm on duty at the hospital in the morning. They'll be expecting me back at the lodging house.'

'I'm not leaving you here. The cabby was right, there's little or no traffic and I haven't seen another cab since we reached the end of Leman Street. We can put ashore in the morning and you can get a train to Bishopsgate Station.'

Daisy looked anxiously at the steep water-men's stairs and the wharf that had all but disappeared beneath a thick coating of snow. The other side of the river was lost in the darkness and the increasing blizzard, and she could barely make out the shape of the rowing boat tied up alongside. It seemed that she had little choice.

23

Guppy brought her a cup of cocoa laced with sugar. 'Here, drink this. It'll warm the cockles of your heart.'

'Thank you.' Daisy accepted the drink with a grateful smile. She could barely speak for her teeth chattering, and she could not stop shivering. Guppy had rowed as fast as he could but it had taken the best part of an hour to reach the *Lazy Jane*, and the climb up the Jacob's ladder had been difficult and dangerous. She shuddered at the memory of the nightmare moments when her feet had kept slipping from the frozen rungs, and she had found herself hanging over the churning black water. Huddled beneath a coarse blanket, she sipped the hot sweet cocoa, but the vessel yawed suddenly and she only just saved herself from falling off the chair. 'What's happening, Guppy?'

He bent down to pick up a tin plate that had fallen to the floor. 'It's all right, miss. Don't worry, the captain knows what he's about. Jay's the best when it comes to navigating dangerous waters.'

'When do you think we'll be able to dock? I have to be at the hospital first thing in the morning.'

Guppy shrugged and turned away. 'It depends on the conditions downriver, miss. If I was you I'd try to get some sleep.'

Daisy glanced round the tiny saloon that was functional but definitely lacked a woman's touch. It was furnished with a table and chairs but nothing that looked remotely comfortable. 'I don't think that's going to be possible.'

'I weren't suggesting you doss down in here, miss. The captain said you was to use his cabin because he's going to be at the helm all night. Jay don't trust any one of us to handle the ship in these conditions.' He took the empty cup from her and placed it on the table. 'If you'd come with me?'

It was a command rather than an invitation and Daisy was exhausted or she might have argued. She followed him out of the saloon and down a narrow passage to a cabin in the stern of the vessel. Guppy hung a lantern from a hook so that it swayed with every movement of the ship, sending its flickering beam to create sinister moving shadows. At any other time Daisy might have found such an environment unnerving, but she was too tired to think and when Guppy left she lay down on the bunk, still fully dressed, and was asleep in minutes.

She awakened to find daylight streaming in through the porthole and she sat bolt upright, gazing round in disbelief. Gradually the events of the last evening came back to her and she leaped off the bunk, but the movement of the deck below her feet caused her to lose her balance and she fell to her knees. Bruised and humiliated, even though there was no one to see her, Daisy scrambled to her feet and edged her way over to peer out of the salt-encrusted glass. She blinked, dazzled by the whiteness of the snowy river-bank and the cold light reflecting off the steel-grey water. They were obviously a long way from the centre of London, and there was no sign of habitation.

She turned with a start as someone knocked on the door. 'Yes. Who's there?'

The door opened and Guppy entered; this time he held out a mug of tea. 'I thought you'd be awake, miss.'

She staggered over to the bunk and sat down, a little too heavily for elegance, but at least she had not embarrassed herself by another fall. 'Thank you, Guppy.'

'There's breakfast in the saloon, if you feel up to eating. Some people find the motion of the ship upsets their stomachs.'

'I'm fine, thank you. But where are we?'

'Too far from London to get you where you want to be, miss. But at least the snow has eased off, although by the looks of things it's pretty thick on shore.' He backed out of the cabin, leaving Daisy to drink her tea.

* * *

Jay was in the saloon when Daisy walked in and he rose from his seat, but she could see that he was exhausted. Dark shadows underlined his eyes and he was unshaven, giving him the appearance of a world-weary buccaneer. He only needed a gold earring in one ear and a cutlass at his belt to complete the look. Daisy was tempted to comment, but she thought better of it. Jay might not think it funny, or perhaps it was too close to the truth. She should be angry with him for not putting her ashore, but he smiled and she felt herself weakening.

'It's good to see you again, Daisy. I'm sorry I couldn't put you ashore as you asked, but the weather conditions made it virtually impossible.'

'Or perhaps you're on the run again.'

'You know me too well.' He resumed his seat. 'Sit down and have some breakfast. Unless, of course, you're feeling queasy.'

'I seem to be a good sailor although this isn't the way in which I would have chosen to find out. Where are we, Jay? I need to get back to London or I'll lose my job at the hospital.'

'By my reckoning the roads are going to be impassable. I'm sorry, Daisy. I didn't kidnap you deliberately. That's not my style, although I must say it's good to see you again.'

There was no doubting the sincerity of his last remark and Daisy felt the last of her anger melting away. Jay always seemed to have that effect on her and it was disturbing. 'I might say the same in different circumstances, but what am I supposed to do now?'

'I'll see that you get home to Little Creek.'

'It isn't my home now.'

'Isn't it?' He met her gaze with a look that seemed to bore into her soul. 'You were happier when I last met you. Do you really want to live in London?'

'Never mind me, Jay. What I don't understand is why you were moored so far upriver? What made it worth the risk?'

'It was a business deal. You don't need to know more, Daisy.'

'I seem to have become part of this venture, whatever it is. I think I deserve to be told the truth, Jay. What have you been doing that makes you constantly on the run from authority? I can't believe it was because of something you did years ago.'

He stifled a yawn. 'I've been up for two nights running. Could we have this conversation some other time?'

'No. I'm sorry but you've done this to me before. I'm not stupid. I know there's more to it than bringing a few articles of contraband into the country.'

'All right. I'll tell you the truth.'

'You could start by telling me how you came to be master of the *Lazy Jane*. You were a poor boy who'd served a year in prison for some petty crime that you did or didn't commit. That's what you led me to believe.'

Jay drained his cup and refilled it with coffee so strong that it looked and smelled like tar water. 'You're right, of course. The truth is that *Lazy Jane* belongs to Tattersall, and it was his doing that set me off on the course I took. He saw me as a useful puppet and he threatened me and my family if I didn't do what he wanted.'

'Why you?'

'I was caught poaching on his estate when I was just fourteen. The squire sentenced me to six months hard labour, but when I came out of prison I found two of his men waiting for me at the gate. They took me to a room at an inn and I came face to face with the man who had sent me to prison in the first place.'

'Squire Tattersall?'

'Yes, the squire himself. I was given a choice either I worked for him or my family would suffer the consequences.'

'But what could he have done?'

'He could have evicted my family from their cottage, or, as he said, he could blacken my mother's name by having it put about that she was a wanton before she married Lemuel, and that she didn't know who my real father was. I didn't believe him and if I'd been older I might have stood up to him, but I'd just come out of a horrific time in the clink, which is something I wouldn't wish on anyone.'

'So what happened then?'

'I was put to work on board the *Lazy Jane* and I learned how to sail her from the master, who was good to me and treated me more like a son.'

'Was the squire involved in smuggling then?'

'He didn't call it smuggling. According to him we were just running errands to the Continent and back.'

'You could have jumped ship.'

'And starved to death in the streets of London or wherever I happened to land? I was young and to be honest I found it exciting. I'm not a saint like Nick.'

'I thought you were his friend.'

'Nick is well respected and he'll devote his life to the village, just like his father. Maybe I take after mine and I'm a wrong 'un through and through.'

'I don't believe that for a moment, but you don't have to do this any longer. You're not working for the squire now. He can't harm you ever again and he relented at the last and tried to make reparation for the wrongs he'd done you and your mother.'

'That's true, but I'm not sure I want to inherit his fortune. The man was a villain.'

'The *Lazy Jane* belongs to you now, and everything the squire had is yours too. You could settle in the manor house and live a life of ease.'

Jay shrugged tiredly. 'I suppose I could, but I'm not sure that a living ashore would suit me. Maybe I'm a born wanderer. Anyway, I need sleep, and you must eat.'

She gazed at the food spread out on the table, realising that she was extremely hungry. She had not eaten since noon the previous day and her stomach growled at the sight of bread, butter and a pot of what looked like strawberry jam. A baked ham and a bowl of apples completed the spread.

'Help yourself, and if there's anything else you want just ask Guppy.' He stood up and made for the doorway, but Daisy reached out and caught him by the sleeve.

'Just a minute. Are we really going to Little Creek?'

'Last night while I was at the helm I had plenty of time to think, and you were right. It's time I went home to see my family, especially now that the old man is no longer there to cause trouble. We're bound for Little Creek, and if the trains are still running you'll be back in London by this evening.'

He left the saloon before she had a chance to question him further. Somehow the thought of returning to Little Creek was more attractive than facing the reality of living in Mrs Wood's lodging house and working twelve-hour shifts at the hospital. She loved her patients and she was deeply interested in the causes and treatment of all manner of ailments, but her experience of nursing the desperately ill in the summer had left her eager to do more than simply washing out bedpans and changing sheets. The news that Mrs Garrett Anderson had recently qualified to practise medicine against all odds had circulated around the hospital, and had been received with a degree of cynicism by many of the senior doctors. But the first barrier was down and maybe, in the not-too-distant future, women would be admitted to medical schools in England. In the meantime Daisy was determined that the lack of opportunity would not prevent her from doing what she could to alleviate the suffering of others, even if it meant taking up a subordinate position to her brother and Nick.

She carved herself a slice of ham, buttered a slice of bread and sat down to enjoy her breakfast. When Guppy brought a freshly made pot of tea she managed a bright smile. 'Jay tells me that we're going to Little Creek. If there's anything I can do to help during the voyage I'm only too happy to oblige.'

Guppy almost dropped the pot as he gazed at her in astonishment. 'Well, I never! With due respect, miss, I thought you was going to be difficult. I mean, you wasn't exactly a willing passenger, was you?'

'No, I suppose not, but I've had a word with the captain and I can see the logic of his decision. I can make myself useful.'

Guppy stroked his ginger beard, eyeing her thoughtfully. 'Now you come to mention it, miss. I believe you're a medical person.'

'I'm training to be a nurse.'

'Well, Cook has a nasty boil on the back of his neck. It's been plaguing him for days. Do you think you could do anything for him?'

'I most certainly can. Let me finish my breakfast and then you can show me where the galley is. I'll need hot water and something to make a poultice. Bread will do.'

'And I've got a splinter that's gone deep into me finger.'

Daisy smiled. 'I'm sure I can deal with that, too.'

There were only three crew members apart from Jay. Guppy was the mate, Ramsden the cook, and Lewis was just a boy who did what he was told, most of the time anyway. He attached himself to Daisy, and she only had to ask for something and Lewis would do his best to oblige. He was the healthiest of all of them apart from Jay, who seemed to be fighting fit. Daisy made a bread poultice for Ramsden's boil and another from soap and sugar for Guppy's splinter. After three days and several applications both were successful and Ramsden's temper improved, as did his cooking. Guppy's finger healed and Jay was full of praise for Daisy's nursing skill, but there remained a slight tension between them when it came to talking about the future. Jay seemed determined to resist becoming the lord of the manor, and although he listened politely to Daisy's arguments, he refused to see reason.

They were in the saloon on the third evening, having enjoyed a filling supper of salt beef stew. 'We should make landfall tomorrow, and I'm a free man.' He raised his glass of wine in a toast. 'The squire tried to ruin me, but he's only succeeded in making me stronger. I can do as I please.'

Daisy sighed. 'You're impossible. You can't go on as before, Jay. You've got your mother and your brother and sisters to consider as well as your tenants. It's not just you now.'

He downed a mouthful of wine. 'I can do both. Ma and the girls will want for nothing, and I might take Jack on as cabin boy.'

'Don't you dare,' Daisy said angrily.

Jay threw back his head and laughed. 'It's so easy to shock you.'

'You wouldn't drag your brother into a life of crime.'

'No, of course not. I just wanted to see your face when I suggested such a thing.' Jay leaned across the saloon table. 'Join me on board the *Lazy Jane*. Don't go back to slaving in the hospital or working all hours for Nick. Sail away with me and we'll conquer the world.'

She stared at him in surprise. 'It's the wine talking.'

He grasped her hand as it rested on the table. 'No, it's not. I'm deadly serious for probably the first time in my life. We make a fine pair, you and I.'

'Don't say things like that.' She snatched her hand away, knocking her glass of wine over in the process and she jumped to her feet. 'Now look what you've made me do.'

'Lewis.' Jay raised his voice to a shout and Lewis appeared in the doorway so promptly that Daisy thought he must have been listening at the keyhole. 'Miss Marshall has had a slight mishap. Fetch a cloth and another bottle of claret.'

Daisy rose to her feet. 'You've already had too much to drink or you wouldn't be talking such nonsense.'

Lewis glanced anxiously from one to the other and scuttled out of the saloon, returning moments later with a dirty-looking cloth.

'Wipe the mess up and clear the table,' Jay said firmly. 'Then you'd better get some sleep. We'll be making landfall first thing in the morning.'

Lewis nodded and began mopping ineffectively at the quickly spreading pool of wine. Daisy took the cloth from him. 'Let me do that, Lewis. You look as though you could do with a good night's sleep.'

'He'll get plenty of that when he goes ashore,' Jay said casually. 'His dad owns a farm in the next village to Little Creek. Benny Sykes was his cousin,' he added in a low voice when Lewis had left the cabin. 'I doubt if his old man will let Lewis come back on board after what happened.'

Daisy wrung the cloth into an empty soup

bowl and continued to mop up the wine. 'I'm surprised that his father allowed him to join your crew anyway. He can't have known what trade you follow.'

'People along the coast accept that smuggling is part of life. It has been for a couple of centuries, and in its heyday everyone would have been involved from the squire to the parson and the farm workers. The fun has gone out of it now.'

'Then give it up, Jay. You no longer need the money.'

He stood up and leaned across the table, kissing her on the lips before she had a chance to move out of the way. 'You are beautiful, Daisy. I think I love you.'

'You're drunk.' She tossed the wine-soaked cloth at him. 'You'd better get us home safely, or . . . ' She hesitated, at a loss for words.

Jay looked down at the red stain that was spreading across his shirtfront. 'Or you'll do what, my love? If this is the worst you can inflict on me I can happily live with that, Daisy mine.'

She headed for the door but Jay sidestepped the table and he caught her in his arms, holding her so close that she could feel his heart beating through the thin cotton of his shirt. His kiss sent fire through her veins and an unexpected surge of desire that she fought with every ounce of willpower. Even so, she found herself giving in to the moment and responding instinctively to his embrace. Julian's kisses had been polite and undemanding but Jay's mouth on hers and the male scent of him roused feelings in her that she could never have imagined. It was only when the click of the door handle made him release her that she had the strength to pull away, dazed and bruised but longing for more. She glanced down at her bosom and was shocked to see the red wine stain on her one and only gown.

She gave Jay a shove as he attempted to move closer. 'Now look what you've done. It's ruined and I've got nothing else to wear. How can I go home like this?' She burst into tears and found herself once again in his arms. This time he was stroking her hair and soothing her as if she were an unhappy child.

'Take it off,' he said when she managed to regain her self-control.

'What?' She stepped away, gazing at him in horror.

'Lewis. I know you're out there. Fetch one of my shirts — the cleanest one you can find.' Jay began unbuttoning the front of her gown. 'Don't worry, I won't tear the material. I have done this before.'

She took a step backwards. 'I'm sure you have.'

'Take it off and Lewis will get it washed and dried before we make landfall. The range in the galley never goes out so the material will dry overnight. Lewis will bring one of my shirts and you can preserve your dignity.'

Clutching the front of her dress together, Daisy glared at him, but the laughter in his eyes and the curve of his lips that only moments ago had sent her senses reeling, brought a reluctant smile to her lips. 'What dignity? I've already lost that, you wretch. How dare you treat me like one of your molls?'

'What does a well-brought-up young lady like you know about fallen women?' Jay's expression was stern but his lips twitched and there was a mischievous twinkle in his eyes.

'Why do you turn everything into a joke?' Daisy demanded crossly. Her confused emotions made her want to laugh and cry at the same time, and she resorted to indignation in an attempt to regain her self-control.

He brushed a lock of her hair back from her forehead. 'If you pout like that I'll have to kiss you again, Daisy mine.'

'Stop calling me that.' She tossed her head. 'You're impossible.'

As if on cue Lewis entered the saloon, holding out a clean white shirt. 'This was all I could find, Captain.'

'That'll do nicely.' Jay took it from him and held it up in front of Daisy. 'Take off your gown and give it to Lewis. He'll wash it for you and make sure it's dry for tomorrow.'

Daisy hesitated. 'I'm not undressing in front of you.'

'What a pity.' Jay began to unbutton his shirt. 'I'll take mine off and hand it to Lewis, but only if you'll do the same. I can't say fairer than that.'

'Shall I go outside, miss?' Bright red in the face, Lewis backed towards the door.

'Just turn your back,' Daisy said wearily. 'You, too, Jay. No peeping.'

They both turned away while she stepped out of her gown and put on Jay's clean shirt. She tapped Lewis on the shoulder and handed him the garment. 'Thank you, Lewis. I really appreciate this.'

Jay slipped off his shirt and tossed it to him. 'See what you can do with this. Although I dare say it's ruined.'

Lewis hurried from the saloon, leaving Daisy and Jay facing each other. His bare torso was well-muscled and his skin gleamed silkily in the lamplight. Daisy had to curb the treacherous desire to walk into his arms and feel the warmth of his flesh against hers. She took a deep breath. 'I'm going to my cabin, Jay. I'll say good night.'

'It's lucky for you that I was born a gentleman or I might be reclaiming what's mine.'

She walked past him with her head held high. 'That doesn't include me. I'm nobody's property.'

'I meant my shirt, of course,' Jay said, laughing. 'Now that would be interesting. Would you like me to escort you to my cabin?'

'Thank you, but no. I think I can find the way.' Daisy let herself out of the saloon and went straight to the cabin, where she sat on the bunk with her arms wrapped round her. The soft cotton of Jay's shirt was cool against her skin and the scent of him seemed to be interwoven in the cloth. She lay down and pulled the covers up to her chin. Tomorrow they would land in one of the creeks and she would make her way through the snow to Creek Cottage. At home in her old room she would forget all the strange and disturbing sensations that she had just experienced. Jay could do as he pleased, but she hoped for Mary's sake that he would see his family comfortably ensconced in the manor house before the call of the sea enticed him away again. Even so, she had to admit that he was disturbingly attractive, and if she were to be honest she had enjoyed her time on board his ship far away from the reality of life on shore, but this brief interlude was almost over. Jay had said he loved her, and she had been tempted to believe him, but he probably said that to all the women who took his fancy. He might marry one day, Daisy supposed, but she pitied his poor wife.

She curled up, turned on her side and closed her eyes.

★   ★   ★

Daisy was awakened by someone tapping gently on her door. 'Yes? Who is it?'

'It's Lewis, miss. I've brought your dress.'

She sat up. 'Come in, Lewis.'

He opened the door, holding the gown in front of him and turning his head away.

'It's all right. I'm perfectly decent.'

'I got some of the stain out, but not all of it,' Lewis said apologetically.

Daisy took it from him and examined the bodice. There was a faint pink shadow but the worst of the stain had been washed away. 'Thank you, Lewis. You've done a splendid job.'

His cheeks flamed but he smiled shyly. 'I tried, miss.'

'Are you looking forward to going home? You

must miss your family.'

'There's ten of us at home. I doubt if they've noticed I'm not there.'

'I can't believe that. Your mother will worry about you, I'm sure.'

'Ma's always got another baby to fuss over. It's Benny's ma who'll be sad, miss.'

'Yes, I'm so sorry for her loss. Does she live nearby?'

'She lives in the pig man's cottage. My dad let her stay on after Uncle Isaiah died.'

'Was Benny her only son?'

'Yes, miss.'

'How terrible. It will be a bleak Christmas for her, but you must tell her that Benny received the very best care at the London Hospital.'

'Yes, miss. I got to go. I'm helping Cook with breakfast.'

'Of course. I'm sorry I kept you from your work.' Daisy waited until the door closed on him before getting up. She took off Jay's shirt and folded it neatly, laying it over the end of the bunk. After a quick wash in ice-cold water she slipped on her dress, which was now warm and dry and she brushed her hair, allowing it to hang loosely around her shoulders.

It seemed important to leave the cabin as she found it and she moved about the small area, tidying it so that virtually no trace of her remained. The memory of Jay's embrace was still fresh in her mind, as were the feelings he had aroused in her, and now she must face him over breakfast as if nothing had happened.

To her intense relief he was not in the saloon,

although breakfast had been laid out as usual. Lewis brought her a pot of tea and some toast.

'Thank you, Lewis. Has the captain eaten yet?'

'I took him some coffee earlier, but we're heading into the creek. We should be at anchor within the hour.' He left her to eat her breakfast in solitary silence, and when she had finished she wrapped her cloak around her and went up on deck.

The air was icy and a bitter east wind tugged at her clothes and slapped her cheeks as the ship glided silently towards the shore. She clutched the rail, squinting as her eyes grew accustomed to the cold white light reflecting off the snowy banks, and the gleam of the pale winter sunshine on the steely grey waters of the creek. It was a black and white landscape, apart from the odd evergreen tree in the woods, and the sudden and startling contrast of the bright scarlet berries on the holly bushes. Daisy had been longing to get ashore and back to normality, but suddenly life on board the *Lazy Jane* felt like reality and returning to Little Creek was a step into the unknown.

It must be the strangeness of the scenery that was making her feel so disorientated. Last time she had been here it was high summer; now she wondered what had happened to the autumn and the natural progression of the seasons. She told herself she was being ridiculous. It was time to say goodbye to Jay and the crew of the *Lazy Jane* and go back to her old life. She returned to the warmth of the saloon. The motion of the ship changed and it seemed as though the wind had dropped, or else they were in the lee of the land as the *Lazy Jane* bobbed gently at anchor. She could hear Jay shouting instructions to Guppy and Lewis and the loud splash as the jollyboat was lowered into the water. Moments later Jay burst into the saloon.

'Are you ready to go ashore?' His casual manner and carefully controlled expression gave nothing away. He might have been a different person from the man who took her in his arms and kissed her so passionately last evening.

Daisy rose to her feet feeling oddly deflated. 'Yes, but how are we to get to Little Creek? It's obvious that the snow is very deep and we have no means of transport.'

'We walk,' he said with a wry grin. 'Unless you want to spend Christmas on board the *Lazy Jane.*'

'We'll never make it.'

'I could carry you.'

'Now you're being stupid.'

'There is an alternative.'

Daisy sighed and shook her head. 'Stop teasing me, Jay. What are we going to do?'

A smile lit his eyes. 'How do you think the squire hid contraband and unwelcome incomers?'

'I have no idea. What did he do?'

Jay held out his hand. 'Come with me and you'll find out.'

24

Ramsden was to stay on board and take care of the ship, but the others disembarked into the jollyboat, with Guppy and Lewis each taking a pair of oars. When they reached the shore Lewis jumped agilely onto the shingle and secured the painter to the nearest tree. Guppy leaped onto the beach, followed by Jay, and they dragged the boat from the water. Daisy found herself hoisted in Jay's arms and deposited on dry land. She wrapped her cloak more tightly around her as she was buffeted by a sudden gust of wind. The overcast sky threatened more snow and there were already deep drifts in more sheltered areas.

'We'll never make it to the village,' she said anxiously.

'We won't even try.' Jay took her by the hand. 'Come with me. It's too cold to stand here chatting.'

Daisy had little chance to argue as he started off across the icy shingle and dived into the undergrowth. For a moment she thought she was going to have to fight her way through a tangle of brambles and hawthorn, but she found herself following him along a well-trodden path. Sheltered from the wind and snow, it was relatively easy going, although each laboured breath felt like shards of ice piercing her lungs and robbing her of speech. It seemed as though they were plunging into a dark forest, but suddenly they emerged into a snowy clearing in the midst of which was a white marble folly, designed to resemble a Roman temple. Daisy uttered a gasp of surprise.

'Where are we?'

'You'll soon see.' Jay led her up the steps so that they were under the vaulted ceiling supported by marble columns.

Daisy watched in amazement as he bent down and brushed away a pile of dead leaves to reveal a trap door, which opened after several tugs on an iron ring. A flight of stone steps led downwards, disappearing into the darkness.

'Wait there a moment.' Jay descended into the gloom and reappeared minutes later clutching a lighted lantern. 'Give me your hand, Daisy. Mind how you go — the steps are slippery.'

'Where does this lead?'

'Don't worry, I've been this way more times than I can count. You'll be perfectly safe.'

She glanced over her shoulder and received a reassuring nod from Guppy. There was little alternative other than to put her trust in Jay once again and follow him into the unknown. To her surprise she felt a *frisson* of excitement as she held his hand and descended into an underground cavern. Guppy and Lewis followed close behind, although Daisy experienced a brief moment of panic when she heard the trap door close, and they were left with only the feeble beam of the lantern to light the way.

'We'll soon be warm and dry,' Jay said cheerfully. 'Light the other lantern, Guppy. We don't want to be left in the dark if this one goes out.' He led the way along a narrow brick-lined passage, his boots squelching in the mud. The smell of damp was masked by the odour of burning lamp oil. Water dripped from the roof, trickling like tears down the walls. Daisy was apprehensive but oddly comforted by Jay's confident attitude. It was obvious that he knew where he was going, and the others seemed equally at home.

'Is it much further?' she asked breathlessly.

'Feel the air,' Jay said brusquely. 'It's getting fresher. Not far now.'

Almost as the words left his lips she could see a faint rectangle of light, which grew larger and larger until they emerged into a summerhouse that overlooked a snow-covered garden. The house beyond was instantly recognisable.

'It's the manor house.' She grasped Jay's arm. 'Why have we come here? I think you owe me an explanation.'

'It's all part of my disreputable past. Let's go inside and see if we can find Mrs Ralston. She'll take care of you.' He turned to Guppy and Lewis. 'You know the drill by now. Enjoy your shore leave.'

'Aye, aye, Captain.' Guppy tipped his cap and winked. 'Good day to you, miss.'

Lewis hesitated. 'It was nice meeting you, miss.'

'And you, Lewis,' Daisy said earnestly. 'Thank you for looking after me on board.'

'My pleasure, miss.' Lewis bowed and backed away as if in the presence of royalty.

'You've made a conquest there.' Jay tucked

Daisy's hand in the crook of his arm. 'Let's go inside and see if I'm welcome.'

'You're master of the house now,' Daisy said, smiling. 'You're the lord of the manor and you don't have to return to your old ways.'

'Perhaps. We'll see.' Jay came to a halt, shaking his head. 'No more back doors for me. We'll enter through the front door, Daisy. I dare say I might get used to this, in time.' He patted her hand. 'Do you see yourself as lady of the manor?'

'I see myself dying of lung fever if we don't go inside soon. It's snowing again, unless you hadn't noticed.'

'I see nothing but your beautiful face, Daisy mine.'

She snatched her hand free. 'Don't call me that.'

He slipped his arm around her waist. 'You do realise that you've been on my ship for several days without the benefit of a chaperone, Miss Marshall. You'll have to marry me to save my good name.'

'You are ridiculous.' They were both laughing when Molesworth opened the door to the main entrance. His eyes widened and his mouth dropped open.

'Good day to you, Molesworth.' Jay ushered Daisy into the hall. He stopped to gaze at his surroundings. 'So this is what it's like to be lord of the manor. I've always had to creep in through the servants' quarters.' He took off his hat and greatcoat and handed them to the startled butler, while a young maidservant hurried up to take Daisy's cloak and bonnet.

'We weren't expecting you, sir,' Molesworth said stiffly.

'Well, as you see, I'm here and so is Miss Marshall. Unfortunately the weather seems to be closing in again, so you'd better ask Mrs Ralston to have rooms made ready for us.'

'There's a fire in the drawing room, sir. Shall I inform Mrs Tattersall that you are here?'

'Mrs Tattersall?' Jay stared at Molesworth, a frown puckering his brow.

Daisy grasped Jay's arm. 'Your mother must be here, Jay. I was hoping that the girls could persuade her to move in.'

'Lead on then, Molesworth. I've been here dozens of times but I confess I've never been above stairs before. You'll have to show me round.'

'I know where to find them,' Daisy said hurriedly. 'Perhaps Molesworth could arrange for us to have some refreshments. My hands and feet are frozen and I'd love a cup of tea.'

Molesworth's disapproving expression softened slightly. 'I'll inform the kitchen, miss.'

'Thank you, Molesworth,' she said, smiling. 'Come along, Jay. This time I can show you the way.'

There was something different about the old house. Perhaps it was the log fire that blazed up the chimney at the far end of the entrance hall, or maybe it was the vases spilling over with holly and ivy that had been strategically placed so that the splashes of colour broke up the austere wainscoting. As they made their way to the drawing room there were signs that children were residing in what had previously felt like a house of doom. A hoop and stick had been abandoned in the passageway together with a bat and ball, and someone had put a top hat on the head of an alabaster bust of Julius Caesar with a striped woollen muffler tied around his neck. Jay did not seem to notice as he strode along at her side, but Daisy sensed his eagerness to see his family and she quickened her pace. When they reached the drawing room she threw open the double doors. Jack was sitting on a rug by the fire playing cards with Judy Begg, while Molly kept Pip and Nate occupied by pushing them round the room on a battered-looking wooden horse that someone must have unearthed from the attic. Mary and Hilda were seated on either side of a roaring fire, but Mary leaped to her feet and ran to throw her arms around her son.

'Jay, my boy. You've come home.'

Daisy smiled to see mother and son reunited, and she went to sit beside Hilda on the sofa. 'Is everything all right at Creek Hall?'

'Yes, as far as I know, miss. We came with Mary because she didn't want to stay here on her own.'

'What about Dove and Linnet?'

'They've got their positions to think of. Dove likes working for the doctor and Linnet is happy where she is. I think she's got her eye on the schoolmaster.'

Daisy frowned. 'But I thought that Dove and Elliot would make a match of it.'

'Everything seems to have changed since that dreadful disease took so many lives. I believe

Linnet has been comforting Mr Massey since he lost his mother, and Dove spends all her time helping the doctor. She's had to step in where you left off.'

Daisy stared at her in astonishment. 'Are you telling me that there's something going on between Dove and the doctor?'

'It's not my place to say, miss.' Hilda jumped up to rescue Nate, who had fallen off the toy horse and was howling miserably.

Jay and his mother were deep in conversation and Daisy sat by herself, feeling suddenly alone. The news that Nick might have an interest in Dove had come as a shock. She realised now that she had taken his devotion for granted, assuming in the back of her mind that one day they would join together in matrimony as well as a working partnership. But did she love him? Or was her affection something that had grown from shared values and being thrown together in the desperate fight against the epidemic that had brought misery to so many?

'Daisy, come and speak to my mother.' Jay's voice broke into her reverie. 'Ma says she's not sure she wants to live here.'

'You surely can't wish to go back to the tiny cottage, Mary.' Hilda sat down with Nate on her knee, giving him a cuddle. 'I wouldn't if I were you.'

'I don't know if I can forget who I was,' Mary said soulfully. 'I'll always be the scullery maid, disgraced by the master of the house. He'll haunt me for the rest of my life.'

Daisy rose to her feet. 'If you allow him to

influence your decision it means you're letting him win. He can't hurt you or anyone now, and he must have had a glimmer of a conscience or he wouldn't have married you.'

'He only did it because he was afraid of hellfire,' Mary said gloomily. 'Everyone knows that I'm not really the lady of the manor.'

Jay put his arm around his mother's shoulders. 'Does it mean so much to you, Ma?'

Mary dashed tears from her cheeks. 'Yes, love. No one knows what I went through before and after I married Lemuel. He called me a whore and he treated you so badly that you took to crime.'

'Yes, my stepfather treated me badly, and I hated the way he spoke to you, Ma. But it was the squire who started me on the road I took.' He led his mother to the sofa that Daisy had just vacated and sat down beside her. He patted the space at his side. 'Come and sit by me, Daisy. You know the story, but Ma doesn't.'

Daisy took her place at his side, and he curled his fingers around her hand. She gave him an encouraging smile. 'Tell your mother everything, Jay. She deserves to know the truth.'

'Go on, son,' Mary urged when he remained silent.

'When I came out of prison Molesworth met me at the gates. I was taken to an inn where I met with the squire, and what he offered me sounded reasonable enough. After all, what chance would an ex-convict have of finding useful employment?'

'What was this offer?' Mary asked suspiciously.

'The squire owned a ship, the *Lazy Jane*, and I paid for my freedom by doing the squire's dirty work. He made a fortune from free trading, as he liked to call it, and I have to admit that I enjoyed the excitement of keeping one step ahead of the authorities.'

'That's how you knew about the tunnel,' Daisy said slowly. 'You brought smuggled goods here.'

'And people, too.' Jay chuckled. 'The squire didn't care how he made his money or who suffered as a consequence of his greed. Although why he chose me to carry out his plans I'll never know.'

'Perhaps he took pleasure in the fact that he could make you do what he wanted.' Daisy raised Jay's hand to her cheek. 'I don't know how he could have treated his own flesh and blood in such a callous way.'

'He was a cruel man.' Mary laid her head on Jay's shoulder. 'I'm so sorry for all that you've suffered.'

'It wasn't your fault Ma.' Jay gave her a hug. 'You did your best for me. Although I'll never understand why you married the old devil.'

'I did it for you. I thought I was doing the right thing by pretending that Lemuel was your father. I wanted to give you a better chance in life, but I know now that I was wrong.'

'I can look after myself, Ma,' Jay said tenderly. 'The squire and Lemuel Fox treated you badly and both of them let you down. You were the one who suffered most and now you deserve better.'

'I know what you're saying, Jay, but this place feels haunted,' Mary said, shuddering. 'I see

413

ghosts everywhere. I remember myself as a young and innocent girl with my whole life before me, and it was ruined by that man.'

'Not all of it. You're still young enough to have a good life, and I'll see that you do. I've been a bad son, but I'll do what I can to make up for the years when I should have been taking care of you.'

Hilda took her hanky from her pocket and blew her nose loudly, and Daisy had to wipe a tear from her eyes.

'Will you give up the evil trade, son?' Mary asked softly. 'I can't live here if you're paying for it by risking arrest and imprisonment or even transportation to a penal colony.'

'Your mother's right,' Daisy said hastily. 'Surely the squire must have left a fortune, even if it was gained from his illicit dealings.'

'I'll think about it, but I'm not making any promises.' Jay rose to his feet as the door opened and the parlour maid entered carrying a tray of tea and cake. 'Anyway, it looks as if we're going to be marooned here for some time, unless there's a sudden thaw.'

★   ★   ★

Jay's prediction came true. Snow was falling steadily and it continued intermittently for the next week with freezing temperatures and no sign of a thaw. Daisy was desperate to find a way to let her family know that she was safe, but the roads were impassable and as far as Toby and her friends in London knew, she had left the hospital and vanished into thin air. She could only hope that her aunt and uncle had not been informed of her disappearance, and she wondered how Nick would react. Would he be frantic with worry because he had tender feelings for her? Or would his anguish be on a less personal level, having lost a valued nurse? If what Hilda had said were true, it seemed that Nick had found comfort elsewhere. Daisy was puzzled, but she had little time to dwell on what might be happening in the outside world. Mary and Mrs Ralston had decided to utilise their enforced incarceration to open up and clean all the rooms that the squire had not used, and there were many. The servants were kept busy running up and downstairs with buckets of soapy water, mops and brooms, and Hilda was left to look after the children. Judy was considered old enough to help with the daily round of housework, but she had made firm friends with Cook and spent most of her time in the kitchen, learning how to prepare food and helping to knead the bread dough. Hilda also preferred to work in the kitchen, possibly because it was the warmest room in the house, and Pip and Nate were placed in the charge of the youngest housemaid, who was only a couple of years older than Judy.

Jay spent most of the day organising the outdoor workers to cut and collect firewood. The sound of an axe on the chopping block echoed round the grounds, breaking the eerie silence where every other noise was muffled by the thick layers of snow. Daisy accompanied them once or twice in an attempt to bring in as much greenery as possible, including large bunches of holly and ivy. It would be Christmas in a few days and it was important to make it a special occasion for all concerned, and in particular the children. Daisy even managed to persuade Jay to cut down a huge pine tree, which they planted in a barrel and placed in the entrance hall as it was too tall to put in the drawing room. That evening they drank mulled wine and played snap dragon, risking burned fingers by plucking raisins from flaming brandy. The adults joined in with the children in a riotous game of blind man's buff, and then Jay whisked Daisy round the drawing-room floor to a tinny tune from an old musical box that Mrs Ralston had found tucked away in a cupboard. Their enjoyment seemed to be catching and soon everyone joined in, even Hilda, who was getting quite nimble on her artificial limb. The spirit of Christmas appeared to have overtaken the malignant influence of the squire, and when Daisy went to her room that night she felt that the house was happy at last. She sang as she brushed her hair before plaiting it ready for bed.

The next day she spent hours cutting out stars from pieces of card, which she found in the squire's study, and with Hilda's help she made paper lanterns to hang on the tree. Judy and Molly cut out strips of wallpaper they had found while exploring one of the unused attic rooms, and Cook whipped up some flour and water paste so that they could make paper-chains. In the same attic Mary discovered a box of toys that had been put away without ever being used, and a dusty portrait stowed away under the eaves, which Mrs Ralston identified as being Sophia Tattersall, the squire's long-suffering wife, who died at a relatively young age. Neither Mrs Ralston nor Mary could give an explanation as to why the squire's late wife had hoarded toys when she was childless, although Daisy thought privately that perhaps the poor woman had longed to become a mother and had refused to accept that it might never happen.

Daisy had the chest taken to her room. The toys might be outdated and covered in cobwebs, but they were in good condition, and that evening, when the children were in bed asleep, she took the smaller items to the kitchen where she washed each one carefully and set them by the range to dry. Wooden soldiers lined up in front of the fire as if on parade, and dolls with porcelain faces and wigs made from human hair, were naked beneath pieces of flannel, waiting for their lace-trimmed dresses and pantalettes to dry on a makeshift washing line stretched between two chairs. Daisy was replacing some brightly coloured building blocks in their box when Jay burst into the kitchen.

'Hilda told me you were down here. What on earth are you doing?' He gazed in amazement at the array of children's toys. 'Where did you get these?'

'Mary came across them in one of the attic rooms, along with a portrait of the squire's late wife. The poor lady must have been desperate for a child.'

417

'And then I came along.' Jay pulled a face. 'I can imagine that didn't make for a happy marriage.'

'I think the squire ruined any chance of that simply by being himself. Anyway, the day after tomorrow is Christmas Eve, so I want to have all these wrapped and put round the tree for the children. We can at least give them a happy time.' She smiled up at him. 'And the tree is magnificent. We just need some more decorations to make it look even more beautiful.'

Jay picked up a drying cloth. 'Here, let me help.' He took a couple of bricks and started to pat them dry. 'I can be useful.'

'I don't doubt it.' Daisy smothered a sigh.

'What's the matter? You look troubled.'

'I just wish I could let everyone know that I'm safe and well.'

Jay pulled up a chair and sat down. 'By that I suppose you include Nick.'

'He's a friend and we've worked closely together all summer, but my brother will be frantic and so will my aunt and uncle.'

'There's just a chance that I could get you to Little Creek, but it's risky.'

'What is it? I can't let them spend Christmas thinking I might have been murdered and my lifeless body tossed into the Thames.'

A wry smile curved his lips. 'I was tempted a couple of times when you were first on board my ship.'

'I'm sure you were, and I was feeling much the same about you when you wouldn't put me ashore.'

'Then I'll try to make amends. If I'd known how long the snow was going to last I wouldn't have left Ramsden on board, but I intend to row out to bring him ashore anyway.'

'How does that help me?'

'The tide will be right in the morning and if the winds are favourable Ramsden and I might be able to take the jollyboat around the saltings and get close enough to Little Creek for you to reach your aunt and uncle's cottage.'

'If that's possible, why didn't you suggest it before?'

'Don't get on your high horse, Daisy. The freeze hadn't set in then, but the snow is so hard-packed now that it might be possible to walk a short distance, and it's a question of going with the tide, which should be just right, as I said, first thing tomorrow morning.'

'I'm sorry. I didn't mean to sound ungrateful, although you did put me in this position in the first place.' Daisy met his frown with a smile. 'I'll risk it if you will.'

He bent down to pick up another wooden block. 'You'll be safe with your aunt and uncle.'

'You're going to leave me there?' Daisy dropped the brick she had just picked up and it fell into the sink, sending up a spray of dirty water.

'Isn't that what you want?'

'Yes, of course. I mean I hadn't expected to go home so soon, not before Christmas, anyway.'

Jay eyed her thoughtfully. 'Perhaps it's time to let you get back to the life you know, Daisy. I can't keep you here for ever, even if I wanted to.'

'And do you want me to stay?' She had to ask the question, and she held her breath, waiting for his response.

'That's neither here nor there. You have to decide for yourself. I'm not going to force you into anything. It's time you went home, for both our sakes.'

The atmosphere in the kitchen had changed subtly and Daisy shivered despite the warmth. It was as if the squire had returned to make sure that whatever hopes were cherished in a person's heart were snatched away from them.

'I've done here,' she said briskly. 'I'd better find something to wrap up these toys. I was looking forward to seeing them open their presents.' Tears filled her eyes and she began to stow the soldiers back in the toy box. When she looked round Jay had gone and she heard the door click on its latch as he left the room.

She stayed up late, wrapping the presents in what remained of the wallpaper and labelling them with the name of the appropriate child. It took several trips to place them beneath the tree, but the end result even drew a smile of approval from Molesworth as he went on his late night rounds, locking doors. But when she was finally in bed, tired and aching from the exertion, Daisy found that sleep evaded her. She was desperate to go home and let everyone know she was all right, but she realised with something of a shock that she wanted to stay in the house she had grown to love, with the people, or perhaps more importantly, the person she most wanted to spend her life with. She had felt the old house awakened after a long sleep and opening its arms to embrace the future, but Jay was sending her back to her old life, and he had made it clear that their brief relationship was over. Tomorrow she would go home and carry on as before, but somehow the spirit of Christmas had evaporated, leaving her feeling alone and bereft.

25

It was still dark when they left the house next morning. Daisy followed the bobbing light of Jay's lantern as he made his way to the folly at the end of the garden, and the hard-packed snow crunched beneath her feet. It was at least two hours before dawn, but it felt like the middle of the night. Daisy had barely slept for thinking about their perilous journey, although it was the ultimate consequences that worried her most. She realised now that the last few days had been the happiest time she ever remembered, and going back to her old way of life was going to prove more difficult than she could have imagined. She knew that Jay thought he was doing the right thing by taking her to her family, and she was eager to see her aunt and uncle, but fate seemed to have taken her on another and unexpected journey. Nothing was certain, least of all her future, and she felt as though she had reached a crossroads — but which way to take? And did she have a choice? It seemed that Jay had decided for her and this would be a final farewell.

'Hold my hand.' Jay reached out to her. 'Just until we get to the bottom of the steps — they're very slippery.'

The air in the tunnel was dank and it seemed to stretch even further than it had when they first came ashore, but the temperature underground had remained constant and it was only when they emerged onto the foreshore that the extreme cold struck her forcibly. Jay seemed impervious to anything other than the business in hand, and having handed Daisy into the jollyboat he heaved it into the water. She could see the dark shape of the *Lazy Jane* bobbing idly on the slack water and she experienced an almost overwhelming desire to ask Jay to turn back, but she was too anxious to speak and wary of giving away her innermost feelings to the man who was suddenly treating her like a stranger. It was hard to forget their previous passionate embraces and yet too painful to remember them in the light of what might follow.

As they drew nearer the vessel Jay shipped oars and cupped his hands round his mouth to call out to Ramsden. He had to repeat himself several times before a tousled head appeared above the ship's rail. Ramsden was anxious about leaving the boat unmanned, but Jay managed to convince him that no one in their right mind would be out on the water in this weather. His reasoning seemed to convince his reluctant crew member and Ramsden climbed down the Jacob's ladder, lowered himself into the boat and took up a set of oars.

Daisy could do nothing other than sit tight and hold on to the bulwarks when the waves grew higher and the small boat careened dizzily and then righted itself. Jay and Ramsden rowed tirelessly, fighting against the wind and the crosscurrents they met as they headed out to sea to avoid beaching on the salt marsh. The first grey light of dawn in the east brought with it an icy blast, but as they headed towards Little Creek they had the advantage of the wind behind them. Even so, it was daylight by the time they reached the shore nearest to Creek Cottage and Jay leaped out to heave the boat onto firm ground. Daisy was preparing to climb over the bulwark when Jay lifted her to the bank. Despite the physical contact he might as well have been hoisting a sack of corn or a barrel of ale, and he set her down without looking at her. An invisible barrier seemed to separate them — it was as clear as glass and just as impenetrable. Daisy picked up her skirts and made her way carefully along the snowy river-bank. She could see a plume of smoke rising from the chimney of Creek Cottage and a light in the window. Set in the midst of the wintry scene it made a pretty picture, but she was shocked to realise it was no longer her home.

Suddenly Jay was at her side, taking her by the arm as she almost lost her footing. 'I'll see you safely to the door.'

'You're leaving me here?' She knew the answer even before he spoke and the last vestige of hope evaporated.

'It's what you wanted, isn't it? You've been worried about your family ever since we left London.'

'Of course I have. None of them knows what has happened to me.'

'Now I'm trying to atone.'

They had reached Creek Cottage and she

hesitated with her hand on the doorknocker. 'Atone for what, Jay?'

He leaned over and kissed her on the lips. 'I'm not sorry for kidnapping you, but I know I did you an injustice. Now I'm going to do the right thing.' He covered her hand with his and rapped on the door. 'I'm returning you to your family, where you belong. Goodbye, Daisy.' He backed away, holding her gaze with a long look, and then he turned on his heel and strode over the icy ground as if his feet had suddenly developed wings.

Daisy's hand flew to her cold lips. She could feel his kiss imprinted on them and she tried to call him back, but she could not form the words, and then the door opened.

'Miss Marshall. Well, I never did!' Linnet stared at her in astonishment. 'You've come home at last. We thought something terrible must have happened to you.'

Daisy glanced over her shoulder and her spirits plummeted at the sight of Jay pushing the jollyboat into the water. He leaped in and picked up the oars, shouting an order to Ramsden as he steered the boat into the deeper water mid-channel.

'Come in out of the cold, miss. You must be frozen.'

There was little Daisy could do, although for a fleeting moment she was tempted to run to the water's edge and call out, begging Jay to return and take her with him. But that would be foolish and dangerous, and he had obviously decided that she was better off without him, or perhaps he had simply been amusing himself and was glad to be rid of her. The unhappy notion convinced her to step inside and close the door on what might have been.

'Where is my aunt? I must see her and explain.'

Linnet's smile was wiped away by a worried frown. 'I'm sorry, miss, but the master and mistress travelled up to London the moment they heard you was missing.'

'Oh, my goodness! How awful. They must have been so worried.'

'I believe the police was called, too. Constable Fowler came to the door making enquiries and he said the coppers in London was looking for you. There's been a hue and cry, miss.'

'I knew they would worry, but I didn't realise it had gone so far. I thought everything would have come to a halt because of the weather.'

'Where've you been, miss? I don't mean to pry, but you disappeared off the face of the earth.'

'It's a long story, Linnet. It all happened so quickly and I couldn't get home. Anyway, that's not important. How can I contact my aunt and uncle? Do you know where they intended to stay?'

'No, but they said they was going to see Dr Marshall.'

'Poor Toby, he must have been frantic, but there really was nothing I could do.'

Linnet eyed her curiously. 'Dr Neville came to the house — quite upset he was when I told him you wasn't here and no one knew where to find you. He seemed very put out. Anyway, if you'd like to go upstairs and change out of those damp clothes I'll make you a pot of tea. Have you had breakfast?'

'No, not yet. Is there a fire in the parlour? I'd like to get warm before I go to my room.'

Linnet moved to bar the door. 'No, miss. I'll light one straight away.'

'But someone must be in there. I saw the candle in the window.'

'No, miss. I was cleaning the grate.'

'What are you hiding, Linnet?' Daisy asked suspiciously. 'Is there something in the parlour you don't wish me to see?'

Linnet shook her head. 'No, of course not, miss.'

'I'll take a look.' Daisy pushed past her to fling the door open and came face to face with Elliot Massey. The small tea table had been set with two places and it was obvious that the pair had been sharing a meal. 'You two have some explaining to do.'

'Don't blame, Elliot,' Linnet cried passion-ately. 'I begged him to stay because I don't like being here on my own. Hattie went to London with the mistress.'

'It was my fault, Miss Marshall.' Elliot stepped in front of an agitated Linnet. 'I shouldn't have taken advantage of the situation, but we're in love.'

'Oh, Elliot!' Linnet breathed, gazing at him with a rapturous smile.

'I don't want to be a killjoy,' Daisy said sharply, 'but it does look as though you've been abusing my aunt and uncle's hospitality, Mr Massey.'

'I know and I'm sorry, but I came calling last evening and it was snowing too hard to risk going home. I know it seems bad, but I love Linnet and I want to marry her.'

'I wish you both well, but that's not what concerns me most. If my aunt and uncle are in London I need to get word to them that I'm safe.'

Linnet exchanged worried glances with Elliot. 'Will I be dismissed? I know I done wrong.'

'No, of course not, Linnet.' Daisy turned to Elliot, who looked pale and shaken. A lock of lank hair fell across his brow and he was visibly trembling as he clutched his hands to his chest. Daisy wondered how such a weakling had managed to win the affection of the two sisters, and yet Linnet appeared to have deep feelings for him despite the fact that the gossips had, rightly or wrongly, paired him and Dove. Daisy managed a shadow of a smile. 'I won't say a word, but the weather has improved a little and I think you should make your way home now, Mr Massey. If the village gossips find out you've been staying here they'll make both your lives a misery.'

'I intend to marry her,' Elliot said stoutly. 'If she'll have me.'

'Yes, with all my heart.' Linnet cast a wary look in Daisy's direction. 'It will be all right, won't it, miss?'

'Congratulations,' Daisy said briskly. 'I hope you'll be very happy, but I need to get to the village post office where I can send a telegram to my brother. I'm certain he'll know where to find Mr and Mrs Marshall.'

'I have my pony and trap in the stable, Miss Marshall.' Elliot took his jacket off the back of the chair and slipped it on. 'If, as you say, the road to the village might be passable I'd be happy to take you to the post office, but I wouldn't advise you to go on foot. We can leave now, if you so wish.'

'Thank you. I can't allow my family to spend Christmas worrying about me.' Daisy thought quickly. There was someone else she needed to contact urgently. 'Would it be possible to get as far as Creek Hall?'

'I can't say, but we could try if you need to see the doctor.'

'I want to let Dr Neville know that I'm all right.'

'And tomorrow is Christmas Eve,' Linnet said enthusiastically. 'We'll be able to celebrate with happy hearts because you've come back to us, Miss Marshall.'

A vision of the huge Christmas tree in the entrance hall at the manor house flashed before Daisy's eyes, and she tried to imagine the children's faces when they unwrapped their presents, but the scene faded as quickly as it had come. 'I'll spend it quietly here, but you are free to do as you please, Linnet. You may spend Christmas with Mr Massey if you so wish.'

Linnet blushed rosily. 'I don't know what to say, miss. Thank you.'

The ride to the village in Elliot's trap was even more hazardous than the trip in the jollyboat. His horse kept slipping on the treacherous road surface and the wheels sunk into the softer snow on the side of the road. Elliot had to leap down and dig them out several times, but eventually they reached the post office and Daisy sent a telegram to Toby at his lodgings. She would have sent another to Mrs Wood to let her know that she was safe and well, but she was short of money, and reluctantly she said goodbye to the curious postmaster and climbed back into the trap.

'I think it's too dangerous to risk the road to Creek Hall,' she said reluctantly. 'I might try to walk there later when I've had something to eat and a change of clothes.'

'Looks like you won't have to, Miss Marshall.' Elliot pointed his whip in the direction of an approaching vehicle.

Daisy recognised Hero and she smiled with relief when she recognised the person on the driver's seat.

'Nick.' She stood up in the footwell and waved.

He reined the horse in and came to a halt beside them. 'Daisy. Where the hell have you been?' He acknowledged Elliot with a brief salute. 'Good morning, Schoolmaster.'

'Good morning, Doctor.'

Daisy looked from one to the other, detecting a slight hint of antagonism between the two men. Then she remembered what Mary had said about Dove having grown close to the doctor, when at one time it had seemed that she was sweet on Elliot. Why, Daisy wondered, was life so complicated when it came to affairs of the heart?

'You have some explaining to do, Daisy.' Nick glared at her, but she sensed that his anger was born of anxiety.

'If you have time to visit Creek Cottage I'll explain everything,' she said, eyeing Elliot warily. He was not above passing on juicy bits of gossip. Some people had called the schoolmaster 'an old woman', but perhaps that was unfair.

'Very well,' Nick said grudgingly. 'I have a couple of calls to make and then I'll come to Creek Cottage on my way home. I hope you've got a good explanation because your disappearance has caused a great deal of trouble.'

'Just a minute,' Daisy cried angrily. 'You have no right to criticise me when you don't know the facts.'

Nick blinked and stared at her in surprise. 'Well, I . . . '

'Help me down, Mr Massey.' Daisy held her hand out to him. 'I refuse to argue in public,' she added, noticing that the postmaster was standing in the doorway of his cottage, taking in the scene with apparent interest. 'Thank you for bringing me into the village, but I'll go with the doctor on his rounds.'

'No, really, Daisy,' Nick protested. 'That isn't necessary.'

She alighted from the trap and climbed up to sit beside Nick. 'But it is. You have no right to

431

judge my actions until you hear my side of the story. Drive on.'

He flicked the reins and they started off very slowly across the treacherous ground. While he concentrated on the road ahead Daisy told him the reason for her sudden disappearance, and he grudgingly agreed that there was nothing she could have done.

'There's one thing I don't understand, Nick.' Daisy turned her head to stare at his stern profile. 'Why are you so angry with me? I thought you would be more reasonable.'

'I was worried about you and I suppose I felt guilty.' He shot her a sideways glance. 'There's something I have to tell you.'

'Yes, I know. Linnet told me that you and Dove are more than friends.'

'I'm sorry, Daisy. We grew close after you left for London, but I still care about you and I was frantic with worry when I heard that you had seemingly vanished off the face of the earth.'

'You don't have to worry about my feelings, Nick. I'm glad that you've met someone who makes you happy.'

'I wouldn't go so far as that, Daisy,' Nick said ruefully. 'I'm very fond of Dove, and she's good company, but . . . '

'It's nothing to be ashamed of. You can't always choose the person you love.'

'But you and I were a perfect match, Daisy. I honestly thought so and my regard for you hasn't changed.'

She sighed with relief. At last it was out in the

open. 'Nor mine for you, but my heart lies elsewhere, too.'

'With Jay? I might have known it. Is that why he abducted you?'

'I've already explained that, Nick. It wasn't planned. It all happened because of a dreadful accident to one of his crew, and then it was the weather that prevented him from putting me ashore. You might say that Jay and I have been thrown together.'

'Does he love you?'

'I think so.'

'If it's true, why did he abandon you just before Christmas?'

'Jay wasn't to know that my aunt and uncle are in London. He thought he was doing the right thing.' Somehow she could not bring herself to admit that her brief romance with Jay might be over. That would be too painful.

'And he's the squire now, or at least he's the landowner, and will continue to bleed his tenants dry while doing nothing to improve their lot.'

'Nick, if I didn't know better I'd think you were jealous. You and Jay were boyhood friends, and you of all people ought to realise that he wouldn't behave like that. He didn't choose to be the squire's son, and he suffered years of abuse from Lemuel without ever knowing why.'

'That's as maybe, but if Jay is going to be lord of the manor he needs to see how his tenants live.'

'Don't you think he knows that already?' Daisy kept her voice even, but she was losing patience with the man she had once thought she might marry. 'Jay grew up in one of the squire's hovels.'

'Then perhaps you ought to see the conditions that some of my patients have to endure.' Nick reined in Hero and climbed down to the ground, reaching for his medical bag. 'Will you come in with me?'

Daisy glanced at the cottage, which was half submerged in a snowdrift. There were tiles off the roof and the woodwork around the windows was rotten, as was the front door. Half the panels were split and the bottom of the door was like a row of broken teeth. Nick held out his hand and she accepted his help as she alighted from the trap.

The interior of the cottage smelled of bad drains and sickness. The walls oozed damp, green mould was spreading up the wall and the packed earth floor was rapidly turning to mud. There was a single iron bedstead in the corner of the room and beneath the tattered blankets Daisy could just make out the shape of an elderly woman. A claw-like hand clutched what had once been a colourful patchwork quilt but was now filthy and faded.

Nick leaned over his patient. 'How are you today, Betsy?'

'Not so good, Doctor.'

Daisy moved closer. 'Can I do anything?'

'Water,' Betsy croaked. 'I have a terrible thirst.'

'Where are your family, Betsy?' Nick asked gently. 'Your daughter usually looks after you.'

'She's gone to beg Farmer Johnson for an egg or two.'

'Is that all you have to eat?' Daisy asked anxiously.

'Water, for the love of God.'

Daisy looked round for a jug and found only an old soot-blackened saucepan hanging above the empty grate. She took it without a word and went outside to the communal pump only to find it frozen solid. There was only one answer and that was to collect fresh snow, but without a fire it would take hours to melt as the interior of the cottage was only a degree or so warmer than outside. Daisy retraced her steps, slipping and sliding on the frozen ground. Nick was tucking his stethoscope into his medical bag and he looked up, his expression grim.

'I'm going to take Mrs Noon to Creek Hall, if she'll agree to leave her cottage.'

'My Nancy will be back in a minute, Doctor.' Betsy's voice was little more than a hoarse whisper. 'She'll get the fire going and cook me an egg.'

Daisy looked round the hovel and was even more horrified than before. The manor house was like a palace compared to this, and the Christmas tree and presents seemed like shameless luxury. 'What can we do?' she murmured. 'Are all the squire's properties like this?'

'You've seen where Jay was born, and to Lemuel's credit it was comparatively well kept, or rather it was when my father owned the land. He looked after his tenants, but Tattersall bled them dry.'

'But these people are starving,' Daisy said in

desperation. 'Tomorrow is Christmas Eve and they have nothing.'

Nick snapped the locks on his bag. 'That's about it. I do what I can, but you'll find at least a dozen families in the village who are in a similar predicament. I can't take them all in.'

Daisy glanced at the thin shape beneath the covers and the old woman's ashen face. 'Will she survive?'

Nick shook his head. 'There's little hope, and Nancy is ill-suited to look after herself, let alone an ailing parent. The poor woman will end up in the workhouse or an asylum when the old lady passes away.'

'You might not be able to help the others, but I can,' Daisy said firmly. 'Will you take me to the vicarage, please, Nick?'

He smiled for the first time since they had met that day. 'I don't think prayers will help in this instance.'

'It's Mrs Peabody I want to see. I know she's a vital force and if she puts her mind to something it will be done.'

★   ★   ★

Grace Peabody stared at Daisy in astonishment. 'You want me to tell all the late squire's tenants that they have credit at the village shop?'

'The squire's tenants and anybody you know who is living in utter poverty. It's time something was done for the people of Little Creek. They've suffered long enough at the hands of a ruthless landlord, and the squire's son will make sure that

436

such a thing never happens again.'

'But thirty shillings a family is a lot of money, Daisy.'

'Jay wants to make reparation,' Daisy said recklessly. 'I can't get to the manor house until the weather improves, but if the shopkeeper will let them have the food on credit I know that Jay will pay him handsomely. It's Christmas and no one should go hungry.'

A slow smile spread across Grace's thin features. 'Well, now! Who would have thought it? Jay Fox, the wild boy turned benefactor.'

'The squire knew that Jay was his son, but he forced his own flesh and blood into an illegal trade. He used his only child to make money for him despite the fact that he was already a wealthy man.'

Grace folded her hands primly in her lap. 'At least the squire atoned for his sins on his deathbed. John told me everything.'

'And now Jay wants to make up for the wrongs that his father did to the people of Little Creek. Will you help me, Mrs Peabody? The shopkeeper is unlikely to take my word alone, but he will listen to you.'

'I'll do what I can to persuade him. Your aunt and I have already done what we could to help the poor, but with the new squire's backing we'll be able to do so much more.' Grace angled her head. 'You obviously have influence with him. Are we to expect wedding bells?'

Daisy felt the blood rush to her cheeks but she managed to meet Grace's inquisitive stare. 'If, and when, I decide to marry, you will be among the first to know, Mrs Peabody.' She rose to her feet. 'Shall we go to the shop together? I want to make certain that Mr Keyes understands the urgency of getting food to everyone in need. Perhaps we ought to make a list of necessities, and then he can make up food parcels to be delivered to those who are unable to leave their homes?'

Grace rose to her feet. 'An excellent idea. Eleanora and I have done something similar, but on a much smaller scale, of course. I'll send for the carriage.'

Mr Keyes was at first sceptical, but Grace Peabody was not going to be gainsaid and she hinted that hellfire would be waiting for someone who refused to help the poor and needy, especially at this time of the year. She quoted the book by Mr Dickens when the miserly Scrooge was faced with the Ghosts of Past, Present and Future, reminding him of his duty to mankind. The shopkeeper buckled beneath such pressure and accepted the list of items that both Grace and Daisy considered to be what the poverty-stricken families most needed.

'I want your word that you'll make up as many of the parcels as you can today, and the remainder must be delivered tomorrow — Christmas Eve,' Grace said sternly.

'But who shall I say sent them, Mrs Peabody?' Mr Keyes eyed her nervously. 'My customers don't want charity.'

Daisy frowned. She had not considered that fact. 'Leave it to me, Mr Keyes. There's plenty of daylight left and I've nothing better to do. I'll call at as many homes as possible and let them know that the new squire wishes to make changes for the better, and he hopes that they will accept a token of his goodwill.'

'Well said, Miss Marshall.' Mr Keyes beamed at her, adjusting his steel-rimmed spectacles.

'The vicar will be visiting many homes today and tomorrow,' Grace said hastily. 'I'm sure he will be only too happy to spread the word.'

'Thank you, Mr Keyes,' Daisy said, shaking his hand. 'I know this will mean a lot of work for you, but you will be well recompensed.'

'It's a pleasure, miss.' He adjusted his spectacles yet again. 'The late squire used to have his comestibles delivered from Maldon, but maybe the new squire would consider using my services.'

'I don't doubt it.' Daisy nodded and smiled. 'A much more sensible arrangement.'

'Then that's settled.' Grace made for the door. 'The sooner we start the better.'

26

Daisy visited as many cottages as she could, but progress was slow and walking through thick snow was difficult and tiring. She had seen Mr Keyes' young son rushing about as he delivered the first of the food parcels and she had noted the expression of delight on the faces of the recipients, although she had seen one woman questioning him and seeming about to shut the door in his face when one of her older children intervened. The ragged boy snatched the package and slammed the door before his mother had a chance to object further.

It was dusk by the time Daisy reached home and she could barely put one foot in front of the other, but she was satisfied that she had done her best. Quite how Jay would react when he was presented with the final bill was another matter, but she knew that Mary would be on her side. Between them they would convince him that his generosity would demonstrate his sincere desire to make amends for the treatment the tenants had suffered at the hands of the late squire.

Linnet had a good fire going in the parlour and there was a tasty stew simmering on the kitchen range. There was no sign of Elliot, and Daisy was too tired to make enquiries. She had made it plain that he was welcome, although she doubted if Aunt Eleanora would have been so accommodating. She sat by the fire and ate her supper, but she could scarcely keep her eyes open. After such an early start and a physically tiring day, she was thinking of going to bed when she heard someone rapping on the door. She sat up straight, suddenly alert. Perhaps Jay had had a change of heart. She jumped to her feet but it was Linnet who burst into the room waving a telegram.

'The messenger boy is waiting to see if there's an answer, miss.'

Daisy's fingers trembled as she opened the folded sheet of paper, and she smiled.

Relieved that you are safe and well. Will remain in London for Christmas. Return when weather permits. Uncle Sidney.

'Is it bad news, miss?'

Daisy shook her head. 'No, not really. My aunt and uncle can't get home for Christmas because of the snow, but they know I'm here.'

'Is there a reply, miss?'

'No, there's nothing I can add.' Daisy reached for her reticule and took out a couple of pennies. 'Give this to the messenger and thank him for his trouble. Oh, and wish him Merry Christmas.'

'Yes, miss. Of course, but what will you do?'

'I'll be all right here. We seem to be well supplied with everything I might need.'

'Elliot has invited me to meet his father in Maldon on Christmas Day, but I'll tell him I can't go. I won't leave you on your own, miss.'

'I won't hear of it. You deserve a day off.'

'Thank you, miss.' Linnet hesitated in the

doorway. 'Will there be anything else this evening?'

'No. I'm going to have an early night. I was up well before dawn so I'm really tired. Good night, Linnet.'

'Good night, miss.'

Daisy sat by the fire for a while, staring into the glowing coals and wondering what everyone was doing at the manor house. Creek Cottage seemed very small and extremely quiet after the chaos of living with so many women and children, let alone a larger-than-life person like Jay, whose presence had transformed the atmosphere in the old house. When she finally went to her room she undressed and put on her warm wrap, but instead of going straight to bed she went to sit on the window seat and gazed out across the water. In a gap between the trees she could just make out the twinkling lights of the manor house, but it seemed as far distant as the moon and equally impossible to reach. Shivering with cold and exhaustion, she climbed into bed and pulled the covers up to her chin. Tomorrow was Christmas Eve. She would walk to the village and make sure that the parcels were being delivered to the right people. She closed her eyes.

★　★　★

She was awakened by the sound of hail hitting the glass panes, but as she sat up in bed she realised that someone was tossing handfuls of gravel at her window. The pale light of dawn

442

filtered into her room and at the sound of yet another volley of small stones, she leaped out of the bed and crossed the floor to fling the casement open. She leaned out. 'Who's there?'

'Come down and open the door.'

'Jay! What are you doing here?'

'Let me in and you'll find out.'

She slammed the window and ran downstairs, shrugging on her wrapper as she went. She wrenched the front door open and Jay rushed into the hall, sweeping her up into a passionate embrace. She struggled at first out of sheer surprise, but the warmth of his mouth on hers and the feel of his hard body beneath his heavy boat cloak made her weak with desire.

'What are you doing?' she gasped when he finally allowed her to draw breath.

'I've come to bring you home. I can't live without you, Daisy. I've tried, but my life means nothing if you're not by my side.'

'This is madness,' she protested feebly. 'We need time to get to know each other better, and we should talk . . . ' She never finished the sentence. His kisses were laced with pent-up emotion equal to her own. Common sense and rational thinking had flown out of the open door like a flock of white doves.

'You love me,' he said hoarsely. 'I know you do, and I love you more than I would have thought possible.' He held her away from him, holding her gaze so that she could not look away. 'I want you with me for ever, Daisy.'

She laid her hands on his chest, holding on to the last vestige of pride. 'You walked away and left me yesterday. What changed your mind?'

He released her, smiling ruefully. 'For once in my life I was trying to do the right thing, but it doesn't sit well with me. I didn't realise quite how much you meant to me until I thought I'd lost you.'

She was naked beneath her nightclothes and it was bitterly cold in the hallway. The front door was still open and an icy blast snatched at the thin material of her nightgown. She folded her wrapper around her, even though it was too late for modesty, and she closed the door. 'Come into the parlour, Jay. There's something I have to tell you.' Taking him by the hand she led him into the room. 'I have a confession to make — I've done something you might not like.'

Jay sat in a chair by the fire, which gave out a little heat even if it had burned down to glowing embers, and he pulled her onto his lap. 'Let me hear this confession and I'll absolve you from your crime. It can't be worse than anything I've done in the past.'

'You're laughing at me, but you might not when you know the truth.' She smiled despite the sudden *frisson* of nerves that made her shiver. 'I told Mr Keyes to give food to the poor, up to the value of thirty shillings for each household, and I said you would pay.'

He threw back his head and laughed. 'I heard about that and I wish I'd thought of it.'

'Who told you?'

'I went to the vicarage before I came here this morning and I hammered on the door until Peabody answered it. We had quite a long chat and he told me what you'd done.'

'I'm sorry, I know I should have asked you first, but I wasn't sure if I'd ever see you again.'

His eyes darkened and he held her close. 'How could you think that? You must know I love you.'

'I knew that you wanted me. There's a difference.'

He lifted her to her feet and stood up, his smile fading. 'I'm not like my father, Daisy. I don't play fast and loose with innocent girls.'

'But you went to the vicarage before you came here? Why would you do such a thing?'

'Because I wanted everything to be above board. My mother suffered at the hands of a selfish man who cared nothing for her or for me. I want to do right by you.' He went down on one knee, taking her hand in his. 'Daisy Marshall, I love you more than life itself — will you do me the honour of becoming my wife? The vicar is waiting in the church and Mrs Peabody and her maid are willing to act as witnesses. Please say yes, because I can't go another day without you, Daisy mine.'

'I will. Of course I will, Jay.' She glanced down at her nightgown and the wrap that had become undone during their embrace. 'But I'm not exactly dressed for a wedding.'

He rose to his feet and took her in his arms. 'You look perfect to me, but I can wait while you put on something a little more practical for the conditions outside.'

'This must be a dream,' Daisy said dazedly. 'Any moment I'll wake up.'

Jay smiled. 'The next time you wake up we'll

be in our own bed at Creek Manor and you'll be Mrs Tattersall.'

'But this is mad. How will we get home?'

'Guppy and Lewis came with me in the jollyboat. They're for us at the church and we'll leave as soon as we've signed the register. If we hurry we'll just about catch the tide.'

'But what about our families? We can't get married without telling them.'

'My mother cried with happiness when I told her that I was coming for you. She said if I returned on my own she'd lock me out of the house. Mrs Ralston has volunteered to help Hilda and Cook to create a wedding breakfast to remember, and the children are bubbling with excitement. You promised them you'd be home for Christmas, and they haven't forgotten.'

'I know, and I want to be with them, but there's my family, not to mention your sisters. They'll be so upset.'

'Then we'll do it all again in the spring. You'll have the most beautiful silk gown and flowers everywhere. Your aunt will cry and your uncle will give you away. We'll invite the whole village, but today is just for us.'

'Then I suppose I'll just have to go with you,' Daisy said, interspersing her words with kisses. 'We can't have the lord of the manor locked out of his own home. This is going to be the most wonderful Christmas ever.' She broke free from his arms and blew him a kiss as she hurried from the room. She would have to make do with her best dress, but that did not matter, nor the lack of a bouquet or bridesmaids — those could come later.

* * *

There was no music to accompany Daisy as she walked up the aisle on her own. Despite the bitter cold, she had settled for a cream silk afternoon gown, trimmed with coffee-coloured fringing, worn beneath a chestnut-brown woollen mantle with military-style frogging, and a matching velvet bonnet. It might not be a wedding dress but it would have to do, and she could tell by the appreciative glances from Ramsden and Guppy that she was looking her best. They rose to their feet, as did Grace and her maid, and Jay was waiting at the altar with the vicar.

When it came to placing the ring on Daisy's finger Jay gave her an apologetic smile.

'This was my mother's wedding ring, but when the thaw sets in we'll go to Colchester and I'll buy the most beautiful one we can find in the jeweller's.'

'Is this a problem, Daisy?' John asked anxiously. 'Do you want to go ahead?'

She smiled and nodded. 'It's just a band of gold. It's the man who places it on my finger whom I love.'

Jay leaned down to brush her lips with a kiss.

'You aren't married yet,' John said, frowning. 'May I continue?'

Jay smiled sheepishly. 'Yes, I'm sorry, Vicar. I got carried away.'

The rest of the service was brief but it seemed to Daisy that choirs of angels accompanied them as they made their way down the aisle, arm in arm. It was snowing again as they emerged from the church and Jay wrapped a heavy boat cloak around Daisy's shoulders.

'You're not travelling back to Creek Manor in this weather, are you?' Grace Peabody asked anxiously.

'They're expecting us,' Jay said firmly.

'And I want to see the children open their presents tomorrow morning,' Daisy added, smiling despite the fact that snow was blowing in her face.

'But the tide is against you now.' John Peabody unfurled a large black umbrella and held it over his wife's head. 'Why don't you wait until later?'

'We're good at rowing, Vicar.' Ramsden pulled up the collar on his pea-jacket. 'Clem and me have coped with worse than this.'

'Then at least come to the vicarage and have some breakfast before you set off.' Grace turned to her maid without waiting for a response. 'Hurry on ahead, Clara. Tell Cook to prepare bacon and eggs for four extra guests, and plenty of toast.'

'Yes'm.' Clara wrapped her cape tightly around her and dashed off into the swirling snow.

'I could do with a bite to eat, guv.' Guppy eyed Jay hopefully.

'Of course.' Jay smiled and kissed Grace on the cheek. 'That's very kind, Mrs Peabody. A noble gesture considering the fact that I woke you and the vicar at such an ungodly hour.'

'Not at all, especially since you've become the village benefactor.' Grace nodded to a woman who was struggling against the snow, staggering beneath the weight of a wicker basket filled with groceries. 'Good morning, Mrs Gilks.'

'Good morning, ma'am.' Mrs Gilks paused, eyeing Jay with a shy smile. 'Ta, for the food, sir. Me and my family will have a good Christmas, thanks to you.'

'The thanks is due to my good lady, ma'am,' Jay said, smiling. 'She's the one who realised how bad things were for some people in Little Creek, but that is coming to an end. I'll do my best to make life bearable for my tenants, and that's a promise.'

'God bless you, sir. You, too, ma'am.' Mrs Gilks bowed her head against the increasingly heavy snowfall and stumbled on towards her cottage.

Daisy clutched Jay's arm to steady herself as they negotiated the icy path to the vicarage. 'That was well said. I'm proud of you.'

'I'm not such a bad chap at heart. You were the first to realise that, Daisy mine.'

She smiled despite the icy shards bombarding her face. 'You may call me that now. I rather like it.'

He stopped to kiss her, raising a cheer from Ramsden and Guppy.

'Come along,' Grace called from the doorway. 'Don't dawdle.'

'It's like being back at school,' Daisy

whispered, giggling. 'But they are very kind and I am really hungry.'

The narrow hallway was dark compared to the whiteness outside, and a smell of beeswax, brass polish and lavender cologne was tempered by a waft of bacon frying and hot toast. Ramsden and Guppy shuffled in, stamping their booted feet on the doormat before following Jay and Daisy into the dining room, where the maid was busy setting the table. The mahogany furniture reflected the warm glow from the fire, and candles had been lit, casting pools of golden light on the white damask tablecloth.

Minutes later they were all seated, heads bowed while John Peabody said grace, and as the last word left his lips his wife reached for the coffee pot.

'Coffee everyone? Or would anyone prefer tea?'

Ramsden and Guppy exchanged wary glances, shaking their heads. 'No, thank you, Mrs Peabody,' they said in unison, reminding Daisy of schoolchildren addressing their teacher.

The maid entered as if on cue carrying a large silver platter piled high with bacon, eggs and sausages, which she placed in the centre of the table.

'We like to be informal at breakfast,' Grace said, handing round a rack of hot toast. 'Do help yourselves. This is a rather odd wedding breakfast, Daisy,' she added, chuckling. 'But my husband and I wish you a long and happy life together.'

'Hear, hear.' Ramsden helped himself to bacon.

'Manners!' Guppy said, nudging him in the ribs. 'Ladies first, mate.'

'Sorry.' Ramsden offered the salver to Daisy.

'Thank you, Eli,' she said, smiling as she speared a slice of bacon and a sausage. 'This looks and smells so good.'

John looked round with a nod of approval. 'I will use this in my sermon tomorrow. We are gathered together to celebrate the union of a young couple, and the true meaning of family.'

'Yes, indeed, Vicar,' Daisy said gratefully. 'You and Grace have been so kind to us. I can't thank you enough.'

'That goes for me, too.' Jay nodded emphatically. 'Until now I hadn't given much thought to the responsibilities I've inherited, but I realise there is much more to running an estate than merely collecting rents. From my past experience I know what it's like to be poor and desperate, and thanks to Daisy I've been able to do something very small for my tenants. I will do better in future with the help of my beautiful wife.' He raised his cup to Daisy. 'I'll toast you in champagne one day, Daisy. But until then you have my undying love and devotion.'

Daisy smiled and kissed him, and Guppy sniffed loudly, wiping his eyes on his table napkin. 'I wish Ma was here to see this. She's a sentimental soul at heart.'

Daisy tried to imagine Clem Guppy's mother as anything other than sour and grim-faced, and failed. She sensed that Jay was thinking the same

451

thing and she dared not look at him in case she burst out laughing. The meal continued with sporadic attempts at conversation by Grace and mumbles of appreciation from Ramsden and Guppy, but Daisy knew she would remember her unofficial wedding breakfast in the cosy vicarage parlour for the rest of her life.

All too soon it was time to brave the cold again. Daisy hugged Grace and thanked her for all she had done, and she was bold enough to plant a kiss on John Peabody's thin cheek, while Jay thanked him once again and shook hands. Despite Grace and John pleading with them to stay at Creek Cottage until the weather improved, Daisy was adamant: a promise to the children was binding, and tomorrow was Christmas Day.

★   ★   ★

The journey home was a struggle against wind and tide, with waves lapping over the gunwales, and Daisy huddled in the stern wrapped in the cloak with a strip of tarpaulin around her shoulders to protect her from the spray. It took the combined efforts of Jay, Clem and Guppy to get them back to the creek where the *Lazy Jane* was at anchor, but finally, after nearly three hours of hard rowing, they managed to beach the boat and clamber ashore, stiff and cramped with frozen limbs and hands. Jay insisted that Ramsden and Guppy must accompany them to the manor house, and they made their way through the tunnel to the summerhouse, and emerged in the snow-covered garden.

'I should go home and let Ma know I'm safe.' Guppy eyed Ramsden, as if expecting him to make a joke of his concern for his aged mother.

'Come inside first and get warm,' Jay said hastily. 'Have a bite to eat and a glass of hot toddy to keep the cold out.'

Ramsden slapped Guppy on the back. 'Another hour or so ain't going to make much difference, mate. A good stiff drink will put feathers on your chest.'

Daisy slipped her hand into the crook of Jay's arm. 'You must carry me across the threshold, Jay. It's the custom.'

'I have it all planned. My mother gave me instructions before I left.'

'Get your wife indoors, Cap'n, afore she freezes to death,' Ramsden said, grinning.

'We ought to enter by the front door.' Jay raised Daisy's hand to his chilled lips. 'But we'd have to fight our way through six-foot drifts to get there, so I'm afraid we'll have to use the tradesmen's entrance.'

'I don't care, Jay. Let's get inside as quickly as possible. I can't feel my feet.'

They trudged through the knee-deep snow and finally made it to the rear of the house where Ramsden and Guppy had already alerted the kitchen servants. Judy was the first to greet them and she came running down the passageway, stopping to cover her mouth with her hands as Jay lifted Daisy in his arms and carried her across the threshold.

'Oh, my!' Judy breathed. 'That's so romantic.'

Hilda was not far behind her and she clutched her hands to her bosom. 'You're married. You did it, sir.'

'I did, Hilda. But I've promised my wife that we'll have another ceremony in the spring, so that everyone can be part of the proceedings.' He set Daisy down on her feet. 'We're in desperate need of food and something hot to drink. Will you take care of my men?'

Cook put her head round the kitchen door. 'They're sitting by the range, sir. Each with a glass of hot toddy. Will I make some for you and Mrs Tattersall?'

Daisy hugged Judy and then Hilda. 'I'd love a cup of tea, please, Cook. And something to eat, too. We haven't had any food since breakfast, but that was hours ago.'

Cook beamed at her. 'You'll find a collation set out in the dining hall, madam. We didn't know what time you'd arrive, so we're saving the best for Christmas Day. I hope that suits you.'

'Yes, indeed. It's so good to be home.'

'Run upstairs, Judy,' Hilda said urgently. 'Tell Mary that they've arrived safe and sound. The fire is lit in the drawing room. We've thought of everything in the hope that you'd be home today, Daisy.'

'Thank you, Hilda. I can't tell you how good it is to be here. I thought I was going to spend Christmas all alone in Creek Cottage.'

'I would have swum there to get you rather than that,' Jay said gallantly. 'Let's go and find my mother so that I can show her that I do listen to her advice sometimes.'

'I can't believe this is happening.' Daisy allowed him to lead her towards the back stairs. 'Just yesterday I thought it was all over between us.'

'That was my fault. I must have been mad, but I'm seeing things straight now, Daisy mine. I'll spend the rest of my life trying to make you happy.'

'I'll remind you of that next time we argue, or when you miss the *Lazy Jane* so much that you can't resist the call of the sea.'

'That won't happen. I've swallowed the anchor — I'm never going to leave you again.' He came to a halt as they reached the great hall and Judy came running towards them followed by Mary and Molly, who was carrying little Nate with three-year-old Pip trying valiantly to keep up with her.

Mary threw her arms around Daisy and held her close. 'You're married?'

'Yes, Mary.' Daisy drew back to reveal the ring on her left hand. 'Thank you for this. I'll return it to you as soon as I can.'

'There's no hurry, my dear. You're my daughter now, the same as Linnet and Dove — I just wish they were here. Jack is coming in from the stables to join us for the wedding breakfast, such as it is, but stores are running low.'

Jay leaned over to kiss his mother on the cheek. 'We don't care, Ma. Whatever you've done will be gratefully received.'

'Well, your room is ready and the fire was lit early on so it will be nice and warm. Why don't you go and change out of those damp clothes and then we'll celebrate properly?'

Suddenly shy, Daisy shot a sideways glance at her new husband. 'I'll join you later, Jay.'

He gave her a smile that would have melted a heart of stone. 'Of course. I'll see you in the drawing room.'

Daisy knew that Mary was staring at her as she hurried towards the staircase, but everything had happened so quickly and now she was a married woman with all that entailed — suddenly she needed a little time on her own. She went to her old bedchamber and found that Hilda had thoughtfully laid out exactly the right gown. The gesture, although small, brought tears to her eyes. Her family were important to her, but so were her friends. She changed into the ruby-red corded velvet gown with frothy white lace at the neck and sat down at the dressing table to do her hair. She wanted to look her best for Jay.

★　★　★

The rest of the day passed in a warm haze for Daisy. The old house was redolent with the smell of boiling Christmas puddings, hot mince pies and buttered rum that Jay insisted on serving to anyone with a fancy for it. With her new family around her and heartfelt congratulations from Mrs Ralston, Molesworth and the rest of the indoor servants, it was the happiest time Daisy could ever remember. If Toby and Minnie and her aunt and uncle could have joined them it would have been perfect, but they were in her thoughts and she knew that they would wish her well, even though Aunt Eleanora would complain bitterly when she discovered that the wedding had gone ahead without her.

The children were bubbling over with excitement, although the younger ones did not fully understand the significance of the day, but it was Christmas Eve and that was always magical, even to adults. When the children were in bed Mary decided to have an early night, and Hilda had gone below stairs to join the servants in a party of their own. This gave Daisy the opportunity to hang stockings from the mantelshelf in the great hall, and Jay helped her to sort the items they had collected to fill them. There were walnuts from the store cupboard, which had been harvested from the tree in the orchard, as well as rosy red apples. Then there were marzipan sweets made by Cook in the shape of exotic fruits and berries, and Hilda had embroidered hankies for Judy and Molly. She had also knitted mittens for all the children, and these too were tucked into the stockings. A sprig of holly added to each one completed their task and they stood back to admire their handiwork.

'It's wonderfully festive,' Daisy said happily. 'And the presents under the tree look so exciting.'

Jay put his arms around her. 'This will be our first Christmas together.'

She stood on tiptoe to kiss him on the lips. 'It will be the best Christmas ever, but don't forget that you promised me a spring wedding with everyone invited.'

'That's a promise I intend to keep, because I love you more than I can say. But tonight I'm not going to share you with anyone, Daisy mine.' He swept her up in his arms and carried her across the marble tiled floor to the grand staircase. Daisy sensed that the portraits of the former occupants were looking down at her as they had on her first visit to Creek Manor, but this time they were smiling.

We do hope that you have enjoyed reading this large print book.

Did you know that all of our titles are available for purchase?

We publish a wide range of high quality large print books including:
Romances, Mysteries, Classics
General Fiction
Non Fiction and Westerns

Special interest titles available in large print are:
The Little Oxford Dictionary
Music Book
Song Book
Hymn Book
Service Book

Also available from us courtesy of Oxford University Press:
Young Readers' Dictionary
(large print edition)
Young Readers' Thesaurus
(large print edition)

For further information or a free brochure, please contact us at:
Ulverscroft Large Print Books Ltd.,
The Green, Bradgate Road, Anstey,
Leicester, LE7 7FU, England.
Tel: (00 44) 0116 236 4325
Fax: (00 44) 0116 234 0205